Praise for Griffith REVIEW

'An always vibrant mix of creative writing, essays, photography and ideas, *Griffith REVIEW* has gone from strength to strength.'
Adelaide Review

'Admirable...a varied, impressive and international cast of authors.'
The Australian

'Intellectual and creative depth...brims with talent.' *The Age*

'*Griffith REVIEW* represents "the long game" in journalism, providing quality analysis in an age of diminishing journalistic integrity.' *Walkley Magazine*

'Admirable insights...witty and cuts through the complexities.'
Australian Book Review

'*Griffith REVIEW* is a wonderful journal. It's pretty much setting the agenda in Australia and fighting way above its weight...You're mad if you don't subscribe.'
Phillip Adams

'It's a cracker, a reminder of how satisfying on every level good-quality non-fiction can be.' *New Zealand Herald*

'An outstanding example of what "zeitgeist" means...uncannily prophetic. *Griffith REVIEW* seems to get better with age.'
Sydney Morning Herald

'Rare, sometimes shocking candour...Editor Julianne Schultz seems to inspire unusual frankness in her contributors. I recommend a long and leisurely reading of this revealing collection. This collection shows Australia and Australians from every point-of-view but the obvious, revealing a diversity of worlds.'
M/C Reviews

SIR SAMUEL GRIFFITH was one of Australia's great early achievers. Twice the premier of Queensland, that state's chief justice and the author of its criminal code, he was best known for his pivotal role in drafting agreements that led to Federation, and as the new nation's first chief justice. He was also an important reformer and legislator, a practical and cautious man of words.

Griffith died in 1920 and is now best remembered in his namesakes: an electorate, a society, a suburb and a university. Ninety-six years after he first proposed establishing a university in Brisbane, Griffith University, the city's second, was created. His commitment to public debate and ideas, his delight in words and art, and his attachment to active citizenship are recognised by the publication that bears his name.

Like Sir Samuel Griffith, Griffith REVIEW is iconoclastic and non-partisan, with a sceptical eye and a pragmatically reforming heart and a commitment to public discussion. Personal, political and unpredictable, it is Australia's best conversation.

GriffithREVIEW31
Ways of Seeing
Edited by Julianne Schultz

GriffithREVIEW 31

INTRODUCTION

7 **In praise of experts**
JULIANNE SCHULTZ: Restoring trust and respect

ESSAY

13 **Reformation and renaissance**
JOHN ARMSTRONG: New life for the humanities

52 **The crumbling wall**
IAN LOWE: Science, certainty and value judgements

74 **More than human, more than nature**
LESLEY HEAD: Plunging into the river

83 **Selling the forests to save the trees**
DAVID RITTER: 'Welcome to Brand Biodiversity'

90 **We, the populists**
ROD TIFFEN: The perils of populism

112 **Word for word**
EMMA HARDMAN: Finding meaning beyond verbatim

143 **What is seen and heard**
PETER ELLINGSEN: Understanding the place of memory

161 **The minor fall, the major lift**
ANDREW SCHULTZ: Music, power and the composer's 'black art'

192 **Exploring the historical imagination**
PETER COCHRANE: Narrating the shape of things unknown

212 **White me**
ROBERT HILLMAN: Learning from theory and practice

230 **The play of days**
JULIENNE VAN LOON: Contemplating play through parenthood

MEMOIR

61 **The bone garden**
MARGARET MERRILEES: Looking after the fences and keeping an open mind

102 **Science without a capital S**
ROBYN WILLIAMS: Battling Grumpy Uncles, Media Tarts and Jurassic Marxists

123 **Language wars**
SELINA LI DUKE: Sometimes, mother knows best

138 **Tunnel vision of the soul**
LEAH KAMINSKY: Learning to hear new narratives

173 **Rebuilding the Stratocaster**
PAUL DRAPER: Synthesising work and play

185 **Death and distraction**
HELEN ELLIOTT: Learning to pay attention

REPORTAGE

131 **In the kingdom of the mind**
TANVEER AHMED: Explaining human behaviour

222 **At the gateway of hope**
HOWARD GOLDENBERG: Back to remote Australia

FICTION

151 **From what I hear**
ALAN VAARWERK

241 **The raft**
AMANDA LOHREY

POETRY

12 **The drought breaks, July 2010**
PETER HANSEN

111 **I want to be editor of the chimpanzee register**
KENT MACCARTER

229 **Monkey business**
CORY TAYLOR

PICTURE GALLERY

33 **Vita Brevis Est**
GEORGE SCHWARZ

More online:
www.griffithreview.com

COVER IMAGE:
Gnats, Chicago 2005. Darren James.

Griffith REVIEW gratefully acknowledges the support and generosity of founding patron Margaret Mittelheuser.

GriffithREVIEW31 AUTUMN 2011

GriffithREVIEW is published four times a year by Griffith University in conjunction with Text Publishing. ISSN 1448-2924

Publisher	Marilyn McMeniman AM
Editor	Julianne Schultz AM
Deputy Editor	Erica Sontheimer
Picture Editor & Production Manager	Paul Thwaites
Associate Editor	David Winter, Text Publishing
Publication & Cover Design	WH Chong & Susan Miller, Text Publishing
Text Publishing	Michael Heyward, Kirsty Wilson, Sarina Gale, Megan Quinlan, Michelle Calligaro
Proofreader	Andrea Lewis
Editorial Interns	Jessica Ballantine, Laura Middlebrook, Alan Vaarwerk
Administration	Andrea Huynh
Typesetting	Midland Typesetters
Printing	Ligare Book Printers
Distribution	Penguin Australia

Contributions by academics can, on request, be refereed by our Editorial Board. Details: www.griffithreview.com

GRIFFITH REVIEW
South Bank Campus, Griffith University
PO Box 3370, South Brisbane QLD 4101 Australia
Ph +617 3735 3071 Fax +617 3735 3272
griffithreview@griffith.edu.au www.griffithreview.com

TEXT PUBLISHING
Swann House, 22 William St, Melbourne VIC 3000 Australia
Ph +613 8610 4500 Fax +613 9629 8621
books@textpublishing.com.au www.textpublishing.com.au

SUBSCRIPTIONS
Within Australia: 1 year (4 editions) $99.80 RRP, inc. P&H and GST
Outside Australia: 1 year (4 editions) A$149.80 RRP, inc. P&H
Institutional and bulk rates available on application.

COPYRIGHT
The copyright of all material published in Griffith REVIEW and on its website remains the property of the author, artist or photographer, and is subject to copyright laws. No part of this publication may be reproduced without written permission from the publisher. ||| Opinions published in Griffith REVIEW are not necessarily those of the Publisher, Editor, Griffith University or Text Publishing.

FEEDBACK AND COMMENT www.griffithreview.com

ADVERTISING
Each issue of Griffith REVIEW has a circulation of at least 4,000 copies.
Full-page adverts are available to selected advertisers. To book your advert, in the first instance please email Griffith REVIEW: griffithreview@griffith.edu.au

This project has received financial assistance from the Queensland Government throught Arts Queensland

This project has been assisted by the Australian Government through the Australia Council, its principal arts funding and advisory body.

INTRODUCTION

In praise of experts

Restoring trust and respect

Julianne Schultz

WALKING across the scorched lawns of the quadrangle of a major university behind a man on his mobile phone, I found it impossible to ignore the increasingly agitated conversation.

'Yes, I know I am listed as a water expert on the university's media directory, but I can't answer your questions. What you want to know about is not my expertise.' He tried to explain the basics of the hydrology of groundwater and the specifics of his particular subset of knowledge.

The caller just needed a quote to round out a story about the drought that had left the country parched for years. It was not that a quote from any professor would have done – but for the agitated expert it must have felt like that. His knowledge was deep and specialised; he was a world expert with countless citations. His expertise intersected with public discussion only at the fringes. Even if he had been asked about the hydrology of groundwater, to comment in a way that made sense to the non-expert, the intellectual beauty of complex calculations and arcane terminology would have to be stripped away. It was easy to see how for him this could feel like betrayal of a lifetime of research.

Knowledge has become so specialised and self-referential that it delivers its own rewards. The best scientists, though, have long accepted that they need to explain their research, to make sense of complexity and to promote breakthroughs beyond the specialist journals. For many this is challenging. For those able to step beyond their specialisation the benefits can be clear and tangible – measured in research dollars, public and political recognition.

Yet even for experts who have completed media training, the public domain is fraught with risk – the unpredictable vitriol of debate is hard to prepare for, and a high profile can be a burden for those who most value peer recognition. Science has its own languages, its own standards of proof, which don't translate easily into a public domain that at best can be nuanced and informed, but disappointingly often is simplistic and inflammatory. Trust and respect are easily traduced in this domain.

This is just as troublesome for those in the humanities and social sciences, even if their language is less technical, their methods more accessible. These disciplines rarely have the benefit of promising breakthroughs that will extend life – but the habits of mind, the standards of proof and depth of knowledge, are at least as specialised. The insights they generate are also at least as relevant to the big questions of the day and help us live fuller lives.

IN THE WET spring of 2010, the consequences of the long-term exclusion of the humanities and social sciences from public discussion and policy formation, which Stuart Macintyre documents in *The Poor Relation* (MUP, 2010), played out with book-burning bonfires in country towns in the Murray-Darling Basin. The drought may have broken but the problem of water in the driest continent remained.

After eighteen months of research, the Murray-Darling Basin Authority's long-awaited draft framework on the 'volume of water required to maintain and restore environmental assets, using best available science and the principles of ecologically sustainable development' was released. The experts concurred that the science was excellent, the report a monumental achievement.

Anyone with even a passing interest in public life could not have failed to notice it was not generally well received by those most directly affected. As officials from the Authority travelled to town after town they were confronted with the stark reality of the distrust of experts. In some towns the reaction was violent, the report was torched, tractors were driven into blockades; in others palpable fear numbed communities already stretched to the outer limits of resilience after a decade without rain. The prospect that even as the drought broke there would not be a return to the good old days was too hard for many to contemplate.

Coastal dwellers whose only exposure to this came from the nightly news could be excused for thinking it was an attempt by vested interests to emulate the rage of the American Tea Party movement – made-for-TV events with self-interest cloaked in inflammatory garb, designed to achieve political outcomes and the maintenance of the status quo.

There were elements of this cynical game-playing, but reading on the Authority's website the record of the dozens of meetings, attended by tens of thousands of people, points to something more fundamental, as Chris Miller from Flinders University has argued: a hunger for genuine consultation, for answers to local and human-centred problems, for research that went beyond the number-crunching derived from simple telephone surveys, for understanding and respect for Indigenous and traditional ways of life, for pathways that make it possible to create a thriving future by working within sustainable environmental limits.

The scientific and environmental research was exemplary, but the glaring gap in the voluminous report was of research that used the full range of tools of the humanities and social sciences, research that engaged with people, that drew on historical and international precedents, that explored the detail of local differences, the psychological response to change, the economic consequences and opportunities, resilience and fear. Research that enabled the progressive leaders dotted throughout these towns to imagine and articulate a different future, research that put the environmental issues in human terms, and helped maintain a place for the people who know and love the lands of the Basin.

The exclusion of this perspective threatened the whole project. In contentious areas the aphorism holds: the whole is only as strong as its weakest link.

The glib response uttered in countless interviews – that there would be no future unless the environment was sustainable – missed the point that effectively making such a major transition could not be left to either the market or policy handed down from Canberra. The non-specialists who live in these communities wanted everyone to know that they had something to add, and that in the era of connectivity they expected their hard-won expertise to be considered.

The changing tone of the consultation process is clear in the reports from the meetings. At first the officials exuded a father-knows-best certainly, but it did not take long for them to switch to more attentive listening. When the Authority eventually committed to another round of 'socioeconomic' research to be conducted over the summer months, it tacitly acknowledged that this research had not been adequately conducted in the first place – although the truncated timelines for the new project beg a similar question.

The danger was that the need for political compromise would again mean that nothing was done, when what was needed was a broader perspective, more persuasive and inclusive approaches, drawing from a wider range of disciplines, incorporating more ways of seeing.

It is striking that the Wentworth Group of Concerned Scientists, who made the health of rivers a matter of such potent political consequence, have in recent years broadened the scope of their work to include social scientists – with striking results – but by the end of 2010 they feared that the science would be swamped by emotion, when both were needed.

This attempt to draw the human and social sciences into a scientific project echoes an earlier attempt to create a place for the humanities and social sciences in the big issues facing the driest continent. In 1970 the heads of the three learned academies – science, humanities and social sciences – decided to work on the Murray River as a 'combined exercise', ranging across natural and human history, ecology and the legal, administrative, economic and political aspects. After several years of symposia that tested the limits of interdisciplinary research, it was concluded that it was time to abandon the assumptions on which the Basin had been managed, lest 'future generations curse us'.

NOT SO LONG ago, socioeconomic research accompanied every major policy proposal or significant initiative. It is still done, but it has lost an authoritative place at the centre of the policy development. Government departments stripped back their in-house research units and expertise dissipated, consultants with econometric models prevailed, the 'social' virtually disappeared.

As Stuart Macintyre points out, even in the postwar days, when a mandarin culture prevailed – uniting leaders from the public and private sectors with the god professors of the major universities in seeking solutions to pressing national problems – the social sciences had to fight to be included. But they were heard and taken seriously – at least until the late 1980s, when rational-choice economic theories came to dominate the policy process and public debate. Then it was expected that people would behave like cogs in a well-oiled machine, so there was less need for social research.

At the time, in a handful of important books, leading scholars pointed to the limits of this thinking. They argued that economics alone was too narrow a frame, that there were matters that the market could not resolve, that there was such a thing as society. Within a few years of the 1991–92 recession we had to have, the benefits of deregulation made most of us richer. It seemed that these eminent professors had been crying wolf. They became easy targets for ideologically motivated commentators. Locked in a political straitjacket, they lost confidence and a respected public voice. Combined with the rise and rise of popular culture, the uncertainties postmodern thinking brought to traditional ways of thinking, and the increasingly narrow credentialising of academic life, scholars in the humanities and social sciences who chose to engage with the public domain were pulled into ideologically defined battles.

As the limits of overreliance on the market become clearer, so does the need for new ways of analysing problems and making sense of the world. The conservative American commentator David Brooks observed, 'The technicians have an impressive certainty…they have amputated those things that can't be contained in models, like emotional contagions, cultural particularities and webs of relationships. As a result everything is explainable and predictable…they can dismiss the poor souls down below…'

Now we know that people individually, in groups and in companies, do not always make rational choices. Behavioural economics may bring the social back into economics, but the problems and issues we are facing – climate change, population size, globalisation, water shortages – are even more diffuse, complex and human-centred. Making sense of them entails creating a space for those from the humanities and social sciences to contribute to the public debate, and encouraging them to speak up and be less defensive.

1 December 2010

Peter Hansen

The drought breaks, July 2010

Again clouds balloon across the sky,

Restoration ladies lifting swelled skirts

to piss in casual passing

on the mud-running gutter of creeks.

Daisies dash across the plain

and dribble along the fence,

songlines from paddock to paddock,

white-capped and yellow-eyed

they dance through saltbush

with the fecund smile of spring.

A growth of moss has purpled the claypans

surrounded by lines of serious silver-breasted rye

and careless crops of copper burr

where, in a depression, a shiny black thistle

feeds on the felted yellow bones

of a ewe and a lamb.

Peter Hansen has spent most of his life working on sheep stations in the Western Riverina, New South Wales. His first collection of poems is *Shearing at Coonong and Other Poems* (Ginninderra, 2010).

ESSAY

Reformation and renaissance

New life for the humanities

John Armstrong

ONE evening I was getting into the crowded lift at my local tube station in Central London, to go down to the train. As the doors closed a middle-aged gentleman squeezed in. I recognised him as a fairly distinguished professor of history from the University of London School of Advanced Study, where I directed the philosophy program. As we descended he suddenly blurted out to everyone and no one: 'That's it; I've had it. What they're doing to our arts faculties is a complete disgrace.' We looked at our feet as he went on about the government, university administrators and the general ruin of intellectual culture.

I don't know what made him snap at that moment. But the professor in the lift has for me become a symbol of the view that the humanities are hard done-by and that they are in decline – or at least in an extended period of trouble – through no fault of their own, but because of bad decisions by others.

In less dramatic ways I have heard this analysis restated many times during my years in Australia: the academic humanities are doing a good job;

they are fine, serious and important disciplines, staffed by able and sincere people. But governments and university administrators set impossible targets, demand crazy workloads, cut budgets, reducing staff numbers and imposing a stultifying managerial regime, and generally forcing the humanities onto the defensive.

There's a simple and morally necessary solution, according to this view: increase our funding, then leave us alone.

When I arrived in Australia, in 2001, this analysis seemed to cohere with a political assumption, even a political blindness. In the years during which John Howard was Prime Minister many humanities academics assumed that he was personally responsible for their situation. A Prime Minister is a terrifying adversary, but also cause for submerged optimism. Howard would (eventually) be defeated and – the thinking went – because he was the sole cause of the troubles, the good times would roll again.

There was in the humanities a generalised, and very honest, inability to imagine John Howard as anything other than an aberration, sustained by deceit and media manipulation, rather than as a man who was exceptionally adept at expressing widespread opinions.

Consequently, there was no self-examination: there was no hint that the humanities might themselves have contributed to their troubles, that they may have failed to win sufficient public respect and admiration to carry weight in national life.

I BELIEVE THE academic humanities require radical reform – not just in their institutional framework but in their intellectual self-conception, their sense of purpose, of mission even; in their habits of mind, their modes of admiration and the direction of effort. Ironically, such reform is needed to *return* the humanities to their grandest, most longstanding ambitions. Wisdom should be powerful in the world: that is why we teach, research, and engage the public.

And that is why this essay is called 'Reformation and renaissance'. I want to show how reform is needed in order to accomplish something magnificent and serious. There is a tendency in the humanities to hear a call for reform as a threat. Calls for reform always seem to come from people who don't especially care about the humanities. I want to change that association and to connect the idea of reform to the pursuit of great educational endeavours.

Taken one way, 'the humanities' is the traditional name for a group of academic disciplines, of which the core members, identified by subject matter, are philosophy, history, art history and the study of literature. (It's an imperfect nomenclature. There are subject areas such as music, fine art, architecture, religious studies and politics that have much in common with the humanities, although they are not usually covered by the term.)

Looked at from a distance it seems obvious that the humanities would, almost of necessity, occupy a central, highly valued place in the collective life of a society. In principle, the academic disciplines called the humanities are concerned with the study of basic human issues: what can we learn from the past that is important to know today; how should we think about experience; what is valuable and why; what is the meaning of life; what is justice? In addition, the humanities are the repositories of all the best stories, the greatest narratives, the biggest adventures in thinking, the finest creative works.

The political and institutional difficulties of the humanities should be puzzling – even disturbing. How can it be that the keepers of so much that is self-evidently important and interesting have arrived at this situation? And is there anything that can and should be done to put things to rights?

THERE ARE DIFFERENT ways to tell whether the humanities are thriving, just coasting along, or in trouble. An institutional yardstick would assess things like the ranking of schools or departments in national and international league tables. It would measure the number of staff employed, or the number of papers published in journals which are well regarded by academics, or the number of competitive grants won – in competition against other humanities academics, and awarded on the assessments made of proposals by high-placed humanities experts.

These are internal assessments. They measure department against department, university against university. Such assessment is fine if you think that overall things are going well, for in that case you can spot local weaknesses or pockets of special success, and set about remedial action or imitation.

But such assessment is fatal if there is drift or decline in a whole field of activity. It gives far too much weight to the views of insiders – in fact, this is all that it measures. And if you think – as I have come to think – that there is a problem within the humanities, then just measuring the view from inside may not be helpful at all.

In politics, one of the most damaging things that can happen to a party is to be captured by its activist base. Their party conferences are euphoric, the activists praise one another and push for policies which thrill them. But the task for a party isn't to delight its activists; it's to earn the trust of the wider world. And it may happen – we know it can happen in politics – that a dangerous gulf opens between the preoccupations of a devoted group of insiders and the concerns of the wider population.

If you want to know how a field of human endeavour is faring as a whole you have to look outwards. You have to look at the need for that endeavour and the potential of the enterprise. The question cannot be: how do the humanities regard themselves from the inside? The question must be: how are the humanities flourishing (or not) everywhere else? This is a question the humanities owe it to themselves to ask; it is a noble question, a confident question – one that springs from a conviction that the humanities ought to be judged in such grand terms.

IN SEPTEMBER 2010 I participated in a daylong discussion at the Melbourne Business School: a key moment in the debate about the future of business education. What qualities of mind and character should the school be fostering through its MBA program? There was a broad consensus that qualities such as imagination, communicative verve, conceptual analysis, awareness of the broad issues of history and – above all – self-knowledge were important. These were seen as valuable not only in themselves, but in helping students towards successful careers in successful companies. For such qualities are not an indulgence, but sources of competitive advantage. Moreover, they have much to contribute to the development of a good economy.

It could be said that an appeal was being made to the humanities. In a deep sense that is absolutely right. The qualities that are recognised as much needed in business education (because much needed in business) are rooted in the humanities. In principle, history, literature, philosophy and art could all have much to contribute here.

But it would be a mistake to think that this need could easily be met by the existing disciplines. For one thing, they have internalised a general suspicion of — even hostility to — the idea of business. I believe that suspicion is unwarranted. But it supports my argument when people object and say that the humanities are right to be suspicious — for that is simply to cut those disciplines off from a place where they could be of great service to the world.

Unthinkingly you could suppose that business, like some wicked tyrant, merely wants to exploit humanities-type intelligence for mean-spirited ends. Bring us your eloquence (so we can make more money); bring us your insights into the narrative of history (so we can make more money); bring us your knowledge of the creative achievements of art...

I don't deny that this could conceivably occur. But it is nothing like what we were talking about. Businesses have to make money; but how they are profitable, what they are like, what they are like to work for, what they produce, what their impact on the world is, how they influence society: these are all open questions, and many different answers are all compatible with the bottom line of satisfying the shareholders. And in any case, business education is now often a route to working for NGOs that face many of the same questions as commercial enterprises: questions of efficiency, management, purpose, dealing with divergent stakeholders.

Business is such a vast and central part of the contemporary world that it would be crazy to write it off as unworthy of serious attention from the humanities. At the same time this suggests a lack of confidence in the worth of the humanities themselves. Surely, if they are so important, they could contribute powerfully to the good education of executives.

My fear is that there's no way the needs of business education could be met by sending students across campus to attend existing humanities classes. In an interesting experiment, the social philosopher Charles Handy taught a class at the London Business School on Sophocles' *Antigone*. It's a good choice for business executives. The central character, Antigone, is caught in a conflict between two kinds of loyalty – to the demands of the state and to her conscience. She wants to provide a proper burial for her brothers who have fallen in battle against their native city; but the ruler of the city forbids this, since the brothers were enemies of the state. Antigone follows her conscience and is condemned to death. The play raises the question: what would you have done? It provokes discussion of more likely scenarios: what would be the equivalent today? Can the same kind of conflict occur in less tragic but still significant ways? And then how would you decide? How would you respond if you were, as might well be the case in the future, in the position not of Antigone but of the ruler?

The play's value is as a starting point for serious discussion. And the discussion gets more serious the more people are willing to bring their own experience, their own ambitions and their own loyalties into play. It depends also upon the determination of the teacher to make this happen – to guide it and judge it and participate.

I don't doubt that there are academics in humanities disciplines who could do this if required. It's just that if they can it's a happy accident. There's nothing at all in the requirements of the job that test for this ability; it has nothing to do with peer approval or promotion or publication or research standing. There isn't an institutional culture that reflects continuously and ambitiously on how to do this as well as possible. Doing it really well – realising the opportunities afforded by the play to maximum effect in the lives of students – is a complex, sophisticated skill.

I appreciate that somewhere in the background there has to be a body of scholarly knowledge – that has enabled translation of the text, that has framed basic ways of thinking about it (Hegel was quite helpful here) and that can flesh out the significance of the speeches. But we must remember that this scholarly base is there to support the kind of discussion that the executives have. It's not an end in itself and its worth should be gauged by what it enables us to do. Further, a single scholarly base can serve pretty much the whole world. In preparing that kind of class the teacher only needs to be able to get such background insight from somewhere – it doesn't matter whether it comes from someone at Harvard or from the classics professor across the campus. Existing knowledge may already be sufficient for the higher purpose.

I recall being sent a collection of graduate papers on *Antigone*. I don't want to mention the university they came from and I don't think it matters – similar collections could have been produced in almost any serious university in the western world. The papers did not represent a local oddity; they were from the academic mainstream.

What they had in common was that they were extremely complicated. The graduate students had gone to extraordinary lengths to show how much high-intellectual matter they had absorbed. Being intelligent meant being difficult. Despite many years of intellectual training in philosophy, I often found it hard to follow the arguments presented. They solved problems I didn't have. It was as if they were saying to me: 'So, you don't know enough about the structuralist appropriation of Greek tragedy – let me help you out.' Or: 'Worried about the erasure of class in nineteenth-century construction of "the classics"? I share your pain.' The concerns stuck me as forced. They were interests that could be raised in the hothouse. I imagined a seminar in which students egg each other on to more and more recherché topics.

The academic ideal of what to do with a major play like *Antigone* is at odds with the value the play has for non-specialists. But the value to non-specialists is not a lower type of value. It's not that the executives Charles Handy was teaching were, sadly, too stupid to understand the high-theoretical games. It's that their needs were more serious and substantial: more real. The aim of complication was not to make the play more important; it was to demonstrate a specialised kind of technique.

This is the impasse that the humanities face. There is a deep need for what they have to offer. But they have evolved – under special circumstances – in a way that makes it difficult for them to respond to and meet that need.

IN HER RECENT book, *Not for Profit* (Princeton University Press, 2010), the eminent American philosopher Martha Nussbaum argues that democracies need the humanities to be strong and pervasive. The humanities, she argues, teach critical thinking, imagination, compassion, and develop individuals who are global citizens – people with a sense of the big order of the world. Nussbaum is right to say that these need to be widespread capacities if democracies are to function well. We need inner resources so that 'class, fame and prestige count for nothing, and the argument counts for all' – as she deftly summarises the lesson of Socrates.

The kind of education she has in mind will, she admits, be costly in resources. It needs to be experiential, participatory; classes have to be small. And all that I heartily agree with. At the same time, Nussbaum argues that the humanities are under continuous attacks from governments that regard education primarily as a vehicle for continuous economic growth, and from students (and their parents, who often influence the choices of their children) who want to get their share – and perhaps a little more than their share – of that growth.

The paradox is that, in order to have access to the kinds of resources Nussbaum says they need, the humanities would have to do a great deal of convincing – and they would specifically have to convince people who are starting from an unsympathetic position. Hence, her book's title is unfortunate. What's bad about profit? It's precisely people who care about profit who need to be brought on board.

In fact, the title is misleading. As the argument develops, it becomes clear that Nussbaum actually agrees with me and my colleagues at the Melbourne Business School. If we want a successful economy we need businesses to absorb the best that the humanities could offer. The economic model that suggests business is all about technicality and applying rules is incorrect. You can't claim that you could further economic growth while ignoring things like imagination, independence of mind, ethics or social responsibility. Properly understood, good education would support a good economy. So, in Nussbaum's terms, it would be for profit. It would achieve many other goods as well; but those goods are not in opposition to the pursuit of profit. She is only opposed to a misguided, unsustainable strategy for obtaining profit.

A similar shift between the apparent claims and details of Nussbaum's argument can be traced in her idea of teaching in the humanities. In her big statements it often sounds as if she thinks that democracy will be well served if the existing ways of pursuing the humanities are merely multiplied: much more of the same. But the detail of her argument points in another direction. It becomes clear that the kind of education she has in mind is not the one that is normally given in the name of the humanities. And so, as she quietly says, large reforms will be needed if the humanities are to rise to serve the great purpose she assigns them.

ONE OF THE obstacles to seizing the opportunity is imaginative and intellectual: there's a deep fear of dumbing down.

'Dumbing down' suggests a tragic split: either you are serious but speak only to insiders, or you speak to the rest of the world but talk nonsense. The phrase implies that it is impossible to speak wisely to a general audience. In this view, humanities intelligence cannot be potent or persuasive beyond the walls of the academy. 'Dumbing down' is contrasted with the conversation of the seminar room, the conference and research journals addressed to a professional audience. This fear is extremely important. If the power of the humanities depends upon their integration with the life of a society and their capacity to speak to the experience of large numbers of individuals, then a conviction that this is impossible is a serious impediment.

'Dumbing down' is a real phenomenon. The question is not whether it ever happens. Rather, what we need to know is whether it is inevitable. Is any attempt to take serious thought outside the walls of the academy doomed?

The central narrative, I think, is this. You understand some issue in the strenuous, refined arena of the academy. To explain the issue to others you must inevitably simplify; but to simplify is to abandon the very things that were important in the first place. The narrative is exemplary in the sciences. Simply put, the layperson cannot understand the real reasons why a particular hypothesis is attractive, or what the underlying principles of explanation and method are. Unless you study the topics carefully for several years, you simply won't understand. You may think you do, but that is delusional.

The sciences only just hold their own against this. Because of the obvious and immense power of technology – which derives from science – there is a fairly widespread conviction that what scientists do is serious and productive, even if we do not understand it. Although even here the conviction is fragile.

In a recent essay in these pages the historian Tom Griffiths made a fine case for the importance of the humanities in helping make science, particularly the science of climate change, more powerful in the imaginations of more people. As he put it: 'Understanding the history of ideas enables a more subtle and discriminating assessment of the public debate about climate change today. There is not only widespread confusion about the science, but also a misunderstanding of how science – or any disciplined knowledge – operates.' I agree, but I am awed by the implications. He places a huge burden on the shoulders of the humanities. As it happens, he has does his share of bearing the load. But it's crucial to see how powerfully this commits him (and anyone who sympathises with him) to courage in the face of the fear of dumbing down. He asserts a public task, on the widest scale: transforming the way not just a few people think but the way a whole society thinks about something as complex as the idea of disciplined knowledge.

The worth of the humanities ultimately depends upon their mattering in people's lives. They might matter because they give help with personal or collective problems; they might matter because they provide emotional or ethical insight; they might help shape a good view of the world; they might (as Nussbaum thinks) sustain democracy; or (as I think) improve the economy; they might (as Tom Griffiths thinks) help us address long-term environmental issues. But all these benefits depend upon the humanities being widely and deeply engaged with non-traditional audiences.

All the specialist work in the world will not achieve these benefits if it remains distant from the public. I don't think that this point is particularly controversial. The controversy comes when you realise that the professional structures and institutional facts of the academic humanities are at odds with this ambition. The ultimate point of research and specialised work is to further those great public educational ends. But that's not how the system works.

NOT SO LONG ago I had a terrifying run-in with a former president of the Australian Academy of the Humanities. I admire his work. He took the view that the humanities were already engaged with the tasks I advocate and already doing an exceptionally good job. He was very angry, and I felt intimidated. I think I now understand what was at stake. As an individual he has tried to do the sorts of things I believe we need to do. My criticism is not of him but of a system that makes him an exception (even if an honoured one) and leaves it to chance whether academics share his ambitions.

The system we have was designed to produce what in the middle of the last century was called a mandarin culture. That is, a cadre of professors who would – like leading scientists – discover the most refined knowledge, which would then, somehow, trickle down to the rest of society. Or, would perhaps simply bypass the public. The top humanities academics would live in the same world as the leading politicians, industrialists and public servants. At the high tables of the universities they would find a single pinnacle. The wisdom of the humanities would thereby be effective in the world, without having to cultivate a general audience. And this was given more plausibility because – at that time – you could just about believe, at least in the UK, that the humanities represented a formalised, ambitious version of the culture of the executive class.

If this ever existed, it belongs now to the realm of fantasy. If the humanities are to be powerful in the world it must be through their role in the lives of large numbers of people.

Hostility to what is thought of as dumbing down is really a confusion of means and ends. Technical specialisation is only a means to something else – ideally, more important knowledge. And the end is that such knowledge should be effective in the world. But to be fitted to be effective in the world, such knowledge cannot remain in its specialised form. This is not an unfortunate concession that has to be made. It is the most noble and sophisticated task.

There are solutions to the problem of dumbing down. It's not a mystery. It's just that the humanities have been set up institutionally in a way that puts the solution out of reach – with rare exceptions.

The solution is to be found in the cultivation of two intertwined practices. The first – and ultimately most difficult – derives from a question most famously posed by St Augustine: 'Why is it good to know that?' The question needs to be taken with the utmost seriousness and pursued as far as we possibly can. It is common currency in the humanities to suppose that your own work is important (leaving aside the damned, who work only to meet administrative demands and who have lost any sense that what they do is important in other ways). But this belief is generally tacit – not surprisingly, because academics are mainly working for the interest and admiration of a peer group who, almost by definition, share a sense of what's important. There are furious battles of ideas; but these are conducted among people who share a background, not before an unconvinced audience.

The second solution is artistry. I spend most of my working life writing books for the commercial market. In the past ten years I've published five books with Penguin UK. My intellectual background is firmly philosophical and I draw continually on my six years of graduate studies. I was educated mainly in the analytic tradition, which places great emphasis on the definition of concepts, the formation and rebuttal of argument, the clarification of ambiguity and a precise sense of the scope of claims – what it being claimed; what is not included in the claim.

In my books I try to write in a way that is not merely accessible to non-specialists; I try to speak to the inner lives of readers. There is a huge difference. Almost every newspaper article is accessible. Whether it is moving, beautiful, serious, engaging is another matter entirely. I devote a great deal of attention to the tone of the writing, to the length of paragraphs, to the flow of each sentence.

None of this has anything whatever to do with dumbing down – the attempt to find an audience by feigning stupidity. My model of writing is based on the best intellectual-literary works I know: *Middlemarch* and *War and Peace*. George Eliot and Tolstoy have an astonishing ability to convey ideas as part of experience. That's what I aspire to.

If it takes two or three years to write a book, writing for an average of two hours every day, and if a book is around two hundred pages in length, that's the equivalent of three days per page. Or about a hundred words a day. In fact, I often write a thousand or more words a day. So nine-tenths of the effort is rewriting. Almost everything gets thrown away.

In my writing practice, research is not a major concern. This is partly because I often feel that, in a technical sense, I already know more than the book requires. What I don't know is why an idea is important or exciting. That's what needs to be worked out. It's discovered by asking myself: why, really, am I interested in a particular topic? What is beauty to me, for instance, or why do I care about the idea of civilisation? I start out with a vague thrill: these concepts seem to me to have immense promise, but I don't know why. I'm trying to uncover what that promise and excitement is. And I'm trying to work out how to share it with other people. A critical resource is recalling – reliving – the experience of not being interested, or of being baffled, or of being bored, of reading books which I found disappointing or which I read out of a sense of duty. I need to listen to my own associations; I need to risk recognising that the development of an idea is tedious – even if it is true.

WHEN I TOOK up a post at the Melbourne Business School some of my fellow academics in the Arts Faculty at the University of Melbourne described it as 'going over to the dark side'.

One of my colleagues at the school was formerly a colleague in the then philosophy departments at Monash and later at Melbourne. She's a philosopher of mind and science. I dropped by her office to talk about the strange fact that we'd both ended up in a business school. Drawing on our experiences we sketched a 'Rome to Constantinople' theory of the future of the humanities. As the Roman Empire developed, the balance of its interests and needs for government shifted to the east. We imagined a migration of humanities talent, with people being drawn to the places where their insights, curiosity and intellectual skills were most needed and appreciated. Would the most interesting historians, we wondered, one day be based in faculties of economics and commerce – where their understanding of the forces that shape the world would be of maximum application? Could the philosophers of the future find their offices in investment banks – where the hardest problems of meaning and value and logical analysis need to be understood and tested in reality?

Perhaps this is not just a fantasy. In recent months I've been involved in a major project on ethical leadership that reaches into the highest levels of executive education. This project – which has substantial external funding

– is based in a business school, although the topics with which it deals, power and ethics, might seem to belong by rights to the humanities. And these are humanities themes; it's just that the official centres of the humanities are not the places where they are being pursued in the most helpful ways.

The program provides intensive education for the most senior managers of major businesses and corporations. Required readings are drawn from the classics of the western canon, and constitute a mini-course in the humanities. The aim is serious: let's read Nietzsche or Tolstoy to see what they can teach us about the meaning of life, the nature of values and the project of articulating your most consequential beliefs. And we are doing this with a sense of practical urgency. We need to get good at this kind of thinking.

Ethics and leadership are deep topics of the humanities. They are also practical matters. They need to be put into action in the world; our understanding of them needs to grow from close reflection on the actual experience of individuals; for, ultimately, the relevant knowledge – the relevant capacities and abilities – is held in the minds of agents. In other words, the education of ethical leadership is a collaboration between people who are in or are about to be in positions of real power and those who think deeply and carefully but at a certain distance from the action.

Why have the official schools of the humanities, on the whole, not been the ones to grasp this opportunity?

Think of the battle cry 'Speak truth to power!' It's an intoxicating slogan – and a misleading ideal. The problem lies in the word 'speak'. What about getting power to listen? What about understanding the limitations and difficulties of power? What about learning from the experiences of power? No. The slogan imagines that the work is done when you have said your piece. You can imagine situations in which this is truly heroic, or when it is the only thing to be done. Or when magically the pure voice of truth carries a great public with it and so becomes the rallying point for serious progress. But such scenarios are far removed from the realties of life in a market-based liberal economy. There may be much about such societies that could and should be better. But the path to progress doesn't lie in just telling people that they don't know the truth.

Still, it would often be more accurate to talk of academic bemusement than arrogance. Bemusement that the styles of thinking, the accumulated knowledge, the subtlety of mind, the refinement of ideas that are so seriously cultivated in the humanities don't seem to be able to get a greater purchase on the way the world works.

APART FROM ANXIETY about dumbing down there are three longstanding strategic weaknesses of the humanities as they currently operate in higher education. There's the problem of the career path. In the core humanities there are not a great many jobs on offer. If you look at the résumés of most humanities academics at most Australian universities, it is clear that getting appointed has been a lifelong task. Mostly, people will have undertaken a relevant undergraduate degree; then they will have done a masters degree; then a PhD. Since a PhD is almost never sufficient for an ongoing post, they will have had various postdoctoral appointments, writing papers and gradually arming themselves for an ongoing position. In other words, between the ages of about nineteen and thirty-two an individual will have had to have made intense continuous effort in order to be competitive for full employment in a humanities department in a permanent post. In my own field, philosophy, only one or two people are raised to professorial level each year. A successful career in the academic humanities requires a lifelong devotion to your subject.

This means that such academics are extremely unlikely to have had significant experience of work outside this structure, other than casual jobs. This is a problem, because – as I've been insisting – the true home of the humanities is in the world, not in the academy. The collective experience that humanities academics bring to their work is a base from which to reach out to the world. If that experiential base is too small, or too unusual, it won't be possible to reach out in an authentic or compelling manner.

ANOTHER ENTRENCHED OBSTACLE can be seen in the political culture of the humanities. Recently I was chatting with a colleague I rather like but don't know all that well. He happened to mention that his politics are – as he put it – far to the left. I have nothing against his opinion. But it struck me as significant that he felt very relaxed mentioning it. He spoke as if it were obvious that I would be sympathetic, although I have never said anything on such matters to him. His ease was a symptom of the pervasive culture of the humanities. It's just assumed that you are on the left, unless you go out of your way to explain otherwise.

It's completely fine – and an expression of intellectual freedom – that individual academics should be able to come to more or less any conclusions about the tasks of government, so long as they don't preach to the students. This principle is securely established. But there is too much consensus among people in the humanities. It is a political monoculture. There are a few exceptions, no doubt. But they really are exceptions.

The monoculture closes off the potential for wider sympathy. A lot of the most successful people I know have no engagement at all with the humanities. The disciplines do not seem to recognise their aspirations, or speak to their ambitions. Such people have a huge impact on the world. I know it will sound strange, even ridiculous – and this is a symptom of our problem – to say that one of the primary tasks of the humanities is to teach grace and dignity to those who are materially successful in the world. This isn't to do with recruiting them to philanthropy ('tell your friends in business to give us their money' is a phrase that sticks in my mind). When I meet a well-off couple whose idea of heaven is watching Formula One, seeing a celebrity at a flashy restaurant and talking about real estate prices, I see the failure of the humanities. The materially successful set the standard for a lot of other people.

There's an anecdote in Tolstoy about a soldier who reads up on the aphorisms of Lichtenberg so as to be able to hold his own at a society soiree. Reactions to this little story are a test of attitude. Does it hint at a criterion of success for the humanities or does it represent their degradation? I think that capturing the imagination of the successful is an essential task; but I feel lonely with this thought.

THE THIRD WEAKNESS is the idea of the peer group – which is very closely connected to research. Martha Nussbaum seems to take it for granted that research in the humanities will automatically advance the educational project for which she argues. But the connection is not clear. It is not at all obvious that most – or even very much – research has any bearing upon her concerns. For instance, education in critical thinking is already perfectly possible – and could be well supplied on the basis of existing knowledge. We could do with a better understanding of how people learn, of cognitive biases, and of the kinds of exercises and examples that are the most efficient from a pedagogical point of view. But this doesn't sound much like the kind of research humanities academics typically do, or want to do, or are trained to do.

The academic peer group is unrepresentative of the people we need to reach. At its best, the peer group functions as quality control. But it surreptitiously does something else as well. It becomes the target audience. And this is the opposite of what we need. We get good at impressing one another but we need to impress people who are not part of the academic circle.

And we need to do this not as an amateur, optional add-on, as something we do in our leisure time, distinct from our core business. In the 1950s and '60s, when the present professional humanities system started to crystallise – around the ideas of the PhD, research and peer group review – there was limited competition in ideas. High culture was the ruling culture. Today, the circulation of ideas is a professional business. Humanities academics live in a competitive marketplace of content. This is dismaying, because idiotic ideas often get prominence while thoughtful, serious contributions are ignored. We could try to protect ourselves, and withdraw from competition. Perhaps government or philanthropists could be persuaded to shield the humanities from the demotic fray. That would be comfortable for insiders. But it would be terrible for everyone else.

This is the essential question for the humanities: can elegance of mind, subtle reasonableness, care for the logic of argument, nobility of spirit ever hold their own in the wider world? Or can these be pursued only in protected, enclosed environments?

If the humanities are to hold their own we have to face competition; we have to get exceptionally good – not amateurishly good – at engagement. When humanities academics approach a problem like decoding

Hegel's *Phenomenology* or understanding the reception of Byron's poetry in nineteenth-century France, there is no limit to the ingenuity, effort and intelligence devoted to the task. There's no amateurism there. No sense of 'who knows, perhaps this will work'; every possibility is examined, every resource deployed.

The urgent problem now isn't that we can't follow Hegel's convoluted sentences or that we are woefully ignorant of what Byron meant to Balzac; our problem is that we live in a world that doesn't know how to be serious about serious things.

For the humanities to gain a central, powerful position in the world (as I believe they should) the politics and pragmatics of communication need to become matters of intense professional focus – and not as theories, but as things we do superbly well. Not just a little better.

The idea of the peer group holds a key to the reformation and renaissance of the humanities. If 'peer' could be redefined, the situation would change – and government, administrators and academics could, in concert, achieve this. 'Peer' simply indicates whose opinion about value you pay attention to. A top-tier journal is identified by asking which journal insiders hold in most esteem. We should say, instead, that the humanities need to win the esteem of outsiders. Therefore, the greatest prestige should track wider esteem. 'Top-tier' could be recast to require significant external interest. We should aim to combine a high level of cognitive sophistication with the achievement of real enthusiasm and interest from a broader constituency.

So we need to listen to and take seriously the responses of people who are not already devotees or insiders. They are peers in the sense that we have to treat them as equals. If that were done we would orient effort in the humanities towards the proper goals. Thus, a PhD should have a non-academic examiner; appointments committees should have non-academic members; journals should have non-academic reviewers. We have to break with the idea that the humanities are or should be structured like sciences (scholarship is the science of the humanities). The goal of the humanities is the creation of knowledge and ways of thinking that are found useful by others, and academics cannot be the final judges of whether this has been achieved or not. A good analogy would be that the humanities seek 'technologies' of living and thinking. Technology requires an underlying science, but the science alone isn't sufficient. You need an intense focus on what works for people, on what needs they have (or could be persuaded to recognise). The interface needs the greatest care.

THE IDEA THAT the humanities should be useful has proved to be something of a stumbling block. But this is for superficial rather than deep reasons. In 2005 I was appointed Knowledge Transfer Fellow at the University of Melbourne. Knowledge Transfer was a statement of general intent: university teaching and research should develop more purposeful and more creative relationships with thinking needs, and thinking strengths, of the economy and civil society. The details in the humanities were not at first clear. The response seemed panicky. It took the form of grasping at random applications of existing research.

I don't want to be harsh about any of the well-intended projects, but I do want to analyse the difficulty involved. So I'll invent an example that serves to illustrate a generic problem. Some famous paintings express tranquillity and peace of mind. And there are times when such feelings might be much sought-after – perhaps in a dentist's waiting room. (My local practitioner has an unfortunate interest in works that convey anguish and despairing rage.) So you could project a Knowledge Transfer research program that places images by Claude Lorraine or Mark Rothko in stressful environments and studies the impact on people's condition of mind.

I don't mean to be down on such a project, but it has an air of desperation about it. It takes some of the noblest and grandest achievements of the western imagination but employs their lowliest strengths. Works that aspire to reveal perfect beauty or instil awe are used to reduce transient tension. It's as if the project is saying: we have given up hope that the grander significance of these things could ever be powerful in the world; but we have to find some utility; anything will do.

This is the reverse of an equal but opposite problem that has, at other times, been evident in the humanities. I recall several occasions when cultural historians have tried to persuade me that neoclassical architecture is the advance guard of fascism. Here, the intellectual is saving the modern world from right-wing tyranny. But the salvation is faked because the threat is unreal.

Actually, the whole episode of critical radicalism that gripped the centre of the humanities for about twenty years under the banner of Theory suffered from exactly this inflated and unreal sense of significance. Put harshly, Theory said to the world: you are stupid and wrong about everything; you won't be able to understand why (read a page of what we write – I guarantee you will find it incomprehensible); now treat us with honour and pay for us. The hatred of the 'bourgeois' world was palpable, and yet it was taken for granted that this hatred should be funded by the state. This arrogance broke a fundamental principle of social relationships: if you want to influence people you have to gain their trust; if you want to be understood you have to speak a language people understand.

Over-modesty and grandiosity have a common theme. Each struggles to find an appropriate idea of utility for what it is concerned with. Each difficulty has a common cause. They start from existing lines of research and discussion, and seek some outlet for that work.

Rather than searching for niche markets for existing interests, we should follow a very different path. The humanities should start from core questions, great questions – and these should be framed practically. Instead of asking 'what is rationality' we should start with 'how can public rationality be improved'. The practical question embraces the conceptual one – you need to know what rationality is if you want to get more of it. Or 'how can the arts help people live better lives' – which includes the questions 'what is art' and 'how should we understand the art of the past', but sets these within a consequential framework.

So, the attempt to solve the great questions leads out directly into purposeful engagement with the wider world. The great questions orchestrate intellectual effort and drive it to practical projects, and to interdisciplinary collaboration. But the collaboration is purposeful – it doesn't start with an institutional worry (how can we get disciplines to work together); it starts with a real problem which needs collaboration.

Continued on page 41

PICTURE GALLERY

Vita Brevis Est
GEORGE SCHWARZ

Untitled 11, 2006 from *Vita Brevis Est*, Digital print 40 x 40cm, edition of 3

Untitled 7, 2006 from *Vita Brevis Est*, Digital print 40 x 40cm, edition of 3

VITA BREVIS EST

Untitled 20, 2006 from *Vita Brevis Est*, Digital print 40 x 40cm, edition of 3

Untitled 14, 2006 from *Vita Brevis Est*, Digital print 40 x 40cm, edition of 3

VITA BREVIS EST

Untitled 12, 2006 from *Vita Brevis Est*, Digital print 40 x 40cm, edition of 3

Untitled 13, 2006 from *Vita Brevis Est*, Digital print 40 x 40cm, edition of 3

VITA BREVIS EST 39

Untitled 18, 2006 from *Vita Brevis Est*, Digital print 40 x 40cm, edition of 3

Untitled 4, 2006 from *Vita Brevis Est*, Digital print 40 x 40cm, edition of 3

Vita Brevis Est (Life is short) images courtesy of George Schwarz.
For further works by this artist, go to www.stillsgallery.com.au/artists/schwarz/

THE MOST CONFUSING idea about the value of the humanities – which has gained many adherents in recent times – is that they are valuable for their own sake. The argument runs: people say that the humanities lack instrumental value and that, therefore, they should not receive public subsidy.

Let's concede (for this stage of the discussion) that, quite often, the humanities are weak on instrumental value. Let us suppose that their contribution to growing the economy, creating jobs, improving medical services, increasing national security or promoting social inclusion is tenuous. But this is not a problem – it is said – because they have another kind of value: intrinsic value. And their possession of intrinsic value justifies public support.

It may not be easy to spell out any powerful, quantifiable practical benefits that follow from appreciating Titian's paintings, reading *The Critique of Pure Reason*, grasping the influence of Turgenev on Henry James or knowing about court politics in the reign of Charles I (to take traditional themes), or comparing the imagined body in different vampire films, speculating on 'why there is something rather than nothing', decoding symbolist poetry or tracing the gendered politics of politeness in eighteenth-century France. But that doesn't matter. The value of these pursuits is intrinsic.

Is this a good argument? We need to clarify a few points. What, exactly, is intrinsic value? Do the humanities actually have it? And, if so, how does this translate into a claim upon public subsidy? The central way of conceptualising intrinsic value is: anything is experienced as possessing intrinsic value to the extent that the appreciation of that thing does not depend upon further benefits which may flow from it.

On this view it is certainly correct to say that the humanities have intrinsic value. But this is not, in fact, to say very much. For intrinsic value is ubiquitous. All entertainment, all hobbies, most social intercourse, all interior decoration and most holidays (to start the list) are pursued primarily for their own sake, without their enjoyment depending upon consequent benefits. Intrinsic value is not a rare or elusive phenomenon. We do not use the term in ordinary conversation, but practical life is deeply interwoven with, and organised to serve, the enjoyment of intrinsic value.

One person thinks it would be nice to spend an afternoon walking in the hills; another wants to read *The Critique of Pure Reason*; a third is going to bake bread; a fourth is heading to the pub with some friends. All are in pursuit of intrinsic value: they like these things 'for their own sake'. Why should just one of these be singled out for public subsidy (other than that fact that it is the least popular)? We could, after all, think well of the reading project – just as we could think well of the other projects – without regarding it as requiring any kind of public intervention.

The 'intrinsic value' defence of the humanities is coy. It's of no significance in debates about higher education merely to note that some activities happen to be liked for their own sake by some people. The decisive claim needs to be much grander, and is more difficult to defend. You would have to claim that the humanities possess an exceptional degree of intrinsic value – so great that societies should go out of their way to foster such experiences and should maintain institutions expressly for the purpose of cultivating these experiences.

Such justification was undertaken in the 1950s and '60s by FR Leavis. He developed an account of the humanities – with English literature at its core, but spreading widely – that stressed the idea of quality of consciousness. Leavis had no doubt that appreciating Jane Austen's view of life, or coming to share the sensibility of Henry James, was of tremendous intrinsic value, far beyond the level of other experiences we may happen to enjoy for their own sake. He made intense efforts to justify these claims. He tried to show how lesser enjoyments arise from shallow and self-destructive inclinations. He waged war on contemporary culture, which he regarded as corrupt and corrupting. He developed techniques of teaching that were designed to educate the student's inner life to a pitch of concentrated sincerity and sensitivity – necessary requirements, he believed, for an encounter with the highest degrees of intrinsic value. He was a tireless public advocate of such an education.

Leavis – it hardly needs to be said – has been completely disowned by the humanities. It is the humanities that have preached the idea that enjoying a novel by Tolstoy is no finer an experience than watching an ad; that it is only a prejudice to suppose that Montaigne is a better writer or deeper thinker than Dan Brown. Such views make any 'intrinsic value' defence hypocritical. All the effort would need to go into convincing people of entirely the reverse propositions. Namely, that activities and preferences are radically unequal, that some are much more worthy than others and, therefore, deserving of special protection and effort. Today, the intrinsic value defence of the humanities is panicked and insubstantial. Fearing being judged on utilitarian grounds, supporters of the humanities clutch at a non-instrumental notion of value. But they have not, for a long time, taken the pursuit and honouring of non-instrumental value as their core purpose.

Any sustained, ambitious attempt to justify the humanities on the grounds of their intrinsic value has to be pursued along the lines Leavis sketched out. That is, you would have to make the claim that some experiences are far finer and deeper than others, and that popular opinion has no authority on what these experiences are. If popular opinion happened to be right about the highest levels of intrinsic value there would be no need for special state institutions: the free market would be the best provider. Obviously we don't need any special institutions to support the enjoyment of Harry Potter. It would be easy to conduct research, analyse the plots and characters, and speculate about social ideology. But none of this is necessary for the appreciation of the intrinsic value of the Potter books – they have been widely enjoyed already, for their own sake. So if you care about intrinsic value, in terms of popular opinion, you would quite cheerfully abolish the literature courses of universities, and leave things to Amazon and the publishing industry. Anyone who believes that there is no difference of intrinsic merit between popular culture and high culture should reject the intrinsic value argument as providing any justification for the academic humanities. Because, from that point of view, the academic humanities are redundant, or just a support system for a minority hobby.

In other words, the intrinsic value defence of the humanities requires an additional premise: high intrinsic value is real, even when unacknowledged. It requires the belief that there can be genuine leadership towards experiences which are of great value for their own sake, but which most people (and the open market) would miss if left to themselves. The humanities as practised today run away from these claims. They want the conclusion (we are special) but not the premises (intrinsic value is hierarchical, unequal).

Let me put my cards on the table. I believe that one of the deepest tasks of the humanities is to seek out, secure and maintain the highest forms of intrinsic value, and to promote the widest possible public devotion to such values. But this is a call to reform the humanities. It is not, in fact, what the humanities do, nor is it what they are set up to do. The humanities systematically reject the idea of high intrinsic value and thereby saw off one of the branches on which they could sit.

CONSIDER THESE STATEMENTS by distinguished humanities academics, reflecting on the value of their disciplines: 'Latin serves to train the mind; it is not merely that one learns to read particular ancient texts: one learns to weigh the meaning of a word, to grasp how words come together to form meaningful sentences; one learns to think.' And: 'Long after students have forgotten the details of the French Revolution, they will continue to know how to express their own views clearly and powerfully; they will have developed the skill of weighing evidence, of assessing the views of others, of taking a long view of complex events: these qualities will serve them well in life.'

These statements advance the view that the value of the humanities does not lie so much in the content they teach as in the qualities of mind they cultivate.

Can we identify the qualities of mind and the resources of character that the humanities seek (or should seek) to cultivate? Some of these qualities of mind and resources of character are not unique to the humanities; but still the humanities may provide for many people the best route to these 'virtues'. And it is misleading to isolate the virtues – their full benefit depends upon their interaction with one another.

This list is not exhaustive; but it should include the following.

Mental space (openness of mind, breadth of mind): this is the ability to work productively with – and take seriously – more than one point of view, or concern, at the same time. This matters when several points of view (or lines of thought, or concerns) are relevant to the matter in hand; but when they do not sit well or easily together, they seem opposed – and may actually be. Notions of incompatibility, incommensurability and incongruity describe the various tensions that may exist among points of view.

An open mind is one that can adjust its internal order in the light of a new idea or fact. But there has to be something significant there already to be adjusted. The finer the existing order, the more powerful and impressive a new idea or fact needs to be if it is to call for and sustain this new order. An open mind is one that is ready to absorb any worthy new fact into an existing serious conception of the world. Thus, having an open mind is not a just a matter of willingness to consider any fact or idea (wherever it comes from); even less is it hunger for novelty.

At its best, openness of mind is a kind of courage. It is the capacity to see the power of a thought when you would rather avoid it. This is precisely what is missing in the facile idea of openness as lack of anxiety – 'I can consider anything.' 'Openness' is a complementary virtue: it is most valuable when combined with a strenuous commitment to logic, hierarchy and evidence.

The ability to learn from the experience and ideas of others: the subject matter of the humanities includes the best that has been thought and said about the human condition, about what has happened in the past, and about what is worthy of care and respect. A great deal of human insight of enduring, if partial, significance is scattered through the traditional materials of the humanities. The hope is that the scattered divergent insights can be retained, accumulated and better understood – and deployed now.

We should be very ambitious here. It's only a start to say things like 'we need to know about the past' or 'seeing how women behaved in 1793 changes our ideas about the construction of femininity' or 'we need to know how people thought about God in the past.' This 'need' should be investigated more stringently. What we need such information for should be at the forefront of enquiry, not tacked on later as an excuse or self-justification – which, frankly, is what it often is in practice.

The understanding and appreciation of values: this has often been seen in a pious and unadventurous light. The aim of the humanities might be said to be the inculcation of compassion and tolerance – the emotional virtues *du jour*. We should be more adventurous here. Probably, almost everyone who undertakes higher education in the humanities is pretty tolerant and compassionate. The bigger ambition is to look seriously at the values we need the humanities to help with – for instance, the merit of taste (the capacity to see and appreciate beauty). What about the value of maturity: the recognition of inescapable conflicts between goods; the capacity to keep the long-term in view; the strength to say 'no' to yourself and others; the readiness to take responsibility for hard decisions that will have negative consequences for some people?

Knowledge and appreciation of values is a kind of fleshing-out. Often the values we have are articulated by vague yet important words – but we don't much think about or understand what they really come to, or what they mean in practice. This issue of is huge significance outside the humanities.

On a great many questions and issues we ought to have a normative point of view – that is, to regard certain outcomes or practices or objects as good, malign, noble, base, beautiful, ugly, ethical, vicious or admirable. These terms are normative: they express moral judgements. But such terms are vulnerable to misuse and are grounded, at least in part, in subjectivity; they are not scientific. Their relation to evidence is weak; they do not derive their authority (such as it is) from consensus, although they seek consensus. They are not provable, although they are not irrational.

A sophisticated, powerful thinker and agent in the world needs to participate in normative and evaluative points of view. But there is a great difference between merely having an evaluative stance – whatever it may be – and being good at normative thinking.

The process by which you become a fine and successful normative thinker (and agent) can be presented in ideal form: first, you become aware of your own normative attitudes – this is complex, because often you do not notice quite where a normative attitude begins, or what role it is playing. Second, you examine the grounds of this normative attitude; you explore its relationship to evidence and argument; you consider its merits and weaknesses. Third, there is a process of revision in which normative attitudes are refined and reconstructed. Fourth, normative attitudes are deployed in the world. The experience this yields takes you back to the start of the cycle, but at a more sophisticated level. This is only the briefest outline of an immensely complex process.

Such a process flourishes in a culture in which normativity is taken very seriously – you are ambitious to form fine normative attitudes – and simultaneously good at examining and understanding the possible weaknesses and limitations of normative attitudes. Ideally, this is not a solitary project but is native to a local culture. It cannot be pursued in a purely theoretical environment. You need to draw upon the lessons of experience.

Normative thinking requires the integration of discursive labour and the accumulation of experience. It is one of the most important areas in which we can see the centrality of the idea of lifelong learning.

Learning from experience: the humanities are typically connected with book learning; they involve library and archival research. This is ironic, because the things they deal with (great paintings, great works of fiction, the dramas of history, the ideas created by great philosophers) often have entirely different origins – those achievements were from broad and rich personal experience.

For instance, Goethe worked out what he thought in the interface between book learning and life learning. We should be creative in thinking about how this can be brought into the humanities. The aim is to help students learn from their own experience.

Working up from suggestion to statement: the capacity for clear, logical thinking is one of the most easily understood of educational ambitions. Often what is needed is the capacity to turn informal, suggestive, muddled material (early stage thinking) into a better-organised presentation – so that the relations between ideas can be more easily grasped. This is the capacity to work up an inchoate line of thought (a hunch, an inspiration, a suggestion) into a more mature form.

This might occur when you take a poem and attempt to turn some of its suggestive poetic thinking into prose statements that can be weighed in the light of reason and evidence. What distinguishes really fine achievements of this kind is that they do not lose what is buried in the inchoate thought; they reveal it more clearly. The basic form of this kind of approach asks: what is the potential significance of this suggestion? Our capacity to see what something could mean, or what someone is trying to say, is of great utility.

The capacity to benefit from seeing the weaknesses of your own work (to take risks and be self-critical): it is natural to overestimate the significance and merit of your own ideas. Self-criticism ideally anticipates and internalises a good external critic. It's crucial in the gradual evolution of better versions of ideas and proposals.

But often the ability to see the weaknesses of your thinking is paralysing; you become cautious, dispirited, and rely too much upon consensus and established patterns. There is a capacity of character, as well as of intellect, which enables an individual to be both self-critical and able to take intellectual and conceptual risks.

This could be developed through the rewriting of exercises and essays, or where the individual student is required to grade their own work; to provide a rationale for the grade; to go back and rewrite the essay or presentation. This could be repeated twenty times if need be. Ideally, this would be done under time pressure – in an open office setting.

The fostering of judgement: a key aspect of judgement is the willingness to assert what is genuinely important in a particular situation. It is at odds with the application of an existing and well-established set of priorities. It involves taking responsibility for your assertion – and hence involves reflecting upon experiences of failure. An interesting strategy here might be to concentrate on intellectual failure (confusions, inability to make progress, lassitude, boredom, pretentiousness).

Healthy impatience: this is the capacity of character, as well as of mind, to push ideas past their current threshold. If everyone is talking about integrity, for instance, your immediate response should be 'what is integrity?' and your second response should be 'let's work it out.' It involves recognising the point at which a lot of people have stopped thinking. It is a conviction that we can almost always come up with much better ways of understanding our present concerns. It's impatience with concepts that don't deliver what people suppose they do. For instance, talk about innovation rarely recognises the fact that it is a process term (something is new) masquerading as an achievement term (something is better).

The non-reductive simplification of sophisticated material: the humanities contain stunning examples of the powerful, straightforward presentation of immensely sophisticated material, as well as the complex presentation of simple material. One of the main features of life is the need for people with sophisticated ideas to be able to communicate what is central and critical in their thinking to people who won't grasp the subtleties through lack of time, lack of aptitude or lack of interest.

Such communication should be the finest achievement of sophistication – because it has arrived at such a solid and clear understanding of a complex matter that the point can at last be presented in a straightforward, convincing and helpful way. You go through complexity to simplicity.

The process here is of an ever improving understanding of what the issues actually are – what the claim is, what the rationale is – so that, eventually, it can be presented in a clean and organised and compelling manner. The relevant exercise might be that of demanding more and more clarification from students in specific set exercises (under time pressure), but with many opportunities to repeat the exercise.

This is a point of difference between the humanities and other disciplines. The best work in the humanities – or the work the humanities deals with – often is simple in presentation (Plato, Tolstoy, Raphael, Mozart, Jane Austen). There are of course great subtleties and sophistications at play, but they are presented straightforwardly. It would be a huge gain for humanity if we could systematically educate people in this capacity.

Confidence in dealing with established misunderstanding: the sources of confidence are twofold. First, the recognition that understanding or explanation isn't a matter of consensus; the fact of consensus isn't compelling in itself. It's simple to state this intellectually. It's a matter of character, however, to be able to use this obvious point in the press of life. But the negative capacity to be independent won't come to much unless it is allied with an ability to engage fruitfully, to deal with, such a consensus. That involves being able to second-guess what the roots of confusion are, to understand the fears or difficulties that are attached to breaking with the established view.

So, in cultivating these capacities, we are not just inculcating heroic oppositional stances. A good question: why might it be attractive or exciting to hold the view opposed to the one you have been arguing for? The aim isn't to teach some particular bit of content. The aim is to inculcate a great quality of mind. So the education should aim at internalising this capacity.

A QUALITY OF mind can be seen as both ability and a disposition. An ability names something you can do. A disposition names something you tend to do.

The aim, then, of humanities education – in this sense – is to cultivate dispositions: the reliable, intelligent deployment of abilities in real-world situations. It is the ability to think carefully – when under pressure, when there are strong countervailing forces, when there is a need to do so, in the service of an important purpose.

What would be the consequences for the humanities if they took the cultivation of such dispositions of mind as their central purpose? It would mean radical revision of teaching. If the point of studying the French Revolution is not so much to accumulate knowledge about that event as to develop abilities to think effectively about complex processes, the emphasis in teaching and assessment should be on those qualities of mind as needed in other situations. If we've learned something about a complex process, let's try using it on something other than the French Revolution. And in research, qualities of mind would stand as the principle of evaluation.

I was recently talking to an engineering student and the conversation happened to turn to ethics. I was surprised by how confidently she handled the topics: she had a well-informed view about utilitarianism and its strengths and weaknesses. Having, in the past, often taught introductory courses on ethics, I was rather envious of her lecturer. I feared that few of my students would have come away with such a good education. How had she come to understand all this? She explained that she'd been watching a series of lectures on YouTube by the Harvard philosopher Michael Sandal. The lectures were so good, she said, it was like watching a brilliant documentary.

There's no reason why all lecturing should not be provided in this way. A hundred or so superb communicators could take over the whole of that task. The more intimate aspect of education – the cultivation of capacities – would then be the primary focus of teaching.

THE STAKES ARE high. We need the humanities to flourish. But this will require reformation: the humanities need to become more eloquent, more focused on other people, more adept at facing competition, more connected to the economy, more sympathetic to aspiration.

If we will it, this is not the twilight of the humanities: it is early morning. We have to shake off our dogmatic slumbers.

John Armstrong is Philosopher-in-Residence at the Melbourne Business School and Senior Advisor, Office of the Vice-Chancellor, at the University of Melbourne. He is the author of several books on art, love and beauty, including most recently *In Search of Civilisation* (Penguin, 2009).

ESSAY

The crumbling wall

Science, certainty and value judgements

Ian Lowe

I GREW up in an era when science had an aura of certainty and solidity: it was 'the true exemplar of authentic knowledge', as the eminent sociologist Robert K Merton put it. History inevitably contains a subjective element, and there are different and legitimate views about the significance of a work of literature, but science was different. At school we learned which chlorides are insoluble and which metals are attacked by hydrochloric acid: no room for subjectivity or different interpretations there. We learned the laws of motion, as set down by Newton hundreds of years ago: not theories but laws that can't be broken. The science was incontestable, so your answer in the school test was either right or wrong. At university, all the physics and chemistry I learned as an undergraduate was solid, unquestioned knowledge.

Science spoke with a particular authority. It has been argued that other disciplines were affected by this perception; some observers think 'physics envy' led economics down the path of mathematical modelling and arcane theories that, applied to financial products, wrought havoc in the real world. That is another story.

Applying science had produced technical marvels that significantly influenced World War II, like radar, culminating in the fearsome weapons that obliterated two Japanese cities and brought the war to an end. Applying science to our domestic life gave us clean drinking water, protection from diseases, cleaner and faster cooking, better communications and a dramatically improved material lifestyle.

Governments cheerfully funded science, confident that the goose would continue to lay golden eggs. The highest-achieving school leavers were more likely to study science at university than arts, law or medicine, let alone courses in economics or commerce. The CSIRO, originally set up to improve our primary industries, extended its work into manufacturing and information processing. Most politicians worshipped the new deity and appeased it with regular offerings, though some were more cautious; Winston Churchill famously said that scientists should be 'on tap, not on top', working as directed.

To some extent, the perception that science produces permanent knowledge still applies in the laboratory. I recall my doctoral supervisor saying in admiration of a distinguished colleague, 'When he measures

---

PREVIOUS PAGE: Mikael Damkier. *Boy and a mask.* www.dreamstime.com

something it stays measured!' That fabled scientist spoke disparagingly of 'those romanticists', a research group he believed to espouse theories that went beyond the solid evidence from experiments. Predictability is not just a perception: ask a scientist to measure something under controlled conditions, the melting point of a specified alloy or the rate of reaction between two chemicals, and you can expect a precise answer. What's more, you can expect the same precise answer from any competent professional. In the artificial world of the laboratory, where all the relevant variables can be controlled, science gives clear and verifiable answers, with little room for subjective interpretation.

THE FIRST CRACK in the wall was the analysis by the physicist and historian Thomas Kuhn of what he called scientific revolutions. He used specific examples: the old earth-centred view of the universe and physics before the development of quantum theory. In each case the old science was working diligently within what he termed the dominant paradigm, a phrase that is now part of the political lexicon. He showed that 'normal science' accepted the existing theory and worked within it, collecting data and solving small puzzles. But the accumulating evidence led to increasing awareness that the prevailing theory was inadequate.

Even then, Kuhn argued, the old theory was not rejected until a new and better theory was developed to explain the observations. In each case, adherents of the old theory were understandably reluctant to admit that their life's work had been in vain. They often tried to find a contorted logic that fitted the new evidence into the old theory. Kuhn concluded the new theory would triumph only when proponents of the old one retired or ceased to have influence, leaving the field to the Young Turks who saw the improved explanatory power of the different approach: a scientific revolution.

I saw two examples of Kuhn's theory in action in the 1960s: the continents and the origin of the universe. The theory of continental drift had been around since the nineteenth century and made instinctive sense, since the east coast of South America is strikingly similar to the west coast of Africa and it looks to the amateur eye as if they could once have fitted together. But scientists could not imagine continents moving around on the face of the earth, and the theory was dismissed as populist nonsense. It all changed when one critical measurement found the sea floor spreading around the Mid-Atlantic Ridge, showing that the continents were actually moving apart. Within about five years, the old superstition of continental drift had become the new science of plate tectonics. This in turn made sense of a wide range of previously puzzling observations, from the continuing growth of the Himalayas (the result of the Indian Plate colliding with the Asian Plate) to the biological parallels in Africa, South America and Australia resulting from the earlier existence of the super-continent now called Gondwanaland.

In the case of the origin of the universe, there were two competing theories at the time, known as the steady-state model and what was condescendingly called the big bang, the idea that the universe was still expanding from a cataclysmic event about fourteen billion years ago. There was no solid evidence, so the two theories were both intellectually defensible.

It was my first experience of scientific controversy when the University of Sydney brought leading proponents of the two competing theories to a physics summer school. After George Gamow expounded the big bang theory, Thomas Gold stood up and told the audience why he could not accept that explanation. The following day the roles were reversed, with Gamow explaining why he could not accept Gold's equally learned exposition of the steady-state model.

The debate raged for another decade or so. The evidence steadily accumulated in favour of the big bang, but some supporters of the steady-state model found convoluted ways to reconcile the new observations with their preferred theory. Eventually one crucial measurement effectively resolved the issue. Calculations based on the big bang theory showed that there would be residual radiation now, at the very low temperature of 4.2 degrees Kelvin (or nearly -270 degrees Celsius), if their model was correct. When that radiation was detected, the argument was resolved.

In more recent times, a parallel was the debate in the scientific community about global climate change. The underlying basic science is well understood. The British physicist John Tyndall showed in the 1850s that carbon dioxide absorbs infrared radiation. Svante Arrhenius, the Swedish physicist and chemist, called it a 'greenhouse' gas in 1892, arguing that it had the same effect as the glass in a greenhouse. Glass is transparent to visible light, but absorbs infrared radiation. So when the sun shines on a greenhouse (or a car parked in the sun) the sunlight warms the interior. The heat would normally be radiated away, but the glass prevents this happening and the temperature rises, desirably in a greenhouse but uncomfortably in a car.

Arrhenius pointed out that the same 'greenhouse effect' occurs in the earth's atmosphere as sunlight passes through and warms the surface, but the radiation of heat into space is slowed by carbon dioxide, water vapour and other trace gases in the atmosphere. Two examples illustrate this effect. A clear night in winter is much colder than a cloudy night. The belt of water vapour on a cloudy night slows the radiation of heat away from the earth into the cold night sky. The large-scale example is the climate on the moon, which is the same average distance from the sun as the earth. The moon has no atmosphere, so the temperature plummets when the surface is not receiving sunlight. The difference between day and night is about 250 degrees Celsius, compared with ten to twenty on earth, and the average temperature is thirty-three degrees lower. There is no doubt that the 'greenhouse effect' exists and makes conditions much better for life on earth. Arrhenius calculated in 1892 that doubling the amount of carbon dioxide in the air, say by burning huge amounts of coal, would increase the average global temperature by four to five degrees.

In the 1950s scientists began to measure the increasing concentration of carbon dioxide in the atmosphere. By the 1970s some were expressing concern that this could change the global climate. In 1985 a critical international conference reviewed the evidence and said that the release of greenhouse gases seemed to be changing the climate.

Both greenhouse gas concentrations and average global temperatures were increasing, but cautious scientists warned that the evidence did not prove a causal link. The Intergovernmental Panel on Climate Change was set up to examine the evidence and recommend responses. Its four reports reflect steadily growing confidence that the recent changes in global climate are a direct consequence of human release of greenhouse gases. This has persuaded most politicians that concerted action is needed.

A small number of reputable climate scientists, a group you could count on the fingers of one hand, still say they are not convinced of the causal link. They have been supplemented in the public debate by a larger group of people, some scientists outside the specialisation but most with no scientific credentials at all, to argue against action. The attention given by the media to those in denial has created a public impression that the science is uncertain, whereas the science has been settled within the relevant community for at least a decade.

THE QUESTION OF the most appropriate response to this knowledge is a more complex matter, and science itself is of limited help. The science tells us that we need to curb the growth of greenhouse gas levels in the atmosphere, but choosing from the possible ways of achieving this involves economic, social and political issues as well as scientific assessments.

I chaired the advisory council that produced the first Australian report on the state of the environment. Our terms of reference allowed us to inform governments and the community about environmental problems, but not to recommend responses. Some saw this as a limitation, but I defended it as ensuring the validity of our report. The science can tell us, for example, if urban air quality is unacceptable. It can tease out the various contributions to the pollution levels. Since the main cause is motor vehicle exhaust gases, there are several possible responses. Each vehicle can be made cleaner, and this can be achieved by regulation or by financial inducements. The number of vehicles in the air shed can be curbed, again by regulation or financial incentives, or possibly by educating the community to recognise the health consequences of polluted air. The pattern of transport could be changed, perhaps by investing in better public transport. The entire transport task could be reconsidered, perhaps by measures to encourage people to work from home or closer to where they live. Weighing up the alternatives is mostly a balance of issues that are involved in the agreed goal; there is no right answer that science can give.

The same argument applies to climate change. We know that we must reduce the rate of releasing carbon dioxide and other greenhouse gases, especially methane. This could be achieved by using cleaner energy supply technologies, by improving the efficiency of turning energy into the services people want, or by phasing out pointless uses of fuel energy. We probably need to pursue all three approaches, but the balance between them is as much social, political and economic as it is technical. Most qualified experts agree that we need to move to electricity supply technologies that put less carbon dioxide into the air than the present system, with its heavy reliance on coal. But there are genuine differences about the alternatives. Professor Barry Brook of the University of Adelaide does not believe that renewable energy systems like wind and solar can be scaled up fast enough to meet our needs, so he supports investment in a possible new generation of nuclear reactors that could avoid the chronic problems of the current industry. I am still sceptical about whether those problems can be solved, so I don't support the idea that

Australia should adopt nuclear power. Unlike Professor Brook, I agree with the argument of the climate change campaign Beyond Zero Emissions in their recent report, *Zero Carbon Australia*, showing how a mix of renewable energy technologies could meet all our needs by 2020. Those two different assessments of the present uncertain situation are both intellectually valid; they are simply differing value judgements.

This leads us to a more fundamental problem. Thirty years ago the American nuclear scientist Alvin Weinberg argued that there is a class of problems which can be stated in the language of science, which are technical questions within science's sphere of knowledge, but which cannot be answered in terms that are acceptable within the scientific tradition. The examples he gave were the operating safety of nuclear reactors and the health consequences of low levels of radiation. If we eventually operate enough nuclear reactors for long enough, he said, we will then have good statistics that would enable accurate safety estimates to be made, but even that hope is probably undermined by constant improvements in designs and operating systems.

In the case of ionising radiation, Weinberg argued, we can't conduct controlled experiments in which we systematically irradiate controlled groups by different amounts and then observe differences in their health. All we can do is monitor inadvertent exposure, and controlled processes like medical diagnostic exposures, and try to infer risk. Even if we had good data, he said, weighing up whether the slight increase in long-term health risk of exposure is justified by the benefits, real or alleged, of nuclear power or nuclear weapons is inevitably a value judgement.

There is a parallel in the approach we take to blood-alcohol levels. We know that alcohol affects our judgement. There is no threshold level below which the increased risk is zero, simply a decreasing risk as alcohol levels reduce. Different societies set different acceptable levels for drivers, trading off the increased risk of accidents against the social benefits of allowing moderate consumption of alcohol. For some classes of drivers, like those in charge of buses, we adopt a zero-tolerance approach. For the wider community, levels like .05 or .08 are simply a balance between competing demands.

Most people accept that we should not be gratuitously exposed to radiation, so there is still concern about the nuclear weapon tests of earlier decades. Much of the unease about nuclear power stems from accidents like the Chernobyl disaster, which spread radioactive debris across a wide area.

Medical diagnostic procedures are usually justified because there is a clear potential benefit that outweighs the risk. Even there, the Australian regulator is concerned about the increasing use of whole-body scans as 'fishing expeditions' in the absence of clinical indications, fearing that it increases risk more than it improves measurable health outcomes. In the 1950s Australians had regular chest X-rays to detect tuberculosis; the tests were discontinued when the disease became so rare that the rate of diagnosis no longer justified the radiation exposure. Deciding how much radiation we can be exposed to is, like the blood-alcohol level, a trade-off between competing demands; science can't give us a right answer.

MANAGING IN THE new world of uncertainty is a challenge to political institutions, but it is also a challenge to scientists. Politicians usually want a clear answer, a yes or no rather than a cautious maybe. When I am asked for expert advice, I get the impression that my reputation as an expert demands an assured response. The American journalist HL Mencken is credited as saying that every complex question always has a simple answer – and it is always wrong.

It is important to be aware of uncertainty and give suitably qualified answers to complex questions. Science cannot say in advance whether genetically modified crops will have a disastrous impact on the natural ecology of a region, or whether a two-degree increase in the average global temperature will destabilise the Greenland ice sheet. The recent admission of this point by the UK's Royal Society was seized on with depressing predictability by the attack dogs of the Murdoch press to vilify those of us urging responsible action to slow climate change. For that reason some scientists are reluctant to admit uncertainty.

Some have a more general worry that the admission removes the cloak of authority from science. I think science actually has the opposite problem: a level of disillusion stemming from unwillingness to admit uncertainty. Scientific authorities confidently told the community that nuclear power was clean, cheap and safe. When it became widely believed that it is dirty, expensive and risky, the whole authority of science was questioned. This could have been avoided if scientists had been more guarded in their support for the technology. While most scientists were reluctant to give public assurances that 'mad cow disease' could not cross the species barrier and affect humans, some yielded to urgings from politicians and told the British public not to worry. The consequent outbreak of variant Creutzfeldt-Jakob disease did serious damage to the idea of scientific authority.

The New South Wales Land and Environment Court now has a process for dealing with scientific uncertainty in cases before it. When experts called by the two sides differ, the court can require them to produce an agreed statement summarising the area of common understanding, those questions on which they disagree and the evidence for the two contending opinions. This is a good model for the future. It recognises that science can't give simple answers to complex questions. In the real world of natural systems, there will always be areas of uncertainty, in some cases impossible to resolve on the time-scale required for big decisions. Scientists should be suitably modest about what we know and what we don't know, rather than overstating their confidence in our current limited understanding. Decision-makers need to assess risks and consider the consequences of being wrong. The precautionary approach should be applied seriously. That is a better approach than misplaced confidence in scientific authority.

Ian Lowe is an emeritus professor at Griffith University and president of the Australian Conservation Foundation. He is the author of many books, the most recent of which is *Voice of Reason: Reflections on Australia* (UQP, 2010), an updated collection of his short writings. His essays have appeared in *Griffith REVIEW: Hot Air* and *Dreams of Land*.

MEMOIR

The bone garden

Looking after the fences and keeping an open mind

Margaret Merrilees

AN old man is sitting by his fireside, candlelight illuminating a halo of wisps around his bald head. He puts aside his *Guardian Weekly* and stares into the fire, toothless jaws working rhythmically. His pre-dinner ration, self-imposed, is five pieces of chocolate.

Why five pieces, when the block is six pieces wide? A personal challenge, no doubt. This is a man who considers the possibilities.

'What are you thinking?'

'Just contemplating life.' He smiles his gummy smile.

His eyes have become bigger in this past year. The blue has faded, but he is wide-eyed in the way of babies who expect marvels. It is a lovely thing to witness.

In the mornings I put my head around his bedroom door and see him lying as he will later lie in death. Each time I am suddenly afraid.

'Duncan?' I call softly.

His eyes spring open. 'Hello?' he croaks. Nothing else moves, but his eyes are alive.

DUNCAN KNEW THAT his long life was coming to an end. He was a realist: a zoologist, a palaeontologist, a farmer. He knew that he was an animal like any other and that death would come to him. Incontinence and immobility were approaching. A number of times he blacked out and fell between chairs, table and fire, then regained consciousness, unscathed. But he knew that his luck might not hold. Another blackout might cripple him. Or, worse, impair his mental capacity. Though he was not at all afraid of dying he was very much afraid of the loss of independence and dignity.

He had little interest in seeking medical help and none in submitting his body for tests and diagnoses. For sixty years he had been lucky enough, or canny enough, to keep himself free from major medical intervention. He was sceptical about the lengths to which modern medicine will go and was a long-time supporter of voluntary euthanasia.

Suicide is no longer a crime in this country but it is still a crime to assist a suicide – in Western Australia the penalty is life imprisonment. At the time in your life when you most need help and companionship, the former is illegal

---

PREVIOUS PAGE: Elisabeth Arena. *Joseph* (*The Bone Garden collection*), detail, 2004. Courtesy of the artist. www.mondoarena.com

and the latter involves great risk for your companions.

Duncan accepted that the rule of law is the best arrangement so far devised by humans for peaceful coexistence. But it only works if we all go along with it. So how should a citizen respond if he or she disagrees with a law? Could a man like Duncan organise his death to be a fitting end to his life? Conversely, could he live his life in such a way as to make his death easy and straightforward?

IN THE 1970S, aged fifty-five, Duncan retired from the Western Australian Museum. He and his wife, Elizabeth, left their three acres near Perth and moved to a farm in the south-west. Much later I asked whether it was hard to turn his back on a career which was satisfying and in which he was well respected. 'But ever since I was a boy,' he said, 'I wanted to be a farmer.'

His professional interests did not end with his retirement. They simply broadened, and in any case his work activities had never been confined to office hours. He once collected chewed bones from the lion enclosure at the zoo and buried them in the garden, so that he could study the tooth marks when the soft tissue was cleaned away. There were other bones too. Belatedly, my sister and I discovered that he was in the habit of robbing the graves of our pets, a latter-day resurrectionist.

At the farm Duncan worked from sunup to sundown, seven days a week. He drew plans for a house that incorporated the best thinking of the time about energy conservation. It would use solar electricity exclusively, and solar hot water boosted by the wood stove. Duncan dug the foundations and the cellar and worked alongside the builders. Once the house was finished he and my mother turned their attention to the yard, and Duncan constructed a vegetable garden with raised beds.

Years passed and the overhanging trees grew bigger. Elizabeth left and Duncan moved his few vegetables to pots on the veranda, where there was more sun. The garden beds became a cemetery for animals, often road kill, which Duncan found or was given. Once the flesh had rotted, he retrieved the skeletons. Sometimes he allowed visitors, especially children, to work on minor specimens, brushing away the soil with small paintbrushes so that none of the bones was lost.

Duncan's specialty was marsupials but he was interested in all bones. A question arose about the vertebrae of snakes and lizards. Is the spinal cord carried to the end of the tail through a bony tunnel or an open channel? He needed a skeleton for study. During that summer three dead snakes were forthcoming, though only two were intact: a dugite and a tiger snake. The ceremonial burial of the dugite, by then stinking, was Duncan's Christmas treat. He believed neither in God nor in consumerism, so he was happy to spend the day alone burying his snake.

His interment method was a layer of flywire followed by a layer of sand, followed by a careful arrangement of the carcass, more sand and another layer of mesh to deter scavengers. In the case of summer burials, including the Christmas snake, he watered the garden beds carefully. Moisture was necessary for the flesh to decay and be consumed by parasites.

The snake disinterments were ceremonial occasions. Neighbours were invited to watch but only Duncan himself was allowed to do the paintbrush work. A snake skeleton, consisting mainly of dozens of vertebrae and tiny detached ribs, is not an easy thing to keep track of. Duncan wanted the vertebrae in order, threaded onto cotton.

Once he had labelled and annotated the results he displayed the bones with great seriousness to anyone who visited, young or old. Part of Duncan's charm was that he spoke to everyone in exactly the same way, regardless of age, gender or background, and simply assumed that they would be interested in the subjects that fascinated him. It never seemed to occur to him that people might be daunted by his fierce intelligence and encyclopaedic knowledge.

Duncan was unfazed by the occasional failure. Birds and bats buried in pots produced nothing. The bones were so fine that they disintegrated. So he tried keeping them in water, using whatever old crockery was to hand. This could be disconcerting for visitors. Duncan would serve them a cup of tea and a biscuit, pushing aside a saucepan full of liquid bones and feathers. For years a dessert bowl held the remains of a mummified rat, only the skull visible beside a pelt of fur. A saucer in the living room still holds a collection of fine bones held together with feathers and threads of dry flesh.

WHEN MY SISTER and I were growing up in our tiny nuclear family, with our nearest close relatives on the other side of the continent, there were three secrets. Like all family secrets, these were complicated burdens.

The first was that both our parents were members of the Communist Party. The secrecy probably arose from the oppressive conservatism of the 1950s, when left-wing books were hidden and children were trained to keep quiet about unpopular political affiliations.

Eventually Duncan faded away from the CPA, because he no longer believed that the party was a grassroots movement. But he never lost his interest in communism (indeed, it was impossible to stop receiving *China Reconstructs* – once a subscriber, always a subscriber). For the rest of his life he collected thick folders of press clippings. He thought and wrote. His ideas evolved and developed and circled back and around. He was generally sceptical about western condemnation of the Soviet and Chinese systems. But in a different mood he wrote: 'Like most people growing up with Abyssinia, the Spanish Civil War, and the obviously growing power of Nazism, we thrashed about for counterweights, and like many of the best of our generation, we saw it in Russia – may we be forgiven for our panicky blindness.'

What Duncan retained was the basic socialist principle that the common good should come before private gain. When he was fired up by the social revolution of the sixties and decided to retire to the land, he envisaged a co-operative enterprise. He spent his last thirty years on land owned by one of the clubs he had helped set up.

By the end of his life Duncan had achieved freedom from ownership, more or less. He had plenty of books, tools, art and music supplies, the use of a lovely (if shabby) house and a little cash saved from his pension. He had no real estate and no investments.

THE SECOND SECRET was that Duncan had tuberculosis in the 1940s. As with communism it is hard now to recreate the stigma attached to TB. Duncan's case was mild and his stay in a sanatorium relatively short, but it must have reminded him of a six-week incarceration for diphtheria in his childhood. Elizabeth's assessment was that the effect of being institutionalised was worse than the illness. She took him home against the advice of the doctors and went out to work while his mother nursed him.

Duncan had been teaching high-school science but, as a TB sufferer, he was no longer welcome in the public education system. After a series of short-term jobs and two interstate moves, he got a position at the University of Western Australia. He did not admit a history of TB – surely one of the very few times in his life that he told a lie.

THE THIRD SECRET was the most inexplicable. It concerned the death – indeed, the very existence – of Jock, Duncan and Elizabeth's first baby, who died of asthma at the age of nine months. I imagine that this became a secret when my sister started to ask questions. My parents probably showed pain and were short in their answers. She deduced that Jock should never be mentioned. Jock was a secret.

Sadly, my parents turned this into a secret from each other and did not share their feelings. My mother never got over the death of her baby and, worse still, she believed that Duncan had forgotten him.

When Duncan and Elizabeth separated, in 1985, Duncan wrote about her departure on the bus to Perth: 'The most devastating and yet most precious memory of my life is seeing Jock for the last time through the hospital window as I was leaving, and waving to him. He was propped up in a cot, fighting for breath, but he saw me wave and smiled back. This was early one night, and we were woken up in the small hours of the following morning by a hospital messenger, to tell us he was dead,' he recorded. 'Waving goodbye to Elizabeth as the bus pulled out this morning and seeing her turn and smile and wave back – again through a window – reminded me poignantly of what she used to be.' In later years Duncan downplayed these episodes. He blamed himself for leaving Jock in the hospital that night and he ruminated about the reasons for Elizabeth's departure. But on the whole he was philosophical. I am reminded of the White Knight in *Alice Through the Looking Glass,* which Duncan read to us when we were little, chortling contagiously. After the knight's umpteenth fall from his horse, this time into a ditch, Alice rushes to rescue him.

'How can you go on talking so quietly, head downwards?' Alice asked, as she dragged him out by the feet, and laid him in a heap on the bank.

The Knight looked surprised at the question. 'What does it matter where my body happens to be?' he said. 'My mind goes on working all the same.'

ONE UNSETTLING AND exhilarating aspect of conversation with Duncan was that his sense of time was of an unusual order, measured in millennia rather than decades, centuries rather than years. He accepted without difficulty the mind-boggling truism that the whole of human history is a small blip in geological and evolutionary time. As a boy his passion was chemistry. Then an imaginative teacher took the class out to gather raw material and Duncan discovered geology. Later he added a second degree in zoology and a PhD in palaeontology.

Duncan's ideas about time were underscored by his appearance. He was tall and skinny and balding and grew a beard long before it was fashionable. He was then about forty, but his beard was silvery and he looked decades older. He seemed already to have done his ageing, so that from then on he simply faded and grew more stooped. A newspaper cutting from 1978 shows him behind his desk in a white coat, a jawbone in one hand, magnifying glass in the other, under the ambiguous caption 'Shedding New Light on Ancient Man'.

Duncan wrote many scholarly papers in his time and popular articles too, since he was always interested in teaching and in making science accessible to non-scientists. After his retirement he continued to read and discuss everything under the sun with anyone available. An exchange of letters with a local Jehovah's Witness led him into two extended meditations. Firstly, how do you prove the theory of evolution? He corresponded with various colleagues, but found that there is a dearth of straightforward evidence: for example, a single layered deposit that would show unequivocally the changes in one species over time.

Secondly, how do you prove the immense age of the earth? For this he turned to the Margaret River caves, in which he had done a lot of his work. His writing brings to life the beauty of the caves, enhanced by a detailed understanding of how they are formed and an estimate of how long each process might have taken. 'At present, the answers can only be guesses. Ten thousand years is only one hundred centuries, and my guess is that one hundred centuries are not nearly enough.'

Mostly, Duncan's retirement interests revolved around politics, the activities of a single species with a short history and a limited future, but fascinating nonetheless. The 'great work' of his last decade was a discursive but disciplined treatise entitled 'Democracy', which pulled together all his readings and musings on social organisation from prehistory onwards.

In other writing Duncan allowed himself more latitude. In a 2002 essay he compared the medieval Catholic Church, the USSR and the present-day USA: 'three giant experiments in social engineering'. The essay ends unexpectedly, with a summary of the findings of two researchers, Richard Wrangham and Dale Peterson, on bonobo and chimpanzee behaviour. Unfortunately, they suggest humans are more like violent chimpanzees than peaceable bonobos. Duncan's plan was that we should unlearn the former behaviour and replace it with the latter. 'I believe we should move purposefully towards a society in which woman-to-woman bonding is the social cement, that is, towards matriarchy. Domestic cattle and wild African elephants did so long ago; *Homo sapiens* is slow.'

Another of Duncan's late essays, a fable, describes an encounter between a mob of calves and an elderly chook, starting with curiosity and ending with mutual panic and stampeding cattle. It concludes: 'Some of the things which alarm us prove to be nothing but terrified chooks.'

DUNCAN HAD AN explosive temper, which he vented mainly on inanimate objects: trailer knobs, combustion engines, mechanical devices of all sorts. Eventually he did away with everything except hand tools, cutting his firewood with an axe and a bow saw.

In earlier years Elizabeth did her best to defuse rows and provide a broader, softer perspective. Duncan knew this. Writing to me about their separation he kept any anger or pain rigidly in check. It was the trained scientific mind applied to the subject of his own marriage. He listed his disappointments, but also described Elizabeth's strengths, such as her gift with people. 'It has been she who has kept me in touch with the people round about; without her I'll hear nothing and know nothing unless I can change my ways pretty radically. All told, I'll have to make some changes in my life, an unwelcome need,' he acknowledged. 'You said a while ago that you don't like *Encounter*. Neither do I, partly because it is dishonest in its bias, but partly because it forces me to review cherished ideas. Cherished practices might be even more distasteful.'

How extraordinary that he should subscribe to *Encounter*, a reactionary English magazine widely believed to be subsidised by the CIA, simply to challenge his own preconceptions. Perhaps he was not so ill equipped, once

Elizabeth left, to change his ways.

He set about the task with his customary thoroughness. He remembered names and asked after children. He wrote down the dates of birthdays and remembered to send a greeting. He got to know neighbours and people in shops. He learned enough Italian to welcome his grandson's new partner. He got the phone connected, learned the violin and formed a string group. He was active in the local arts council and the Bush Fire Brigade. He handed out how-to-vote cards for the Greens in his conservative timber-milling town. He was open about what he believed but always prepared to listen to another point of view. He made a place for himself and the community accepted him. He might have come with the hippies in the 1970s but, as one friend and neighbour put it, he looked after his fences and he stayed.

Duncan travelled interstate rarely and overseas only once, much earlier in his life. His one trip to Perth in his last decade was for Elizabeth's funeral. By the end his life was a round of small chores and observations: firewood, the weather, the rain gauge, visits from animals. The rest of his day consisted of reading, writing, painting and, increasingly, gazing at the fire or dozing. At night he lit the stove – a ritual requiring nine different grades of kindling – cooked his dinner and gave the wind-up torch fifty slow turns.

Duncan enjoyed visitors when they came, but didn't greatly mind when they went away. He lived his round with great contentment. When asked, he said that he had done everything he had ever wanted to do. He had sent his snake skeletons to the Museum. His achievements were complete. 'Except,' he said, 'for sorting the Musica Magica scores for the library.'

Given the piles of paper of every description, in every direction, this was a considerable understatement. Later he added, in a burst of candour, 'and I probably won't get around to that.'

WHAT, IN LATER years, became of Duncan's explosive temper? When they moved into full-time farming Elizabeth was concerned that he did not have the temperament to cope with cattle and sheep. But perhaps it was the animals that taught him patience. Thirty years later he would write: 'For many years I had the privilege of caring for a small herd of cattle.' The privilege.

The cattle were his day-to-day companions, along with chooks and sheep. He knew their idiosyncrasies. He spoke to them, always quietly, so that they would come when he called and let him move them from paddock to paddock.

He toasted stale bread in the oven as a treat for the sheep. He had only to stand in the paddock and shake the paper bag for them to come running.

Towards the end of his life Duncan wrote about an earlier incident, the death of one of twin wethers, the last two sheep on the farm. 'As soon as I began to drag the dead sheep on to the carry-all platform, even more as I began to drive away, the survivor erupted into what is best described as a frenzy. He set up a continuous bawling, and ran around the tractor and up and down. When, with difficulty, I had got through the gate and begun to drive away, he ran about inside the gate, looking through it, and bawling. I could still hear him long after I was out of sight.'

Another person might have left the dead sheep in the paddock. Duncan did not, and nor did he forget the experience.

Because he had no pets there was nothing to deter the native animals (not to mention the rats) from moving in closely with him. A family of Splendid blue wrens took crumbs and hopped on to his hand. Geckoes hunted on the outside of the kitchen window at night. He knew them individually and observed them as keenly as he observed everything. When one dropped its tail, Duncan kept a log as the new tail grew and sent his observations off to a gecko expert. He spoke every day to four resident kangaroos so that they would come up to the fence with their joeys.

During his last summer a snake moved in. In the logbook he first noted its presence on 26 February. The following day it was sunning itself from 3 to 6 pm, and the next day it had moved into the ferns at the northern end of the veranda. On 4 March he wrote: 'Mainly sunny…Snake seems definitely to have a neck. Now holed up under ramp.' The neck identified the visitor as a tiger snake, rather than a dugite.

On 6 March he recorded: 'Snake holed up under ramp again or still. He's very secretive, slides under cover as soon as aware of having been seen.' Over the next few days Duncan noted the snake's basking habits and size ('girth now c. 4cm diam.'), but then did not see it again. On 13 March he concluded that it had gone, since its former basking places were sunlit but unoccupied. 'So: snake Feb 26 – Mar 10, then moved camp.'

Would it have come when he called? I don't doubt that he spoke to it.

SUPPOSE THAT DUNCAN, having reached the age of eighty-seven, did not wish to push his luck any further. Suppose that he organised a peaceful and painless way to end his life. Imagine that it happened like this.

For months, for more than a year, he and his daughter, when she is staying with him, talk about every aspect of death, from the metaphysical to the pragmatic. How might it be achieved? There are endless logistical complications. What if someone drops in? And what about the standing order for fresh bread every Thursday? The baker has been kind, and wraps the bread in tissue rather than plastic. It won't do to leave the bakery with two unpaid-for loaves at the end of the day. But if you cancel the order in advance won't it arouse suspicion?

Most worryingly of all, how will your companion fare after you have gone? You will be placing her in jeopardy. How can you protect her from prosecution? Clearly it will be safest to pass the death off as natural. A natural death will not be a surprise to the doctor.

But, despite all this thought, Duncan and his daughter fail to see that to conceal the manner of his death will be to create yet another secret or, rather, a reverberating chain of secrets. The daughter will have to lie, and so will her partner and sister, even to the people nearest to them, loved and respected friends, family and neighbours. Such lies and secrets tear holes in the social fabric.

The anxious talking goes on and on. Has he considered every eventuality? Has he rehearsed every step? One day, exhausted by logistics and emotion, the daughter protests: 'I don't know! I don't know who I'll ring up once you're dead.' And, in desperation: 'I've never done this before.'

They laugh. The whole idea is absurd. Too big. Too forbidden. Too everything. But shouldn't it be too ordinary, to warrant all this angst? We are animals. We die.

Duncan's family gathers for a bonfire under a cloudy full moon and he totters down the paddock to supervise and to deliver an incantation. He drew this composition, he explains airily, from here and there: his time with the Sea Scouts, his memory of Latin orations.

As the flames leap upward, so let our aims…
As their light dispels the darkness, so let our understanding…
As the flames die down, so let our peaceful old age.

After the visitors leave, Duncan is uncharacteristically withdrawn for a day, but then emerges in the evening most cheerfully to eat dinner and play Scrabble.

The next day is wintry, with lashing rain and gale-force winds. Duncan decides that this is the time to go. He has been reading in his armchair beside the fire, but abandons his book on the Bayeux Tapestry (the account is 'interesting but lightweight, not worth finishing'). Since it is Thursday, his daughter's partner drives heroically into town to get the bread, risking trees across the road and a farm track flowing like a creek. But then, rattled, she leaves the bread on the counter, and doesn't realise till she is nearly home. Duncan smiles benignly and says that bacon and eggs, cooked exactly so, will do instead of fresh bread and vegemite. He follows that with chocolate biscuits and brandy.

As night falls, he and his daughter light the candles. They wish each other loving but nervous farewells, not at all sure that this will work, not quite believing.

'Good luck.'

'And you.'

And then, propped in his armchair with his daughter holding his hand, he ends his life.

Suppose that he dies with his eyes open, in every meaning of the phrase? As those eyes lose their focus he turns his head slightly to one side, towards the blurry light of the candles. Lastly, he turns again to the fading glow of the fire, his companion of thirty years.

IT DID NOT really happen like that. The daughter and even her partner would be liable to prosecution.

But Duncan did die peacefully in front of the fire. We buried him the next week in the local cemetery, alongside many good neighbours. It wasn't the vegetable garden, Duncan's preference, but it was better than cremation. This way he can be dug up in time and his bones given to the museum.

I wanted to run up and down, bawling like the old wether, and sometimes I did. But meanwhile, in the restrained way of our culture, we had a celebration – secular, of course. We made a memento: a photo of Duncan with his sheep and an extract from the *Rubaiyat*, which we found, handwritten, clipped to his will:

While the rose blows along the river brink
With old Khayyam the ruby vintage drink
And when the Angel with his darker draught
Draws up to thee – take that, and do not shrink.

The wind has been with me all day, whispering and gurgling. A deeper background sound is the branches moving in the tall trees, interrupted occasionally by the impossibly sweet trill of a bird.

There is nothing else to hear in Duncan's house: no traffic, no humming appliances, no television. The last voice I heard was at midday, when I wound up the radio and listened to the news and the four-day forecast. Tonight, besides the wind, and the scratching of the pencil on the paper, I can hear the crackle of the kitchen stove, an occasional explosion of sap or damp wood, the murmur of the kettles. I can hear all this, and so vividly, because I am wearing my father's hearing aids.

I have inherited other riches. I know how to light a fire. At present I don't use more than two or three grades of kindling, but I expect to expand that number in time. And I see that there is no need to be afraid. In particular, there is no need to be afraid of ideas, not even the biggest and wildest ones.

Margaret Merrilees is an Adelaide writer whose work has appeared in *Meanjin*, *Island*, *Wet Ink* and various anthologies. http://www.margaretmerrilees.com

ESSAY

More than human, more than nature

Plunging into the river

Lesley Head

PERFECT September dusk. Tide low, water still. We scrunch wet sand beneath our shoes, facing the rocky cliff opposite. A hooded human in a light-coloured coat enters left, across the water. The figure slowly walks, stretches, crawls, lies, curls – crossing our field of view, always just on top of the water. A black head at the waterline some metres in front is the only clue. The scene is accompanied by a flautist standing in the shallows, and later by readings from historical diaries that echo off the cliffs. We are all captivated, savouring the surreality along with the brackish whiff of the river and the thickening darkness. But we also wonder: how are they doing that?

Over dinner, some of the engineering and performative intricacies emerge. The raft was supported by milk crates with plastic bottles half full of water, calibrated to provide exactly the right amount of flotation. The tide and sunset times could be predicted, in order to bring the audience to the stage at the precise time. This art had a lot of science behind it. The stillness after a windy afternoon was perfect, but just lucky.

This was just one in a set of artistic performances in the Bundanon Siteworks field day. Participants who had spent time in residence responding to that beautiful place near Nowra, gifted to the nation by the Boyd family, had their intimacy ruptured by those who came to experience some of the outcomes. The next day we were joined in conversations between artists and scientists about the future of food and water in a time of global warming. One thread in that conversation was distress and anxiety about climate change and the future, and the failure of society to take seriously what scientists are saying. For some scientists, artists were the messengers who would translate these arcane truths via stage, page or screen into something intelligible to the general community. Most of the artists were too polite to say so, but I don't think they saw their mission as being the public relations arm of science. There is plenty of empirical evidence to demonstrate that education about the facts is insufficient to generate changes in social practice. Notwithstanding differences of opinion about the purpose and role of the arts and sciences,

---

PREVIOUS PAGE: Kate Clark. *Bully*, 2010, Canadian White Wolf hide, clay, foam, thread, pins, rubber eyes, wood, paint. 21 x 10.6 x 13.7cm. Photo: Katsuhiro Saiki. Courtesy of the artist. www.kateclark.com

Siteworks puts a bridge across the river dividing the two cultures. There is much to be learned from the conversation: how the geomorphologist Steph Kermode reads landscape history in a stratigraphic section; how the performance artist Barbara Campbell camouflages the audience and gets them to think like a bird or a nest.

But framing an opposition between sciences and the humanities misses the point, wastes time and effort. This is not to deny the profound differences in how they go about things, nor the significant differences within what we call science and the arts. There is an eerie similarity in the twentieth-century incarnation of both science and arts: they frame the human as separate to the rest of nature. They are not facing each other across that divide; they are both facing the same direction, albeit equipped with different tools. At a time when human activities have become so deeply embedded in earth surface processes that even the molecular composition of the atmosphere bears our signature, the most urgent task for all fields of human endeavour is to reframe our relations to the more-than-human world. We don't need more modernist constructions like bridges; we need a different mode of relating to the river, a conversation about what it is like to all be standing on the same bank. In a sense we are all looking at the figure in the hooded coat (the performance artist Tess De Quincey). She is on the river, but not exactly in it. She is of the river, but not of the river. We, the audience, are looking at an Arthur Boyd painting, and feeling almost in it.

THE NATURAL SCIENCES took their subject matter to be the nonhuman world, excluding from their field of view various forms of human influence. They named their leading journal of science and technology *Nature*. The social sciences focused on human actors and agency, helping, in the words of the historian Tim Mitchell, 'to format a world resolved into this binary order' by constituting phenomena such as 'the economy'. The humanities defined themselves around our species, taking scholarship into the human condition as their raison d'etre. This binary formatting of the world developed a spatial logic – seen, for example, in the divide between nature and the city. When we preserve nature, we preserve it 'out there'. The city is seen as the place of culture, for better or worse, but totally separated. It can represent both the highest forms of human civilisation, in which people ascend far above the state of nature, and also a fatally flawed place that is 'anti-nature'.

Accumulating empirical evidence over the past few decades challenges each of these perspectives in different, albeit consistent, terms. Human difference was shown by evolutionary ecology and genetic research to be the contingent outcome of a few stray genes that seized the moment, and the behavioural consequences that reinforced various moments, rather than a divinely ordained status within creation. Archaeological and palaeoecological evidence demonstrated, in Australia as elsewhere, that 'nature' had been neither stable nor pristine. Climates became colder, hotter, wetter, drier. Sea levels rose and fell, creating new configurations of land and seascape. Humans were participants in Australian ecosystems for tens of thousands of years: burning, hunting, choosing some plants over others, transporting plants and animals to different parts of the landscape in the course of everyday life. Contemporary ecologists have discovered contingency and dynamism, expressed in the idea of novel and emerging ecosystems – new configurations and assemblages not seen before in the fossil record. In these ecosystems, species occur in combinations and relative abundances new to a particular biome as a response to human action. (These are different from modified ecosystems that require human maintenance to continue, such as agricultural systems.) Examples of novel ecosystems include the rain-shadow tussock grasslands of New Zealand, and salt-tolerant communities in salinised areas of southern Australia that combine native and alien species. Ecologists also began to venture into urban spaces, slowly letting go of their reluctance to work in areas dominated by humans.

Critique of the human/nature binary has been a feature of scholarship in the humanities and social sciences over the past twenty years. There have been widespread attempts to unsettle and dismantle it, as well as necessary work in analysing its extraordinary resilience and embeddedness in our thinking and institutions. While the natural and historical sciences were establishing the pervasiveness of human influences in space and time, human geography and other human sciences have over the past several decades rediscovered nonhuman nature and the environment as objects of enquiry, with rich literatures on animals, forests, water, gardens, zoos and urban wildlands, to name but a handful. The materiality of the nature in cities was explored through such lenses as water, clay, food networks and backyard gardens. This work demonstrated that diverse ways of seeing mattered. According to how we think of nature, we might want to put a fence around it, create a bureaucracy to look after it, kill it, eat it, plant it, or remove it. We have, for example, attempted to protect nature in bounded, purified spaces such as national parks and wilderness areas.

So, the natural sciences are discovering people, and the human sciences are considering the nonhuman world more systematically. Scholars are still groping with the implications of these findings and new perspectives. This is the challenge for the twenty-first century, and it is not easy. We talk of the 'post-humanities' to signal the decentring of the human subject, and the 'more-than-human' to acknowledge both the pervasiveness of human influence and its interaction with nonhumans (plants, animals, rocks, weather). The clumsiness of these terms illustrates the difficulty we all have in shifting our modes of thought, language and practice.

Concepts that have served us well now look a bit rusty. 'Human impacts', for example, was a crucial concept in identifying anthropogenic climate change in the long-term climatic record, and is now in common parlance. Human activities now use a quarter of the earth's terrestrial ecosystem production, and between a third and half of the land surface of the planet has been transformed by human development. But the concept of 'impact' positions humans as outside the system under analysis, as outside nature. A key contradiction persists: we maintain dual ways of talking about things (human impacts, human interaction with environment, anthropogenic climate change, cultural landscapes, social-ecological systems), while the empirical evidence increasingly demonstrates how inextricably humans have become embedded in earth surface and atmospheric processes. Agents of 'disturbance', such as humans and fire, must now be understood as a normal part of ecosystems, rather than an external influence. To argue that we need to stitch back together – or to build bridges across – systems or ways of thinking serves only to underscore their ontological separateness, rather than to overcome it.

The accumulating body of research in which the signal of anthropogenic climate change has been identified is one of science's most important contributions of the past half-century. It can be read as a triumphant moment for what James Scott calls the 'high-modernist optic', requiring perspectives both backwards and forwards in time, using evidence from microscopic to global scales. Yet this research also shows us how we might need to think differently about climate change. The emphasis on the moment of collision between two separate entities (the 'impact' of 'humans' on 'climate') has favoured historical explanations that depend on correlation in time and space, to the detriment of the search for mechanisms of connection, rather than simple correlation. This is particularly important to how we think about the future, since removal of the 'human' is presumably not our solution of first resort. Responses to climate change will require human action, in association and assemblage with many other types of agency. On the other hand, we do need to hold onto an appropriate sense of human power and responsibility. The historically demonstrated power of human activity lays on us the means and responsibility to find solutions. Further, climate change is not separable from the present and quarantined to some time labelled the future. There will be continuities with the present, as well as discontinuities. We are already both there and not there, just as there is no past baseline of stability.

Climate change does not stand alone, either as an environmental issue separate from peak oil, biodiversity conservation or food security. Nor does it stand apart from more-than-climatic things such as public debate, media scares, altered financial instruments or new policy frameworks. When people adapt or respond it is often not to climatic factors, but to these assemblages.

THE NORTHERN HEMISPHERE, home of most more-than-human scholarship, itself creates a culturally specific framework that should not be assumed to apply universally. Binaries are particularly resilient in Australia because we have a temporal boundary entrenching the other divisions. The year 1788 establishes for us a boundary of belonging, between Indigenous and not. This is applied in much of our thinking about plants, animals, peoples and land use practices such as agriculture. In Australia the battle to include humans in conceptualisations of nature is not yet won. Many Aboriginal communities are still struggling against environmental management regimes that ignore or erase their presence in the landscape. In such a context they can find the concept – both anthropocentric and dualistic – of 'cultural landscape' a powerful political tool. This unfinished business also affects settler Australians who, research shows, still broadly understand themselves as outside nature. We can thus accurately conceptualise many Australian contexts as needing a more-than-nature approach, rather than a more-than-human one.

We have learned much from Indigenous ways of seeing for several decades now, and have drawn on these to dismantle the binaries. A recent example is provided by Jessica Weir's *Murray River Country: An Ecological Dialogue with Traditional Owners* (Aboriginal Studies Press, 2009). Weir argues that 'modern' thinking, which separates nature and culture, is not only false but also disables our responses to ecological devastation. The crisis in Australia's largest river system, described as being 'run' from computers in Canberra, results from historical over-allocation of water for irrigation, together with prolonged drought over the past decade or so and projected intensification of droughts under climate change. Aboriginal people, on the other hand, have 'respect for country' as a main concern. Weir positions the traditional owners, members of the Murray Lower Darling Rivers Indigenous Nations alliance, as 'amodern' in their relations with the nonhuman world. That is, they are embedded in intimate relationships of mutuality, respect and connection that mix human bodies with rivers and kidneys with lakes.

A big challenge here is how far amodern thinking gets us along a path of practical healing for the river. Are we really ready for the less interventionist approach of letting the river do the work? This is an argument also put forward for the Shoalhaven by a traditional owner, Richard Scott Moore, when he argues we should 'let the river be'. Amodern thinking may mean we have to accept things we cannot fix, and first grieve appropriately (as Weir suggests in part of her final chapter, called 'Acknowledging Ecocide'). We could then move on to living with the new and changed reality, such as that of a dead river. This is surely a tough ask for us moderns – to concede defeat and stop the eternal busyness around trying to fix things.

I am mentally arguing with Jessica Weir and Richard Scott Moore as we wander across the floodplain at Bundanon, considering its depositional history under the instruction of Steph Kermode. There are many influences on its past: climate and sea level change, episodic extreme floods, Aboriginal burning, vegetation clearance by early European farmers, the building of the Tallowa Dam. Local residents and fishers of longstanding have attested today to 'loss' – of fish, oysters, peace, quiet. What would it mean now to 'let this river be'? And why do we give the river primacy in the nonhuman landscape? What makes it an entity separate say to the groundwater, or the water transpired into and through the vegetation? What makes us structure our conceptual landscape around it, rather than around the sandstone topography or the ebb and flow of vegetation communities? Who is to say this river minds being siphoned off to be shared with greedy Sydneysiders?

WE STILL HAVE work to do in coming to terms with the rage and grief of Australia's colonial heritage. But if we misdirect this work as nostalgia for a lost paradise we are also disabling constructive engagement with our future. If Australia has particular problems with binaries we may also have the means to move beyond them, arguably to make a contribution to reframing modernity that will extend beyond our shores. In our everyday engagements with the messiness of our cultural and ecological hybridity we are all sowing the seeds of that crop. We don't yet know what it will look like, but its unruly possibilities might be cause for quiet optimism.

Bundanon and its companion property, Riversdale, are typically weedy places. Though we want to focus on the pristine beauty of the sclerophyll forest, we can only do so by squinting. Fireweed flourishes in the paddocks, lantana clusters along the riverbank. These are declared noxious weeds and conventional management wisdom calls for their removal. It must be a headache for those whose core business is maintaining and fostering the artistic heritage of the place. That heritage is partly one of colonialism – as we were reminded on the Saturday night when a group of young Aboriginal girls reclaimed the sandstone homestead in dance. Do those of us who are not Indigenous stand in the same ambiguous place in the paddock as the coral trees, recommended for removal in regional weed management strategies? Or can we articulate a new and different sort of belonging for ourselves?

Diego Bonetto's Bundanon performance, *Weeds 'R' Us*, saw the audience being served nettle soup and mallow tea. Bonetto challenges the binaries by articulating a more welcoming view of Australian nature than is provided for in most understandings of which plants belong here. His contribution to the Bundanon blog reflects this affectionate view of weeds: 'The strongholds of nature, the untameables, the unruly, the ones actually fighting back – blow after blow, seed after seed – our human prospective [sic] of what environment should look like…Nettle is everywhere, *Urtica dioica*, a blessed plant who fed human for millennia, and we will re-appropriate this and more, mix it with native edibles and create what could be regarded as a cross cultural appreciation of the bounty nature has to offer…'

These are fighting words, confronting to most conventional understandings of Australian environmental management, although they have much in common with Aboriginal people's views of introduced animals and plants, as documented by the anthropologist David Trigger.

There are many contradictions here, whether we are discussing weeds, rivers or climate change. And it is important that our discussions acknowledge our contradictory positions. But the main divisions are not between science and the arts. For those of us who grew up with western thinking, the challenge of reconceptualising human relations to the more-than-human world is our most profound and important. It will not occur as a purely cerebral activity, but as a process of engagement with the dilemmas of everyday practice. To undo the destructive practices of modernity, and reconstitute them into something better, we will need everything in the Enlightenment toolbox, science and arts included. But they will be most effective plunging into the river together, rather than attempting to bridge it.

Thanks to the organisers of the Siteworks at Bundanon program for the invitation to speak, and for the stimulation provided by the work of the Siteworks Laboratory participants.

Lesley Head is a geographer and an ARC Australian Laureate Fellow. She is the director of the Australian Centre for Cultural Environmental Research at the University of Wollongong.

ESSAY

Selling the forests to save the trees

'Welcome to Brand Biodiversity'

David Ritter

LONDON Excel, situated in the now gentrified old docklands of the British capital, is a huge empty space designed for the meeting convenience of the global insider class. Inside the conference centre the street is kept distant as delegates, dwarfed by outsized internal walkways, gather to talk, listen, network and access their PDAs, cloistered from the great metropolis' polyglot commotion.

In July 2010, London Excel hosted the inaugural Global Business of Biodiversity Symposium. The halls – 'large enough to accommodate two 747 jumbo jets' – easily swallowed the thousand or so embodied suits who attended the curious event. Among the throng were bureaucrats, academics, civil society, UN staffers and a few politicians, but most came from private enterprise. The vibe was commercial swagger meets moral self-satisfaction, a combination epitomised by the corporate social responsibility ethic of 'doing well by doing good'.

Between sessions management consultants compared notes with scientists; venture capitalists traded cards with environmental campaigners; bureaucrats took advice from businessmen. Life on earth, it seems, is redolent with the promise of new products and markets that will also deliver ecological salvation. 'We must,' the audience was told by one keynote speaker, 'put a price on ecosystem services, including cultural and spiritual services.' According to a different presenter, 'we should probably be thinking about biodiversity more like a real estate market: these are very distinctive and unique assets.'

'We need,' said the boyish and charismatic British Parliamentary Under-Secretary for the Natural Environment, Richard Benyon, 'to work together to "brand" biodiversity.' 'Only if we put the right price on nature,' another speaker argued, 'can we hope to save it.'

Among the schemes that received the most attention at the Business of Biodiversity Symposium was REDD – Reducing Emissions from Deforestation and Degradation – an idea at the top of the global agenda to revalue the natural world. The REDD concept is simple enough. Forests function as colossal natural carbon sinks, but they are being destroyed at a staggering rate: a frenzy of demolition that accounts for an astonishing 17 per cent of annual global emissions. We are destroying the remaining intact forests of the world at the rate of an area the size of one soccer field every two seconds. The greatest drivers of destruction are global agribusiness commodities, including timber, palm oil, beef and leather, pulp and paper, and soya. REDD contemplates funding being made available for the developing world to decrease deforestation, in order to reduce greenhouse gas emissions, while also conserving biodiversity and preserving indigenous peoples' rights.

Enjoying public support across the political and economic spectrum, REDD is the great hope for both forests and climate, though exactly where the money should come from is controversial. Despite the great recession, some billions have already been committed from the public coffers of certain developed nations – including a relatively modest contribution from Australia. However, it is widely believed that, in the longer term, capital will have to be derived from the private sector, through the creation of forest credits available for trade within global carbon markets.

Already, investment funds are sizing up the growth potential in REDD. London-based Canopy Capital is a private equity firm dedicated entirely to 'the development of new ecosystem services markets'. The target market for

Canopy Capital is 'responsible investors that need to deploy capital sustainably to create wealth worth having'. Like so many of the increasing number of corporate interests associated with REDD, Canopy Capital makes effective use of stunning images of rainforests in its promotional material. The juxtaposition of hyper-finance with primordial images, wrapped up in slick public relations, is striking. 'Welcome,' as one advertising agency puts it, 'to Brand Biodiversity.'

ACCORDING TO REDD'S often repeated 'product narrative', tackling deforestation is a ready remedy for climate change, the knack being to make forests worth more alive than dead. In the United Kingdom, Prince Charles (demonstrating, it must be said, a great deal more leadership on climate change than many of the world's elected leaders) launched an ambitious project to kick-start REDD funding. The Prince's Rainforest Project recruited a suite of celebrities who participated in a beautifully designed public campaign. The resulting film features a sequence of speakers, including Harrison Ford, the Dalai Llama, Pelé, princes William and Harry, and even Kermit the Frog, all of whom are accompanied by a computer-enhanced Argentinean horned frog as mascot, with which they interact.

The final word is given to Kermit, who concludes – with all the pathos that can be invested in an overwrought puppet – 'we need the rainforests… everybody does.'

Meanwhile, on the other side of the Atlantic, a different style of branding has been applied to REDD by a business–NGO coalition under the ungainly moniker Avoided Deforestation Partners. In Washington the message is all about domestic economic interests and US unemployment figures. 'Did you know,' the voiceover in one Avoided Deforestation Partners video begins earnestly, that 'saving forests can save American consumers billions' and 'can protect American jobs'? The tone is unnervingly close to the kind associated with advertisements for novelty kitchen appliances. 'Tropical forests,' the promotion concludes: 'the affordable climate change solution.'

IN A MECHANISTIC, econometric and mass-consumption age it seems to be thought self-evident that the riotous complexity of nature must be transmogrified, through scientific and economic alchemy, into quantifiable units of value. REDD will entail a vast global exercise in carbon accounting, including the establishment of baselines and monitoring, reporting and verification of avoided deforestation. Satellite monitoring, accompanied by 'ground truthing', is expected to play a central role. In addition to requiring tremendous technical expertise, imagining that the entrenched politics, culture and economics that produce the world's appalling rates of deforestation can all be transformed within a few years requires confidence bordering on faith, particularly given that some of the last great forests are found in some of the least-well-governed countries on earth. As *The Economist* recently observed, given that the Democratic Republic of Congo does not know, to the nearest million, how many people have died in its civil war, it is hard to know how its government can be expected to provide a reliable account of its forest-carbon stock.

GEORGE SAUNDERS' SHORT story 'Jon' (2003) is a futuristic narrative of adolescents who have grown up in confinement, as a focus group under the quasi-benevolent control of a brand agency. The teenagers are only able to evoke reality through brand references: 'Though I had many times seen LI 34321 for Honey Grahams where the stream of milk and the stream of honey enjoin to make that river of sweet-tasting goodness, I did not know that, upon making love one person may become like the milk and the other like the honey, and soon they cannot even remember who started out the milk and who the honey, they just become one fluid, this like honey/milk combo.'

The satire echoes the fundamental reconstitution of social meaning that is occurring in relation to biodiversity. Valuing every hectare – every molecule – of rainforest on earth for its carbon, leading ultimately to the creation of intricate global financial markets, necessarily contemplates a radical re-envisioning. According to Pavan Sukhdev, the study leader of the transnational Economics of Ecosystems and Biodiversity project, who addressed the Business of Biodiversity Symposium and visited Australia in

August 2010, there is no alternative to putting an economic value on biodiversity. Sukhdev told his Sydney audience: 'if you don't, then there'll be other things, there'll be other uses of land which are measured in economic value terms. And this will result in trade-off choices being made, which means that nature would be destroyed.'

The revolution in our sensibilities and ways of conceiving is stark. In our most ancient traditions, animals and plants were seen as gods and ancestral spirits incarnate. In later eras the utility of nature was self-evident to nomadic, farming and fishing peoples, who were embedded in landscapes and humbly dependent on the bounty of the seasons. Even in modernity, secular eyes have proven capable of seeing the transcendent beauty of nature as warranting veneration and preservation, albeit that the reverence has often been more honoured in the breach. 'To me,' Wordsworth wrote, 'the meanest flower that blows can give / Thoughts that do often lie too deep for tears.'

PRAGMATISTS WILL INSIST that if the valuation – even the commodification – of nature is what is required to halt deforestation and the more general despoliation of the environment, so be it. Practical efforts, the argument runs, should not be delayed because of arcane anxieties about how the wonder of creation is articulated. Perhaps worrying that the notion of 'ecosystem services' is ontologically and culturally desiccated, or blindingly anthropocentric, is indeed nothing more than intellectual extravagance. But when you change how you understand a thing, you modify its nature. What the philosopher John Searle called 'brute facts' – such as forests and their destruction – are incontrovertible, but our social construction of external phenomena is transformed with every linguistic twist and turn. Indeed, the hope of many who advocate for REDD and for the ecosystem services agenda more generally is precisely that: if we conceive of nature in econometric terms we will change how we act, fundamentally shifting political economy to a sustainable footing. It will be an inevitable consequence of the incorporation of nature within the liberal economic universe.

Writing in the middle of the twentieth century, the great Hungarian social theorist Karl Polanyi considered that the commoditisation of the natural world could only lead to disaster. According to Polanyi, because land had not been brought into being by human beings it was a 'fictitious commodity'. Dealing with land as a commodity, he argued, was contrary to the essence of the thing, an iterative contradiction that would inevitably have deleterious social and environmental consequences. In relation to REDD, the Polanyian analysis may be prescient. If the utilitarian rationale of reducing carbon emissions from deforestation – prioritised on the basis of underlying cost logic about the relative pricing of different abatement options – becomes the paramount justification for forest conservation, what happens if you find that you can achieve the same result more cheaply in some other way? What if it turns out that there is a cheaper and nastier means of achieving the same end? Why pay more for biodiverse natural forests and the preservation of forest peoples' rights, for example, if it is demonstrated to be more fiscally advantageous to sequester carbon with plantations that can themselves be readily harvested for pulp and paper?

Motives are fundamental. It is possible to envisage a version of REDD designed to stimulate sustainable development pathways, with the starting point being the preservation of biodiversity and the recognition of Indigenous peoples' rights. But whether or not REDD or any other economic mechanism for preserving ecosystem services is effective in environmental terms will depend on the real objectives behind the design. As Chris Lang, editor of the trenchantly sceptical *REDD-Monitor*, has commented, 'REDD could involve the biggest ever transfer of control over forests – to international carbon financiers and polluting companies.'

SINGING LOUDLY FROM the same hymn sheet, members of the chorus may still worship different gods. REDD is supported for diverse reasons. Environmentalists, scientists, celebrities and British royalty may well want to 'save the rainforests' for their intrinsic significance, as well as for more pragmatic reasons, but the private sector is in a structurally different position. Power generators and fossil fuel companies, private equity fund managers and management consultants, agribusinesses and carbon traders: all have as their ultimate goal the maximisation of profit. Inevitably, these firms see REDD as an opportunity for commercial and strategic advancement, and their imperative must be to secure the establishment of an international mechanism that offers the best opportunities for mercantile gain. Imagining that corporations – mandated by law to optimise returns for shareholders – are motivated by altruism is not to see the wood for the trees. Undoubtedly, global politics and economics needs reconfiguring if we are to deviate from our drastic unsustainability, but if life on earth is to be remade we must continually ask: on what terms, and for whose benefit?

Author and campaigner David Ritter is the head of biodiversity at Greenpeace in London. Formerly one of Australia's leading native title lawyers, his most recent work includes *Contesting Native Title* (Allen & Unwin, 2009). His weekly blog appears in the *Global Policy Journal* and his essay 'Fishing like there's no tomorrow' was published in *Griffith REVIEW 27: Food Chain*. This article was written in a personal capacity.

ESSAY

We, the populists

The perils of populism

Rod Tiffen

IN October 2010 Australia's Director of Military Prosecutions, Brigadier Lyn McDade, brought charges against three Australian soldiers, resulting from an incident in which six people were killed – one Taliban insurgent, but also four children and a teenager.

Australia's most famous talk radio presenter, Alan Jones, led a vociferous campaign against the prosecutions: 'The government should revoke the powers of this woman, and these charges should be withdrawn...Join the campaign to stop the prosecution of our troops doing what we sent them to do.' Jones frequently and vehemently denigrated the prosecutor, noting she had never been in combat or commanded troops in combat, quoting one listener who said McDade was trying 'to big-note herself; she has no idea'. Jones believes that the parliament should respond to the national anger about 'the obscenity of charging these people'.

Jones's style in this episode embodies the central elements of populism. There is an assumption that the truth is known and clear, and that no one of good faith could doubt or dispute the facts. There is a lack of respect for – indeed, a disdain for – due process, and a refusal to even countenance that these institutional processes (set in place under the Howard Government, not the Rudd Government as Jones asserted) might serve an important and legitimate function, or that there may be other dangers involved in so blithely recommending political interference in the (military) judicial system. There is the demonisation of the individual, 'this woman', seen as the villain, ascribing to her without evidence unworthy motives, and damning her legal expertise because of her lack of practical combat experience. There is an insistence on in-group virtue, an inability to believe that our troops could have done anything wrong. There is a lack of empathy or willingness to appreciate the feelings of the out-group, the Afghan victims and their families, or to contemplate how this might complicate any sense of 'what we sent [our troops] there to do'.

The populist strain in Australian politics and media has become more marked in recent years. When politicians are criticised for being populist it

---

PREVIOUS PAGE: Zina Saunders. *Sarah Palin Bags a Big One*. Created for a gallery display of women's political art. Courtesy of the artist. www.zinasaunders.com

means that they are pandering to what is popular, reinforcing public prejudices irrespective of their validity, over-simplifying and distorting policy options, taking the politically expedient rather than optimal or principled course. In Australia now, populism is a style rather than an institutionalised movement, but in other countries populist parties have played and continue to play an important role.

Historically, populism has described a type of political movement that is ideologically ambiguous, whose views do not fit neatly into a binary left/right opposition between state and market. Many of these movements arose in rural areas. Such agrarian populism often espouses 'producer economics', wanting security of income, to be insulated from the vagaries of prices fluctuating with strength of demand and protected from unfair foreign competition. 'Right' and 'left' populism are distinguished less by their economic ideology and more by the nature of their targets – typically, ethnic minorities or weak or deviant groups for the right; and powerful groups, such as business interests and large corporations, for the left.

Over the past two years Sydney newspapers have used the word 'populist' almost invariably without elaboration, and simply as a self-evident term of criticism. Often there is disagreement about what is dubbed populist – my charismatic speaker can be your demagogue.

In the *Daily Telegraph* nearly all references, particularly by its columnists, were critical of 'left' populism, moves by the government to tax mining companies or public criticisms of banks. In the *Sydney Morning Herald* almost all uses of the word were about 'right' populism: for example, hardline stances against asylum seekers or punitive attitudes towards crime.

THE MOST IMPORTANT populist groups in contemporary democracies are the radical right-wing parties of Western Europe, where the proportional-representation electoral systems make it easier for new parties to emerge and quickly gain a substantial legislative presence.

The most famous have been Jean-Marie Le Pen's National Front party in France, Jörg Haider's Freedom Party in Austria and the Swiss People's Party. In the latter half of 2010 the formation of governments in two of the countries most associated globally with enlightened social policies depended on the decisions of far-right populist groups. The Sweden Democrats, who ran on the slogan of 'Keep Sweden Swedish', hold the balance of power with 6 per cent of the vote. Geert Wilders, who ran a campaign to stop the so-called Islamisation of The Netherlands, won a concession that the conservative government will ban the burka in exchange for his support.

Such parties are always greeted with particular alarm in Europe because they appear to evoke the past. But it would be wrong to see them as a contemporary equivalent of Nazism or fascism, however distasteful their ideologies. Moreover, while there has been some political violence on their fringes, at least so far it has not been central. Despite the intolerance and xenophobia they espouse, these movements do not in the foreseeable future constitute a great threat to democracy, and certainly not one needing anti-democratic methods to combat them.

Though great publicity greets every success of these parties, it should not be thought that their course is always onward and upward. Indeed, they have suffered serious reverses. When they became part of governing coalitions in The Netherlands and Austria they were unable to translate their platforms into attractive and workable policies, and their support fell drastically at the next election. One of the nice things about bigots is that they tend to fall out with each other, and these parties are particularly prone to splits. Their impatience with, and contempt for, institutions means not only that they find it difficult to translate their slogans into policies, but also that they produce more than their share of scandals.

Populism takes different shapes, according to whatever grievances are animating the movement in a particular country. Populist parties tend to centre on a strong leader whose individual characteristics can shape their platforms. While most such movements tend to be anti-gay, the Dutch far-right leader Pim Fortuyn was openly homosexual.

They tend to have a cluster of issues in common. The most basic is the way they draw a sharp line between in-group and out-group. Most commonly this manifests itself in hostility towards immigrants and minority groups. The most obvious and ugly result when right-wing populists come to prominence is that hostility to ethnic minorities increases. A second cluster, sometimes overlapping, concentrates on crime, calling for stricter law and order, more punitive attitudes to criminals.

There is more variety and confusion in their attitudes towards government spending, especially the welfare state. Typically, there is resentment of those they consider unworthy welfare recipients, and hostility towards anything regarded as social experimentation or unorthodoxy that defies common sense. In addition there is a low opinion of 'bureaucracy', and a readiness to believe there are vast amounts of government waste. These are mixed in with calls for lower taxation and a belief that government budgets should always be balanced, although typically there are also calls for greater government spending in their own favoured areas.

THE FIRST AND most obvious damaging consequence of these right-wing populist parties is the way they raise the political temperature, mobilising discontents and directing hostility towards targeted out-groups. But another aspect of populism has its own negative consequences. According to the leading scholar of European politics Hans-Georg Betz, populism can be described not only in terms of ideology but by its characteristic style of argument. This is marked by a pronounced faith in the common sense of the ordinary people; the belief that simple solutions exist for the most complex problems; and the belief that the common people, despite possessing moral superiority and innate wisdom, are denied the opportunity to make themselves heard.

Populism thus not only reduces the scope for tolerance and compassion in public life, but also for reason and dialogue, as evidenced in the Jones tirade about the Australian soldiers' military prosecutions. Because their favoured way is seen as the way of common sense, populists view all else as unacceptable, leading to an intolerance of alternatives – ideas that only fools or knaves could favour. The elevation of common sense often leads to a suspicion and rejection of expertise; and, although they are hardly alone in this, their political debate tends to proceed through the denigration of opponents, rather than the examination of evidence. At its worst, populism promotes betrayal narratives and conspiracy theories, the belief in evil forces that have betrayed the public.

The populist style of argument is most evident in the rise of the Tea Party in the United States and its favourite 'mom', Sarah Palin. In the American political system it is almost impossible for new groups to break the grip of the two major parties, so this is an internal Republican battle.

A distinctive aspect of American populism is the pronounced disgust with politics-as-usual. Government is pictured as full of self-serving hypocrites, experts who lack common sense and elites whose activities run against the interests of the people.

Palin contrasts 'real Americans' with 'East Coast elites', and claims that 'everything I ever needed to know I learned on the basketball court.' At her best, Palin's themes are leavened by a becoming homespun modesty. The eminent American journalist David Broder described this as her 'pitch-perfect populism': 'I do want to be a voice for some common-sense solutions. I'm never going to pretend like I know more than the next person. I'm not going to pretend to be an elitist. In fact, I'm going to fight the elitist, because for too often and for too long now, I think the elitists have tried to make people like me and people in the heartland of America feel like we just don't get it, and big government's just going to have to take care of us. I want to speak up for the American people and say: No, we really do have some good common-sense solutions. I can be a messenger for that.' But these pleasantries quickly give way to more sinister expression of such themes.

The Tea Party takes its name from the Boston Tea Party of 1773 – which, with its rallying cry against the British colonists of 'no taxation without representation', was a pivotal moment in the build-up to the American War of Independence. It is thus a symbolically powerful, if substantially absurd, name for the movement, which calls on 'American patriots' to 'take back' their country.

The anti-colonial imagery is less appropriate when the patriots are being asked to take back their country from other Americans. But rationality is not a major inhibition. An estimated one-quarter of Americans believe Barack Obama is not a Christian and was not born in the country. If he were born elsewhere, he would be ineligible to be President, and leading Republicans have encouraged this vocal minority. Sarah Palin said, 'I think the public rightfully is still making it an issue...I think that members of the electorate still want answers.'

A defining characteristic of the Tea Party is the way its members rejoice in the militancy of their rhetoric. When the Republicans had been criticised for being the party of no, simply opposing everything, Palin proclaimed her movement 'the party of Hell No!' After Obama's health care package was passed, she tweeted, 'Commonsense conservatives and lovers of America: Don't retreat, instead – RELOAD.' Soon after, her website featured pictures of Democrats in the crosshairs of a rifle sight.

A NEW FEATURE of American right-wing populism is that it is intertwined with Rupert Murdoch's Fox News. Fox has abandoned any pretence that its role is simply to report politics. Increasingly it acts as a player, one that has abandoned most senses of professional journalistic standards and constraints. It constantly promotes the Tea Party; and, while the most obvious feature of Fox is its partisan bias, its constant vilification of Democrats, perhaps even more important is the way it is a force within Republican politics, making the task of moderates in the party much more difficult.

Fox now has on its payroll four of the five leading potential Republican contenders for the 2012 presidential nomination: Palin, Newt Gingrich, Mike Huckabee and Rick Santorum. This creates its own complications. When an editor from another network wanted to interview Palin, he was told he would first have to get Fox's permission.

The network already had leading personalities, such as Bill O'Reilly and Sean Hannity, who were famous for their right-wing views and the way they used their programs as vehicles to promote them. But their 2009 recruit has, if anything, eclipsed them in both public profile and the extremity of his views. On 28 August 2010 Glenn Beck again made his own news by staging a Restore Honor rally in Washington, and attracting around 90,000 people.

In his first eighteen months on Fox News, Beck and his guests invoked Hitler 147 times, Nazis 202 times and fascists 193 times. These mentions were usually in reference to Obama. He claimed in one broadcast that the President has a 'deep-seated hatred for white people or the white culture'. For Beck, progressivism, which he has called a cancer, is the enemy. Alluding to the mission of Jewish Nazi-hunters he says, 'To the day I die I am going to be a progressive-hunter.'

There has been widespread debate about the partisan effects of these developments. A Republican moderate, the former Bush speechwriter David Frum, forecast that while it would help the party in the mid-term congressional elections by mobilising the base, it will hurt it in the 2012 presidential and congressional elections, when turnout is much higher, by taking it away from the mainstream. The first part of his prediction proved correct in November 2010. But more important than whether Beck and his comrades at Fox News sway any votes is the way such rhetoric compounds intolerance and polarisation.

IT WOULD BE easy to sit back, as Australians are wont to do, and deplore the craziness of Americans. There is nothing as extreme and irrational as the Fox News and Tea Party rhetoric in Australian politics. But, arguably, there has been a similar trend towards anti-intellectualism and distrust of expertise in Australian public life. When the Murray-Darling Basin Plan was published in October 2010, angry farmers at one rally burned copies of it. This book-burning passed without condemnation, or even comment, by any politician or commentator. Barnaby Joyce, Leader of the Nationals in the Senate, has said he used Productivity Commission reports as toilet paper. Global warming, in particular, seems to have aided an increasing distrust of science and expertise in Australian, as in American, public life. There have been many media people peddling conspiracy theories. To the Liberal Senator Cory Bernardi the science is simple: 'The earth is actually not warming. We still have rain falling, we have crops still growing. We can go outside and we won't cook.' Tony Abbott was equally dismissive: it was just 'crap'.

While Australian populism draws on similar grievances and factors as populist movements in other western democracies, it occupies a different place in the Australian party configuration. Except for Pauline Hanson's relatively short-lived One Nation party, it is not marked by the emergence of new entities. What is perhaps most notable about populist issues in Australia at the moment is that the parties tend not to stake out explicit pro and con positions so much as seek to outdo each other in responding to – and at the same time reinforcing – the public mood. This was the case in New South Wales state politics for several years, where one party tried to outbid the other in a law and order auction, both seeking to demonstrate their superior toughness on crime.

AUSTRALIAN AND AMERICAN populist rhetoric share a similar counterposing of the elites and the people. According to Glenn Beck, 'on one side we have the elites, and on the other side we have the regular people.' The elite label was similarly used constantly to attack the democratic credentials of critics of the Howard Government.

The two labels, populist and elitist, capture curious ambivalences about our attitudes towards democracy, reflecting the shifting associations between popularity and virtue. 'Elite' has a positive set of connotations to do with achievement and excellence. But in political discourse it carries connotations of exclusivity – of feelings of superiority to, and disdain for, the popular and ordinary.

'Populist' has a similarly long lineage and convoluted mix of meanings. Its roots lie in an upper-class distrust of democracy and distaste for popular culture. While the contemporary usage focuses on politics, the cultural uses to some extent run in parallel. In the arts, high culture is extolled as more authentic and deeper. A populist approach is derided when it implies that commercial success is achieved, and aimed for, at the expense of more artistic motivations. But this easily slides into a smug superiority towards anything popular. For some defenders of public broadcasting in Australia, for example, the assumption seems to be that the size of the audience is in inverse proportion to the height of the brow, a recipe not only for snobbery but for justifying failure.

Democracy celebrates the wisdom of the people, and popular support is the ultimate justification for a government and, often more problematically, for its policies. But again there is an ambivalence, captured in the contrasting postures in which leaders indulge. One common stance is to insist – bravely – that they will do what is right, what is in the national interest, irrespective of the political consequences, and not pander to what is popular. But equally commonly they adopt the stance – always humbly – of listening to the people, and showcasing their responsiveness.

Julia Gillard was ostentatiously listening to the people before the 2010 election when she paraded her concern about the most obvious example of populist politics, asylum seekers arriving by boat. The classic symptoms are present in abundance. Sympathies are determined with a strict demarcation of in-group and out-group. There is no sense of proportion in relation to the total number of immigrants arriving in Australia. Both parties – and the media – act as if the number of boat arrivals is principally or even only a matter of pull and not of push. There is almost no attention to conditions in the countries that 'boat people' have arrived from. All sides demonise people smugglers, as if highlighting their evil deflects the human plight of the asylum seekers. There is a determination to 'protect' Australia's borders by processing people offshore, whether or not that is more cost effective than other options.

Again, in 2010, the similarities between the major parties were more marked than the differences. Neither was prepared to concede the populist ground to the other.

IN UNDERSTANDING THE increase in populism, and acknowledging the likelihood that it will continue, we need to appreciate both the demand and supply factors. The demand factors come from the resentments and insecurity generated by socioeconomic conditions. The pace of change and its relentlessness, the complexity of a globalised world and the challenges that confront it all contribute to political disenchantment. Such feelings are far from universal. They are most likely to be present in groups feeling left behind by change, or when economic conditions are less buoyant. But there is likely to be a substantial constituency susceptible to populist appeals in the future.

Two factors are noteworthy. One is the disconnection between the sources of the anger and the targets against which it is politically expressed. Sometimes it seems as if there is free-floating resentment, ready to be attached to whatever scapegoat is to hand. Before the 2010 election Labor politicians stated how strongly people in Western Sydney felt about boat people. Whatever real grievances residents of that area have, boat people have done nothing to add to their problems.

The second is to understand the restorationist rhetoric in which their complaints are often framed. Populists frequently and fervently profess patriotism, but it is a patriotism expressing alienation from the actual country, from the present. They want to restore their country to a simpler, purer imagined past, to take it back from those who somehow have taken it away. This is the politics of estrangement masquerading as expressions of intense attachment.

While social conditions provide the fertile soil in which populism might grow, we need also to examine how such sentiments are fertilised, and here we need to look at trends in contemporary politics and media. The supply side has increased in tandem with political professionalism and ruthlessness, and with media shrillness.

The parties have become ever more calculating and cynical in their pursuit of political advantage. They are relentless in their determination to attack each other. The result is a constant stream of invective, nitpicking and slanderous character attacks. The fatuousness and hypocrisy of this posturing no doubt discourages many from tuning in to political debate.

But the parties have not only become more aggressive: they have also become more defensive, less willing to offer targets for the other side to attack. This caution has led them to depend on polling and focus groups as counsels of conformity. Increasingly they are unwilling to challenge public perceptions, whether these are soundly based or not. Instead we have both sides escalating rhetoric that caters to such prejudices.

Developments in the media have moved in parallel to exacerbate the trend towards populism. The 24-hour news cycle has become more intense, and as a result the total amount of information becoming public has probably increased. But, if anything, it has worsened the fragmentary way in which political arguments and evidence emerge, rather than enabling wider perspectives and aiding comprehension. And not only are the pressures for journalistic productivity increasing, but marketing seems to be ever more to the fore. Patriotism may be the last refuge of a scoundrel, but it is the first instinct of many news executives. The search is always on for stories that fit and reinforce existing public opinion.

Just as importantly, there are ever more outlets where the strength of opinion offers more commercial and personal reward than the uncovering of information. Commercial talk radio, the sensationalist presentations of the tabloid newspapers and the large number of columnists who rely more on opinion than analysis together form an ever louder echo chamber escalating the sensation *du jour*.

We are faced with a party logic and a media logic attuned to reinforcing rather than challenging public prejudices. Each abets the other in a chorus of conformity. Together they form an outrage industry that absents proportion, reason and reasonableness, and where it is difficult – soon, perhaps, near impossible – to have a measured debate of policy options. It is unlikely that populism will beget a significant radical-right party in Australia. But with the current mix of political and media incentives, the populist mood in Australian politics is not likely to change. Those whinging elites will continue to have much to be unhappy about.

Rodney Tiffen is Emeritus Professor in Government and International Relations at the University of Sydney, where he was a member of staff for three decades before his recent retirement. His most recent book, co-authored with Ross Gittins, is *How Australia Compares* (second edition, Cambridge University Press, 2009).

MEMOIR

Science without a capital S

Battling Grumpy Uncles, Media Tarts and Jurassic Marxists

Robyn Williams

SCIENCE is one of the few human constructs designed to test its own veracity continuously. There is no point in time at which we all nod, wise men with beards, women with six-figure IQs, and say: 'That's settled...next!' All aspects of scientific enquiry are always under review.

But it's not as simple as that.

When I was an ABC cub, in the early 1970s, I was regaled by History Men and Counter-Culturists with the view that Science had lost its capital S. Science was, like everything else, conditional, even if we agreed that most of it was considered settled, more or less: the earth is round, dinosaurs are dead and duodenal ulcers are caused by germs, not stress.

Popper did not apply universally. In many fields, not only Freud's, you couldn't do experiments to prove or disprove a theory. Powerful interests, the wise men cautioned, governed research; and if the military-industrial complex didn't like it, it didn't happen.

Accordingly, during the 1970s and '80s, my colleagues gave science a hard time. I did it in a slightly frivolous manner, running hoaxes and satires. Norman Swan did it by exposing fraud and duplicity. The late Peter Hunt did it by showing how partial the use of scientific knowledge was in the management of forests and mines. Matt Peacock did it by exposing the horrendous effects of asbestos on human health.

Science was another 'self-perpetuating priesthood', and to get a fresh idea expressed the old professor had first to die. You might wait for decades. And, finally, in some benighted nations, if the tyrant didn't like it, the field lapsed: in the 1930s Joseph Stalin had Trofim Lysenko, and crops failed; decades later Thabo Mbeki had Peter Duesberg, and too many people died from AIDS.

We wanted our audience to think twice when authority was wheeled in on its throne to pronounce the infallible truth. The Academy wasn't quite the same as the Vatican, we implied, but there were resemblances. It was often political, always complex.

Such is youth.

The more I saw of the 'fringe', the more annoyed I became by their self-seeking, often deeply anti-intellectual intransigence. While the crystal-stroking, herbalist folk in chunky cardies and ponytails (as Mike Carlton notoriously described them) got massively ripped off, so science itself became more self-critical and professional in the best sense. What worried me was the political naivety.

IN THE 1990s and the present century the world changed dramatically. Yes, there were internets and webs, and almost instant and universal communication. This meant that the longevity of scientific falsities shrank. At least, in academia. But science communicators also flourished, freed up by the new willingness of institutions desperate for funds, to maintain profile: they let their boffins speak. Paul Davies, Tim Flannery, Mike Archer, David Suzuki, Jane Goodall, Sylvia Earle, Brian Cox, Stephen Hawking and others became famous. There was plenty of science on TV. It was often over-produced to within a nanometre of its life, but you got the point. It was *there*.

Science seemed secure, even popular. There were embarrassments, such as the disarray in physics, which couldn't get its quanta and its relativities in one box, and had to wave red-faced at all that dark stuff – but scientists had a terrific tale to tell about the natural world and were listened to with respect.

By 2007 all this had changed. There was no explosive event, no tipping point that anyone noticed. But the consequences have been enormous. It's as if a thought bomb went off in *Dr Who* and half the globe's brains turned to custard. Governments have wobbled, prime ministers (actual and potential) have fallen and the President of the United States is threatened by the Mad Hatter's Tea Party.

It is another consequence of the new communication technology, in tandem with the old: say anything you like, tell any lies you fancy, and they can have as much currency as the sayings of any old-fashioned sage. Instantly.

Three main areas bore the brunt of the new politics: health, evolution and climate. The journal *Nature*, shocked, put it this way in March 2010: 'Climate scientists are on the defensive, knocked off balance by a re-energized community of global-warming deniers who, by dominating the media agenda, are sowing doubts about the fundamental science. Most researchers find themselves completely out of their league in this kind of battle because it's only superficially about the science. The real goal is to stoke the angry fires of talk radio, cable news, the blogosphere and the like, all of which feed off of contrarian story lines and seldom make the time to assess facts and weigh evidence. Civility, honesty, fact and perspective are irrelevant.'

That last line is crucial: 'Civility, honesty, fact and perspective are irrelevant.'

I have been producing and presenting *The Science Show* on ABC Radio for thirty-five years. The change in tone – when civility, honesty, fact and perspective became irrelevant – was chilling.

When Ian Plimer's *Heaven and Earth* (Connor Court) was about to be published, in 2009, I knew it would make a splash. Accordingly I sent it to three professors hoping that one of them would find the time when not up a mountain or locked in committees to record a review. All three were climate experts of high standing.

Within days of my deadline all of them suddenly delivered. I decided to put their comments to air, in different programs. One, Kurt Lambeck, then the president of the Australian Academy of Science, appeared on *Ockham's Razor*; the other two, David Karoly from the University of Melbourne and Malcolm Walter from the University of NSW (an old friend of Plimer's), on *The Science Show*. The reviews shredded *Heaven and Earth*.

After they were broadcast I received an email from Plimer demanding airtime for a response. I replied that it wasn't customary for book reviews to be followed by replies from disgruntled authors but he could have an *Ockham's Razor* to himself. 'Immediately?' he demanded.

'Well, no,' I replied. I was in Corsica, wouldn't be home for three weeks and our science programs don't have locums, so they were already pre-recorded. He would have to wait until I returned.

A couple of days later Plimer appeared at the Sydney Institute. He announced that the ABC was refusing to have him on. His comments, via the institute's podcast, went around the world.

On my return from Europe I duly recorded his scripted talk. He repeated his main lines from *Heaven and Earth* debunking climate science, ignored the arguments his three critics had presented and attacked the ABC for keeping him from its outlets. Ian Plimer had, however, on the publication of his book, appeared on most of our frontline programs. At length.

I was astounded that the man I'd been instrumental in awarding a Eureka Prize to, for his campaign against creationists, was now willing to emulate Rush Limbaugh. He knew what I had promised. He knew the ABC had been generous to him.

MY CONCERN IS about the science. My job is to report what authoritative sources say about the latest, tested evidence. I am past caring what the consequences of that evidence may be, although proof of pixies, faked moon landings or CIA bombings of the World Trade Center would be rather perplexing. If it is credible work, on it goes.

I report the latest paper on climate rather like a financial journalist reports the value of the euro. If it's 58 Australian cents, then so be it. We say so. You'd hardly say it's 28 cents too often, without being sacked. The consequences of misleading the public on matters of fact can be really harmful.

But the value of the euro is not absolute. It changes from day to day. It is influenced by arbitrary factors, such as 'confidence' or flighty investors. Scientific evidence tries to frame nature: what's really out there. It builds on immense edifices of previous investigation. It is still conditional, but usually very robust.

Until now you dismissed that rigour at your peril. But science in many issues underpins politics. Look at water, rivers, genetic modification, forests, fishing: divisive issues with consequences, with winners and losers. Rather than addressing the issues head-on, it is much easier to torpedo the scientists, unused as they are, gentle souls, to brawls on the hustings.

So Sarah Palin announces that fruit-fly research is a waste of money. Rush Limbaugh tells his millions of listeners, 'The four corners of deceit are government, academia, science and media. Those institutions are now corrupt and exist by virtue of deceit.' Ray Evans, reviewing *Climate: The Counter Consensus* by Bob Carter (Stacey International, 2010) in *Quadrant* magazine, avers on carbon dioxide, warming and the human influence: 'These two arguments have no evidence to support them. None.'

'Death panels' are conjured by opponents to President Obama's health bill, suggesting that the commie systems in the UK and Canada have triage committees ready to sentence your granny to execution if she is deemed unacceptable for treatment in public hospitals. They even said Stephen Hawking would not be alive today if he lived in England (he does!). This led Professor Lawrence Krauss to write in the *Scientific American*: 'The increasingly blatant nature of the nonsense uttered with impunity in public discourse is chilling. Our democratic society is imperilled as much by this as any other single threat, regardless of whether the origins of the nonsense are religious fanaticism, simple ignorance or personal gain.'

'Democratic society is imperilled': that is what's at stake. The Deputy Leader of the Opposition, Julie Bishop, had it right when she compared political parties to football teams in conflict. She did not take the next step: politics is about power, not achievement; winning, not legislation; noise, not meaning. Governments here and abroad are paralysed. Programs are in stasis. Debates are stymied by monstrous mendacities. Obama is a Muslim? The Earth is cooling? Medicare kills pensioners?

What is happening? Naomi Oreskes and Eric M Conway suggest the campaign has been orchestrated by a few think tanks using techniques of the 'mad men' on Madison Avenue, knowing that the scientists' replies would unfailingly be prolix, contorted by pious attempts at fairness and, worst of all, published in journals the public never reads. In *Merchants of Doubt: How a Handful of Scientists Obscured the Truth on Issues from Tobacco Smoke to Global Warming* (Allen & Unwin, 2010), the two academics describe how it was done.

Richard Girling summarises it in a review in the *Sunday Times*: 'A tiny, unqualified minority, they [the contrarians] succeeded in skewing every debate. By promoting doubt, they persuaded editors that, in the name of "balance", their propaganda deserved equal weight to the painstaking work of independent scientists. Peer-reviewed research was routinely dismissed by the sceptics as "junk science". Perversity and invention were erected in its place. The contrarians are far-right political ideologues who cut their teeth in the Cold War. When the Soviet Bloc collapsed, they looked for a new threat to the free world and found it in the environmental movement. They compare it to a watermelon: green on the outside, red in the middle. For them, regulation is the enemy of the free market, the slippery slope to socialism, which must be blocked at whatever cost...Oreskes and Conway have exposed the lie.'

Climate science is replete with uncertainties. No one knows how high temperatures may rise, whether the effects will be drastic or otherwise, and how quickly remediation may work. There is plenty to debate, even before we consider policy options and their consequences.

But how do you spot a wilful distorter or his arguments in advance? They are of several types: Grumpy Uncles, Tory Media Tarts, Foaming Shock-Jocks, Jurassic Marxists and the Busted Bitter. They may be combined in assorted ways.

Grumpy Uncles look like Wilson Tuckey on stilts. They have 'seen it all' and know that previous millennial warnings came to nothing. Been there...

Tory Media Tarts suffer from Attention Deprivation Disorder. Nigel Lawson and a couple of his fellow lords from Thatcher's time (Christopher Monckton) add a *Brideshead Revisited* cachet to the list of dissenters.

Foaming Shock-Jocks we all know about. The trick is to tell the professional (and sometimes rational) contrarians from the sociopaths who really mean it.

Jurassic Marxists feel green politics is a bourgeois push to deprive the world's poor of the rich comforts we enjoy. The journalist Alexander

Cockburn and Martin Durkin (maker of *The Great Global Warming Swindle*) may be members.

The Busted Bitter (and often Twisted) were once supreme in their fields but fell out with their employer – university, media outlet – over money or status. Having recovered from the insult they now fly the world appearing on well-funded platforms with almost anybody knocking *'government!'*

If you haven't spotted which type your interlocutor belongs to, test their argument. Characteristically, the climate sceptic displays the following signs: no level of evidence is ever enough. (You may go back a thousand times and they will always have a blocking tactic.) They invariably are linked to a lobby group, often with powerful political connections: *Quadrant*, the Institute of Public Affairs, the egregious Senator Fielding (whose combination of creationism and climate doubting seemed not to put Plimer off one bit). They are entirely against anthropogenic global warming – only 100 per cent attitudes are entertained. (Most of us are not 100 per cent either way about anything, except a free drink.) Peer review is an echo chamber of old mates and academies are glorified hospices. The greater the renown of the scientist, the more they will be rejected by 'sceptics' as authority figures (as I used to do in the 1970s – I recognise the slippery debating trick). Lines are repeated shamelessly, like pollies on a stump speech, despite the arguments and facts having been crushed a hundred times before.

If the scientists seem consistent and numerous in making the case on climate, it's only because they are rabidly chasing the same research dollar. (This can be attached to virtually any finding at any time.) If you find sceptics' anti-climate tirades in reactionary magazines, free-enterprise think tanks and the right wing of conservative parties then there's a chance, just a chance, that it's ideological. (That they appear hardly anywhere else is, of course, a coincidence or a plot.)

There are two final gambits to look for if the above hasn't worked. Look for the overturning of philosopher David Hume's ideas on causality. Those billiard balls may not rebound tomorrow, despite having done so for the whole of recorded history, and carbon dioxide may fail to have any effect beyond today's concentration, two centuries of research notwithstanding.

Then you can call all the climate scientists and their adherents 'religious deviants'. As Cardinal George Pell put it: 'Some of the hysteric and extreme claims about global warming are also a symptom of pagan emptiness, of Western fear when confronted by the immense and basically uncontrollable forces of nature. Belief in a benign God who is master of the universe has a steadying psychological effect, although it is no guarantee of Utopia, no guarantee that the continuing climate and geographic changes will be benign. In the past pagans sacrificed animals and even humans in vain attempts to placate capricious and cruel gods. Today they demand a reduction in carbon dioxide emissions.'

Any one of these easy-to-administer tests show up an unblushing sophistry designed to obliterate any climate scientists offering evidence of any kind, hampered as ever by an unawareness of inevitable uncertainty.

MY JOB IS the pursuit of truth. Or so they tell me. Just as I will look at today's listing and tell you that the euro is worth 59.5 Australian cents, I will report what is published on climate science in the finest journals or summarised by the top international academies of science, including our own, because it is their function to assess the state of play in a field. It has been my experience that all these sources point in the same direction. Climate is changing, we are responsible and the problem is real. I cannot help what experts say. I am biased towards authority – reliable, proven sources.

But I will seek out dissenting voices. Not just because I'm a child of the 1970s and those hirsute counter-cultural renegades, but because the world is a complex place and we need to probe interesting ideas outside the mainstream. Accordingly, our science programs have featured Matt Ridley (a 'luke-warmist'), Freeman Dyson (a climate critic), Don Aitkin (a sceptic), Nigel Calder (a dissident), Jennifer Marohasy (an indefatigable critic of greens) and the more conspicuous sceptics from within science itself. A broadcaster must engage with unfashionable ideas. These may prove to be, as were the claims of Vaclav Havel and others antagonistic to socialist 'truth', dead right in another age.

There are only a limited number of occasions on which you can have a fellow saying the same thing, pushing the line of the lobby. We do not, in the programs I present, feature Greenpeace or the Australian Conservation Foundation or the anti-GM groups (or very rarely); we also try to avoid Institute of Public Affairs and Heartland Institute spokesmen (though some of our 'sceptics' are paid by them, or have been).

Such are the complexities. Such are the trials of science in public. Lord Robert May, the Australian who became both president of the Royal Society of London and Britain's chief scientist, warned ten years ago that this would be the 'Century of Uncertainty'. He wrote: 'Pockets of aberrant opinion may hold out, with proponents either ignoring decisive evidence and experiments, or alternatively inventing ever more baroque ways of modifying their views to accommodate facts…It is important, although often difficult, at each stage in the evolution of such a landscape to maintain a clear sense of its geomorphology. Unfortunately, the media's praiseworthy aim of always presenting a "balanced" account can have difficulty tracking such an evolving landscape. The temptation, whether in print, radio or TV, is to present the "two sides", as if reporting a sporting event.'

For those of us in broadcasting it has become trickier than ever.

Democracy has, in the past two years, resembled a sporting event – one without an outcome and with too much brawling. We should remember previous eras with similar turbulence, when lies – often big ones – became easy to tell. It is likely that the stakes, both politically and environmentally, are as high today as they were then. Let us try to ensure that the sons and daughters of Goebbels do not end up creating a world as ghastly as it was when I was born.

Robyn Williams has presented *The Science Show* on ABC Radio National since 1975. He is the author of ten books and is a fellow of the Australian Academy of Science and a visiting professor at the University of NSW. His essays have appeared in *Griffith REVIEW: Making Perfect Bodies, People Like Us* and *Hot Air*.

Kent MacCarter

I want to be editor of the chimpanzee register

You know, chimps?
They sure as Christ know you
That genus with answers
They've scoped you for years
Yes, you. For millennia
Chimps with hammers
Chimps with bones
Twirling them like batons
In the marching band
That is your DNA
I want to be editor of the chimpanzee register
Tagged in XML
Pencilling in code
Of who's here
Who's not
Focusing the lens
On why you are
Summoning the chimps
Just to be sure
It's too hot to be naked
Solely on paper
So unzip
Unzip
Try this on
Or disappear

Kent MacCarter was born in the US and lives in Melbourne. His first collection of poetry is *In the Hungry Middle of Here* (Transit Lounge, 2009).

ESSAY

Word for word

Finding meaning beyond verbatim

Emma Hardman

> 'Letters are signs of things, symbols of words,
> whose power is so great that without a voice
> they speak to us the words of the absent;
> for they introduce words by the eye, not by the ear.'
> – Isidore of Seville, *Etymologiae*, c. 600

WHEN I tell people I work for Hansard, the conversation generally goes like this: *Ahh,* they say, *So, you...* They raise their hands and tinkle their fingers. They are miming stenography or Computer Assisted Transcription (CAT).

No, I say. CAT writers – and steno writers before them, and pen-and-paper shorthand writers before that – take down speech at the speed it is spoken, in real time. The stenotype machine – which is like a shorthand typewriter – replaced paper-and-pencil shorthand in the mid-to-late 1970s in Hansard. In the 1980s steno became CAT. The difference between a CAT machine and a stenotype machine is similar to the difference between a manual typewriter and a word processor: same keys, same method, same shorthand language – different technology. Steno creates shorthand in ink on paper; CAT produces shorthand on a screen, which is changed by software into words. Steno or CAT is what you see in American courtroom dramas where a woman sits between the judge and the lawyers, using what looks like a mini typewriter and, if asked by the judge, reads back what has just been said: *I did it, your Honour. I killed him*. There are no stenotype machines used in federal Hansard any more, and only a few people who do CAT.

Oh, so you must know shorthand?

No. Although many Hansard editors do. Until the 1980s, Hansard reporters would take down everything that was said, in shorthand, with a pencil and paper. They would take their transcription back to an office, where they would dictate it to a typist, editing the report as they read it out. In those days, it was a lot less verbatim than it is today. 'Tidying things up' was an

---

PREVIOUS PAGE: Jack Pierson. *Abstracts*. Word sculpture installation.

important aspect of Hansard's brief – rewriting whole paragraphs, restructuring speeches, clarifying arguments, changing vocabulary and generally 'nicing' it up. The typed pages would then be edited and proofread again before being printed.

You must be a fast typist? They are ready to be impressed.

I figure they've earned it for maintaining their curiosity. *You see,* I say, *Hansard is not a verbatim account. It is not a direct transcript. We transcribe what they say and we edit it, but it is more than that.*

Now the look of shock and suspicion – which is encouraging: it shows that people have a sense of ownership of the words of the people they have elected to govern. They want direct access, transparency, between the people and their government, and this is something they expect as their democratic right. And I wholeheartedly agree.

When I tell them that it takes one of us an hour and thirty minutes to transcribe seven minutes and thirty seconds of parliamentary proceedings – together, known as a 'turn' – they are appalled. I can see the unasked question in their eyes: *Can't they hire people who can type faster than that?* They are restrained enough to say only: *But what on earth are you doing?*

I try to explain that we are making the written record more accurate.

More accurate than what was actually said?

No, 'more accurate' as in reflecting the meaning of what was said more accurately than if we just wrote down everything they said word for word.

So, you take out the ums and ahs?

Yes, but it is more than that.

I try to describe how we transform spoken language into written language and how this is not the same as verbatim transcription. I talk about how people don't always say what they mean, how speech consists of not just words but also facial expression, pauses, intonation, gesture, context, pace, volume; writing is just ink on paper. Sounds go out of a mouth and Hansard transforms the meanings such that they can enter someone's eyes. The momentary becomes enduring; time becomes matter. It is an act of translation.

I am still facing a dubious look. *Whatever gets you to sleep at night*, I can see in their eyes.

EMMA HARDMAN: Word for word

HANSARD IS A 'rational verbatim' report. This enigmatic term evolved from Erskine May's *A Practical Treatise on the Law, Privileges, Proceedings and Usage of Parliament* (1844). The modern Australian Commonwealth Hansard mission statement, derived from this Westminster antique, is: 'To provide an accurate, substantially verbatim account of the proceedings of the parliament and its committees which, while usually correcting obvious mistakes, neither adds to nor detracts from the meaning of the speech or the illustration of the argument.'

It sounds clear enough. But how do you know what *substantial* is, in *substantially verbatim*? How often is *usually*, in *usually correcting obvious mistakes*? How do you know if a mistake is *obvious* or not? And what about adding or detracting from *the meaning of the speech or the illustration of the argument*? By what standard?

Writing is 'the graphic counterpart of speech, the fixing of spoken language in a permanent or semi permanent form'. The first words for 'reading' in Greek and Hebrew also meant 'to convince by argument or rhetoric, to call out, to recite'. Up until quite recently – the Middle Ages – reading *was* speech. No one read in their head, as we do now. Even when alone, reading and writing were spoken. Before the ninth century, scriptoria in Western Europe were very noisy places. Everyone was there to read and to write, and both of these activities by definition meant speaking the words aloud.

The rise of Carolingian minuscule – a script that introduced punctuation, capital letters and spaces between words in Western Europe – meant that the reader did not have to work out where each word and sentence began and ended. Where there were three modes – sight, hearing, speech – there became just one: sight.

By the thirteenth century, silent reading was as entrenched as reading aloud had once been. The new practice of silent reading sent rules to the other extreme. In the scriptoria, all spoken language was banned and scribes were required to communicate with each other in sign language while working. Scriptoria fell silent.

Stephen King says that 'writing is telepathy', and the British writer, translator and linguist Anthony Burgess, author of *A Clockwork Orange* (1962), observed: 'Thoughts, desires, appetites, orders have to be conveyed from one brain to another, and they cannot easily be conveyed directly. Only with telepathy do we find mind speaking straight to mind without the intermediacy of signs…The vast majority of sentient beings – men, women, cats, dogs, bees, horses – have to rely on signals, symbols of what they feel and think and want.'

TODAY IN HANSARD the majority of editors use voice-recognition software (VR). The editor sits in the chamber only to 'log' what is going on: a kind of minute-taking. They are not typing everything that is said; it is all being recorded by the broadcasting department. The editors are in the chamber to write down who is speaking when. And you won't find many of those colourful interjections that are flung across the chamber in the transcript, because they only go in if they are responded to by the person who has the floor. After seven minutes and thirty seconds, the next editor on the roster comes in and the first editor goes back to their office, puts on their headphones and calls up the audio of the proceedings they have just witnessed. As the sound goes in their ears they speak what they are hearing into their microphone, and VR produces those words on the screen. We call this 'voicing'. When you voice, it works best if you speak fast, because the technology uses context: the more word groups it has at once, the better its 'guesses' about what you said and what you meant.

'Words' don't actually exist in spoken language. Although we might think we say *the warmth there was*, what we actually say is closer to *the warmpth air was*, which VR has to make a stab at and might come up with *the warm there was* or *the war there was* or *the war path was*. *This data* sounds the same as *this starter* or *this Tartar*. We rely heavily on intonation, non-verbal signals and contexts to decipher the speaker's meaning.

Language is not simply a means of communication; it is also a crucial part of the entire process of cognition. We use words to designate objects and their location in space. Through grammatical constructions we express relationships and ideas. Language is fundamental to perception, memory, thinking and behaviour.

Our brains devote a vast amount of space and energy to language functions. There is reading, writing, speaking, listening, hearing, body language, gesture, facial expression. Each of these involves motor functions as well as cognitive function: you move your jaw, hands, face, lips and tongue to speak; you move your hand, arm, head and eyes to write; and you move your eyes to read.

We tend to think of language as one thing. You can say (or sign) the word *dog*, you can hear the word *dog*, you can write the word *dog* and you can read the word *dog*. It still means the same thing. But reading, writing, speaking and hearing are all different processes, physically and neurologically. When a conscious human subject is scanned using positron emission tomography (PET) and asked to perform similar but subtly different language tasks, different areas of the brain light up, depending on whether the subject is hearing words, seeing words, speaking words, even generating verbs.

The same part of the brain lights up when a subject is speaking, no matter what the language. (This is the same part of the brain that lights up when the subject is a sign-language speaker, whichever the sign language.) When reading or writing, it is another part of the brain – again, it is the same, no matter what language.

The alphabet is no more than three thousand years old, but speech is as old as humans. We tend to think of writing and reading as natural upshots of speech; however, the relationship between written language and spoken language is arbitrary. The English alphabet has five symbols for vowels: a, e, i, o, u. But English has twenty-three vowel sounds: fifteen single sounds and the rest diphthongs (double vowel sounds, as in *eye*) and triphthongs (as in *our*). The acrobatics performed by the brain to hear these sounds and decode them into bits of meaning using the Latin alphabet (a, b, c, d, e…), or vice versa, to use only five symbols to cover twenty-three vowel sounds, is an incredible feat.

LIKE ANY OTHER kind of translating, Hansard editing is problem-solving, a constant balancing of many rules. The main rules we have to deal with are: a Hansard transcript should be *clear, readable and grammatically correct*; it should accurately record what the speaker *said*; and it should accurately record what the speaker *intended*.

These three rules are often mutually exclusive. And add to this roughly a thousand pages of others – relating to punctuation, grammar, usage, spelling, hyphenation, capitalisation – contained in the *Hansard style guide*, the *Hansard editing guide* and the *Hansard form guides*, not to mention our other staple, the Macquarie Dictionary, all of which contain rules that are often in conflict with each other.

In the passage from a speaker's brain to the brain of a reader of Hansard, there are many channels that meaning has to pass through. The editor has to find the most direct and clear path through these channels, changing what the speaker said into something that has the same meaning but consists of marks on a screen – letters and numbers and symbols in space; no longer sound waves passing through air. It is a fabulously circuitous route.

The first hurdle is the speaker's intention: what the speaker thinks or means, before they even move their mouth, those pre-verbal firings of electricity in the brain.

Then there is the speaker's attempt at a transformation of those electrical currents and snapping synapses into words – still not spoken. We can never reliably recreate our cerebral intentions: there is always a gap between intention and action. This gap, the gap between thought and speech, between meaning and words – the gap we fill with language – is tiny, and huge. It is a black hole that all words fall into, and it represents the entire endeavour of communication, of writing and reading and conversing with each other. This gap is the attempt at telepathy that Stephen King and Anthony Burgess speak of. To say or write what you feel and experience and see and hear, to communicate what you mean, is a subject that philosophers have spent lifetimes trying to untangle.

After this, there is what the speaker actually says. The speaker might say *We did not do that*, when they meant to say *We did do that*. This may seem like a big error – to say the opposite of what you meant to say – but it is surprisingly common. A verbatim rendering of this would be *We did not do that*, but a Hansard editor will have taken into consideration all of the surrounding utterances, the context, the tone, the political alliances of the speaker, the body language (perhaps the speaker was distracted at that moment, by someone entering the chamber), and deduced that the speaker really meant to say the opposite of what they said.

Then there is what the editor hears. It took me a while to realise that it is worth listening to that confusing phrase, that swallowed word, just one more time, even though you're sure you won't be able to hear any more than you did the first five times because, miraculously, on the sixth listen something has popped in your brain, something has changed, and it is clear what is being said. Everything is the same, but your brain has processed and focused on every detail until it finally homes in on the one thing you were not able to understand. They are saying *when you look at this data* not *when you look at the starter*. They are saying *refugia* not *re the future*. And this might shed new light on the rest of the sentence or paragraph.

Then there is what VR hears the editor say – and this is easily fixed, but makes for some fun: *catch lick priests or deigned* for *Catholic priests ordained*; *who were turpentine indisposition* for *who were there at the time in this position*; *2000 and Sikhs* for *2006*; and *Collette Ding and burying parent emissions* for *collecting and burying their emissions*.

IT IS AT first counter-intuitive that a verbatim account of the proceedings of parliament could be less correct than a 'rational verbatim' translation. But the verbatim translation of 'verbatim' cannot be done in one word; you need three: 'word for word'. We can say the most confusing things, yet the listener extracts the right meaning. Every moment, our brains glide over misspeakings, repetitions, stumblings, mumblings and a general inability to express ourselves clearly, to put our thoughts into speech. We are also interpreting winces, pauses (does the speaker pause because they have lost their train of thought, because they are adding emphasis, or because they have just realised that they are reading from the wrong sheet of paper?), throat clearings, gestures, the expression in the voice, the emphases. It is impressive how accurate the human brain is when it tries to extract meaning from such confusing data.

Here is an average piece of spoken language written verbatim:

> In terms, of, um, sorry, just to, I mean, in terms of this very first one, you can really see here. Um, Peter, would you, thank you. In terms of this getting, getting out of canoe, it initially didn't, at first it really strikes me that really bush stores what it seems to be is it seems to be

quite a powerful idea in that sense in as much as it would seem too if it's really very much improving one aspect of those communities being a store that really really reduces the two I guess but it also as well and it would seem is providing an example of a business prize beyond what the really small list of examples of the jobs you have got in those communities right at the very present moment which are providing a really a role model. What it is is that. Do you agree with that?

Gibberish, right?

Here is a Hansard-style edited version, the result of close attention to context of topic, of issues and of intonation; to pauses, pace, emphasis, common sense, what was said before and after, who the speaker was and what was happening in the room (a PowerPoint slide was being shown):

In terms of this first graph – getting out of the 'goo' – it initially strikes me that Bush Stores seems to be quite a powerful idea in the sense that, if it is improving one aspect of those communities, being the store, that reduces the 'goo'. But it also would seem to be providing an example of a business enterprise beyond the small list of examples of jobs which are providing role models in those communities at the moment. Do you agree with that?

This is not elegant prose. But it makes much more sense. It is an effective translation from one mode to another, a written representation of what was said and what occurred.

A Hansard editor must have a passion for the nuances of words, phrasing, punctuation, usage, grammar, vocabulary, syntax – and a broad general knowledge. You must know (or know where to look to check) that the *bee's knees* refers to the knees of one bee, not the knees of many bees (which would be *bees' knees*). You receive your *just deserts* not your *just desserts* (it comes from the verb 'deserve'). It is *grisly remains* not *grizzly remains* (unless all the other bears have left the campsite and only one *grizzly remains*). And if the speaker says *It's not rocket surgery*, the editor must decide if it should be rendered: *It's not rocket science* or *It's not brain surgery*, or if it should be left as is.

EMMA HARDMAN: Word for word

HANSARD TAKES OUT false starts, redundancies, verbal tics and unnecessary repetitions. We get rid of all the *ums* and *ahs*, the *ahems* and *errrs*. We get rid of 99 per cent of the *Mr Speakers* and *Mr Presidents* that bookend so many utterances in the House of Representatives and the Senate. Other verbal tics that are candidates for deletion are *very, really, actually, certainly, however, surely, of course, so, therefore, and, but, because* and *I think*.

Hansard editors routinely put in things that were never said and leave out a whole bunch of stuff that was said. Most of this stuff is 'form'. Form is procedural text – replacing what was said with standard descriptions. For example, when we hear something like this:

President: *Is leave granted to move that? Leave is granted. You can now move it Senator Nettle. You move the postponement to the next day of sitting? That's 810 in your name?*

Senator X: *That's right.*

President: *The question is that that motion be agreed to. Those of that opinion say aye, those against no. I think the ayes have it.*

The transcript will read *Question agreed to* – a phrase that wasn't even said. This kind of translation is crucial in representing accurately what has happened in parliament: a bill has been passed or a vote has been taken.

ONE OF THE things that sucks up a Hansard editor's time in the desperate dash to get their turn finished in an hour and thirty minutes is checking. We check spelling, punctuation and grammar. We check the names of organisations and departments, television stations and mining companies. We check the date the second reading debate is being resumed from. We check the spelling of Princess Leia, the Fonz and Jabba the Hutt. We check page references, committee titles, names of countries. We check Aboriginal language names, acronyms (there are thousands of these in regular use) and the names of the Auburn under-eights netball team.

We discover that *seedoor* is CEDAW: the Convention on the Elimination of All Forms of Discrimination against Women. We need to ascertain what the *sugarloaf salient* is, what a *retention lease* is, and what *bitterns* and *vuvuzela* mean, to know how to spell them and to verify that what we think we heard makes sense in the context. And we check names, even if they seem obvious. Invariably, the *John Smith* whose name you neglect to check is *Jon Smythe*.

We check quotes. And politicians quote a lot. They quote from newspaper reports from fifteen minutes ago to three hundred years ago. They quote from television shows, movies, radio interviews and songs – in June 2008, Mr Raguse, the then member for Forde, *sang* the first verse of Redgum's 'I Was Only Nineteen'. They quote TS Eliot, Henry Lawson, Shakespeare, Emily Dickinson, Socrates and Ronald Reagan. They quote from Senate committee reports and from *Hansard*. They quote from legislation, letters and emails, international treaties, scientific studies, websites, annual reports and advertising material. And they quote from *subsection two, paragraph two of the legislation* and Hansard has to work out that what they meant was Section 146A(2)(b)(ii) of the Cross-Border Insolvency Bill 2008.

AS A LOVER of language I had always been aware that spoken and written language are different. Spoken language is looser; you can get away with more. You don't have to think about spelling or punctuation when you speak. And most people are aware that body language plays a larger part in communication than we consciously perceive. But how profound the differences are was unexpected and fascinating. What I love about my job is being with the words and meanings in an intimate way; wrestling the spoken word into the written; translating one to the other; and being the closest thing there is to a telepathist, a medium between one brain and many other brains. The transcript that Hansard produces is not word-for-word. But nor is it a painting, a collage, an artistic interpretation of what went on. It is a clear, well-framed photograph.

References at www.griffithreview.com

Emma Hardman is a Canberra writer and editor. She works as a Hansard editor at Parliament House. Her first novel, *Nine Parts Water* (UQP, 2007), was shortlisted for two national literary awards. She is currently working on a novel set during the the flu pandemic of 1918-19.

MEMOIR

Language wars

Sometimes, mother knows best

Selina Li Duke

WHEN my son told me he was going to Beijing to study Mandarin after graduating, he also said, with a mischievous grin, 'See? I'm a good Chinese son after all. Are you happy now?'

It was far from an admission of defeat in the battle of the generations, or a concession to relentless pressure from a pushy (Asian) parent. He was going to backpack all the way to Beijing, staying in hostels featured in the Lonely Planet, meeting young adventurers – including 'hot chicks' – from all around the world. And he wasn't going to think about anything as mundane as getting a job, though knowing the language of an economic power would no doubt add to his eligibility for one.

Still, that he was so motivated to learn Chinese as to go to China to do it surprised me. As a child and a teenager he was never interested. His eyes would glaze over whenever the words 'Chinese lessons' were mentioned. No way was he going to give up his weekend sports, parties or sleepovers to attend tedious Chinese Saturday schools. He would forgo treats, lose pocket money, eat vegetables, clean toilets – anything rather than learn a language he did not identify with. Though half-Chinese he is all-Australian by birth; his friends, even the Chinese ones, speak English. He happens also to look more European than Asian. He surprised me once with a reference to the 'Asians' at his high school who 'always stick together'.

But I did want him to have a connection to my other cultural world, to understand at least a little of what *gong-gong* (grandfather) or *yi por* (maternal great-aunt) were telling us as we munched on our *char siu bao* (roast pork buns) at the dim-sim restaurant in Hong Kong. Without knowing their language he would always look upon them as inscrutable, and their world as exotic and Other.

I also wished for him the pleasures that I have experienced – of acquiring extra perspectives that come with knowing another language, perspectives that have enabled me to appreciate the beauty of a culture as well as see through the crap. So much of a culture, good or bad, is untranslatable.

PREVIOUS PAGE: Clay Butler. *There goes the neighbourhood*, 1994. Courtesy of the artist. www.sidewalkbubblegum.com

IT TURNED OUT that such wishes were very much in tune with the thinking of the times. When I arrived in Australia, in the early 1980s, the word 'multicultural' had become part of the political and media lexicon, not just as a description of the changing society but also as a kind of ideology (albeit a highly debatable one) to aspire to. It was only in my readings of Australian history later that I found out about the attitudes of previous periods: how 'assimilation' was the dominant theme of social planning, and minorities – indigenous as well as newcomers – were expected to conform to the mainstream Anglo-Celtic ways, which would include ditching your mother tongue.

By the 1980s linguists had also turned away from the belief that the young brain has only a limited capacity for language learning, and that if it is shared by more than one language the proficiency in each language would suffer. Instead, they talked about linguistic universals, about the 'deep structure' of all languages and how knowing one language actually enhances the acquisition of another. There have been many studies too to show the cognitive and intellectual benefits of acquiring a new language, how it boosts brainpower and communication skills – indispensable qualities in the quest for that Holy Grail of all parents, their offspring's academic success.

Also, as Australia became more engaged in trade with Asia, there was the growing recognition – if a little grudging – of the economic benefits of being 'Asia-literate'.

And so, from the day my son was born, I was asked, first by the nurse in the maternity ward and later by 'ethnic' as well as Anglo-Australian acquaintances, 'Are you going to teach him Chinese?'

'Yes, I will,' I would say. But as you have probably gathered from the preceding paragraphs, I turned out to be a total failure. The result of my efforts, twenty-four years later, is that my son is a typical Australian in language ability: a monoglot. Through the years he has mastered the names of a few dim-sim dishes, and a smattering of Chinese words and phrases of an irreverent nature, but that is all.

'What have I done wrong?' asks the mother who feels she has not measured well on yet another yardstick of parenthood. While I do not really lose too much sleep over that failure (as distinct from other failures), the topic of can-your-son-speak-Chinese comes up all too often during social occasions and I have sheepishly to face up to that failure again.

IT WAS NOT until I had to teach my own language that I realised how little I knew about it, for I know it as though by instinct, and not with any analytical or conceptual understanding. People said, 'You don't have to know how – just talk to him in your own language while your husband talks to him in English.' (This is known as the OPOL method: one parent, one language.) Okay, but when do I start talking to him in my language – from birth, so that he becomes a 'simultaneous bilingual'? Or when he is two or three, after his first language is established, so that he becomes a 'sequential bilingual', which according to experts is just as good?

A straw poll of friends and acquaintances could not produce a definitive answer. (There was no such thing in those dark days as online parents' forums.) Being a cautious person, I decided to delay my Chinese input until my son was two or three. But unfortunately, in my case, later means never. By the time he could get about in his first language, it was a struggle to get him to listen to me in his second. To get the terrible two- or three-year-old to do what you want him to – to get immediate results, in order to save your sanity – you begin to use only the language he is accustomed to, the language used by all his friends, his dad, his extended family in Australia and his favourite TV characters.

What's more, in the past few decades, for reasons yet to be fully agreed upon, this language has become a language for the world. Some boast about the glorious 'flexibility', 'logicality' and even 'masculinity' of the English language, while others believe its ascendancy is merely the result of historical circumstances, of British imperialism in the nineteenth century and American power in the twentieth, in the same way that Latin was once used throughout Europe because of the might of the Roman military and, later, of the Roman Catholic Church.

These days, even kindergarteners and first-graders in Beijing and Shanghai are learning English. English has become the first foreign language for most of the world, a kind of lingua franca whenever different nationalities meet, whether at a science conference in Helsinki or a beauty contest in Mexico

City. The complacent, monolingual Australian thus sees little need to learn the language of other peoples, and many an ethnic parent gives up nagging her Australian-born or -educated offspring to learn her native tongue. What is the use of forcing Cantonese or Tamil or Tagalog on your children when it is not going to be used outside the home, anyway? It is far more urgent that they get ahead in the mainstream society, by first getting the world language right.

Indeed, it is by no means easy to get that language right, even for the native-born. Listen to all the squabbles between 'experts' about what is the best teaching method for early literacy: 'phonics' or 'whole language'; 'traditional', 'functional' or no grammar. And just as your child has muddled through primary school, you begin to hear the war cries of those who want to keep Shakespeare on the English syllabus and those who want students to study pop lyrics. You look at the assignment he has to do for English as a 'subject', the essays and interviews and presentations, and realise its enormousness and complexity. Then there are the maths assignments and the social studies projects, and music after school. After needling him constantly to complete these tasks in time (in competition with hanging out with mates, soccer, cricket and Nintendo) the wearied mother cannot bring herself to nag about anything else.

IN MY CASE there is also the further issue of which Chinese language to teach. Born and bred in Hong Kong, I speak Cantonese, a language of the south. Yet Mandarin is the obvious choice for people wanting to learn Chinese. It is the language of Beijing and of central government since the Qing Dynasty. Its premier status was affirmed by both the Nationalist government (established in 1912) and the Communist government (established in 1949). The latter especially had enunciated laws and imperatives aimed at the spread of Putonghua (the 'common language', the official name for Mandarin) to the furthest corner of the land. Jiang Zeman, President of China from 1993 to 2003, once remarked that there are 'too many languages' in the nation, decrying their profusion as a barrier to modernisation and unity. So, while the Chinese constitution includes guarantees about minority-language rights (and there were substantial if erratic efforts to achieve this in practice, especially for the larger and more 'assertive' minorities in politically sensitive areas), the overarching theme of Chinese language policies has been the promotion of Putonghua as the standard language for the whole nation.

History is full of stories about how coercion was used by speakers of a dominant language to bring speakers of other languages in line. This happened in authoritarian as well as democratic regimes. According to the linguist Andrew Dalby, in North America 'the speaking of native languages in school precincts was punished down to the 1950s, as it was in Australia even in the 1970s.' It was as though the maintenance of your (indigenous or minority) mother tongue posed a threat to the purity of the mainstream culture, a sign of disaffection and rebelliousness.

These days, the more persuasive tool of education is the language engineer's stock-in-trade. When a language is designated as the medium of instruction in schools across the land, the spread of its use is guaranteed. The broadcasting media, state or private, also plays a pivotal role. China Central Television dramas are a powerful instrument in the spread of Putonghua across China. And the linguist Nicholas Evans notes, 'Rupert Murdoch's Star Channel is doing more to spread Hindi into remote Indian villages than sixty years of education campaigning by the Indian government.'

Historically, as a dominant language takes over more and more spheres of everyday life, and fewer and fewer children in minority groups learn their parents' native tongues, the decline of these tongues is set in train. At the beginning of European colonisation of Australia there were about 250 different indigenous languages, but in 2005 a national survey found that only 145 were still spoken, of which most were 'severely or critically endangered' and only eighteen were considered 'strong'. Nicholas Evans observes that the same kind of language death has occurred in North America and South Africa. Other areas of language extinction include 'much of Brazil under the impact of Portuguese, in Siberia under Russian, in the Sudan under Arabic, throughout Indonesia under Indonesian, and in even quite remote parts of Papua New Guinea, under Tok Pisin, the newly developed national lingua franca.'

All over the world, linguists and anthropologists like Evans are frantically documenting dying languages, often in nursing homes where the very last speaker resides, so that the voices of entire peoples, in all their moods and cadences, do not fade into silence, and the unique experience and knowledge they articulate are not lost to the rest of humanity. Sometimes, even governments get in on the act of minority-language maintenance, committing a modicum of funds and resources to the cause. It may be token, a sop to bothersome minorities, or a genuine attempt to support 'diversity' and 'linguistic ecology'. I have the feeling, however, that the decline and eventual death of many languages, especially those without a written culture, will be hard to stop. I wonder what the global landscape of languages will be like in one or two hundred years; what voices – if any – other than those of economic and political power will be there in our once splendidly polyphonous world.

RAISED IN HONG Kong, with an anti-Communist upbringing and colonial British education, I never had any great emotional connection to Mandarin, the language intoned by those stony-faced men of the National People's Congress as they stood or clapped like robots against the luridly red backdrop of the Great Hall of the People. Even as I was sometimes seduced by its mellifluous sounds in films and songs, and through classes and tapes, it was a language I could not call my own. When it came to choosing a Chinese language for my son, I hesitated to put Mandarin above my mother tongue of Cantonese. I started with the latter, but a few months later, when pragmatism reared its head and he hadn't learned much Cantonese anyway, I would try to start all over again in Mandarin. But the result would be the same: glazed eyes, yawns, wriggling bottom.

And so the years went by. Years one to six, according to education experts, are the foundation years, when children, with their still supple, 'plastic' brains, may learn one language and then another (up to seven, some linguists say) without apparent effort and without developing an accent. Some academics are more generous, pushing this age boundary to twelve. By the time my son was a teenager I had practically given up. I would just be happy that he got through school and university, with or without the advantage of a second language.

Am I glad that he now wants to learn Mandarin in Beijing? Yes, I think it is worth applauding any effort that will broaden the mind and open it to ways of seeing other than those of a narrow pop-culture world, or indeed anything that is an intellectual challenge (a huge one for my son, considering that he has to start from near zilch at twenty-four).

That he chose Mandarin over Cantonese does not bother me too much anymore. He did say he would tackle Cantonese after he has mastered Mandarin. After all, the two are linked by a common writing system, the script of the Han people (the majority, ruling race in China). It sounds like a pipe dream, but it is a nice thought.

In any case, by one method of assessment a language other than a national language needs about a million speakers for it to be 'safe' and not in danger of becoming a museum piece. By that measure Cantonese is not going to die out very soon. Seven and a half million loud and strident Hong Kong residents are Cantonese speakers, producing Canto-pop and Canto-films for China and the overseas Chinese world. Indeed, notwithstanding a 'patriotic' lobby that wants to replace it with Mandarin as the medium of instruction in schools, Cantonese is still so mainstream in Hong Kong that it is a kind of bullyboy to other regional dialects of the south. It saddens me, for instance, that I have not heard my mother's dialect of a southern rural county, considered 'peasant' and inferior in Hong Kong, spoken there for many years.

AT THE TIME of writing, my son is struggling on his rather expensive beginner's Mandarin course, offered by a reputable university that is nonetheless out to get foreigners' money. He has to learn forty new characters a day, not just the sounds but the writing. He is embarrassed that the Brazilians, the Germans, the Koreans and the son of a Saudi diplomat on the course seem to be doing better than he is. I am glad he is learning a precious lesson in life: if you make the mistake of not listening to your mother when you're young, you pay dearly later in life.

Selina Li Duke has published children's picture books, short stories and essays in anthologies and journals, and a book of personal essays, *With Barbarian Ghosts* (Southern Cross University Press, 1998), which draws on her experience as a migrant.

REPORTAGE

In the kingdom of the mind

Explaining human behaviour

Tanveer Ahmed

AS a junior medical student I walked the waxed, antiseptic-smelling corridors of Sydney's Royal North Shore Hospital dressed in an oversized lab coat. One of the first patients I was encouraged to see was a middle-aged woman from the Central Coast. A retired schoolteacher, she had been transferred after an unusual heart attack. As I began my examination, I felt an atypical collapsing pulse on her wrist, and remembered that the textbooks called this a water hammer. When I placed my stethoscope on her chest there was a rapidly rising and falling whoosh across the left side of her sternum, the aortic area of the heart. She had a damaged valve in an uncommon location.

But before I heard the so-called heart murmur, a term that made me think of bodily organs whispering sweet nothings, it was clear, even to a novice, that something else was unusual. When I asked her to remove her hospital gown, she did so with great enthusiasm, revealing her droopy, ageing breasts. I was taken aback, not yet accustomed to the power of my professional status. I felt awkward standing next to her husband, who muttered dryly, 'How come you're never like that with me?'

I mentioned the experience to one of her treating doctors, more as an amusing anecdote than because of any clinical significance. Although the registrar laughed, something also clicked and he ordered a barrage of tests.

A week later he told me that my encounter had led to the discovery of a tiny lesion in the frontal section of her brain, observable only on expensive MRI scans. It was probably the result of a small stroke that occurred around the time of her heart attack. Barely perceptible, it had subtle effects on her interactions, particularly her social inhibitions.

I remember the episode clearly, even though it was early in my training. It focused my interest on our essentially social nature – how the vast bulk of our brain exists to process and react to social information; how primed it is to recognise, interpret and respond to the input of others, which lays down patterns governing behaviour. I have always been interested in the extent to which we are individual or collective beings, and how feeling is as fundamental as thinking.

In the decade and a half since that consultation, the study of the brain and how it regulates behaviour has become one of the most fertile fields of discovery. Barely a week goes by without a declaration of the relevance of neuroscientific findings to everyday life. A picture of a brain scan in pixel-busting Technicolor usually accompanies these proclamations, often connected to announcements from new disciplines with the prefix 'neuro'.

Neuro-marketing allows advertisers to pinpoint the parts of the brain that light up in response to particular products or tailored messages. Neuro-economics looks at how we make economic decisions and their relation to brain functioning. Even some philosophers have embraced neuro-ethics, in which ethical principles are examined using brain scans to determine people's moral intuitions when they are asked to deliberate on classic dilemmas. France has become the first country in the world to devote a government department to looking at the policy implications of our burgeoning knowledge of neuroscience, led by Associate Professor Olivier Oullier.

My own field, psychiatry, has benefited enormously. While the specialty was once the bastard child of medicine – lacking prestige and credibility – a growing interest in mental health and the way brain chemistry affects our emotions has lifted it into the mainstream. During the 2010 federal election, Australian of the Year Professor Patrick McGorry and the Brain and Mind Institute's Professor Ian Hickie became two of the most prominent doctors in the country. While this goes some way to making up for years of neglect, it also suggests a growing expectation of a marriage of the biological and social sciences.

IN MY LIFETIME, three and a half decades, more has been learnt about the brain than in the whole of human history. We now know there are more than one hundred billion nerve cells, and each of them has many thousands of synaptic connections – channels of chemical communication – with its neighbours. We know an increasing amount about the anatomy of the different functional centres that make up the brain, their varying responsibilities, how they execute their duties and even how they evolved. We are beginning to understand how memory, which lies at the core of the subjective self, is dependent upon the strength of the cell networks formed by our experience, thoughts and feelings.

We could even be on the verge of a new Enlightenment – one in which the concept of the individual autonomously making rational decisions is usurped by a new, more complex understanding of the forces that shape human nature. This process may be accelerated by the global financial crisis and the frailties of our systemic assumptions that it exposed.

It is rare to hear about human nature in discussion of politics, yet it is the foundation of the underlying conflict. Debates about human nature have often been restricted to criminality and other social pathologies, as if only bad people failed to conform to the behavioural model of modern economics. But most policymakers agree that whether addressing business regulation or competition in schools, *Homo economicus* served well enough: given choice, people will act in their own interest, and by so doing make the system work better for everyone. This is a useful, but flawed, shortcut to understanding human behaviour.

The most influential thinkers of the earlier Enlightenment were consumed by the question of how to balance reason with the primitive and softer elements in our nature. Adam Smith's greatest influence, David Hume, was adamant that reason 'ought only to be the slave of the passions'. For Hume, emotions drove people to apply reason, to satisfy basic desires for food or sex, or more complex behaviours such as curiosity and ambition.

Smith, too, offered a sophisticated analysis of our instincts for fairness and social sympathy in his first book, *The Theory of Moral Sentiments* (1759). Despite being the Zeus of market rationality, Smith's arguments for these forces to balance self-interest were lost in the laissez-faire hubris of the recent decades leading up to the financial crisis.

John Maynard Keynes reintroduced this concept in the 1930s when he referred to 'animal spirits', coining the phrase to describe a range of emotions, impulses, enthusiasms and misperceptions that drive economies – and ultimately unwind them. In *Animal Spirits: How Human Psychology Drives the Economy, and Why It Matters for Global Capitalism* (Princeton University Press, 2009) the economics professors Robert J Shiller and George A Akerlof, the latter a Nobel Prize laureate, argue that those who subsequently interpreted Keynes's thought 'rooted out almost all of the animal spirits – the noneconomic motives and irrational behaviours – that lay at the heart of his explanation for the Great Depression'.

Passions, or animal spirits, relate to the hybrid make-up of our brains. The human brain is not really a single organ, but three brains in one: a triune, in the famous Yale neuroscientist Paul MacLean's theory of brain evolution. A primitive 'lizard' brain, designed millennia ago for survival, lies at the core and straddles the roots of ancient dopamine-reward pathways, the channels of pleasure, curiosity and desire.

Around this reptilian base evolved the limbic cortex of the early mammalian brain. This is where kinship behaviour and the nurture of the young – characteristic of all mammalian species, and particularly evident in our own social behaviour – is rooted.

The third part of our brains is the overlying cortex, the size of which differentiates us from other mammals. Subsequent evolution within the mammalian species is marked by a continuous expansion of this cortex, and by extraordinary growth of the frontal region, the part that was damaged in the uninhibited patient I examined as a medical student. This distinguishes us within the primate lineage behaviourally and physically: it is the place where information from our three brains is brought together, analysed and distilled. This hybrid apparatus blends emotion and reasoning, just as Hume and Keynes surmised long before magnetic resonance imaging made it visible.

THERE ARE TWO areas that brain research is illuminating which challenge how we organise society. One is our essentially social nature: we are herd-like animals who show a strong tendency to conform with group norms. The human brain is much larger than other primates' because of the development of our remarkable capacity for social skills: empathy, co-operation and fairness. There is growing evidence that we are more like nodes in a relationship network than discrete entities. It is through our capacity for empathy that awareness of how our behaviour is judged by others emerges. From the to-and-fro with other individuals we learn to navigate as citizens in a social order.

The second area of astonishing discoveries is in the plasticity of the brain. Dr Norman Doidge, a psychiatrist and psychoanalyst, has become a literary superstar around the world with his book *The Brain that Changes Itself* (Scribe, 2008). We are not, in computer-speak, hardwired: our brains can change well into old age. Parts of the brain can learn new tricks. We can shape our brains to create new habits that we might have thought we were incapable of; we can learn to see things from new perspectives and react in a different way.

The implications of this for policy development are considerable. For example, it is now well known that early childhood deprivation can scar the brain, leaving a mark that is visible to imaging technologies. This informs much of the focus on early childhood education and intervention. The scars – disadvantage etched on the brain – mean that those who trumpet the individual's capacity to triumph over their environment must confront significant limitations. On the other hand, Doidge's notion of neuroplasticity tempers extreme beliefs of environmental determinism and suggests that we can remake ourselves.

Much of this modern brain research is affirming for social democrats. By highlighting psychological frailties, such as our preference for immediate reward when it is available before our eyes, and the way this contributes to market epidemics, a powerful case can be made for regulation, paternalism and social measures to promote feelings of security. Hence the popularity of the concepts promoted in Richard H Thaler and Cass R Sunstein's book *Nudge: Improving Decisions about Health, Wealth and Happiness* (Penguin, 2009) and its associated invention of a new political philosophy called libertarian paternalism. As Associate Professor Olivier Oullier observes, this is a way of encouraging a certain behaviour, such as not smoking, but making people feel like they were empowered to make the choice themselves. A combination of advertising aimed to shock with bite-sized portions of relevant information has been shown to be the most effective method.

The persistent mantra of choice is undermined by social psychology findings that show how bad people are at predicting what will make them happy, or even remembering what has made them happy in the past.

There is ample evidence from brain studies that humans have a fundamental instinct for fairness, just as Adam Smith believed two and a half centuries ago – undermining those who believe inequality is minor collateral damage in the generation of wealth. But Smith's notion of the invisible hand of the market ensuring an equitable order without regulatory interference is on weaker ground away from the tight-knit agrarian communities of yesteryear, and in the hyper-global world of multinational corporations and instant communications.

There is, though, much from our insights into the brain that also offer support to those on the right of politics. It is true that we are programmed for self-preservation amid scarcity, so self-interest is our primary motive. The modern world of abundance, with its relentless flow of novel and cheaper opportunity, is a great challenge. The economics historian Avner Offer writes in *The Challenge of Affluence: Self-control and Well-Being in the United States and Britain Since 1950* (Oxford University Press, 2006) that wealth breeds impatience and impatience undermines wellbeing. We struggle to make decisions for the long term; conservative philosophies that stress the importance of social institutions which have evolved over time and reflect a natural order, like the family, church and other civic institutions, protect us from ourselves. Offer refers to these as 'commitment devices' and points out that, as we become richer, we mistakenly think we do not need them. Social institutions and cultural taboos are ways in which generations hand down tacit knowledge about human nature. They should be protected from social engineers.

THERE ARE LIMITS to how much we can apply neuroscience to policy. Even the most sophisticated neural imaging cannot differentiate between physical pain and the pain of social rejection. Even in the simplest of tasks the brain functions as an integrated unit, with many parts seemingly working together. The findings of a particular part of a brain lighting up in the isolated, controlled environment of a lab should be taken with a grain of salt.

But it would be disingenuous to discount the growing knowledge about the brain and human nature, and whether it might contribute to a more substantive meeting between the various sides of politics and policy. Conservatives cannot discount the importance of social context, inequality and the limits of market rationality. Likewise, so-called progressives need to be wary of the capacity of the state to empower communities, and more interested in the role of social norms and civic institutions. Our brains evolved in small, homogenous communities but are now faced with extraordinary diversity in a fast-changing, globalised knowledge economy. It is a period of great creativity, change and more than a little bit of danger. We can be better equipped by a more nuanced knowledge and acceptance of the flaws that science, the highest application of reason within our animal brains, is shedding light upon.

This subtler perspective on human behaviour is something my patients remind me of every day. They are a jumble of primitive instinctual beings, striving for love, approval and meaning, for whom economic self-interest plays only a tiny part in explaining why and how they behave.

Tanveer Ahmed is a psychiatrist and a *Sydney Morning Herald* opinion columnist.

MEMOIR

Tunnel vision of the soul

Learning to hear new narratives

Leah Kaminsky

IN midwinter Julia shuffled into my office and slowly lowered herself into the chair beside my desk. It was a cold, wet Melbourne morning and patients were starting to pile into the clinic, sheltering from the wind. The clock on the wall showed fifteen past nine and I knew I was in for a busy day.

In the waiting room people had peeled off their coats and scarves. Dripping umbrellas huddled in the corner stand. Everyone sat flipping through old magazines or chatting quietly on mobile phones. A small child at the play table was building a tower of blocks, his construction demolished every so often by an angry coughing fit.

Julia placed a paper coffee cup on my desk. She wore an orange floral shirt, crimson pants and a pink crocheted poncho: not the standard outfit for a ninety-year-old great-grandmother. I glanced up at the screen, scanning her long list of illnesses and operations. They read like a litany of woes: osteoarthritis, osteoporosis, hypertension, hypercholesterolaemia, abdominal aortic aneurysm, ischaemic heart disease, appendicectomy, hysterectomy, bunionectomy. Not bad. Then I checked her medications: Lasix, Lipitor, Norvasc, Fosamax, Aspirin, Metamucil, Ostelin, Stilnox, Zoloft. Perhaps I should think about cutting some of these back, but not this visit. There was no time. I started printing out the scripts she had probably come in for and prepared myself to guide her gently out of the room; I needed to get a move on and see the coughing child in the waiting room before he infected everyone else.

Julia reached into a string bag and pulled out an envelope, her knobbly fingers trembling as she opened it. She fumbled with a letter inside, eventually managed to pull it out and cleared her throat, demanding that I turn away from her medical record and listen. 'We are delighted to accept your application to participate in this year's Senior Olympics in the over-75s 50-metre Breaststroke,' she read. 'Please ask your doctor to fill out the attached medical documents and return to us as soon as possible.' She handed me the forms and sat waiting, hands folded in her lap.

I had to stop myself from snorting. I wondered if I should run a dementia screen, send her off for blood and urine tests, arrange a brain scan. Composing myself, I asked: 'Are you sure about this, Julia?'

'Yes, doc,' she answered confidently. 'Besides, I'm guaranteed to win the race.'

I pulled up the Mini-Mental State Exam on the screen and started interrogating her: *What is the time, day, date? Where are we right now? Count backwards from 100 by sevens.* To my amazement, Julia scored full marks. I picked up my stethoscope and carefully checked her blood pressure, listened to her heart for murmurs, her lungs for fluid, measured her blood sugar, made her point back and forth rapidly from the tip of her nose to my finger, asked her to walk heel-to-toe in a straight line. She passed with flying colours.

Nonetheless, I was very reluctant to sign off on her fitness to participate. Julia was ninety, after all. What if she had a heart attack or a stroke in the water? She might slip on the edge of the pool and break her hip, or suffer severe pain and muscle cramps during the race.

Still, I initialled the papers, stood up and signalled that the consultation had ended. I was running way behind schedule, so I opened the door and held my hand out, gesturing towards the waiting room. Julia hauled herself up, shoved the forms in her bag and left my office, a huge smile on her face.

'Good luck!' I said, rolling my eyes behind her back.

I AM ASHAMED to admit that on that wintry Monday morning in my office with Julia, under the pressure of the brimming waiting room, I had a relapse of a condition I call 'tunnel vision of the soul'. I started developing this affliction when I first became a medical student, many years ago. It is a crippling ailment in which you see only things that are straight in front of you. You focus on the sickness and cannot see the person. Your peripheral vision is blurred, so you don't notice your surroundings unless you deliberately turn your head to look. The onset can be insidious, the symptoms barely perceptible. It is contagious in my profession; in fact, I think it has reached epidemic proportions.

During the consultation that day with Julia my tunnel vision returned with a vengeance. I was looking at her through the narrow lens of scepticism and so-called professionalism, and I saw a fragile old woman on the verge of death. I failed to listen to what she had been trying to tell me.

Up until that morning I thought I had been cured years ago when, during my training as a hospital intern, I began to read the poetry of Dr William Carlos Williams and the short stories of Dr Anton Chekhov while on night duty. Their lens on the world coaxed me to return to writing – something I hadn't done since high school. With a trembling pen, I began to heal my own wounds and to try to make some sense of what I had experienced as a young doctor. Since then, my medicine has always fed and informed my writing, and I feel that, more importantly, writing and reading has somehow made me a better doctor, opening my eyes so that I am better able to see my patients as human beings, each one with their own unique narrative.

Jerome Groopman, a professor of medicine at Harvard Medical School and the author of *How Doctors Think* (Scribe, 2007), writes: 'The wise doctor probes not only the organs of his patient but also his feelings and emotions, his fears and his hopes, his regrets and his goals. And to accomplish that most important task of applying wisdom, the physician also needs to take his own emotional temperature, to realise how his own beliefs and biases may be brought to bear in his efforts to secure a better future for his patient.'

Writing can be a means of distilling the experience of being a doctor.

Abraham Verghese, a professor of medicine at Stanford University and an alumnus of the fabled Iowa Writers' Workshop, believes that although the humanities and medicine may seem disparate worlds, for him they are one. 'Doctors and writers are both collectors of stories,' he says. Both careers have 'the same joy and the same prerequisite: "infinite curiosity about other people".'

There is a long tradition of physician-writers. Apollo managed to combine a dual career as the Greek god of both poetry and medicine. Copernicus, Maimonides, Bulgakov and Chekhov were all physicians who purloined their patients' narratives. Many contemporary doctor-writers, such as Oliver Sacks, Norman Doidge and the Australians Peter Goldsworthy, Nick Earls, Karen Hitchcock and Jacinta Halloran afford us a glimpse of the world through the eyes of a person who deals daily with existential matters and traumatic situations.

UNTIL RECENTLY, THE physician was embedded in the patient's narrative. The ultimate role of the village doctor, present at every rite of passage in a person's life, would be to sit vigil at their deathbed, often simply holding a hand as a way of saying *I am here — I will stay with you till the end.* Nowadays, with all the bells and whistles of medical technology, the last thing many patients hear before they die is the muffled farewell beep of the ECG monitor in the intensive care unit. 'As for last words, they hardly seem to exist anymore,' Atul Gawande wrote recently in his *New Yorker* article on palliative care, 'Letting Go'.

To combat this dehumanisation of medicine, many medical schools have introduced courses in Narrative Medicine and Medical Humanities. Dr Felice Aull, editor of the Literature, Arts, and Medicine database at New York University School of Medicine, observes in the mission statement of the NYU Medical Humanities website: 'The humanities and arts provide insight into the human condition, suffering, personhood, our responsibility to each other, and offer a historical perspective on medical practice. Attention to literature and the arts helps to develop and nurture skills of observation, analysis, empathy, and self-reflection — skills that are essential for humane medical care. The social sciences help us to understand how bioscience and medicine take place within cultural and social contexts and how culture interacts with the individual experience of illness and the way medicine is practiced.'

In this vein, Danielle Ofri, an associate professor at New York University School of Medicine and editor-in-chief of the *Bellevue Literary Review*, says: 'On rounds each day, I always carry ten copies of a poem or essay to distribute to the team. But when the moment comes – as we are finishing the case presentation – I'm always overcome with hesitation. It feels supremely awkward…I'll read the poem aloud. My fantasy is that [the students] will jump for joy at the end, bursting with insight and inspiration. Most often, however, there is just silence; awkward, painful silence. I'll never really know, but I'll just have to hope that it plants some seed or thought in a few of them.'

I wish I'd had a consultant like Professor Ofri when I was a medical student.

Every patient has a story to tell. It's just that as a doctor you need to look beyond the massive MRI and CT scanners to see that.

SEVERAL WEEKS AFTER our fraught consultation about her swimming race, Julia returned to see me. The apple tree outside the window was in full blossom and the sun shone into the room.

'How did it go?' I asked her, wondering if she'd even made it into the pool.

Julia fumbled in her pocket, then pulled out a gold medal and placed it between us on the desk. She beamed. 'I won!'

I sat there in disbelief.

She placed her hand on mine, as if to reassure me. 'I never had any doubt I would come first, my dearest,' she said. 'The way I see it, I had it in the bag before I even started. All I needed to do was simply finish the race.'

'How's that?' I asked, puzzled, preparing to repeat the dementia test.

'Well, doc,' she answered with a little shrug, 'I was the only entrant.'

Leah Kaminsky is a GP and a Creative Fellow at the State Library of Victoria. She was the Eleanor Dark Flagship Fellow for Fiction in 2007 and is an MFA student in Fiction Writing at Vermont College of Fine Arts, US. She is the editor of an anthology of prominent physician-writers, *The Pen and the Stethoscope* (Scribe Publishing, 2010). Her collection of poetry, *Stitching Things Together*, is published by Interactive Press (2010).

ESSAY

What is seen and heard

Understanding the place of memory

Peter Ellingsen

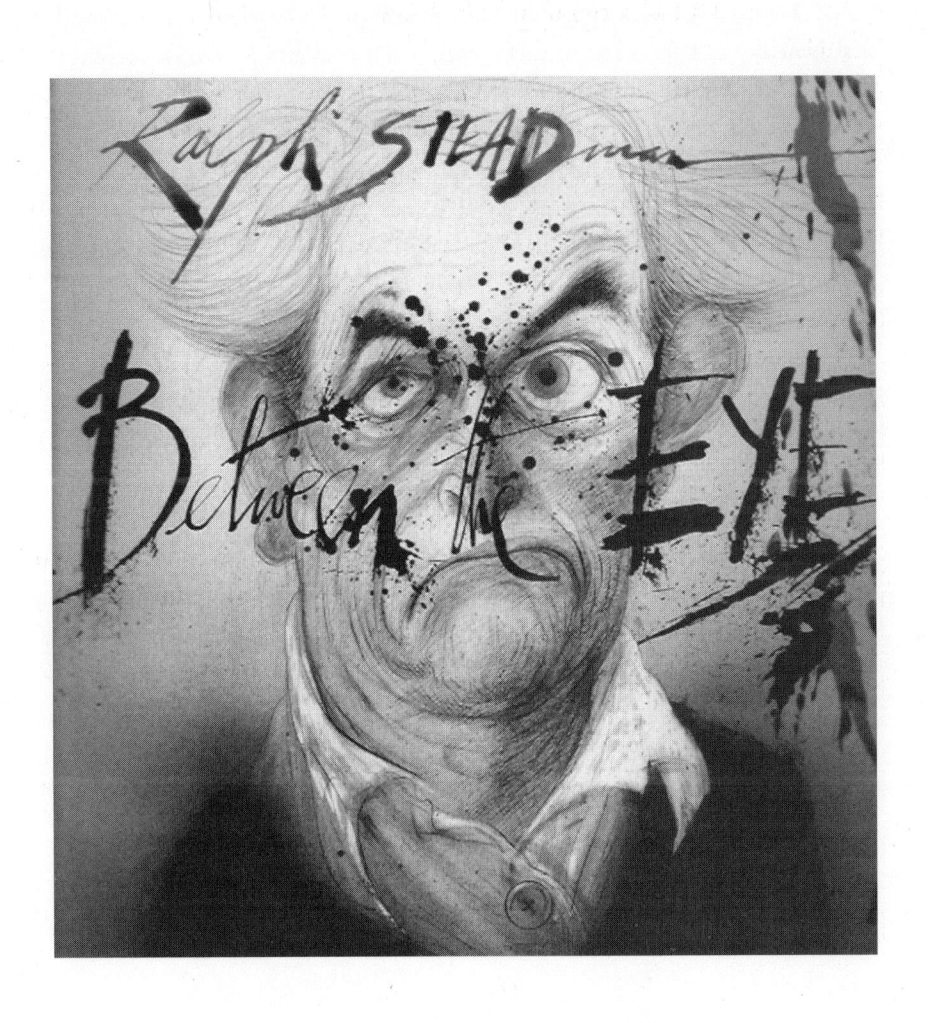

> 'What are these blinks of an eyelid, against which
> the only defence is an eternal an inhuman wakefulness?
> Might not they be the cracks and chinks through which
> another voice, other voices, speak in our lives?
> By what right do we close our ears to them?'
> – JM Coetzee, *Foe* (1986)

NEARLY ten years after my mother's death I can still remember her telephone number. I thought of it recently while walking my dog in the park. Or, rather, it thought of me, leaping unexpectedly in to my mind. I don't have a particularly good memory and hadn't thought of the number since she died, but those digits have a life of their own. Science would probably explain it with pictures showing a part of my brain lighting up. But no scientist would be able to tell me why the number entered my mind at that moment. More than three centuries after the Enlightenment inaugurated the Age of Reason, memory, and the past it is meant to represent, remains a puzzle.

When it comes to memory – which is to say, what identifies us – we are, like the teenager in the 1970s pop song, 'working on mysteries without many clues'. Science and its technologies, which I thank God for when I go to the dentist, is not much use when it comes to what I might be, beyond an organism. This is because I am not identical with my physiology. The memories that make my story mine alone – that set me apart – reside in countless nuances that science has no method of measuring or monitoring. Yet, if these nuances are ignored, I am set adrift. I am, in that sense, a stranger to myself: linked to, but not the same as, the observable processes that keep me alive. Why does my memory rescue some scenes from oblivion, while others that I try to forget hang on?

I used to think that memory could be explained by social structures, that what stayed in my mind was what my working-class family, with its need to keep its place and its silence, left unsaid. But this isn't right. What my family kept hidden is not explained by what it lacked materially. My mother had little interest in objects and did not crave entrée to higher levels of society. Raised in Broken Hill, she was a new arrival to Melbourne and like many outsiders readily gave her past away in favour of the future. The future she

---

PREVIOUS PAGE: Ralph Steadman. *Between The Eyes*, offset colour exhibition poster, 1984, 76 x 51cm.

wanted, but could never speak of, was one without certain memories. They were not class-bound reminiscences. My mother was proud that her mother took in ironing to pay the bills and her brothers went on the swag during the Depression. The past that my mother wanted to leave behind involved a childhood that began with her father's death and built up to a camouflaged feeling of unfairness in love. My mother would remind me how easy I had it compared to her. She was talking about loss and her exile from a desired, adoring gaze. Hers was a personal rather than a class conflict, one that had more in common with Freud than Marx.

But it was many years before I understood this. Like my mother, my inclination as a young man was to flee – to move away. For many years I worked as a foreign correspondent. The stories in the newspapers I wrote for seemed to account for what went on in the world. I was happy to see the events that I wrote about as facts, even though some facts – a medical discovery, for instance – needed an expert to interpret them. Then, in 1993, I encountered a series of events that were not just beyond what I knew, but beyond any facts that purported to explain them. Sitting in an English courtroom I heard how two ten-year-old boys had taken a two-year-old toddler, James Bulger, to a Liverpool canal, where they tortured and murdered him. In court the only question that mattered, why, remained oblique because of the assertion that the ten-year-olds were 'bad seeds'. There was no evidence of psychosis – just biological blame.

The same assertions were aired during the trial of Rosemary West who, with her husband, Fred, sexually abused and disposed of at least ten young women, including her own daughter. Dubbed the House of Horrors murderer, West sat a few metres from me in Winchester Crown Court looking, in her pressed blouse and cardigan, like my Auntie Glad. West's guilt, like the boys', was undisputed. What was in question was motive, an explanation for behaviour that seemed unthinkable. The answer, for the media and for the court, was to blame's West's crimes on genetics. This reversion to the mad-or-bad formula was similar to nineteenth-century psychiatry's classification of lunacy as an inherited condition. Defaulting to biomedicine shut the question down, and that may have been the intention. To see such excess as anything other than an organic, banal evil would have created more anxiety. It left me wondering whether the science that claims to understand us is actually used to seal the lid on uncomfortable human truths.

THERE ARE INNUMERABLE ways of recounting a life, both to ourselves and to others. They all toy with memory and describe childhood as a fraught love affair. I wanted to know what those family romances consisted of – how we are made and unmade by what we remember and forget. I didn't anticipate objectivity. Objectivity, along with uniformity, is what science looks for, but it is not to be found in human subjects, whose minds and memories are already saturated with judgement. What would, I wondered, an account of a life be like if it was not foreclosed or forced to fit within supposedly rational parameters?

I knew that the stories my family and I told, no matter how truthful they tried to be, depended on reconstructions from the vantage point of the present. This didn't make them inauthentic, but it did make the way we all construct memory and identity more complex than either the facts that I found in journalism or the science that says we are our biology. Science has never found the biological substrata of human suffering, just as the eyewitnesses I quoted in journalism never offered more than facts fashioned out of necessarily partial memory – memory that, I now realise, was full of holes hollowed out by the infinitesimal small wounds that prompt us to lie to ourselves. I wanted to find another space from which memory might come, a space full of words, ongoing beginnings, yet with an end in sight. Both of these, beginnings and endings, are frontiers arising from language and the way that it serves as our boundary, and the possibility of beginning anew.

These questions led me to psychoanalysis and to ten years' training to become a psychoanalyst – someone whose function it is to be surprised by words. Psychoanalysis is not like organic psychiatry or psychology. It doesn't erase the mind and memory from mental treatment by separating off the disturbed individual from the disturbance. Rather, psychoanalysis is curious about the complex motives and intentions that surround distress, and how they are inscribed and deciphered in language. Analysts listen to the eruption of that underworld of emotion as it arises in speech, usually from dreams, slips of the tongue and symptoms. Sometimes it can be alarmingly literal, with words we have heard and then turned into weapons to scar our bodies with. Or, more commonly, it is the fortresses we erect in our minds as we try to flee memories that, though they might not be historically true, are true for us.

This is the complexity that science does not address: the way we act not only in response to what we see, but also what we fear and, because we are afraid, deny. It seeps out in symptoms like anxiety, and in unexpected words – words like those that spoke my memories and sheltered my secrets.

Secrets like my mother's body being the first female body I looked at – not just axiomatically at birth but later, entering puberty, when I peeked through the cracks in the wall of the bathroom my stepfather had built at the rear of our house. My mother's body shaped what female bodies were for me, and what I would later seek out. I don't remember thinking of her body as beautiful, possibly because she didn't. My mother's only way of liking the body she kept sheathed through summer, never going to the beach so as not to reveal her varicose veins, was to see it in the past. She found ways to continually stumble across an old, torn photograph of herself at seventeen, kicking her leg high in a chorus line of theatrical amateurs. It was a long line of girls and her question to me was always the same: 'Which girl am I?' It bought delight to her – like the punch line of a joke. It opened up possibilities. In the photograph she could be other than she was: an unrecognisable figure from a past that she was now free to invent. The question made me uneasy, not just because I might pick the wrong girl but because I had to search for my mother when she was the sexually active age I was then.

I am still drawn to black-and-white postwar photographs: Sidney Nolan's sparse Parkville studio, Jack Kerouac's monochrome New York. Ian McEwan suggests in his novel *On Chesil Beach* (2007) that we are all fascinated by the era when our parents courted. This might be true, but I'm also drawn to photographs of that era because of how spaces are different, how they lack gadgets and a sense of 'lifestyle'. They depict people not accustomed to being watched; whatever performance exists is outside the urgency of camera range, in landscapes where little is expected. Faces, posture and possibility inhabit the setting on equal terms. The space devoid of objects is an invitation to create, to see the options that emptiness provides. My mother feared emptiness, as this is where memory digs in. So she filled herself with select images like the dancing girl, and with photographs that made new memories. When I was the same age as Bulger she dressed me up in unfamiliar finery and had a photographer snap shots that made me look like someone else. These were the memories she wanted to keep, rather than the reality of our lives.

MY STORY, THOUGH individual, is incidental to the media culture I once inhabited. And yet its account of hiding secrets and running from the implications of unconscious desire has an unwelcome, universal quality. We drag our past, with its undigested emotional baggage, along with us, and in retelling it we can't help but evoke the narrative form Freud stumbled across in his case studies. These narratives allow the speaker to inject the present into the past, so that memory can influence contemporary time. They are always concerned with love, in the sense of the longing felt for a place and a person that won't ever let you down. This is a dream from which it is hard to recover. Freud discovered it accidentally, by listening intently to what people said but did not themselves hear. He thought his case studies would be science, but when he reread the accounts he named them novellas.

Maybe this is what the science of the psyche is? There is no guarantee that any science of today won't be the alchemy of tomorrow. And when it comes to the particular science that purports to account for memory and mind, what we find is less explanatory and has less predictive power than fiction. This is especially so with organic psychiatry and psychology, disciplines that struggle to meet science's holy trinity of blind, controlled and randomised trials. Rather than proof, psychiatry and psychology have what in the US is called 'proofiness', accounts that only seem rigorous. They rely on drugs that are unspecific in their effect and, in the case of antidepressants, no more effective than a placebo; and on questionnaire-based behavioural modifications, whose effects are short-lived.

But mostly, in their eagerness to be scientific, psychiatry and psychology attempt to stitch up the subjectivity of the individual: that is, they want to foreclose the ambivalence of being. They don't want to hear the ebb and flow of memory, the structure of dreams and stories that people tell to explain themselves to others. Nor are the disciplines comfortable with how the unconscious doesn't distinguish between past and present, an intermingling that makes memory unreliable. Yet this is precisely how the mind functions. It can be seen in the way young people locate themselves in both the past and present tenses at the same time: 'I hadn't seen him for ages, and I am, like, "What do you mean?"' This irrational speech, devoid of self-consciousness, reveals the sliding between now and before that occurs in memoir.

The mental health industry has largely given up on the inner world for an inferential world that portrays emotional states as little more than a chemical imbalance. The appeal is the supposed precision of organic medicine, and the confidence (and funding) this elicits from government. But science is at its most persuasive when it is deductive, proven from universal laws. The biomedical model in psychiatry can't claim this basis. Instead, it is inductive, often naively so, in that it infers universal laws from a number of observed cases. And even in these observed cases — say, a depressed person being treated with medication — it is not certain what is being seen. While some symptoms appear to abate with antidepressants, no one knows why. The notion that these drugs, selective serotonin reuptake inhibitors like Prozac, function by influencing the concentration of neurotransmitters, such as serotonin, in the brain, is a theory riddled with contradictions. Not only is there no causal, scientific evidence linking depression and serotonin levels: some drugs can alleviate depression yet have little to do with the regulation of serotonin.

Psychiatrists, as the Stanford anthropologist Tanya Luhrmann explains, are trained to identify suffering without being able to do much more than hand over a biomedical lollipop. This is the price the dominant discourse in mental health pays for seeing — allegedly scientifically — a category of illness, rather than a person: a patient is the category indicated by their symptoms. But psychiatric symptoms, which are descriptions of behaviour, are not from science, if that term is still true to its Latin root of *scientia*, knowledge. Psychiatric symptoms come from the American Psychiatric Association's *Diagnostic Statistical Manual of Mental Disorders IV*, whose categories are prey to — even the outcome of — haggling between interest groups. Rather than describing mental disorders, the manual creates them, often because drugs are available to allegedly treat, and so define, them.

IN THE ARENA of psychiatry, science and rationality are said to be central. I prefer the landscape in which language surprises, opening up secrets that are the real software of our life. Secrets, I came to realise, derive from fantasy, from rivalry, hatred and desire. Whether we like it or not, they are unconsciously passed on from one generation to another.

My mother fashioned me out of a desire she did not understand and never explored. It wasn't just the biological urge to reproduce. My psychic existence, the thousands of tiny messages that I absorbed into something I called memory, reflected what I heard and saw. This is the family romance referred to earlier, and it roars inside us. It meant that I was my mother's way of erasing the disappointment of my father, and repudiating him.

My mother lost my father well before he died, when she woke up to the fact he was a damaged alcoholic. It left her full of rage, but it was not for the outside world any more than she could take into account the childhood neglect that explained my father's failures. Her anger was directed at what she saw as personal betrayals, slights that began with wearing hand-me-downs, her younger and prettier sister's preferential treatment, and her father's early death. My mother could not, as Virginia Woolf and Jeanette Winterson did, recast herself through words on a page; nor did she understand the danger of succumbing to the slickness of your own narrative. She stuck to her story and, in so doing, preserved memories that slowly ate her away.

Science erred in its predictions about acid rain, but there is no mistaking the corrosive effect of toxic memory. Unspoken memories destroy us, as the families of soldiers understand. But it is not enough to just open your mouth. As I found when a journalist, and Freud found in the case history of Dora, the first story you are told is never true. Narrative truth is more a means of exchange than an indication of what happened.

This is what we do when we try to understand puzzles like memory: we exchange fragments of what occurred and what we wished for, invariably with attention directed at those we imagine we are addressing – and this is seldom the person standing in front of us. Deciphering memory means going beyond the familiar story we call our history to unravel how and why we repeat what we don't remember. Telephone digits that linger on, I now believe, are like the flaws in love that require us to think more about our intentionality than we do about our pain.

Peter Ellingsen is a Melbourne-based psychoanalyst and writer. He is former foreign correspondent with *The Age*, *Sydney Morning Herald* and *London Financial Times*. He co-authored *Cries Unheard* (Common Ground, 2001) and completed a Monash University PhD thesis on the history of psychoanalysis in Australia. His essay 'China on my mind' appeared in *Griffith REVIEW 22: MoneySexPower*.

FICTION

FROM WHAT I HEAR

ALAN VAARWERK

BUT what if the cops see us?
But what if you run out of money?
But what if you miss your bus?
But what if it rains and you don't have a jacket?
But what if your house burns down while you're out?
But what if you trip over and graze your knee?
But what if he turns out to be a jerk?
But what if you're allergic?
But what if you fall asleep?
But what if your computer crashes?
But what if you get pregnant?
But what if you get mugged?
But what if you get married?
But what if I'm wrong?
Then where will you be?

*

IN the evenings you and I would go down into the little laneway. Sometimes I would buy us coffee or soup, although towards the end when money got tight you were happy with tea from a thermos. We'd sit on the bench outside the glass-fronted Laneway Bar and you would tell me the unauthorised biographies of the patrons moving their hands and mouths inside.

 A middle-aged man, bald except for a grey ponytail, argued with the bartender over a bottle of wine. He was in the film business, you decided, because of his moisturised face and the way he held his hands.

 A large frizzy-haired woman with ridiculously long fake fingernails sat at the window, talking animatedly to an Asian couple. The couple nodded and laughed, and the woman waved her arms in circles and knocked over a bottle. The Asian man bought them all champagne and they clinked their glasses. I suggested they were teachers at the same school. You shook your head. No, they didn't know her – look at the way the man's hand rested on his partner's thigh. After about an hour the Asian couple left the bar. The woman skolled her glass, moved to the next booth and started a conversation with a group of backpackers.

A year ago, on my birthday, we went into the Laneway Bar for dinner and sat in the window. You fidgeted and played with your food. I thought your appetite had gone, but you just said the noise of the bar was off-putting. You felt crushed under the weight of it, too much a part of the world. You preferred the distance.

One time there was a young man, about my age, sitting in the window booth. You liked his suit, said I should wear one more often, that they made my shoulders look good. On the table in front of him was a small parcel with a ribbon around it. When a woman entered the bar and sat down with him, he didn't look up from his beer. She too gazed at her hands, and they both sat still, in silence. What do you think he did wrong? I asked. Maybe he's not the one apologising, you replied. Maybe it's nobody's fault. Maybe their relationship is just in its last days. And then you put your hand behind my head and kissed me on the mouth. I asked you if you were cold, and you said no more than usual.

At the far end of the laneway stands a massive neo-gothic building of black marble and wrought iron whose slab-sided immensity leaves the laneway in perpetual shadow. I don't remember its tiny windows ever having been lit in the evenings, but I have only really taken notice of the building since I've gone back to the laneway without you. I've been sitting at the same bench across from the Laneway Bar, but all its patrons seem blank and silent. You wouldn't have had this problem. I've been finding it hard to concentrate lately, to keep from looking back towards the building and its dark windows, trying to spot movement behind the glass.

*

MY wife Helen and I were making love one evening when she said in a serious voice, 'Would you say you are *disorientated*?'

'What?'

'*Disorientated*. Is that what you'd say?'

'I'm fine.' I breathed into the curve of her neck. 'Why, is something wrong? Am I hurting you?'

'No, no,' she murmured. Her fingernails traced little circles on my back. 'I was just wondering whether the word was *disoriented* or *disorientated*.'

Not long after becoming pregnant for the first time, Helen told me that she felt tormented by words. A name, a phrase, seen by chance throughout the day, would reverberate in her mind, twisting and contorting and rearranging itself, growing larger and louder until she felt her head would burst and a tirade of tortured phonemes would echo off the walls. She made me promise not to book her in to see a shrink. She said it was the baby brain – she just needed to clear her head. 'It's not you, darling, I promise,' she told me, nuzzling my whiskers. 'My brain just spins too fast for some reason. I can tell you *magenta* spelled backwards is *atnegam*, and makes the anagrams *ant game*, *neat mag* and *a tan gem*. But I can't tell you why.'

My legs were starting to ache as I frog-kicked against the doona. I felt Helen's hips and shoulders slacken. '*Disorientated* sounds funny,' I grunted.

She breathed deeply. 'It does. *Disorientated*. *Detatneirosid*. *Diode Tainters*. But I swear I hear it all the time. Although I usually say *disori-ented*. *Dis-ori-en-ted*. I think. Don't I?'

'I don't know, love,' I said through clenched teeth. By now I was doing little more than rocking against her pelvis. 'It's a free country. You can say whatever you want to say, however you want to say it.'

'But that's not enough.' She sighed, pushed me out of her body and rolled over to her side of the bed.

*

I THOUGHT taking the scenic route would be the best thing to do. I thought it would be a nice change from the washed-out scrub of the motorway, a small change of scenery on the way to a big one. In reality, it just meant an extra hour and a half in the car with no radio reception and a daughter who wasn't talking to me.

'You made sure you picked up all your books before we left?'

'Mhmm.'

'Wouldn't want to be missing a book on your first day.'

She said nothing, just gave an exaggerated sigh. I ran my hands along the top, then the bottom of the steering wheel.

The road cut through farmland, completely flat as far as the eye could see. I fiddled with the air vents, redirecting the plastic-smelling air away from my face and onto my hands. I wondered whether it was hot or cold outside, and touched my fingers to the window.

'Look at that, love,' I said, nodding up towards the sky. Out to the east five long chopped streaks of thin cloud fanned out from the horizon. 'Condensation trails, by the look of it. Contrails for short. Not often you see so many in one go. They're made of water vapour, not smoke: did you know that?'

My daughter still did not say anything. I stared at the road. After a few minutes she uncrossed her arms and leant her head against the window. I took this as a positive sign.

'Must be an airport over that way.'

'Maybe.' She looked up. 'Or maybe they're the trails left by nuclear missiles. Maybe every major city has been fried while we've been driving through the middle of nowhere.' She snorted bitterly. 'That *would* be a shame.'

I adjusted my grip on the wheel. 'Don't be silly. It's just planes.'

'That's how the world's going to end. Everyone will see the bombs or the meteors or whatever and say, "Nah, it's probably nothing."'

'For Christ's sake, it's just common sense.' I changed gear too quickly and the engine whinnied. 'Nobody's launching any nuclear missiles. Stop being silly.'

'You don't know that. You've got no more proof than I have. You can say you told me so once we get there, whatever. But right now you've got nothing.'

She sank into her seat with a huff. I played with the knobs on the air-conditioning, and tried to imagine how the rest of the trip would go. I would make a mental list of conversation starters in my head, and rattle them off one by one. Then, eventually, she would cheer up or the radio would come back, and we would hurtle on towards our destination. Anything after that, the arrival, the unpacking, the journey home, seemed purely imaginary, as though there would only ever be this car, this road, this chilly air.

The contrails had all but dissipated into the atmosphere. I squinted to make out their paths, and began to think that perhaps the world really had ended.

*

THERE'S an unattended bag on the seat in front of me. It's probably nothing, not even worth mentioning, really. I'm guessing it was already there when I got on the train — I mean, I didn't see anyone put it down. The carriage is full of schoolkids, so maybe it belongs to one of them — although most of them seem to have backpacks and this seems more like a sports bag. It's pretty well chock-full of something or other. I want to reach across and open it, take a peek inside. But if it does belong to someone, well, that would be rude. The last thing I want is some cocksure footy boy berating me for touching his things.

Still, Bags Without People Don't Make Sense, right? What if there's a bomb in there? Surely I would hear ticking or something? Maybe that's a myth — I don't really know anything about bombs. Somewhere in the carriage, tinny R&B strains from minuscule speakers. I've heard you can detonate a bomb remotely with a mobile phone. A schoolgirl squeals as her friend tries to pull her hair.

If this thing were to explode I'd be the first to go. I suppose being this close I'd disintegrate immediately. I guess that's good — I'd barely even know what had hit me. I hope there'd be enough left of me to identify. I think about my girlfriend. Who would tell her? Would she see the news and, knowing I'm usually on the train around this time, connect the dots? Or would she not know, try calling me, think I was ignoring her, get pissed off, come round to yell at me and hear the news from my next-door neighbour? I wouldn't want to do that to her. Maybe I should call her.

No. This is stupid. It's just a bag. Be Alert, Not Alarmed. Besides, I get off the train in an ordinary outer suburb. Tactically speaking, surely they would wait until the train got into the city to detonate, if only to do the most damage. On balance, I'm pretty safe. And a little embarrassed at how much of a comfort I find this.

Jesus Christ. When did I become such a prophet of doom? I never cared much about anything when I was younger. The biggest argument I ever had with my mum was because I thought she worried irrationally. Now I get into my car and unconsciously check to see there's nobody crouched in the back seat waiting to garrotte me; I deadlock the door when I'm home by myself; I get funny feelings about bags on trains. I wonder how I would look through the eyes of the schoolkids. Would they see me the way I've always imagined myself – savvy, together, confident – or am I just another grown-up living in fear?

I get off the train and walk home through the park. It's a postcard autumn afternoon; the sky is the deepest, clearest blue and the breeze tugs at my skin from all directions. I want to savour this. I find a park bench and sit for a while, listening to the invisible lorikeets clamouring in the bottlebrushes, until the sky goes purple and the dusk blurs my vision.

I arrive home just as the news is starting on television.

★

I'M not an ignorant person, but there are lots of things I seem to not notice. Like how Alex never wanted to stay at my place, at least not after the first few times. We only lived a few kilometres apart, so I assumed he simply liked his space. Plus, Alex lived in a proper house, as opposed to above a butcher's shop in a flat that smelt constantly of meat. That was another thing I didn't really notice. The smell itself isn't that unpleasant – sweet, and sort of cold – so long as you don't think about the severed legs and hanging, dripping torsos from which it emanates. Maybe that was a matter of simply growing accustomed.

It was a nice enough butcher shop, I guess. Two Maltese brothers ran the place, old-style butchers who'd cut meat straight off the carcass right there in front of you – their circular saw made my fridge rattle. I had been living above that shop for just over a year when I took Alex through for the first time. He was the one who directed my attention to the sign above the door. On a white rectangle of Perspex a brown cartoon cow, wearing a bib and licking its lips, sat on a chopping block while an enormous knife sliced its hindquarters into perfectly formed T-bone steaks.

'That's fucking gross,' he said, as though I had put it there. 'How does that thing not creep you out?'

I told him it was something I hadn't really noticed.

After that it felt like the thing had somehow awakened. I couldn't enter or leave my building without looking up at the wretched creature, slavering over its own rump. What kind of cruelty was this, a poor animal parading its innards for the buying public? Who promotes their business in this way, sugar-coating torture with childlike cartoon imagery? I began to feel uneasy around the grinning Maltese butchers and their white aprons. My gut clenched when I heard the circular saw. Like a crooked picture frame or a dead pixel on a screen, the sign filled my mind's eye.

One night, after an argument with Alex, I got drunk and decided it had to go. Standing on a milk crate beside the front door I looked up at the poor cow, at its bulging, glassy eyes. I wanted to stroke its nose, tell it I was sorry, that I wasn't like the other people in the building. The sheet of Perspex made a groaning noise as I wrenched it off the wall.

If I'd been hoping for some sense of satisfaction, I didn't get it. One problem out of the way, a new one presented itself like a punch in the stomach: what to do with the sign. I couldn't leave it outside or put it in the bin, anywhere it could be seen by the butchers or dusted for fingerprints. I couldn't take it to Alex's, not tonight. I suddenly felt very tired. Without a better solution, I carried the sign upstairs.

No matter where I put the thing it felt conspicuous. What if the butchers came up in the morning to ask if I'd seen anything? I kept getting up and moving it. Bathroom, kitchen, laundry. I ended up sliding it under my bed, the only place I felt certain it was out of sight.

But still I saw it. Those wild eyes, the stench of meat. I had brought them closer to me. I lay flat on my back in the darkness, trying as hard as I could to forget that image, that moment when animals stop smelling like animals and start smelling like meat.

★

IN the bathroom, two bluish-green towels hang side by side on a rack. One is cool and slightly damp, strands of hair woven into the turquoise fibres.

The other has been dry for a long, long time.

★

THE hospital was built on a hill to avoid the floods, which meant it could be seen from pretty well anywhere in town. My mother's sprawling bougainvillea on the back fence did a good job obscuring the view of the tan brick monolith, but still the hospital's thin, silver smokestack jutted into the sky. She would sit on our back veranda of an afternoon and watch as the rescue helicopters swooped in overhead, tilt her head to listen to whether the ambulance sirens were coming in or going out. She liked the hospital, said she felt safe knowing it was there.

Once, when I was very small, my older brother and I were walking the dog along the Racetrack, a narrow strip of grass that ran behind the hospital's loading bay. From here it looked more like a factory than a hospital, with gas tanks, roller doors and vans rumbling past. From somewhere in the middle of it all, the chimney shot skyward, black smoke belching from its top.

'Why is there smoke?' I asked.

'Don't you know?' My brother was pulling long strands of kikuyu grass out of the ground. 'That's what happens when someone dies in the hospital. They take you to the furnace and they burn you up.'

'No, they don't.' An image crept into my mind: a pile of bodies, of arms, legs, faces. Dirty, sooty bodies, shovelled into the furnace and out into the air. I fought the urge to hold my breath. 'I don't believe you.'

'They do too. You ask anyone.' This from the boy who told me the pinkie finger was the Rude Finger, and that the tree root we kept tripping over in the backyard was part of a dinosaur skeleton. I had believed him those times too.

I asked my mother when we got home if it was true, but she said the furnace was just where they burned their musty old sheets, and to stop being silly. My brother rocked with laughter – 'Gotcha! Gotcha!' – his victory made complete by my gullibility.

The victory is still his this afternoon, as I help my mother into her towel-covered easy chair, the last light of the day filtering through the venetians onto her yellow, skeletal arms. Out the window, the sun sets behind the hospital on the hill. Black smoke rises from the chimney, and I think of the bodies, imagine their sooty particles clinging to my lungs. I chastise myself silently. Stop being silly. I close the windows, breathe deep, but I can't shake the smell of dusty death from the air.

Alan Vaarwerk, born in 1988, is a short-fiction writer and aspiring editor who lives in Brisbane.

ESSAY

The minor fall, the major lift

Music, power and the composer's 'black art'

Andrew Schultz

ENGAGEMENT with the fundamentals of music and sound deeply influence the formation of a composer's aesthetic. There is such a thing as musical logic, which is based on a mix of physical factors around sound, psychoacoustics and cognition, and complex culturally specific factors that shape the musical experience for individuals and in society. Musical logic can at times seem stupid – even wilfully anti-intellectual – but it functions in a way that is not primarily based in verbal language or scientific thinking. It is its own domain, and the best definitions and explanations of musical logic are always seen in the work itself.

As a composer I have tried to put my arguments in musical form: in the native language of the ideas. My development has come from experience as a composer, performer, listener and thinker – what I have learned and how I have learned it have led to my aesthetic position, which itself is an organic thing and constantly transforming. An aesthetic position can emerge from inherited traditions or be the result of a more conscious activity, filtering through what is important in search of musical elements that could form a kind of bedrock: 'musical truth', to adapt Theodor Adorno's term. To some my point of view may seem conservative, to others radical, but these critical judgements are themselves based on extraneous and often ideological thinking outside the musical domain.

The nature of the musical experience varies, depending on the role you have in the cycle: composer or creator of musical ideas, performer or interpreter, listener or audience. Yet the roles are malleable. The difference between performer and composer is unclear in many types of music; a composer may be a listener or performer; and audiences engage with music in many ways and at many levels of attention, not just the apparently concentrated but passive role in a concert venue. A composer learns much by listening and performing as well as by actually composing. A composed work unperformed has not been realised – its information is dormant until performed and heard.

Composing is a solitary and imaginative internalised activity; performing may be solitary but is often group-based and has at its basis an external physical activity, the production and communication of sound; listening may

---

PREVIOUS PAGE: Trish O'Brien. *Naked cello*. Courtesy of the artist. www.jettyimages.com.au

seem to be solitary and internalised but at its peak level of experience, in a live performance, it is a highly communal and socially engaged activity. Some may see a hierarchy in the triangle – a composer at the peak struggling with creative ideas; the performer transmitting the ideas; the audience attentive but submissive. Yet they are specialised and interdependent roles. Each has its distinctive character and rewards.

The affective nature of music for a listener is well documented and the focus of considerable research. Much of it has emphasised the way the brain deals with music perception: is it an intellectual or an emotional reaction, or a combination? Where does the locus of musical experience situate itself in the brain? Some such research can seem naive – as if the affective response to music were unanticipated and accidental. Like any of the senses, hearing allows access to strong responses. Just as a gentle touch can induce pleasure, a foul smell revulsion or a comic sight mirth, why would we be surprised to find that music – a subset of sound – can induce equally potent responses in the absence of language?

HISTORICALLY, MUSIC HAS often been perceived in terms of its affective power. Plato allegedly described music as a 'moral law' and saw the personal power of music in social and political terms. Two centuries earlier Ibycus described Orpheus as already famous: his harp and voice seem to be a weapon of entrapment, able to block out the fatal lure of the Sirens' songs, enchant the Underworld and tame wild beasts. King David is another harpist who, according to the Old Testament, connives his way to power and authority with seductive music therapy, opening the heart of the disturbed King Saul: 'seek out a man, who is a cunning player on a harp: and it shall come to pass, when the evil spirit from God is upon thee, that he shall play with his hand and all shalt be well.'

The fascinating connection of music, power and religion continues into the Renaissance, Reformation, Counter-Reformation and beyond. Luther embraced music for its psychological power: 'next to the Word of God, the noble art of music is the greatest treasure in the world. It controls our thoughts, minds, hearts, and spirits.' Then the Catholic Council of Trent,

1562 which, in an attempt to draw music back into a form where language clearly dominates, formulated in Canon 8 that music must avoid 'vain delight to the ear'.

Faust – the alchemist, musician, scientist, and the black-artist *par excellence* – emerged as real characters metamorphosed into creative ideas. *Faust* as a story of individual power seems almost a parallel to Orpheus and David, in the sense that power and expression reside in an individual and manifest in a sometimes musical way. Hardly surprising, then, that the Faust story became a key narrative of Romanticism – individual artists shaping themselves and hence transgressing social and religious conventions.

And so to the modern realisation of the fears explicitly expressed by the Greek philosophers and hinted at in the Council of Trent: the malevolent potential of music. Music causes armies to march in time, provides a glorifying soundtrack for mass destruction, inspires nations to aggressive and jingoistic pride, and fires the masses up for protest and revolution. There is the legacy of nationalistic musical works of the nineteenth and twentieth centuries, the propagandising use of popular music in the French Revolution and the intensity of Hitler's involvement with Wagner. Hitler claimed a close and protective friendship with the Wagner clan, wrote as a young man a draft of a Wagnerian operatic epic and purportedly carried a copy of the score of *Tristan und Isolde* into battle.

Much of composers' postwar resistance to engaging with the affective dimension in music, and the inevitable resulting distancing from the wider musical audience, seems to be traceable to that relationship. There is a famous photo of Hitler ('Uncle Wolf') with two of Wagner's grandsons, Wieland and Wolfgang, which shows Hitler protectively embracing the young men, who fondly link arms with him. The implicit story is that music has become a tool of social control – don't give a tyrant the chance. Who except the most vain composer would want to allow themselves or their work to be a part of tyranny?

At least for a period after World War II it seemed as if many composers of the *avant-garde* shared the view that music of a certain type can unleash forces that are socially reckless, and wanted no part of that. In the postwar period the sentimental and affective dimensions of music were a kind of taboo for many composers, in part a reaction to the totalitarian exploitation of music in the preceding twenty years. Cerebral approaches to music were highly valued in the elite, following a lineage of abstract musical thought and obsessive stylistic refinement from Schoenberg, Webern and Boulez. If now we can see that a communicative musical experience would be lost in such approaches, it did not seem so at the time. Better if music is more of a science than an art, then, and if it becomes expressive confine that expression to a generalised *angst*.

The power of music seems to have been accepted for a long time, but as a means for social and political manipulation its development can be traced to the period around World War I. In 1926 the liberal German intellectual Charles Diserens wrote *The Influence of Music on Behaviour*, a utilitarian view of music in a social context: 'Our purpose then is to study the influence of music on the organism. We approach music from the practical rather than the aesthetic standpoint, regarding it as a necessity, a possible means of re-education and human reconstruction for all, rather than a mere subject of unproductive pleasure, or an object for criticism from the learned few.'

How ironic that totalitarian, anti-liberal regimes held a similar fundamental view to Diserens and his Frankfurt School colleague Theodor Adorno: music was a means of social control. What ominous words 're-education and human reconstruction' are in the context of Hitler and Stalin. Both tyrants insisted on the creation of music with social value and embodying national virtues, and then censored what fell outside that edict. Adorno also shared a view that music was a tool for social change and for ideological reasons championed the opposite music to Stalin and Hitler. Music had become a brutal ideological battleground and is only now recovering.

It's not far from Diserens' behaviourist view to some contemporary manifestations and exploitations of the power of music in the commercial world. Music is used to placate airline passengers at the moments of highest anxiety, when they land or take off; to stave off social discomfort in an elevator; to engender happy feelings that may lead to shopping excess in a supermarket; and to create earworms, through jingles or advertising, that burrow deeply into the mind and cement a brand's message. And in much recent film, theatre or television, music is often merely a signpost for triggering emotions, supporting mood, creating the right feel and so on. All are implicit proof of music's power, even if in the quest for commercial advantage they undervalue music's inherent potential.

MUCH, BUT NOT all, of music's power to move lies in its sonic fundamentals. Consider the military use of sound bombs for civil control. They consist solely of a loud explosion, without any destructive effects. They function purely on a psychological level and are a very effective means of engendering fear and obedience.

But how much of the reaction is instinctive and how much is learned? Babies have been known to cry for hours after being surprised by a loud noise, suggesting that a distressed response to a sudden loud sound is innate. Yet for an adult hearing a sudden sound, such as an explosion in a war zone, the knowledge of risk may lead to a more refined but equally dramatic reaction, as they seek safety. An adult with even more knowledge – that is, one used to sound bombs as a device for civil control – may not seem to react at all. So an initial reaction may or may not be instinctive – on a continuum ranging from primal to tempered by knowledge to completely intellectually controlled.

This is relevant to music and the way it is heard because music has both physical properties (as do all sounds) and culturally specific attributes. The physical properties of sound are widely understood as mathematically constant. Sound consists of waves of vibration travelling from a source to a receptor. Although the sound waves are invisible to the eye, they are a real physical phenomenon, just like light (which also cannot be touched). On their trip to being heard they may encounter obstacles or acoustic factors, which may alter the character of the sound. The journey affects the sound we perceive, as does the nature of the receptor. Put an obstacle between the sound and the receptor, and its path will be diverted; put the sound in a resonant chamber and it may produce echoes or other enhancements to the sound. The sound may be enhanced, reduced or transformed by its journey. Our process for receiving sound involves physically capturing the sound by the ear and transferring it to impulses that the brain interprets. We can hear more than one tone at once, but create too many individual tones at once and what we hear becomes unintelligible – although the ear seems to initially (but not indefinitely) search for meaningful information even in a babble of sound.

This is well documented and understood but we take it for granted at our own risk, as the composer's, the musician's and the listener's roles are fundamentally about creating, communicating and experiencing subtleties of the physical nature of sound and interpreting those subtleties. Understanding the limitations of sound production and reception is also important, as there are biological limitations to our listening. If we ignore these fundamentals the capacity of music to communicate is severely restricted.

At key points in music history a return to sonic fundamentals has occurred and shaped the way music has subsequently developed. We may in the past forty years have seen such a move. Out of the postwar European musical *avant-garde* emerged a primarily American movement of experimental music. It followed a quasi-scientific methodology and engaged strongly with the potential of electro-acoustic music in the 1950s and '60s. Central to the thinking of various composers (John Cage is the most well known) was the idea that music exists in multiple ways in a pluralist society and that aesthetic assumptions should be challenged. Experimentation was important – the idea that a defined conceptual process should be established to 'create' music. So a score may be a set of verbal instructions or a game-like scenario in which music would happen as a result. The ideas were important across the arts and philosophy, even if, ironically, some of the music was uninteresting. The ideas themselves are an odd mix – libertarian social philosophy paired with a sombre scientific outlook – but they unquestionably focus attention on the fundamentals of the musical experience.

The American composer Alvin Lucier (born 1931) has a unique and fascinating approach to experimental music that has bearing on the nature of the musical experience and its relation to sound. I came into contact with him in the early 1980s, when he spent a semester at the University of Queensland, where I was a PhD student. An example of Alvin's work is a piece with the wonderful name *Still and Moving Lines of Silence in Families of Hyperbolas*. The concept of the piece is to show the physical presence of sound waves in a room, to the extent that they are absolutely vividly experienced as physical phenomena, as if they were visible. In a performance I participated in with

Alvin, the work in part consisted of a single sustained sine wave being generated electronically from a loudspeaker, while I sat with my clarinet. Over about fifteen minutes I would play very slow, soft, long and evenly spaced notes, moving progressively, by tiny increments, from a semitone below the sound to a semitone above. In all I was able to find about ten to fifteen tiny or microtonal steps to eventually go up a semitone into unison and then as many steps above. The sound waves produced by my clarinet and the sine wave generator interacted in quite amazing ways. As the two tones got closer to being in perfect unison the physical properties of the sound waves changed and became more physically apparent. At the point where they were slightly out of unison the interaction of the two tones produced an extraordinary effect of beating: rapid pulsation waves of disturbed air. Quite uncomfortable to listen to – like the sound of bird's wings beating a path near your head. Then, at the point of absolute unison, the sound waves moved into a beautiful parabola. As the performer I could feel the two sound waves merge in and out and around me. After the concert one audience member (a distinguished musician) explained that she had had to leave the performance because she found the physical sensations of the sounds being created, though extremely soft, unbearably painful and nauseating. I would never have guessed that very soft sounds could have such oceanic force.

The intensity of the experience helped me to appreciate why for centuries so many people have reverted to supernatural explanations of the force of music. Some members of the audience said that they had found inner details and interest from the experience, and found it artistically rich. I found that baffling for some time, as the piece was impoverished in conventional artistic terms. My conclusion, having observed similar reactions to comparable pieces since, is that the human brain will construct a great deal of meaning even where the source material does not actually possess it. The imaginative properties of the listener, in other words, are a critical part of the music experience.

THIS AND OTHER similar experiences have shown me several things regarding music and consciousness. First, the physical properties of sound are almost infinitely powerful in their effect on consciousness. Second, shaped to a rich aesthetic experience in musical expression, the force of sound can be enhanced; but done badly it is less than the raw sounds – a single bass-drum beat on its own can be more potent than a misplaced drum beat in an orchestral work. Third, listening is an imaginative process not purely confined to what is being heard – the brain may manufacture meaning and ascribe value within a set of cultural expectations. Fourth, there are paradoxes in listening – soft can be more potent than loud, and less can be more. Fifth, there are significant inherent limitations in our hearing and listening. Last, there are culturally specific and social influences in our cognitive listening processes that shape and even pervert the way we experience music.

Our biology shapes the musical experience far more than we realise; you could even propose bio-aesthetics as a new field of study. Charles Ives' 1931 exhortation to a concert audience – 'use your ears like men' – could be recontextualised in light of this, to 'don't use your ears like men', because the human listening capacity is limited. Perhaps one day we will have prostheses to improve our listening as well as our hearing.

Of particular interest to me are our physical limitations in listening to music. This is distinct from limitations a listener might have due to a lack of cultural knowledge or misinterpretations of the artistic content of a work. We have limits in our listening ability, just as we have limits in other activities.

For example, our range of hearing deteriorates with age – a child can hear a larger range of pitches than an adult and an elderly person can hear less at the ends of the pitch spectrum than either. You may have noticed the secret-ringtone phenomenon: the high-pitched mobile phone ringtone an adolescent can hear but a middle-aged parent cannot.

There are other limitations in individual listening with implications for composers. The 'cocktail party effect' – a term used to describe our ability to hear mass sound environments and connect to single or multiple lines of interest – applies to music. Even expert listeners have limits to the number of independent lines of music they can hear before the character of the music changes from contrapuntal to a dense mass of sound. Also, as the listener cognitively creates the musical experience, the speed of perception is limited, just as it is in taking in visual or verbal information. That has repercussions for a composer in the pacing of events and even the internal structure of musical ideas. Further, quirks of the imagination can occur in listening, as they do with optical illusions in vision. The ear, it seems, can create inner experiences – we may perceive meaning and even manufacture aural impressions that are not actually present. Limitations in memory are also relevant. Our short-term observation of events and capacity for recall of these events may not be adequate to deal with all of the information in a complex composition.

If one listener is this complicated, what goes on when multiple listeners hear the same piece? Collective responses to music can range from extremely extroverted to completely silent and yet either can signal a high level of engagement. The familiar spectacle of a rhythmic writhing mass at a rock concert can at times look a bit like the schooling behaviour of fish. Some sort of mirroring and collective, non-verbal decision-making seems to occur. By contrast, sitting at a chamber music concert recently I noticed that many of the audience were listening with their eyes shut; I think they were awake and sentient and listening in a deeply relaxed, almost meditative way. By cutting out visual stimulus you can almost become a part of the sound and be highly aware of tiny aural nuances that may otherwise pass by. But are we more or less alone when we listen to music in a group with our eyes shut?

Perhaps an extrovert rhythmic and physical response to music is achieving something similar – feeling oneness with music through highly kinetic group behaviour. To what extent does some kind of quantum entanglement, or mirroring behaviour, affect the listening experience? It should puzzle anyone who has sat with a group of a thousand others in a performance: why do we behave as though one? Why do we sometimes engage almost involuntarily and at other times without cohesion? Does the size of the group have an impact on the behaviour and does the volume of the music influence it?

The brain is puzzling, and the music bug seems almost addictive and viral in its affective and contagious qualities; indeed, at times music in a mass environment can produce disinhibiting effects more typical of alcohol or other drugs. The nature of shared sound is powerful and wonderful.

In music, style is the final frontier. Musical exploration of new ideas has led to massive expansions in complexity in all areas of pitch, rhythm, and tone colour. But, with a few notable exceptions, conceptually driven stylistic expansion – manipulating conventions of style – is taboo. Where a composer engages with it, it can engender ignorant criticism, as I have discovered with two large-scale works, *Journey to Horseshoe Bend* and *Going into Shadows*. Is style a representation of a kind of tribalism – like passion for a football team, do we feel the need to belong to artistic teams? If some studies conclude racism is hardwired, do we have similar incipient artistic prejudice? Is our passion for group behaviour so strong that we find music a marker of group identity? Why is it, when our modern experience of music is so plural, that we look for stylistic uniformity in single works of music? My feeling is that where we learn certain listening behaviours at a young age we are very resistant to transgressing them later. In fact, patterns of listening behaviour around style are rather like etiquette – a very complex social formation of shared behaviour. To demonstrate a lack of affinity with etiquette singles you out as a breaker of social taboos, an outcast.

You may be wondering which of these facets is a permanent feature of human listening and which are culturally specific. Further, which of these limitations may decline over generations? Can we improve our listening *en masse*? Should composers aspire to be listened to by an audience in the distant future with superior listening capacity? That would be in the same way that a composer may write challenging music whose novel performance techniques over time become assimilated and accepted as normal. For example, will our listening ever improve sufficiently to interpret a more fast and complex rate of activity? Yes and no. We may improve individually and collectively but there are limits of biology that preclude improvement past a certain point.

The Leonard Cohen song 'Hallelujah' illustrates the power of simple things. Like other Cohen songs, its true affective domain is not primarily in the music. The key to the song is the exceptionally interesting and engaging way the music functions in relation to the words; Cohen's poetry is magnificent and, while populist, has the knack of catching attention and allowing multiple levels of interpretation. Multiple interpretations are important because they trigger an imaginatively engaged response from listeners and hence a kind of personal ownership and identification. The words provide a powerful level of metaphor echoed by music that is easy to sing, falls within a functional vocal range and is constructed so that there is time to absorb the key ideas. That the song's text plays on musical terminology ('the minor fall, the major lift' and 'the secret chord') is itself a level of meaning that engages attention. Art about art appeals because it makes us think about what we are hearing on several levels. Play the music on its own and it's not much; place it in its social and textual context and there is abundant expressive force.

In Beethoven's Piano Sonata in E Major, Opus 109, the communicative impact is purely musical. It is fascinating that it was written by a composer who had been deaf for two years. The piece draws on profound insight into mental responses to music, a highly evolved inner voice and a physicality of performance touch or muscle memory that Beethoven must have experienced as a pianist. He hears through his fingers and through his highly developed imagination, not his ears. There are five or six particular moments in the Theme and Variations movement that are engulfed in musical expression. Beethoven's music progresses from tuneful and waltz-like simplicity to a huge expressive range, with double trills and passage work that teeters on the edge of losing its balance before returning to the opening theme. The movement shows a detailed understanding of the way a listener perceives and holds musical ideas. There is no great pride or conceit in the music – no ideology or facile fashion – just a determination to permit creative flow and imaginative invention within a carefully constructed and well-understood formal structure.

These are not abstract concepts – the success of the affective dimension of Beethoven's music is based on an exploration of inner listening, rather than any technical argument or intellectual device. The mastery of technical musical language is subsumed to allow an expressive and communicative end. The expressive objective is personal and internal for the listener. Musical logic is paramount in the work and musical logic is a force derived from sound, not language. Definitely not a 'black art', but one that exists in its own sensory domain of knowledge and communication, which words alone can only struggle to fully convey.

This piece was extracted from a speech given at the University of New South Wales in October 2010.

Andrew Schultz's music has been performed and recorded internationally by leading musicians. He has received many commissions, including from the major Australian orchestras. Andrew has held residencies and academic posts in Europe, North America, Asia and Australia, and is a professor of music at UNSW. www.andrewschultz.net

MEMOIR

Rebuilding the Stratocaster

Synthesising work and play

Paul Draper

'In my music, I'm trying to play the truth of what I am.
The reason it's difficult is because I'm changing all the time.'
– Charles Mingus

I FOUND myself collecting guitars. It was an imperceptible transition. Two decades ago I'd owned just a couple of instruments at a time, as working tools of the trade when I was a professional musician, composing, playing and recording for a living. After I joined Griffith University and its Conservatorium of Music, in 1995, this process slowly waned as my academic responsibilities grew. Somehow, though, guitars crept back into my life, each an extraordinary portable artwork and collectively an ever larger inspiration that seems to be approaching critical mass.

At the time of writing this piece I own ten guitars. Not only am I collecting them – I'm analysing, listening to, modifying and rebuilding them (the web being an incredible research tool). And the unique music of each instrument is starting to surface. The hot-rodding fetish is driven by a quest to find the right voice, the music that wants to emanate from each guitar. The guitars are dictating a practice regime that listens to the instruments themselves: for example, throwing away the plectrum and wrestling with extracting a certain language from an electric guitar with fingers, flesh and nails; suddenly exploring exotic Eastern scales because there seems to be a resonance in a particular maple guitar neck; exploring pathways that had never occurred to me in my former professional life, but now the guitars are wanting to tell me something.

They niggle more and more: is it time to rebuild my musical past in a way that makes sense, that still serves my students, faculty and academic career? A bit confronting, really – I haven't 'lived' musicking for fifteen years or so, like a sportsperson needing the regular physical engagement and execution: practising, rehearsing, performing, composing. This new collecting and rebuilding of guitars has taken me by stealth.

Perhaps it is akin to Guy Claxton's notion, in *Hare Brain, Tortoise Mind: How Intelligence Increases When You Think Less* (Ecco, 1997), of the 'undermind'

PREVIOUS PAGE: Reinterpreted ukuleles by Greg Weight, Reg Mombassa and Paul Worstead. From the exhibition *Hula Dreams*, Gallery East, Sydney, 2004. Photo by Greg Weight.

or subconscious hard at work on resolving matters, if you let it. Yet there is still something about the metaphysics of the situation that is intriguing, overpowering. While music has always been central to my life, a driver, I am beginning to realise that the ways in which I have seen this have constantly changed. In the early days the guitar was utilitarian, simply a conduit for the execution of (hopefully) original ideas; at later stages, perhaps more a symbol of 'project-based outputs' or academic engagement. But, most recently, it is a love affair with the instruments themselves, each with such wonderful physicalities and personas that I seem to be listening to them in new ways.

I decided to write about it, to plan for it, and to change direction in a manner that aims to recapture the past, incorporate the present and challenge a future fusion for the two.

I'M A BABY boomer who grew up in the sixties. Fresh out of school, as an eighteen-year-old guitarist, I bypassed university and joined a rock band, promptly heading off to Melbourne to find fame and fortune: good times, cold weather, Lygon Street, Aussie Crawl, Skyhooks, Countdown, shared band houses, and life in pubs and on the road. We never quite cracked the big time, whatever that really means in the stardom-or-bust vernacular. Maybe this was to do with my attitude to money and pay scales – somehow those record company deals never seemed to quite add up. In any case, I became interested in adding more strings to my bow, and there was no way to avoid the fact that this would require an arsenal of practical skills and musical technique. I owned various guitars through this time, but they tended to come and go depending on immediate needs or fashion whims, and I am sorry to say that most of them are not still with me.

I relocated to Sydney in the late 1970s, feeling the need for a change of scene and better musical chops. New fusion musics were emerging and Sydney had a burgeoning jazz scene, along with a Conservatorium of note that offered programs led by the jazz stars of the time. I auditioned and enrolled. Trouble was, I didn't much like it and I didn't agree with how they taught. It seemed much more connected to the teacher's past rather than my own gigging present and imagined future. This is something that has stuck with me for a long time, and what I later came to understand as 'problem-based learning' became a centrepiece for my doctorate. It was also a focus for my own curriculum designs, where theory and practice aim to be driven by and understood through personal contexts – 'student-centred learning', as the current jargon puts it.

I found this first taste of academia disconnected from working. So I sought private tuition from a number of younger gigging fusion players with serious practical credentials, dropped out of the Sydney Con and, for the next five years or so, played and practiced harder than I ever had before. I began to focus more on lucrative but demanding session playing in the recording sector, and moved back to Brisbane in the early 1980s to take up a number of recording and touring offers. This was at the birth of the CD, digital sound, the PC and MIDI (the musical instrument digital interface). The last of these changed the music business almost overnight. Where once there were many large local bands and crews, suddenly there were small duos with backing tracks everywhere in pubs. Software like Band-in-a-Box undercut the live acts by a huge margin and, moreover, many audiences didn't seem to notice or mind.

In the recording scene the same transition was underway. I jumped in, using my experience and love of traditional recording studios to build a small facility in Brisbane, probably one of the first affordable home studios in town. Guitars were still very much in my life, but now they were accompanied by a growing array of technologies, including synthesisers, computers and effects devices, as well as designs for acoustics and isolation spaces. I had successfully exited the dying live scene and reached the new technological frontier. It was at this time I spied and bought a lovely black Fender Stratocaster (still with me today, but now rebuilt): nice to look at and good to play, but essentially a stable vehicle to retrofit with pitch-to-MIDI convertor technology. This meant that I could directly control and play much of the digital technologies and synthesisers directly from the guitar, subsequently opening up more film soundtrack work that could be completed efficiently and cost effectively.

I became what they call in the music business the producer – in this case, of a lot of original music in the next decade or so, and across many sectors:

for bands, solo artists, advertising agencies, radio, TV documentaries, films, local council and state government projects. I began to find myself delivering in-service training to schoolteachers who were receiving bucket loads of computers and music software that they had no idea what to do with: the 'education revolution' of the late 1980s.

It was this trajectory that led me to deliver my first invited lecture on film music and recording technology, at a Brisbane tertiary music school in 1990. That seemed to go well, and was followed by regular casual teaching. I started full-time work at the Con in the mid-1990s, as a lecturer in music technology – the technology moniker stuck. I somehow became the default 'PC guy' because of my work with computers, while my rock, R&B and jazz music never really got much of a look-in at what was then a mostly traditional classical-music institution. From time to time this annoyed me, but the idea of scaling and teaching what I had learned as a career musician was an exciting challenge at age forty-two. An idea of legacy was emerging, and I loved teaching and being part of a team to bring the conservatoire into the twenty-first century – something that we still seem to be doing.

I WAS MOVING out of the professional recording industry, and so too was the rest of the world. The dotcom bubble burst around the turn of the millenium and with it came the digital download revolution, the 'file sharing is a crime' outrage from corporates, lawsuits against university students, and eventually the complete unravelling of record company control of musicians' intellectual property (some might say loss of livelihood, but many statistics would seem to refute this). This so-called digital independence also changed the ways in which we aspire to train future generations of artists. Rather than expect a principal position in an orchestra, or a lucrative pop record deal, we have in some ways turned full circle: craft and portfolio career skills have become favoured buzzwords, along with a new one called 'web 2.0' – meaning Flickr, YouTube, user rankings, 'folksonomies' and the idea that artists can be successful in the 'long tail' economies of an interconnected world.

The design of online ('flexible' or 'blended') learning has been a research interest throughout my academic career. I had to build and establish higher education credibility, and in 2000 I completed a doctorate in education entitled *New Learning: The Challenge of Flexible Delivery in Higher Education*. Drawing on this work, and influenced by web 2.0, in the early 2000s my efforts turned to building online multimedia, podcasting and music communication platforms at the university. I lobbied for the creation of a professional doctorate-by-research in music. In 2005 we introduced a Doctor of Musical Arts (DMA), which these days is bursting at the seams with candidates developing practice-led research aspects of their music.

Taking on the conservatorium's research dean portfolio, in 2009, has allowed me considerable scope for reflection. Steering research and university reporting responsibilities for an academic team and assuming responsibility for research postgraduate candidates has afforded me a bird's eye view of complex viewpoints that I now deal with every day. Might this be linked to my recently morphing perspectives about my own music and my guitars? For example, we develop and assist some outstanding people to attain their doctoral qualifications in the arts though multi-exegetical theses that incorporate creative works. Yet it remains problematic for academics to be recognised for their own creative works. That makes me want to approach the future in a different way.

A COLLEAGUE SUGGESTED that it might be time for me to think about a monograph. Probably considered *de rigeur* for someone who is a professor, this usually means something like: 'an academic must publish monographs over the course of his or her life. These scholarly treatises provide evidence that the academic is carrying out research in the field and analysing already published information. A monograph usually brings new light to the subject, and it may contain breakthrough research. It also further refines the academic specialty of the author, and establishes the author as an authority on the topic.'

On the face of it, this approach sits uneasily – 'scholarly treatise', a book, yet more text outputs substituting for music making? Perhaps, like many other artists in the academy, I found myself slowly drifting away from practising arts simply because of academic demands: my PhD, grants, administration, strategic planning and so on. It's odd, too, in the light of so much talk and gathering of research 'equivalent' outputs across the university sector in Australia from the moment I started in the sector – from the 1998 Strand Report, *Research in the Creative Arts*, to the Howard Government's *Research Quality Framework* and Labor's *Excellence in Research for Australia* (ERA) initiative in 2010.

Despite these attempts to chase the idea of 'practice-led research', I see and hear around me that many academic artists struggle to keep up their chops or significant 'alternate' research outputs (artworks, new music, films), given the demands of ever-interconnected, 'flexible', policy-driven, compliance-oriented university life. It may be easier for some to produce and count journal articles – and, in my case, also immerse myself in recording albums for academic colleagues.

Not that I'm complaining. On the contrary: working in the university over the past fifteen years has taught me much about reflection, analysis, planning and research, while challenging my assumptions and intellect.

Again recalling my colleague's recent suggestion to 'think about a monograph', I want to work this through, consider its shape:

mon·o·graph [mon-uh-graf, -grahf] – noun
1. a treatise on a particular subject, a biographical study or study of the works of one artist.
2. a highly detailed and thoroughly documented study or paper written about a limited area of a subject or field of inquiry: scholarly monographs on medieval pigments.
3. an account of a single thing or class of things, as of a species or organism.

I want to flesh out what seems to be emerging as a plan for my next eighteen months or so. But broadly – as way to fuse and re-examine my music in the light of the intervening decades of experience, and to think about the project in terms of 'practice-led research', one end point being the production of an album of original music I've decided to call *Monograph*.

My Fender Stratocaster, after twelve months of consideration and tweaking, is now complete. It is one of many guitars in my collection, all with individual stories, but this guitar has emerged as the CI for the project (Chief Investigator, in grant-speak). Beautiful, inspirational and, for me, a seminal moment: the guitar's transformation becomes a metaphor to understand the transition from professional musical life into the academy, and back again, drawing on the two. This guitar, in its original form, was at my side in every musical undertaking since the mid-1980s. It was a lot uglier then, with a MIDI interface strapped across its brow, but always a wonderful workhorse.

One half of the instrument is now located in the present and the future. It represents what I have learned in the academy as well as what I have brought to the academy. Every single electronic and metal component has been carefully thought through and replaced, tweaked and sometimes rejected before moving on. Twenty-first-century technology, specialisation and refinement is remarkable, compared with the earlier decades in which the guitar originally operated. In tandem with eBay's international reach, search engine power and web 2.0 culture, this makes the restoration a revealing and reaffirming exercise. It brings together new meanings for the idea of 'music technology' (beyond computers and the 'PC guy'), as well as helping me to remember and acknowledge central musical truths.

The historical aspects are retained in the timber – both the neck and the body are untouched, genuinely road-worn relics of the past life, twenty-five years ago. The wood resonates with every note, blazing venue light, sounds of audiences, loud music, the recording studio sessions, the film soundtracks, my own sweat. All are in the neck and the body: the maple and basswood, in the dings, markings and battle-scarred wear and tear. The guitar is not only a remarkable artwork in itself, but also a living musical personality that continues to inspire and reward, whether through just gazing at it, or in playing it and revelling in the glorious sounds it makes. It also smells wonderful, vividly reminding me of many musical settings: dingy bars and beer, sleek recording studio air-con, sunny outdoor concerts and crowds that go back forever, late-night jams on the porch...

ONE SATURDAY NIGHT, after much playing, the Stratocaster felt done. Where to next? This was still under-realised, a vague feeling in the back of the mind, a few notes on an A4 ream in my studio. Next morning I got up to read the Sunday papers with coffee, something I hadn't done for a while, having been immersed in either work or the guitars. For some reason I turned to that awful 'Body & Soul' liftout, opened at the back page and read my stars (sad but true). It said, 'tomorrow is the first day of the next seven-year cycle...forget everything, await tectonic change, this is the beginning of the rest of your life.' On it went, no oblique comments here, no, no. The page screamed at me: *Be prepared, you poor bugger!* So I put it away and tried to read something else, but couldn't put this seven-year itch out of my mind.

Later, I was talking with friends, both senior American academics, at dinner prior to them returning overseas. I mentioned the seven-year idea and they lit up. They started taking about 'seven-year cycles', both retrospectively and forwards. They asked about details – 'is it a five plus a two?' – and offered all sorts of other confusing but intriguing comments. I've never been into astrology or numerology, but the older I get the more I notice that I tend to look for and respect omens. I wasn't sure what my friends' comments meant, but I went back to my notes for *Monograph*.

I'd already been jotting down vague concepts for the music, a possible album structure, some ideas for what roles the guitars might take, and what stories they might reflect upon as a monograph about my university career. This worked arbitrarily in decade-like slices from my start at the university. I reworked the notes, now figured across three seven-year cycles. Like a road map (and a graphic artwork), a 'five plus two' approach lined up – stunningly – with events and people; the first period overlapped and captured the transition from professional musical life into the university, during those years from 1990 where I worked as a casual lecturer alongside gigging and studio work. A better plan was emerging, but from somewhere in the back of the mind, from intuition, and one very different to the ways in which I've worked more recently, with planning and explicitness.

I'VE BEEN PLAYING every Friday, my research day. Jamming, blowing, improvising, working out the guitars and chop-building with a drummer, a close friend, at his recording and teaching studio in Brisbane. Now we're starting to record and work on some really good stuff. When I mention 'research day', there's been this quick, faint smile that passes across academic colleagues' eyes. Just for a second, but it's as if this is somehow false. Because of academic responsibilities and union agreements that offer a shopfloor model, research time tends to be conceptualised in somewhat nonsensical weekly workload allocations – usually Fridays at the Con. But I tend to do long slabs of intense research activity on weekends and in the evenings. I keep on talking up my Friday research days, though, and especially the playing that happens, the jamming, recording and development of musical ideas. And I notice that colleagues no longer offer the faint smile, but ask me how it's going. MP3s are starting to circulate – and, more importantly, my musical confidence and chops are improving by the week.

Several academic writing themes are emerging about 'improvisation, composition and instrumental technology', and the notion of a parallel between 'jamming' and 'proper' research. That is, when we set out for a new research project or grant bid we review a lot of literature, file, distil, build our arguments and choose core items, then 'remix' an outcome. So too in musical improvisation, as I am finding: investigate the sources (practice, fingers, guitars, metronome, chord structures, musical analysis); improvise, play and record, drawing upon a lifetime's aural library constantly stimulated through physical update; listen; evaluate, remix and produce the output of this research as music.

I recently submitted my first Academic Studies Leave application. I intend to do some traditional writing, and my literature reviews indicate that the field is ripe for work about the nexus between musical improvisation and composition. Moreover, there's my potential contribution to the widening of universities' public and academic profile in the creative arts, through my own ways of seeing 'the artist in the academy': my transition from professional music and casual teaching to a continuing appointment, under Vice-Chancellor #1; to building an academic career through PhD, teaching, designing and convening undergraduate and postgraduate programs, under Vice-Chancellor #2; to establishing a research centre and new doctoral programs, and gaining my chair, with Vice-Chancellor #3.

It will be a series of musical concept performances and the album *Monograph* that reflects on events and people over twenty-one years. And a thank-you note to all.

'WRITING ABOUT MUSIC is like dancing about architecture,' Laurie Anderson once said. This was a belief I once subscribed to, being more interested in art than its critical analysis. However, recent experiences are telling me that the truth is a good deal more fuzzy: working through my instrument collection in intellectual and tacit ways is opening up pathways that I hadn't considered. What will emerge is still unclear, but it is becoming more than a simple binary of practice-and-play or listen-and-write. The writing helps think it through and gets filed away in the undermind, often unexpectedly raising its influence at the point I'd once imagined to be pure inspiration and improvisation. At other points it clarifies, or takes a position on what has occurred in the past, and so rolls the imagination into the future.

I think I've made peace with the 'dancing about architecture' view. Writing and publishing reflections, the processes, the artefacts and so on, seem more and more to be a natural process that highlights an idea of practice-led research in music. It is neither an art critic's point of view nor that of the artiste too busy to write, but a blend of the two stances that tries to speak directly to other academic artists as an authentic group of peers (rather then across disciplines, trying to argue an 'equivalency' to ARC science-based research awards, seeking carrots from the feds and the university sector).

Ultimately, though, I believe the work will be judged not with the forebrain by others, but by something much deeper and primal in human beings' understandings of, and responses to, the music itself. And this is something I have seen so often. Senior managers and academic leaders from all backgrounds talk the talk and walk the walk in research, federal funding, outputs, key performance indicators and the like. In day-to-day work this often appears to translate to one-size-fits-all for artists' academic activities.

Yet human nature, something fundamental, comes to the fore when we experience music, when these same people attend concerts, talk about records and relive their past through music's incredible power. There is not a person I know, not a senior colleague I have worked with, who does not retain a childlike enthusiasm and reverence for the music in their lives, somewhere, sometime. The associations, the memories; the futures it can make, the Esperanto it shares.

Some kind of new fusion is coming for me. I intend there to be interesting research pieces for other musicians along the way but, mostly, I want the music to speak to everyone who listens and contributes their own inner meaning.

I'm still collecting guitars and they are collecting me – sweeping me up and steering me toward new music, new thinking and, I believe, a reconciliation between two careers that, until now, I'd thought of as work and play. My most recent discovery has been the French-Canadian Godin guitar. Mine doesn't seem to need modifications or personalisation just yet, but time will tell. It has a glorious deep-blue flame top that plays wonderfully, with its hybrid electric–classical flat neck and huge humbucking pickups. Godin guitars speak of the old world – rock, jazz, ethnic and classical instruments built with great craftsmanship and love. But they also look to the future, with a vision unrivalled in the contemporary guitar-manufacturing industry. My new guitar features transparent yet twenty-first-century-powerful electronics that provide for direct computer connection (much more elegantly than those I'd forced upon my poor black Stratocaster in the 1980s). A conduit from the mind and the fingers to digital – into software recording, production, remix and onward to the web. And, I hope, to be downloaded into the hearts and minds of others.

References at www.griffithreview.com

Thanks to Glyn Davis and Brydie-Leigh Bartleet for their encouragement and being a sounding board, and to Fred Haefele's inspirational *Rebuilding the Indian* (2005).

Paul Draper is a professor of digital arts at Griffith University and research dean at the Queensland Conservatorium. He serves on international boards, including Pearson Education (Aus.), the *Journal of Music, Education and Technology* (UK) and the Association for the Study of the Art of Record Production (UK).

MEMOIR

Death and distraction

Learning to pay attention

Helen Elliott

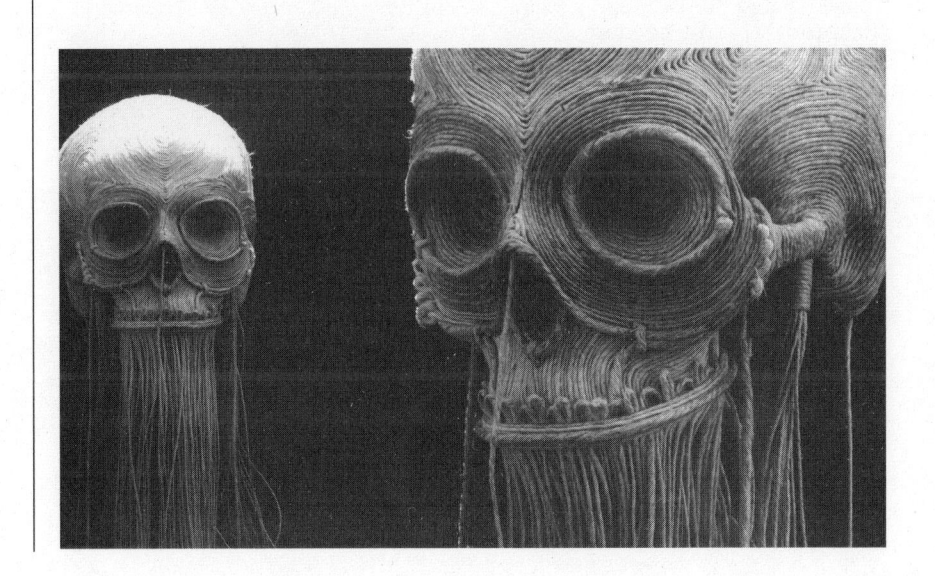

HER subject is distraction. She's written a book about it, published by one of those intimidating American academic houses. She's American and has that attractive twangy accent I can never place. South coast? Boston? With her, though, it's not about the accent. She's very, very smart and the Radio National interviewer is very, very taken with her.

So am I. Google my name and 'distracted' will be riveted to it. I was about to do some reading when that twang lured me across the kitchen tiles, nearer to the radio. Witty, that capacity to morph into your subject. But she's not just a witty snare; she's saying fresh things about a scrappy and infinite topic. I unscrew the still hot one-cup espresso machine, empty the grounds into the compost and, despite my recent swearing off at two, make my third coffee for the day. While I wait for it to spit and gurgle at me I empty the dishwasher. I can't rush out with the overflowing compost, because I'll miss what she is saying and already I don't want to miss a word.

She's making the interviewer laugh. *Oh-oh-oh-oh!* He has an elegant lilt and black lines of TS Eliot slide down my peripheral vision. Was it *The Waste Land*? How many years since I've read that? I still have my original copy. I think.

They're talking about language, about the anachronistic meaning of the word 'distraction', the way it was used for around three hundred years. Not so long ago it meant being *pulled away* or *being pulled in pieces*. That's what she says. Yes! I remember! I can even see the book, *Latin Roots*, with the cracked cover in a weird black-green colour that made my mouth dry. That book was in some shape when I got it third-hand, after two boys. The Latin root *distrahere* means to pull asunder.

There was, she says, a recent American survey of people working in offices that attempted to track their attention spans. What? The results must be wrong. I tear some paper from the roll and wipe down the bench. After seventeen years it never looks clean. The survey indicated that workers are interrupted every three minutes. Every three minutes? And if they're doing something that requires detailed attention it might take as long as twenty-five minutes to get back into it. Workers spend 28 per cent of their day being distracted.

PREVIOUS PAGE: Jim. *Untitled*, papier maché, natural rope & tea bags. Courtesy of the artist, Flak Gallery and Galerie Bailly contemporain. www.jim-skullgallery.com

I'm the cartoon cat that's fallen on its head. Twenty-eight per cent? Exclamation marks bounce off my eyeballs. Companies are interested in this study, because the time their workers waste costs billions every year. Translate global into millions every second.

Then there's this: she says — or the interviewer, who seems to have read her book, says — that it isn't just outside interruptions that cause these minor bleeds every three minutes. The workers distract themselves. Their email pings; their mobile drums; they need to look up a result or Facebook, or monitor an online discussion.

She's set me off like a metronome. How right she is; concentrated work is not possible in offices. I know this because there have been times in my life when I've had to work in those glass and steel cylinders that shimmer on the horizon when I take the freeway from my snug little suburb into the city. As I get closer they take shape, looming like independent colonies. One of them has pointed ears *à la* Batman, and every time I near the end of the freeway I expect an image of Jack Nicholson playing the Joker. He's an actor I dislike. Still. People who know about architecture tell me that the Batman building is a fabulous example of creative architecture.

That's what they tell me, but I'm cautious about rushing to admire the newly made buildings we live and work in, especially these public buildings, facades agitated with bling, angles calculated against serenity. When I'm in them I don't feel awed or uplifted. Disconsolate and nervy, more like it.

If I think about all the people who work in these buildings, all these individuals going about their one precious life as ardently as I go about my one precious life, I feel a distant, but glacial prick. It's closely related to that stupefied panic I have whenever I've watched archival footage from World War II, where lines of people are standing on the edge of trenches waiting to be shot. Or being shot. *Bang. Oblivion.* Each separate soul. Just like me. Who were they? What were they feeling, thinking? Disbelief? Acceptance? Distraught? The word that used to be an alternative to distract. These days I can't look at anything violent.

I was thirteen when I read Anne Frank's *Diary* and it left an invisible tattoo. I turned sixteen, seventeen, eighteen, sometimes delighting in myself and in the world, just as she did, so sometimes I thought about Anne and about how she never knew what it was to turn sixteen. How could this happen? That there was once a girl exactly my age, just as dazzled with life, expecting to live just as I expected to live…and then she didn't. *This happened.* I knew Anne Frank. I knew what she was feeling but, despite my empathy, my *famous* empathy, I'll never understand what she faced. That's like trying to pocket the wind.

What luck that I can work from home, where no one can distract me every three minutes.

I turn off the gas and pour my coffee into a small white bone china cup that has gold laurel leaves, handpainted, winding around the rim. It's called Golden Laurel and was made in Derbyshire when dishwashers were a pair of slim hands in pink rubber gloves. She's using the word 'hopscotching' to describe how we navigate the new, technological world. *Fragmentation, sound bites, split-focus* all sound lumpy compared to *hopscotching*. Hopscotching cascades with images: children, barelegged, short tartan – tartan! – skirts flying as they leg across the pattern to wherever the tor has landed. I used to love the chance and the exhilaration of that game.

The interviewer just called her Maggie, but I missed the introduction and have no idea who she is, other than that she has written the distracting book they are discussing. The interviewer is galvanised by the subject, so much so that he forgets himself, and the whole thing threatens to dissolve as he shambles in like an intellectual elephant just as she's starting to say something. *Oh-oh-oh-oh!* Do shut up. He's a brilliant and learned man, but I've listened to him for years and I know his patterns of thought and I know – and mostly agree with – his opinions. (We're both calcifying.) Because of this I'm always tolerant of his foibles, but today I'm sailing towards impatient. Maggie has only twenty minutes. Let her speak!

I bang my cup down in its saucer and the golden laurels threaten to crack.

She starts speaking about intellectual restlessness. Her thesis, as far as I can gauge, is that while technology is amazing and helpful (*tonic*, she says – lovely), the way we use it is changing the physical capacities of our brains. As she speaks my own brain highlights in mercury. Neuroscientists are coming to believe that our constant hopscotching may be physically altering wodges of our brains in such ways that we are no longer capable of reflection or of the deep thinking that results in difficult problem-solving. She cites two things that cause my brain – currently in a humming state of orange alert – to skid to a halt. One is that fifteen-year-old American children rate very low on critical thinking (although, hooray! Australian children perform far better) and are lining up for huge doses of adult ADHD medications. The other is that a high percentage of long-standing internet users in America did not realise that paid content is common online.

She means, I imagine, marketing, advertising masquerading as independent scholarship, something I expected people automatically assumed every time they read on the net. I never trust it face-up, particularly the first arrival from Google, but she is saying, what? No! Over 60 per cent of people, of *educated* people, read everything without scepticism, without doubting what the professional, visually attractive text says. But I suppose that in a world in love with the image, the text *is* the image. So if a piece of text looks attractive it has a greater chance of being believed.

Like people? What about all those studies done confirming that pretty people of both sexes do better in every way in the world: rail against it if you like, but it seems we're hardwired for prettiness.

When I was a child I believed everything I read. Print — black marks haunting white paper, transforming themselves into indelible truth — was my daily miracle-in-progress.

As I listen I'm trying to get a mark out of the kitchen bench with an organic cleaner that is worse than useless on seventeen-year-old white laminate. Was it the raw beetroot I grated last night? I'm going to use more raw beetroot because I read, somewhere — or maybe I heard it somewhere? — that it is one of those foods. You know. Foods packed with all these as-yet-unidentified antioxidants and enzymes that prevent or cure cancer. My friend has cancer. Should I mention raw beetroot? Everyone gives her advice. I think she might die of advice. Or goji berries. I saw them in the supermarket today. My sister-in-law's sister reckons goji juice saved her life, but she didn't have cancer. She had ennui. You don't turn your face to the wall and die of that these days.

Lobotomise? She, Maggie, said that? My shoulders slump. Is she, too, becoming a cliché: Jack Nicholson again, this time just crazy, as in *One Flew Over the Cuckoo's Nest*? (Why is Jack Nicholson embedded, *embedded!* in my head like a sinister ectoplasm?) Maggie is saying that by switching tasks constantly, by this incessant mental and even physical movement we are in danger of lobotomising our brains. A lobotomised world is lying in wait. Another dark age.

She's not talking about one dark age, nothing one-dimensional about this, but about all the dark ages through history that were often brought about by an intense technological revolution. Our cultural habit, as we lose literacy, is to turn to more technology. What did she just say? Collective forgetting?

The art historian (and endearing snob) Kenneth Clarke says that the hallmark of civilisation is its claim to permanence.

I'm listening hard because, despite the cliché, what she says is exhilarating. I feel like a code-cracker. Bletchley, here I come. I hadn't even known there was a Greek dark age. Of five hundred years. Five hundred? I try to screw that down into memory as I rub at the beetroot stain, which I now see is going to remain a memory for as long as the house is standing.

Maggie believes – and she has excellent research from the best universities, to back her up – that our new skimming habits of mind are destroying and undermining brain function at this deeper level. We no longer have the ability to wrestle with texts and finally will not be able to solve complex problems. She is speaking about the architecture of the brain, of how it requires a keystone and then careful building. The keystone she calls attention. As she speaks, I see it exactly. ATTENTION. In rich, uppercase orange.

The neuroscientists who have been studying nothing but attention for the past decade believe that it is an organic thing, in the same way that our circulatory or respiratory systems are organic. They have isolated three separate but interacting networks – mental processes – at the centre of their subject.

One is focus, the spotlight on whatever is at hand; the second is awareness of the details of what it is; and the third, and most important, is an executive cortex, putting into action the learning. After each learning activity the brain alters physically.

I am curved across the bench, chin resting on hands, head drooping close to the radio. Listening. Last time I listened like this it was to hear the fistula doctor working in Ethiopia, Catherine Hamlin, the only contemporary woman who could be a saint. She shook me up so much that for months after I wanted to offer up my silly life to some higher cause. That was a few years ago. I never give the radio all my attention. If I am in the kitchen, the bathroom or even the bedroom and want to listen to the radio, I always make the most of time, *make the most of time!* and do something practical. Cleaning in the kitchen and bathroom; taking the clothes from the chair and folding them away if I am in the bedroom. I enjoy order.

I used to listen to the radio as I cooked, but for the past few years I've noticed that the concentration required means that I only half-hear the radio. Now I listen, half-listen, to music. I've accepted that multi-tasking, or as Maggie calls it, multi-skilling, is admirable. In a complicated and teeming life I took for granted that it is the only way to be effective – unless, of course, living in squalor doesn't worry you. Multi-tasking is a way of controlling time by layering it. Making the most. But in the layering ATTENTION starts to crumble.

What's this? Connectivity soup? Now there's a metaphor that sings. It seems that although we're more connected than ever, we're more isolated than ever. The critical points Maggie pursues in her book are the need to pay attention to our intellectual selves and to our relationships. She suggests that if we cannot think deeply, we cannot relate deeply. With email and Facebook, with this instant capacity to connect electronically, we're no longer interested in the less thrilling but deeper, and perhaps calmer, relationships. Round and round we swim, twinkling our little lights at one another, in love with the noise and exhilaration of the moment but disabled when we find we want to explore more profound places. She touches on the lack of physicality in relationships and I think of the fractional chill whenever I come across one of those smiley faces in an email: antidotes to emotional intelligence.

Maggie's twenty minutes are up and the interviewer parachutes into the next topic, which sounds like yet another exposé of American nefariousness over the past decade. I'm sure it's all true and I'm sure I'll agree with whoever is doing the exposing, but I don't want to listen. I just don't want to *know*. Being righteously outraged is exhausting.

I rinse my cup. Do I pay enough attention to living?

Helen Elliott is an author and former journalist. Her essay 'Encounters with Mrs L BA(OXON)' appeared in *Griffith REVIEW 11: Getting Smart*.

ESSAY

Exploring the historical imagination

Narrating the shape of things unknown

Peter Cochrane

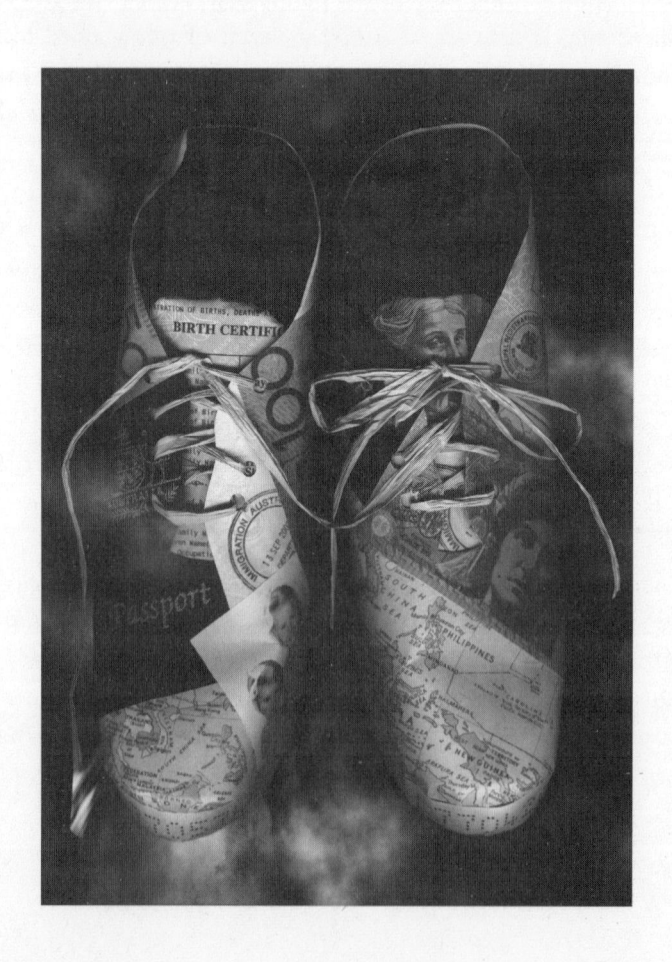

PETER COCHRANE: Exploring the historical imagination

IT has been said of George Macaulay Trevelyan that he was gifted with a 'vivid pictorial sense'. True enough, but consider for instance an extract from the opening to his biography of Earl Grey, *Grey of Fallodon* (1937):

> Fallodon has no rare and particular beauty. It is merely a piece of unspoilt English countryside – wood, field and running stream. But there is a tang of the north about it; the west wind blows through it straight off the neighbouring moors, and the sea is visible from the garden through a much-loved gap in the trees. The whole region gains dignity from the great presence of the Cheviot and the Ocean. Eastward, beyond two miles of level fields across which [Grey] so often strode, lie the tufted dunes, the reefs of tide-washed rock, and the bays of hard sand; on that lonely shore he would lie, by the hour, watching the oystercatchers, turnstones and dunlin, or the woodcock immigrants landing tired from their voyage.

Vivid and haunting, yes, and most certainly pictorial, but the passage is much more than this. In these few lines we are introduced to a life of aristocratic distinction. The paragraph suggests the magnificence of the estate, and even the nomenclature of nature – the hardworking creatures, the oystercatchers and 'woodcock immigrants' – hints at class and privilege, as do Grey's leisurely hours in the dunes, and the juxtaposition of the vista from the garden with the moors and the ocean. And yet we may note that vigorous word 'strode', for all this will later form the backdrop to the vigour of Grey's long and ferociously committed political career in London.

So much is achieved here in so few words, embedded, seamlessly, in the so-called vivid pictorial sense that distinguishes Trevelyan's work. It reaffirms the way in which the historical imagination is an amalgam of literary finesse and historical vision, the oneness of the part and the whole. But if vision is the informing purpose or master metaphor or Big Idea that holds a fine work of history together, then imagination is the reflective eye that knows the

---

PREVIOUS PAGE: Shayne Higson. *Proof of Identity*, 2003. Winner of the 2003 Hermann's Art Award. Lightjet print. 100 x 76cm. Courtesy of the artist.

territory framed within the vision and ranges freely over it. It is the eye that holds both the vision and its episodic content in a kind of continual focus and fluency. It is an eye of reason; it both apprehends and comprehends. It is the hold on an intricate design. And more.

HISTORY ESTABLISHED ITSELF as a professional, university-based discipline partly by disowning its age-old association with literature; by declaring itself a systematic branch of knowledge based on rigorous scholarship; and by branding imagination, dramatisation and good storytelling as practices best consigned to the peddlers of fairytales, romances and mythologies, or to perjurers at law. A particular kind of academic authority was asserted at the expense of more creative possibilities, though not without challenges from within academic history and beyond – exemplified, respectively, by Trevelyan and his great-uncle Thomas Babington Macaulay.

At the same time literature was also inclined to a more exclusive idea of itself. Romanticism associated imagination with 'feeling', sentiment, nature, the passions, rapture even; with the business of transcending 'reason'. Mary Wollstonecraft identified imagination with the rebellious, Promethean character of mankind and contrasted it with reason-centred humanity. 'Imagination,' she wrote, 'is the true fire stolen from heaven to animate this cold creature of clay.' Imagination was about life energy, but life energy of a particular kind: the inner self, the finer sentiments, the higher self that transcends all material concerns.

Wollstonecraft's views were in part shaped by the course of the French Revolution. Her hopes for the revolution were dashed. Her belief in the possibilities of revolutionary action was gone. She was recoiling, repulsed by the 'extreme, calculating rationalism' of the Jacobins. She would remain ever the social rebel, but her faith in public action was now supplanted by a belief that social progress would have to come through individual change, through searching out the enduring truths of the heart.

As Richard Holmes reported in *Footsteps: The Adventures of a Romantic Biographer* (1985), Wollstonecraft's miniature manifesto on the powers of the imagination prophesied the creative works of the next generation of Romantics, notably those of Coleridge and Shelley.

Coleridge, too, would write a passage on the imagination that would become famous and, in a way, help to lock the concept of the imagination into that binary position — opposite reason, calculation and analysis.

Coleridge's famous reverie on the imagination is nothing more than a quick word sketch scrawled in a notebook in the midst of a bumpy journey. It was November 1799. The poet was on board a coach, coming home from his first enchanting encounter with the Lakes District. He and Wordsworth had hiked about and gazed in wonder. On the journey home the all-night coach was not so rough as to prevent sleep and Coleridge hardly stirred until dawn, when he looked out the window and hurriedly reached for the notebook, jotting down a description of birds in formation over the wintry landscape:

> Starlings in vast flights drove along like smoke, mist, or any thing misty without volition — now a circular area inclined in an Arc — now a Globe — now from complete Orb into an Ellipse and Oblong — now a balloon with the car suspended, now a concaved Semicircle — and still it expands and condenses, some moments glimmery & shivering, dim & shadowy, now thickening, deepening, blackening!

The image haunted him for years to come. He pondered its symbolic mystery. He recalled it while climbing over Scafell Pike in 1802 and he reworded it twice in his Notebooks in 1803. In effect he adopted the image, took it on as a powerful metaphor for his own imagination — a protean, pulsing, spontaneous thing, given to 'vast flights', signifying, presumably, the gamut of emotions and associated images; all, he says, 'without volition'.

More than a century later, when describing Coleridge, Virginia Woolf was happy to rely on the poet's own symbolism, associating birds and flight with imagination and creativity. He was 'not a man, but a swarm, a cloud, a buzz of words, darting this way and that, clustering, quivering, and hanging suspended'. The essence here is ancient: 'The poet is a light and winged and holy thing,' wrote Plato. The idea persists today. We still speak of 'flights of fancy' and 'flights of the imagination'. And with that, of course, we seem to have moved an awfully long way away from the business or the practice of history.

Talk of flight or wings suggests both freedom and power, protean vision, spectacular movement of mind, mental aerobatics – mastery of imagery, language and narrative reach – all, no doubt, associated with the status we give to the novelist, the playwright or the poet: elevated, sighted like a hawk, unanchored, unearthed in ways most cannot manage (or imagine). Flight is what we ordinary mortals cannot do and, as a metaphor, it measures the kudos we extend to those world-makers, the fabulous storytellers, the fictive or filmic imaginations at whom we marvel.

Shakespeare's hymn to the 'poet's eye' in *A Midsummer Night's Dream* makes no mention of wings or flight, and yet that eye, it seems, moves like Coleridge's starlings:

> The poet's eye, in a fine frenzy rolling,
> Doth glance from heaven to earth, from earth to heaven,
> And, as imagination bodies forth
> The form of things unknown, the poet's pen
> Turns them to shapes, and gives to airy nothing
> A local habitation and a name.

Both poets recognised an apparently contradictory feature of their imaginative work – it was, to a point, spontaneous and perhaps even unwilled, yet it was also disciplined, systematic and ultimately deliberate in its transformation of thought into words or word pictures. And we must not miss the centrality of wordplay here – 'the poet's pen…gives to airy nothing', something out of 'nothing' – the way it comes down to literary art.

Coleridge used the phrase 'without volition' to describe the spectacle of wild flight. What exactly does 'without volition' mean? Such a craft as poetry can hardly be 'without volition'. The poet's note on starlings evoked untamed movement (like Shakespeare's 'fine frenzy rolling'), yet that flight was supremely co-ordinated by some majestic affinity that creative minds – teaming with narrative schemata, images and their word equivalents – seem to share. The creative imagination unites spontaneous creativity with the deliberate work and reworking of composition, with a mastery that is anything but spontaneous. It is a mergence, an effervescing fusion, of memory, emotion and intellect. As Dickens noted: 'My own invention or imagination, such as it is…would never have served me as it has but for the habit of commonplace, humble, patient, daily, toiling, drudging attention.'

In the modest, slightly mocking self-praise that Shakespeare gives to Holofernes in *Love's Labour's Lost* we glimpse, I suspect, something of the Bard's sense of his own powers, the workings of that extraordinary mind:

This is a gift I have, simple, simple;
a foolish, extravagant spirit full of forms,
fissures, shapes, objects, ideas, apprehensions,
motions, revolutions: these are begot in the
ventricle of memory, nourished in the womb of
pia mater, and delivered upon the mellowing
of occasion. But the gift is good in those in
whom it is acute, and I am thankful for it.

The *pia mater* is the transparent covering of the brain. The term, which also figures in *Twelfth Night,* is a reminder of what a remarkable knowledge Shakespeare had of the anatomy and physiology of the brain, and of medicine in general. There are some seven hundred references to medicine and mental states in Shakespeare's plays and poetry; they are – even by our own standards, says one writer in the *New Scientist* of 20 January 1990 – remarkable for their accuracy. And Shakespeare was a generalist. His medical knowledge was but a small fragment of a vast store of memory covering vocations, customs, law and the legal process, sex, love, the royal courts, aristocracy and diplomacy, as well as a great familiarity with low life, and a prodigious knowledge of the Bible and mythology. His store of memory teamed with general knowledge, with the language to do it justice, with the vision to see the story and the creative power to put it all together on the page. This was 'the gift'.

It was the flight, the 'airy nothing', the 'without volition', the free association, the 'motions', the wildness of the literary imagination – the Romantics so timely in their insistence – that scared historians off, affirming their attachment to the hard facts to be found in the archives and encouraging them, until recently, to see their discipline as a social science rather than a branch of literature.

The rift settled into a sharp though not unchallenged distinction, a set of binary opposites – fiction and non-fiction, hot and cold, heart and head, fancy and reality, emotion and reason – literature and history. Historians were better loaded up with weights than liberated by wings and so, for well over a century, the weighted keepers of objective knowledge held the centre. But their authority rested, finally, on propositions about objectivity that were riddled with self-deception and denial. The centre could not hold. Twentieth-century historians were constantly wondering whether their discipline was a humanity or a social science. In the first half of that century they were inclined to think the latter; by the closing decades, the former. As Ann Curthoys and John Docker argue in *Is History Fiction?* (UNSW Press, 2006), 'the 1980s and 1990s would become a kind of Herodotean period of extended thinking about history as literary form; and of historians engaging in literary experimentation in imaginative and innovative ways.' This 'extended thinking' must surely extend all the way to the much saluted but rarely interrogated concept of historical imagination.

What are we doing when we imagine as historians? How does imagining differ from cold hard analysis, grilling the documents, pattern-spotting, critiquing rivals? Is it just the soft fringe of a hard discipline – here a few emotional insights into character, there a bit of scenery-evoking (atmospherics, that 'vivid pictorial sense', the novelist's empathy on loan), flounce and frills, stuff best consigned to narrative history for the trade market? Or is it in some cognitive sense a form or a part of analysis in its own right? Is the historical imagination fundamental to the practice of history?

INGA CLENDINNEN ARTICULATES better than most the complexity of the historian's task. Many of her essays over the past decade or so have touched on historical practice and the state of the discipline. The diversity of her subject matter in these essays belies an underlying, passionate cause – to define and defend the historical project, to spell out the strict limits of what is possible in history, and to explore and to maximise the 'recuperative' possibilities within those limits. Her writings are a must-read for anyone interested in the historical imagination, for she clearly articulates the oneness of the empirical and the creative aspects of history, the literary and analytical unity, the seemingly paradoxical notion that doing history requires a complete and strict subservience to the facts in the historical record as well as a capacity for richly imagining the past. History has to stick scrupulously to the facts – the surviving scraps from the past that we call the historical record – and yet history at its best will deliver up, out of those facts, a 'richly imagined, richly populated and *previously unknown* world'. How do we do that? How do we keep ourselves nice, pure and yet, somehow, engage with the imaginative dimension of the craft to deliver up something of these lost worlds, something lost, now regained, something vivid *and* new?

Clendinnen's persistence in exploring this paradox, I think, comes out of a particular political or politicised context: on the one hand, the postmodern assault on the discipline of history and, on the other, the fundamentalist broadside – the pretensions to exactitude and the crude empiricism of Keith Windschuttle and his supporters in politics and the media.

Clendinnen's history is meticulously grounded in the extant texts and yet, finally, it transcends them – extracting from what is there more than what is there. 'Imagination is a form of courage,' wrote the novelist Janet Frame. That applies to history as much as to fiction, but in history it is also a discipline in its own right; indeed, it begins with the 'discipline of context'. Great history is imagination disciplined by facts.

Take, for instance, this case study from Clendinnen's much-celebrated book *Dancing with Strangers* (Text Publishing, 2003). The spearing of Governor Phillip at Manly Cove in 1790 is an iconic moment in Australian history. Phillip had landed with a small party, two boats, hoping to make contact with a large party of Aboriginal people – Australians – who were feasting on the carcass of a whale. There was a sequence of exchanges distinguished above all by the language barrier and the limits of comprehension, although some meaning could be deciphered here and there. How did this exchange end up with Phillip badly injured, a spear through his shoulder, and the boat parties making a frantic retreat?

Drawing solely on the British accounts – for there are no others – Clendinnen describes with great care a complicated pantomime acted out between the British, led by Phillip, and the Australians, for whom the demonstrative Baneelon did most of the (mostly unintelligible) talking. The dramatic high point is the moment when an unknown warrior spears Phillip, and the British make that hasty retreat into their boats and row for home, deeply shocked and revisiting the encounter in talk and thought (and later in writing), trying to make sense of it.

What did happen? Firstly, Clendinnen examines the British accounts, extracting as much reliable information from them as possible, about the sequence of events and the details of behaviour at each step along the way to the spearing. This is a meticulous process requiring an ear for inflection, nuance, silences and, importantly, the innocent but significant discrepancies between one account and another. The objective is to conjure as precise a description of sequence and action – that is, of the immediate context – as is possible from multiple, varying and in some ways contradictory accounts.

Next, Clendinnen takes careful note of the assumptions of the British commentators – what they make of the Australians' actions and motives at each and every point along the way. She notes how the British accounts, notwithstanding some residual puzzlement, are shaped by racial assumptions that deny the Australians any real agency: the 'natives' are irrational; their 'actions are purely reactions to British actions'. Unlike the British, they do not have 'conscious agendas'. The why, as posed in these accounts, is answered with what she identifies as the 'panic/accident hypothesis'.

The next step is what Clendinnen calls the 'silent-film strategy', the task of considering the sequenced actions without the 'authoritative British voice-overs'. Clearly her intense engagement with the record has arrived at a point where a certain visualisation is possible, a picture of events, doubtless somewhat fogged by the lens of time but a visual sequence nonetheless and, this time, 'silent', allowing the historian to look again in order to fathom the meaning of what she sees, in particular to understand the Australians' intentions. This is a kind of 'double vision', she says, a second way of seeing the actions that comprise the event.

From context, detail and, finally, visualisation, the historian is able to imagine an entirely different interpretation of what happened, a 'silent film' in which the sequence makes sense in terms of the 'retrieved intentions' of the Australians, the second vision in that double vision: the superior account confirmed by reference to, and consistency with, the record. In this account Clendinnen makes entirely new sense of the strange reticence of Baneelon and his compatriots, of Baneelon's subsequent performance as a kind of master of ceremonies, of the gifts exchanged and the puzzling refusal when Phillip asks for an unusual spear, the spear that is ultimately hurled at him by, it now seems, a carefully positioned warrior.

What the British concluded was 'panic' following a cautious reconciliation was most likely the culmination of a hastily improvised ritual spearing in which Phillip, the Governor, was singled out to pay a penalty for various outrages committed against the Australians, not least the kidnapping of Baneelon just months before. (He was there by virtue of having escaped.)

This is opportune payback arising from a conscious Australian agenda, seizing the moment when the British unexpectedly drop in at Manly. As Clendinnen concludes: 'Having inquired into this and other events, I am coming to think that Australian politics was not tradition-bound, as sentimentalists choose to think, but flexible and opportunistic, as is often the case in societies where warriors and hunting prowess stands high.'

The 'silent film' or 'double vision' strategy works in this instance precisely because the established sequence and actions – derived from an intense engagement with the available texts – make far more sense when the opportune-payback interpretation is applied than the reactive natives-panic hypothesis.

Clendinnen's method here is a clear, step-by-step exhibition of the historical reasoning and imagination at work together. It is all the more helpful because her terminology identifies the way that rigorous empirical work shifts at a certain, advanced point in the inquiry, onto a visual plane that carries interpretation through to explanation.

But this moment is something more than visual: it is the situation on that beach loaded up with the uncertainties of the moment, with possible motives, with intentions, with anxious contingencies, and with the intensity of feelings (as best we might intuit them), some hidden, some explicit, feeding into this uneasy encounter between strangers who must guess as they go. It is the imagining of the still fluid context, with its spontaneous possibilities. It is the historian immersed in the unfolding plot, of unclear direction, with outcomes as yet unresolved, more or less unpredictable. It is the immediacy of the past, the still fluid context of that present back then. It is the visual, yes, but the visual loaded with transcendent understanding.

The phrase 'the still fluid context' comes from the English historian Hugh Trevor-Roper, who argued for the importance of the historical imagination as the capacity 'to restore to the past its lost uncertainties, to reopen, if only for an instant, the door which the *fait accompli* has closed'. By 'still fluid context' he meant a past circumstance or situation in its unresolved condition, before the *fait accompli*, with all those uncertainties, all the contingencies and their possibilities, plans and ambitions – hoped for, wished for, fought for – still in play: 'History is not merely what happened,' he wrote. 'It is what happened in the context of what might have happened.' When Barbara Tuchman was asked how she wrote *The Guns of August* (1962), about the first month of World War I, she said, 'I wrote as if I did not know who would win.'

Grace Karskens has achieved something similar in her recent book, *The Colony* (Allen & Unwin, 2009), where she has, through meticulous and wide-ranging research, mapped the variety and ubiquity of the Eora presence in Sydney over some thirty to forty years of colonisation. And behold! Another Sydney town, a vision no historian had hitherto comprehended or seen or delivered up to a readership. The fascination of *The Colony* is the openness of Karskens' evocation – a colonial town loaded with cross-cultural relationships of such variety; relationships that in their totality amounted to that 'still fluid' time, with the richness of possibilities that preceded what was eventually seen as the *fait accompli*, so much so that these preliminaries have been all but forgotten or, at least, never comprehended in their meaningful totality or, indeed, in their transition to something else.

The great English historian EP Thompson expands on this way of seeing in his essay 'Historical Logic':

In investigating history we are not flicking through a series of 'stills', each of which shows us a moment of social time transfixed into a single eternal pose: for each one of these 'stills', is not only a moment of being but also a moment of becoming: and even within each seemingly-static section there will be found contradictions and liaisons, dominant and subordinate elements, declining or ascending energies. Any historical moment is both a result of prior process and an index towards the direction of its future flow.

The historical imagination entails a lift out of the texts, to a new vision that is both from and beyond them; it is the perception of these energies in process – closely described episodes framed by panoramic grasp. To convey it fully, to get it down, the historian requires something of the generalist skills we noted earlier – a rich and varied store of memory (that composite of education and experience and wide general knowledge) combined with the capacity to see a new story and the creative power to put it on the page:

> ...begot in the
> ventricle of memory, nourished in the womb of
> *pia mater*, and delivered upon the mellowing
> of occasion.

Imagination is the creative faculty of the mind wherein new images and conceptions – things and ideas hitherto unknown – are summoned into the world. The natural home of the imagination is supposedly fiction or art: Dickens' London ('Fog, fog everywhere...'), Patrick White's Voss (in that landscape of desert and mind), Picasso's diffracted faces. But conjuring new images and conceptions has a vital place in other disciplines too – in physics, for instance, or in geology or evolutionary biology. Charles Darwin was emphatic about the importance of the imagination in his work. The young Darwin had his own phrase for this transcendent way of seeing. Long before he wrote *On the Origin of Species* (1859) he called it the 'eye of reason' – an insight as important to history as it is to science.

Perhaps the most quoted instance of Darwin reflecting on imagination appears in his *Voyage of the Beagle* journal (1839) following his observations of the Pacific coral reef known as the Enewetak Atoll. At that time Enewetak was no more than a ring of coral on the fringe of a sinking island mountain. Darwin theorised that corals can only live near the ocean's surface and that in nature's artful way coral polyps built upon previous generations of coral reef as their land base sunk, a process possible because the simultaneous sinking and building took place over fifty million years or so. So coral builds upon coral imperceptibly, life building upon death, inexorably. Darwin's presentation of his counter-subsidence theory in *The Voyage of the Beagle* journal sparked a passage that would become almost as well known as anything he later wrote in *On the Origin of Species*. Here was a rare moment when he was demonstrating his imaginative powers and theorising them at the same time:

> We feel surprised when travellers tell us of the vast dimensions of the Pyramids and other great ruins, but how utterly insignificant are the greatest of these, when compared to these mountains of stone accumulated by the agency of various minute and tenders animals! This is a wonder which does not at first strike the eye of the body, but, after reflection, the eye of reason.

The 'eye of reason' is a wonderfully evocative notion. As Darwin explicitly says, this eye is not the eye of the body. It is the eye of the mind, reason's womb, that is being conjured here, and it is this eye that is required to imagine the counter-subsidence artistry of the corals.

What we need is more than the vision, in the ordinary sense, to see motion or patterning across geological time. The object is change fashioned so intricately and so gradually that the eye we require is one that ranges across eons and makes the invisible visible. We see the 'silent film', sped up so we can grasp it in the mind. The only way of seeing this properly is through a narrative of formation. Darwin elaborates:

> The organic forces separate the atoms of carbonate of lime, one by one, from the foaming breakers, and unite them into a symmetrical structure. Let the hurricane tear up its thousand huge fragments;

yet what will that tell against the accumulated labour of myriads of architects at work night and day, month after month?

Darwin is speaking of a transcendence of sorts, an imaginative reach that follows upon these reflections, an awesome choreography. The perception is itself a culmination of a reasoning process. Darwin hypothesises particular acts ('organic forces separate the atoms one by one'); he sees a great number of these acts as a single combined action ('myriads of actors at work night and day'); and – here is that transcendence, the imaginative process at its apogee – he sees, as if in a silent film, how this endless action accumulates into one event, albeit over fifty million years. This is the silent-film strategy in mega proportions, yet somehow compressed so as to be manageable, mentally, visually. It is time-lapse cinematography of the mind. It is why some writers have talked about the Darwinian 'sublime' – the wonder that is embodied in this vision and the experience of grasping it, a powerful reminder that the Romantic impulse and reason can be entirely compatible. Through an act of the imagination Darwin 'projected a sense of nature's ecological complexity that was otherwise unavailable to him' – or anyone else, for that matter. And he had the literary skill to convey his vision persuasively (upon the 'mellowing of occasion'). This, surely, is 'the gift'!

Long before Darwin used the term 'eye of reason' Immanuel Kant grappled with a closely related problem. The sequentiality of Darwin's imaginative act bares comparison with Kant's attempt to articulate imaginative perception. Kant cited the pyramids and asked: How do we see any one of them? How do we 'apprehend' the parts of the object and yet also attempt to comprehend the entirety of the object? Like Darwin, he asked his readers to apprehend the elements sequentially (diachronically for coral, spatially for the pyramid) *and* to 'comprehend' the whole thing, the big picture (the inter-relatedness of the totality in the case of the pyramid; the process, the narrative of formation, in the case of coral). But here, Kant argued, there is a considerable problem, for in coming closer to see the detail you inevitably lose the vision or grandeur of the totality. The sublime moment for Kant is the moment when the mind both apprehends and comprehends at those two levels. The corporeal eye cannot do this, but what we now call the eye of reason can.

Imaginative history is like this. Though confined to historical rather than geological time, it comprehends discrete episodes in relation to a much greater totality. It is microscopic and panoramic, precise and poetic in its re-presentation of detail, and comprehensive in its vision or its grasp of the context in which detail is located. The eye of reason in history inevitably means envisioning holistically, and beyond the orthodoxies of fashionable contemporary interpretations. It means grasping connections, patterns, processes, evolutions. It implies a kind of imaginative sublime. It is a flash of vision and a structure of deep understanding. The historical imagination is a paradox of groundedness and transcendence. It is weights and wings. It is that Kantian moment when the dynamic interplay of the vision, the narrative of formation in its totality and its particularities, is seized and held in the mind, and thereafter refined and perfected in the artistry of the writing.

Perhaps this achievement bears comparison with fully seeing a Monet – the apparently formless ensemble of blotches seen up close and their relation to the exquisite landscape we see on stepping back: from ferment of colours to triumph of form. The truth about patterns and connections between discrete facts in history is that they are not invented, and yet seeing these patterns and grasping the importance of these connections entails a process of imaginative construction that goes far beyond the intrinsic properties of the documentary record. It requires a magisterial capacity for reflection and integration; it is not so much about selection as it is about recognising and naming hidden patterns and pulses, those 'declining and ascending energies', the imminence in a moment, or a season, or an epoch.

WHAT TREVELYAN'S FAMOUS paragraph does so well for the part, EP Thompson's *The Making of the English Working Class* does even better for the whole. *The Making* was published in 1963 and soon recognised as both a literary masterpiece and a vision of Britain's past that was not only original but also possibly unprecedented in its boldness, its informed moral passion and its breadth. The prose was eloquent, percussive and passionate. Critics conceded the poetic richness of the language. Defenders thrilled to the sheer human vitality of the wit and imagery, noting (crucially for my purposes) how the literary achievement was indivisible from the theoretical achievement.

It is almost fifty years since *The Making* was published. Time enough for historians to, quite legitimately, find flaws and limitations that somewhat more tightly frame the achievement. And yet the book has stood the test of time.

The principal achievement of *The Making* is the imaginative reach of Thompson's project combined with the prose, made radiant by his moral passion. The reach is heroic in its poetry, its vividness and originality. As Terry Eagleton has pointed out, the book superbly reveals how the formation of the working class in the Industrial Revolution entailed the creation of a 'counter-public sphere': counter to the bourgeois public sphere that preoccupied mainstream history. 'In the Corresponding Societies, the radical press, Owenism, Cobbett's *Political Register* and Paine's *Rights of Man*, feminism and the dissenting churches, a whole oppositional network of journals, clubs, pamphlets, debates and institutions invades the dominant consensus, threatening to fragment it from within,' writes Eagleton.

It is this grand vision, packed richly with the fruits of the most intricate and painstaking research, that is the imaginative achievement – an extraordinary exercise in the reconstitutive imagination. It is the retrieval of a previously unseen 'underworld' (unseen in any comprehensive and holistic sense). It is an exercise in network construction that takes the reader way beyond the relations of face-to-face groups to a kind of imagined community (an oppositional network) of national proportions. So, for instance, early in the piece Thompson draws into summary form some of the connections that constitute a fragment of his vision. He begins with the artisan Thomas Hardy: a brief biographical profile gets Hardy to London, married, ensconced in his trade and busy in his role as first secretary of the London Corresponding Society. He then moves to a snapshot of the way this network fanned out:

> One of his colleagues, a Chairman of the LCS, was Francis Place, on his way to becoming a master-tailor. The line between the journeyman and the small masters was often crossed – the journeyman boot and shoemakers struck against Hardy in his new role as a small employer in 1795, while Francis Place, before becoming a master-

tailor, helped to organise a strike of Journeymen Breeches-makers in 1793. And the line between the artisan of independent status (whose workroom was also his 'shop') and the small shopkeeper or tradesmen was even fainter. From here it was another step to the world of the self-employed engravers, like William Sharp and William Blake, or printers and apothecaries, teachers and journalists, surgeons and Dissenting clergy.

'Dissenting' being the apposite word, for Thompson is summoning up – to the extent his vast scholarship enables – an entire 'underworld' of dissent, of resistance. He sees that evolving sense of working class commonality that, with the publication of *The Making*, will both disrupt and reshape our understanding of the industrial revolution. His summaries comprehend for us the big picture, so that we might better apprehend or situate the parts within. He goes on to do this, for instance, with London:

> At one end, then, the London Corresponding Society reached out to the coffee-houses, taverns and Dissenting Churches off Piccadilly, Fleet Street and the Strand, where the self-educated journeyman might rub shoulders with the printer, the shopkeeper, the engraver or the young attorney. At the other end, to the east, and south of the river, it touched those older working class communities – the waterside workers of Wapping, the silkweavers of Spitalfields, the old Dissenting stronghold of Southwark. For two hundred years 'Radical London' has always been more heterogeneous and fluid in its social and occupational definition than the Midlands or Northern centres grouped around two or three staple industries…

But, of course, the Midlands and the Northern centres and other regions will have their moments too. Progressively that fluency of focus between the vision and its detail, contexts within the context, will accumulate, building the imaginative achievement into something sublime – both from and beyond the historical record. It is the eye of reason in which the particularities of geography and political culture are framed by the panoramic vision.

METHOD, OR WHAT Thompson calls 'the discipline of context', is where imaginative achievement both starts and finishes for this historian. It is in the discipline of context that 'each fact can be given meaning only within an ensemble of other meanings,' he writes. This requires a magisterial capacity for reflection, selection and integration, for recognising and naming hidden patterns and pulses, networks, affinities, whole spheres of relationships; not the creation of contexts but their retrieval – the reconstitutive imagination in action. It requires, too, 'a sensitivity to tone, awareness of the inner consistency of the text and of the significance of imagery'. Where the discipline of context engages with the poetic (literary artifice), we find the wellspring – the point of anchorage and the point of take-off – of the historical imagination.

For his later study of the eighteenth- and nineteenth-century ritual of humiliation called 'rough music' Thompson noted that he needed not one hundred instances which were imperfectly understood but a much smaller number, ten, or even five, 'in which one can disclose something of the personal history of the victims, the flagrancy of the offence, the kinship relations in the neighbourhood, the insights afforded by some revealing phrase in a deposition'.

These are the micro-studies, the vivid, path-breaking episodes within the totality of the vision. 'History,' wrote Thompson, 'is made up of episodes, and if we cannot get inside them we cannot get inside history at all.' He was a contextualist striving to understand the complex nature of beliefs and behaviours in another time, and fully alive to the extraordinary difficulty of retrieving that otherness from such a distance.

When the historian Iain McCalman wrote in *Darwin's Armada* (Viking, 2009) about Darwin's sojourn in South America and how his reading of Lyell's *Geology* came together with his observations in the Andes, he noted the kind of movement that the 'eye of reason' entailed. McCalman wrote of 'a mind sweeping forward over the entire western coastal terrain of South America, then back through the recesses of time.' In a similar way, we may observe in *The Making of the English Working Class* both the vision and its episodic content in continual interaction, a mind moving freely across time and place over a span of more than half a century of dramatic change, from pre-industrial radical traditions to the experience and material lives of the working classes, and the growth of class consciousness through institutions such as trade unions, friendly societies, religious and educational movements, political organisations, periodicals, intellectual traditions, patterns of community and structures of feeling. We both apprehend and comprehend that 'counter-public sphere' coming together, progressing, faltering, fluctuating, evolving across time.

THE ANTHROPOLOGIST RENATO Rosaldo has argued that Thompson's radical underworld is a literary invention, the product of the author's 'melodramatic' imagination. Rosaldo has suggested that history in *The Making* is the portrayal of conflict simplified into a battle between good and evil. Rosaldo's critique is postmodern in the sense that the achievement in *The Making* is reduced to a literary fiction; it comes down, finally, to passionate artistry (of the melodramatic kind) rather than brilliant analysis.

Rosaldo's observation of Thompson's artistry is in some ways insightful but ultimately misleading. He rightly draws our attention to passages that powerfully portray persecution and suffering, to passages where Thompson quite clearly takes sides, and where his preference for radical spirit over ameliorist purpose is unmistakable and his own presence as passionate historian is unsubtle. But what Rosaldo does not seem to grasp is the analytical achievement. Obsessed with the melodramatic, he is indifferent to the book's vast, deep scholarship. He privileges the 'melodramatic imagination' over the reconstitutive imagination, the understanding that arises from an epic encounter with the historical records. It is as if the 'defensive ideology' of the 'free-born Englishman' or the 'moral economy of the English crowd' or the pitiless, inhibiting dogmas of Methodism were the inventions of a novelist. The critic rightly draws our attention to some features of the literary artifice – for what is historical imagination without it – but he singularly fails to link these features to the scholarly achievement or to inquire into the composition of their crafted unity. It is not a question of passionate artistry or brilliant analysis – imaginative achievement in history comes from the engagement of the two. It spirals, like a double helix, out of their fusion, their working partnership, in the discipline of context.

The American historian Stephen J Pyne, in *Voice and Vision* (Harvard University Press, 2009), writes: 'Style is not merely decorative or ornamental, any more than are feathers on a bird. Style performs work. Whatever its loveliness or ostentation, it is what allows the creatures to fly, to attract mates, to hide from predators, to be what it is.' The observation recalls a line from Julian Barnes's 1984 novel, *Flaubert's Parrot*: 'form isn't an overcoat flung over the flesh of thought…it's the flesh of thought itself.' We are reminded that there's only one true rule – style must reconcile with subject and poetics with historical vision.

What Rosaldo takes to be melodrama is in fact prose made radiant by political passion, wielded, as it happens, by a historian who knew that the research must be immaculate if the politics and the passion are to persuade. The richness of the language, the vitality of the wit and imagery are, therefore, indivisible from the historical achievement – the originality of the vision in all its hitherto unfamiliar particularity. As it was with Darwin.

We cannot acknowledge Thompson's radiant prose without, at the same time, acknowledging the breadth and precision of the research, the stunning act of retrieval that is central to the achievement in *The Making of the English Working Class*. Imagination in the discipline of history is the capacity to see the vision and its parts in continual focus and fluency, and to *render it as literature*. It is the hold on an intricate design and its particulars. It is anchored in the record, recuperative in essence, and yet it soars above that record and, inevitably, is companion to outstanding achievement.

References at www.griffithreview.com

Thanks to Inga Clendinnen, Mary Cunnane, Greg Lockhart, John Hirst, Brian Hoepper, Stuart Macintyre, Iain McCalman, Ros Pesman, Suzanne Rickard, Deryck Schreuder and Julianne Schultz for critical commentary and discussion along the way.

Peter Cochrane lives in Sydney. His most recent book is *Colonial Ambition: Foundations of Australian Democracy* (MUP, 2006), the 2007 *Age* Book of the Year and co-winner of the inaugural Prime Minister's Prize for Australian History. His other books include *Australians at War* and *Simpson and the Donkey: The Making of a Legend*. His discussion of biographical narrative 'Stories from the dustbin' appeared in *Griffith REVIEW 19: Re-imagining Australia*.

ESSAY

White me

Learning from theory and practice

Robert Hillman

IN the course of an average Australian lifetime, a white lifetime, face-to-face communication with Indigenous Australians might be fairly limited. In my own case, five fairly talkative decades have yielded only three brief conversations. The first was with a sister and brother, Esther and Terry, students at an outer-Melbourne high school where I taught in the 1980s. They must have thought my earlier attempts at engagement a bit tedious because they rolled their eyes when I approached them in the playground. I spoke about the need to eat something a little more nourishing than lollies for lunch. 'Like what?' said Terry. 'Like a salad roll, maybe.' 'We did.' 'Oh. Well, that's good.' Esther offered me a jelly snake and off they hurried, wishing to be where I was not.

The second conversation took place in the early 1990s outside the supermarket in Smith Street, Fitzroy, when a man by the name of Mickey with a fabulous sense of entitlement demanded a hundred dollars for his autograph, which I hadn't requested. I said no. Mickey said, 'Better idea. Buy me a flagon. Can yuh?' I bought him a flagon of Seppelts from the supermarket's bottle shop and he sauntered away singing the chorus of 'The Gambler', his trademark tune.

The third conversation, on a St Kilda tram, was more protracted; was, in fact, five conversations, but since the entire five employed the same words, the same questions, the same responses, I think of them as just the one. At that time, the mid-1990s, a group of Aborigines had established a type of tent embassy in Cleve Gardens, at the intersection of Fitzroy Street and Beaconsfield Parade, right beside the route of the number 16 tram and not far from St Kilda Beach. The park was dominated by a number of ancient Moreton Bay Figs, and under these trees a construction of cardboard, orange blankets and black plastic sheeting was reassembled after each episode of windy weather. It was the contention of those occupying the little park that the Moreton Bay Figs rightfully belonged to the Wurundjeri people, as did all of the land on which the City of St Kilda stood. The High Court decision in the case of *Mabo v. Queensland (No. 2)* was only four years old, and the Native Title Act still younger, but the Cleve Garden Aborigines apparently felt that their moral

---

PREVIOUS PAGE: Richard Bell. *Life on a mission*, 2009. Acrylic on canvas. 240 x 360cm. Courtesy of the artist and Milani Gallery. www.milanigallery.com.au

right to the little park should at least be advertised.

I caught the number 16 tram on the Esplanade above Luna Park at 3.20 each weekday afternoon. At 3.24, the tram made its scheduled stop opposite Koori Park, as the Moreton Bay Fig plantation had come to be called. For five consecutive days, a guy I came to know as Danny in an unravelling Rasta snood, an Everlast tracksuit and French Star sneakers sprinted from the park, jumped aboard the tram, travelled three stops to St Kilda Junction, then jumped off. Why he needed to board the tram and travel a kilometre at 3.24 each day I never discovered. The tram was rarely full and Danny was always able to find his way to where I sat reading EP Thomson's *The Making of the English Working Class* in an impressive edition with a bright red cover. Our conversation went like this.

Danny: You like readin'?
Me: Yep.
Danny: Name's Danny.
Me: Robert. [Handshake]
Danny: Got a place back there.
Me: In the park?
Danny: S'good. Close to the beach.
Me: Ah!
Danny: Saw yuh yesterday, didn't I?
Me: Yep.
Danny: Got any spare change? [Danny pronounced this as one word, 'sparechain']
Me: Sure. [I handed over a couple of two-dollar coins.]
Danny: On ya, bro. Gotta get off. See yuh!
Me: See yuh!

These few conversations, and no more. Aborigines do not come to the parties I'm invited to; do not eat at the restaurants I frequent; do not appear at any of the professional gatherings of writers I attend; do not sit beside me at the cricket or the football; do not live next door to me in Carlton; do not enter the supermarkets at which I shop, nor any other venue of commerce familiar to me; do not share a class with my children; do not date me, marry me, bear my children; do not send me emails about books I've written; do not telephone me. If an official Australian version of apartheid were in force that restricted contact between white me and black them, it could hardly be more effective in its mission than this accidental apartheid that makes me no more than a blur to the original inhabitants of my native land, and they so unfamiliar to me.

This needn't bother me, this lack of contact with Aborigines, but it does. It bothers others, too. If you have a native land, best strive to know its complexity; what it gets right, what it fucks up; its fears, frenzies, phobias; its rewards. There are a number of muddled stories of my native land that I've known since I was a kid – gold in the topsoil here and there, sheep everywhere, a man in a metal suit with a six-shooter, men in slouch hats dying in droves in the North Aegean – that alter over the years but remain engaging. But the story of the black men was always a shambles for white me. The black men were here when the ships came, but in a way they were not; they were pissed off, but patchily, never forming a magnificent army of national resistance; they lived in the desert and understood things that a white man could barely fathom, but the things they knew – the path taken by an escaped convict who had left no tracks at all, where to find water where there was no water – were fascinating, yes, but not fantastic. A teacher in my high school in rural Victoria told the class that the North American Indians were more advanced than the Australian Aborigines because the Indians rode horses and used bows and arrows. I shot up my hand. 'What about the boomerang?' The teacher replied, 'A boomerang is a stick.' His retort set a tone of mild denigration that has troubled me ever since. It seemed wrong that our teacher had not taken the opportunity to make the black men more vivid to us.

What became more vivid was not the black men themselves, but the injustice that burdened them: the land from which the Aborigines had harvested such bounty had, by a process that blended insinuation and armed robbery, been gathered up by a determined people even more advanced than the North American Indians. Dispossessed, abused, humiliated, demoralised, they became the people I was unable to know or understand other than in the context of argument. My politics took over as the governing reference of my commitment to fathoming Aborigines. But allowing my politics to fashion the questions I asked had shortcomings. 'Injustice' became a slogan. Everything I read about Aborigines had to find its home under a heading. A sequence of slogans is not a narrative.

AT AROUND THE time of John Howard's dismissal of any obligation to issue an apology to Indigenous Australians for a couple of centuries of abuse, I was living with a woman who spoke with Aborigines every working day of the year. She ran an outreach agency in Collingwood where the majority of her clients were homeless blacks, and before that she'd managed an Aboriginal community in Western Australia. Her clients adored her, but on a bad day might still toss about terms like 'stupid white cunt' and threaten to have her kneecapped. The abuse didn't bother her; the more inventive insults delighted her. She said, 'It's just the dope,' or, 'It's the piss.' What I knew about Aborigines remained a mess, but I was feeling my way towards a Pearsonian model of tough love. I thought her forbearance left her open to exploitation and felt offended on her behalf. She told me once that she'd spent months looking for a house for a black couple and their baby, only to have the family wander off in a week.

'In a week! Don't they care how much trouble you took? Doesn't that drive you nuts?'

'No. Stop talking about it.'

She came to wince at my responses to incidents like that. They made me seem impatient and ignorant, and it was at that time important to her that she should like me. I was a version of the concerned white man who wants Indigenous Australians to prosper, but who quickly becomes exasperated when they don't. When my friend said, 'Stop talking about it,' what she wanted me to understand was that my goodwill was an easily exhausted resource, and unreliable. Her own way of thinking about Indigenous Australians had nothing to do with mere goodwill. She had overcome the temptation to place Aborigines in a category of the marginalised, or in a category of any sort. They were, to my friend, as various in character as non-Aboriginals, but burdened in a way remote to the experience of non-Aboriginals.

In each of us there is a neglected graveyard of the convictions that once excited us, convictions interred with the questions that expressed the liveliness of our interest. One of the overgrown headstones in my personal graveyard reads, 'The Inevitable Victory of the Proletariat!' and another, 'You Can Live on Lentils!' But we retain our original enthusiasm for maybe two or three early convictions, and return to them, in a struggling way, again and again. The predicament of Indigenous Australians vexes me. I think for some time I have wished Aborigines to flourish by being more like me. I've wanted them to buy houses in the shining place where I live, and hail me at the supermarket, join me on the sofa at parties and say, after a genial howdy, 'Global warming, fuck me, what do you do?' In spite of all that I know of their burden, all that I've read, I seem to have an irreducible conviction that it will all be okay if more Aborigines would only read Kant and Hume and Sartre and maybe a selection of contemporary writers of fiction I'd like to foist on them. My criticism of the federal and state programs (well intentioned, some of them generous) that are supposed to benefit Aborigines has been that they are unimaginative, but my own schemes for Aboriginal advancement are just as unimaginative, although in a more imaginative way.

I met a man at a dinner party, an ex-AFL player, who'd spent some years travelling to Aboriginal communities in the far north to talk about Australian Rules football. By this time my slogans had evolved into theories, in reverse of the usual process that sees theories expressed as slogans. I'd sucked the raw and the cooked out of Claude Levi-Strauss and the nourishment produced a brainwave: the intractable cognitive structures of Indigenous Australians make it impossible for them to negotiate the alien binary structures of European culture. The 'gift' of a house does not establish the reciprocal challenge of valuing the house, because the gift of a house contradicts the social urge to take off at will; reciprocation would amount to alienation of liberty. I put this formidable coup of reasoning together with the argument of Alan Moorehead's *The Fatal Impact* (white man, big ship, tropic climes, booze, syphilis, catastrophe) and uttered these words, with which I must live, to the footballer: 'Primitive people are doomed from the moment that a white man extends his hand and says, "Good morning, I intend you no harm."' The footballer wanted to know to whom I was referring when I said, 'primitive peoples'. I said, 'Aborigines,' and he changed the subject.

I remained attracted to the theory (discredited by cultural anthropologists, as I learned) because it appeared to establish fate as the greatest of all culprits in the playing out of the tragedy. Politically, philosophically, fate is a bimbo, but a goddess in a literary context. I began to think of the Aborigines as a tragic people who might be represented in a whopper novel as an Arcadian race honouring their god with dance and song even as the well-armed priests of a fresher, fiercer deity anchored their ships off shore.

The conception had shortcomings outside the literary context – it suggested that the Aboriginal people were doomed, and that the richness of their heritage, the vigour and variety of all that they imagined, their deeds and ambitions would be unavailing, would be swept away in a diaspora of unrelieved suffering and misery. But the suggestion was forgivable because they would live in art forever, these condemned people: live in the novel. Tragedy immortalises. Oedipus, the regent of a dopey little state in the blithering long-ago, is now famous in song and legend, and in the annals of psychopathology.

FOR ME, FOREVER, data is what it is and never what it might be. And this is true even when the data catalogues atrocity. The number of European Jews who were murdered by the Nazis before and during World War II is horrifying, but numbers are not a narrative any more than are my slogans. In his memoir *If This Is a Man* Primo Levi created (and 'created' is a crucial word) a narrative of suffering and human wretchedness that bows your head to your chest with sorrow. And your head stays there, in a certain sense, for the rest of your life. What we honour with our sorrow is in part the success of the writer in fashioning his story, and the writer himself, herself, honours those he or she writes about by writing well.

The superficiality of my theories about the situation of Aboriginal Australians persisted until 2009, when I was encouraged by a friend to read Howard Goldenberg's recent memoir, *Raft* (Hybrid). Goldenberg is a Melbourne-based GP who has spent part of each of the past twenty years serving as a locum in Aboriginal communities all over Australia. *Raft* is his record of the joy, the madness and the sorrow of those twenty years.

Goldenberg's grasp of the predicament of Aborigines is distinguished from my own in this important regard: he knows what he's talking about. His work has taken him to more than forty Aboriginal communities in five states, most of them represented to the broader Australian community as sites of despair, which some are. Goldenberg finds the language to describe the despair in ways that eclipse my enthusiastic conception of a structuralist black tragedy: 'When I arrive in Hall's Creek, I am greeted by a passing parade of silent figures…floating noiselessly like spirits along the streets of their own town…At night it is the opposite, the people are heard, but dark-skinned in the moonless dark, not readily seen. They cry out hoarsely, harshly, sounds of abuse, the odd scream, cries punctuated by peels of riotous laughter.'

A tour of the underworld demands composure, and Goldenberg maintains the poise of a consoler whose responsibilities extend to bearing witness: 'Elijah…can barely speak or move his facial muscles. He cradles an ice pack against his right temple and cool towels swathe his forehead and cheek. I remove these coverings and find blistered skin and raw patches where the skin falls away in sheets…His aunt who has sat impassively by him, now speaks: "He copped a kicking. They kicked him all over. Then they threw a kettle of boiling water over him."'

And: 'A nurse asks me to see Zachariah. He came in with a spot of pus on his left elbow. When she started to mop up the bead of pus with some moistened gauze, the skin fell away…The more the nurse cleaned, the deeper and wider became the exposed area, until the bones of the elbow were exposed…'

And: 'A phone call from the local Aboriginal Health Centre warns of the imminent arrival of a man who fell asleep and rolled into a fire and stayed asleep. When they bring him into the hospital, he is barely awake. We roll up the charred fabric of his trousers, exposing a white "sock" of pallid, bloodless muscle tissue that has been cooked.'

Goldenberg is a man liberated in his sympathies, in the same way that my friend in the outreach agency was in hers. He diagnoses a patient, Jonathan, with a respiratory illness so severe that the man must be flown from his community to the hospital at Alice Springs, nine hundred kilometres away. Goldenberg attends Jonathan on the flight, mopping up the vivid green sputum that his patient sprays over himself and his doctor in his paroxysms of coughing. A week after delivering Jonathan to hospital, Goldenberg telephones to enquire about his one-time patient's condition and is told that he has left the hospital, discharged himself weeks or months too early. 'Doesn't it drive you nuts?' I said to my friend, and she said, 'No. Stop talking about it.' Goldenberg ends the story of Jonathan by quoting the nurse who answered the phone: 'He left this morning. Jonathan's going home to his own country.'

Witness to some of the most appalling things happening in Australia at any given time, Goldenberg lets the horror speak for itself. At one settlement, a young man dances for the visiting Prime Minister, but later plunges into a booze-fuelled ecstasy of violence:

'That night, the young dancing man drinks, fights with his young wife. She too has been drinking. The man stabs her many, many times. She falls, apparently dead. The violent young man goes into the bush with a rope and he hangs himself.

The young woman survives.

Now she faces a new danger: her husband has died following a fight between them. She hears that the clan elders deem her culpable in his death, and decide she must face the death penalty.

She can never return to her husband's camp or clan. She must fly to refuge on the remotest island of her own clan.'

The mayhem, the madness, the pity of it bows down even those who have made it their mission to buoy the raft on which so many desperate people struggle to survive:

'I witness scenes that distress even veteran workers in these communities. In Mutijulu once, I met a nurse who said, "I'm leaving, my time is up."

I wondered whether she had completed a contract.

"No," she said. "You know when your time is up."

"How do you know?"

She looked away, fell into silence, then replied, "The horror. You can't take any more."'

Any doctor serving the Aboriginal communities of remote Australia is in something of the situation of a medic in a nineteenth-century wound-dressing station. The casualties keep coming, the damage to flesh and organs is awful, and the hopelessness of it all must become overwhelming. Goldenberg worries aloud about the small benefit (in the greater scheme of things) of his time and skill in this war of self-harm: 'I have found myself uncomfortable in many ways. I have felt helpless, and confused by my helplessness; irrelevant and occasionally absurd. I have experienced shock and moral disorientation. Numb hopelessness followed, then a phase of toxic resignation. Later came a calmer state of acceptance, which left me open to encouragement; and mostly now I maintain a poised refusal of acceptance.'

The steady patience of Goldenberg's ministrations does not go unrewarded. He experiences the grace of gratitude from people who have grace as the only gift they can offer. He is listened to raptly on Elcho Island when he sings a Hebrew psalm, his own gift. And he is sometimes permitted to come close and gaze on the remaining, still perfect fragments of men and women whose ancestors thrived in the best of all possible worlds.

GOLDENBERG'S BOOK TAKES its title from Rod Moss's 1990 painting depicting a number of identifiably Aboriginal figures, men and women, in an arid landscape, a ramshackle corrugated iron humpy in the background. Moss's painting quotes Gericault's 1819 masterpiece *Le radeau de la Méduse* (The Raft of the Medusa), displayed in the Louvre. Gericault's picture shows the last of the survivors of the foundered French vessel *Méduse* adrift on a raft in the South Atlantic after memorable incompetence on the part of the ship's captain. *Le radeau de la Méduse* is work of profound pessimism; all of its suggestions direct the viewer's thought to the perfidy of individuals and classes, and to the savagery that lies coiled within us. Moss's work is not pessimistic; rather, the viewer is asked to reflect on the sorrow of it all, and the pity. A female figure in the foreground cradles a male figure who may be dead, may be dying, may be just completely out of it. Two figures behind gesture towards the horizon above the arid plain, or else toward something missing from the picture. But nothing in the picture suggests that any of the human figures is pleading for rescue, or expects it. If there is any sense of something desired, it is that which is missing, whatever that may be.

Goldenberg's book, disguised as a casual collection of episodes in the Never Never, is actually a deeply considered work of art that honours Aboriginal Australians with its craft and its humility. It brings to the literature of the Aboriginal burden a peculiarly Jewish sensibility, a Jewish comprehension of what people are compelled to endure. Exposed to that sensibility and craft, I understood what a further decade of employing slogans and fashioning theories wouldn't have revealed: that Indigenous Australians have not been waiting with bated breath for me to work it all out to my own satisfaction. I realised for the first time that it's not about white me.

Robert Hillman is the author of four novels and the award-winning memoir *The Boy in the Green Suit* (Scribe, 2003), and the co-author of *My Life as a Traitor* (Scribe, 2007). His essays have been published in *Griffith REVIEW*: *Family Politics*, *Divided Nation* and *After the Crisis*.

REPORTAGE

At the gateway of hope

Back to remote Australia

Howard Goldenberg

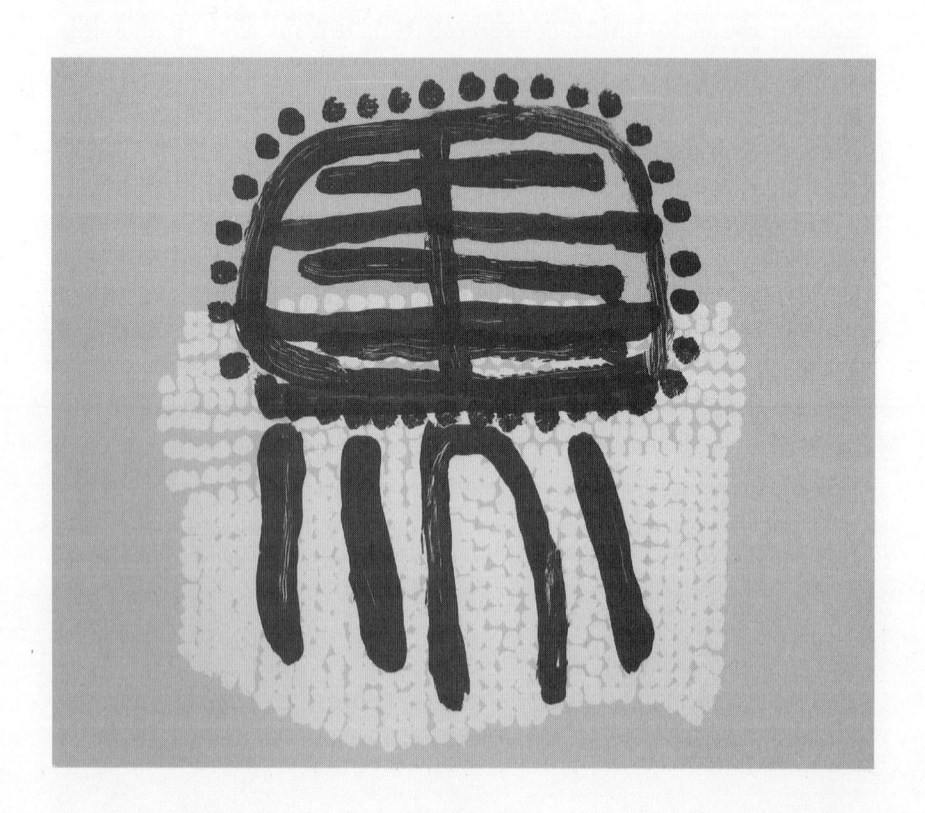

Aboriginal and Torres Strait Islanders are advised that the following piece contains the names and voices of people who have died.

ON a number of occasions over the years 2005 to 2007 I worked as a relieving doctor in the Kimberley. Three times I was in Halls Creek, and once each in Balgo, Ringers Soak, Mullum and Fitzroy Crossing. In these desert places I saw degradation and I contracted a condition new to me: a sort of hopeless resignation.

Later I made single working visits to the coastal communities of Bidyadanga, Lombadina, One Arm Point and Beagle Bay. Here I contracted a reverse condition: a sort of elated hopefulness.

From time to time I'd visit headquarters in Broome. *Unreal city.* Tourism and natural gas have overthrown a town that overthrew the tribes. The gas and the resorts exert their gravitational pull, and tides of people flood in and flood out, distorting life in the town. Blackfellas who merge into the employed classes, and thrive as citizens, remain cultural question marks – as do the smaller numbers who clutch bottles in brown paper bags and congregate in the parks, going nowhere in a go-ahead town. Neither group is a reliable signpost of Indigenous wellbeing. Unreadable, Broome town is unrepresentative even of itself.

I went to each community to allow a longer-term doctor to take a breather. I banked on extending the doctor's tenure and usefulness. I saw myself as a sort of rescuer for the real rescuers, those doctors who came and stayed. The metaphor was of a raft saving people from shipwreck.

I went to work as a doctor; soon I found myself writing a book, *Raft*. The book sold out. I hoped that I had not done just that myself. Now, in 2010, I was going to the Kimberley to work once again. I wondered what I'd see, how much I'd blush over the judgements I had written.

PREVIOUS PAGE: Weaver Jack. *Nanarra*, 2007. Screenprint 49.5 x 39.5cm. Courtesy of the artist and Short Street Gallery, Broome, WA. www.shortstgallery.com.au

BIDYADANGA: IN 2007, I saw a gateway of hope here. Excited, inspired, I wrote hopefully of the community. This time I try to look beyond the gateway. I go to work again at the clinic. Dr Larni – bright, idealistic, solid, practical Dr Larni – who told me she wanted to stay, has gone. I look around: lots of nurses, none familiar.

I start seeing patients. The receptionist greets me: 'Hello, Howard. Welcome back.' She remembers me from my earlier visit. Her name is Christine Shovellor. 'My family's band is playing tomorrow night. Come along and listen.'

The staff are new, but the atmosphere in the clinic is the same: still the informal respect, the calm, opportunistic medicine. The patient – here, now – presents an opportunity to improve health. Beyond the need of the moment, beyond filling a prescription, bandaging a finger or suturing a laceration, the nurses seize the chance to do something broader and deeper. They look at that whole person who is the patient: does her family suffer from diabetes, heart disease, violence? Are her immunisations up to date? How's her blood pressure, her blood sugar level, the penicillin cover for her rheumatic heart disease?

Throughout the Kimberley they have a new computer system for health records. As it is new there are teething problems. There are grumbles about its slowness from computer sophisticates and tremors from the computer-naive. I am one of the tremblers. But, thanks to the tiny Polish-Jewish pharmacist in Broome who created the system and enforces it doggedly, the old chasms of inconsistent medical records are closing. Wherever a patient moves in the Kimberley, her medical data precede her. No matter that she has no mind for drug names, and the names and nature of her tests remain elusive, and her frames for time are not linear or calendrical: we health people can retrieve the information we need.

I ASK A teacher at the school: Do you still have the walking bus that visits every household, every morning, and pied-pipers the kids to school?

'No. Its time has passed. There's a new principal, new ideas. The old head has been moved on.' Incredible. All too credible. And disappointing.

The swimming pool, gleaming sapphire in this red country, is closed.

The temperature will reach 30 degrees today, but the pool is closed for winter. Too cold, says the teacher.

Another disappointment: last time I was here they had a 'no school, no pool' rule. What does the closure do to school attendance?

Later, another teacher at the school gives cheering information: 'In the days of the walking bus school attendance was eighty per cent. Now it's ninety per cent plus.'

The teacher has children of his own at school. Ambitious, gifted, highly motivated, these kids are in years nine and eleven. They study a specific curriculum by correspondence. I wonder why.

'It's not that the school's not good enough. It's a matter of subject choice. Country schools can't offer Indonesian and French and other subjects that my kids want.'

I ask the teacher where he's from. 'Near Beechworth, in northern Victoria. Before that, Newcastle.'

When will he be moving on?

'I plan to stay. We are making our lives here. When my term's up the department will move me on for a bit, but I'll wait out my time, reapply and return.'

OUTSIDE THE CLINIC, something is missing. Wandering on foot through town, running the tracks in the early morning, there's something I'm not seeing: where is the litter? Where are the carcases of derelict vehicles? Bidyadanga is one remote community that doesn't mock its Tidy Town sign.

Bidyadanga is a dry-ish community. (Is there any place that is truly grog-proof?) Bidgy is dry not by fiat but by assent. The locals do not permit alcohol in town, except in the precinct of the old Mission. Some hangover from communion wine. And you can take grog beyond town, to the beach.

On my first night I'm invited to a send-off party in the Mission precinct for some veteran nurses. Whitefellas and blackfellas attend; alcohol is consumed legally and moderately.

The next night I drive down the beach to listen to the Shovellor Band.

My nightlife is picking up. A mixed audience of some hundreds sits, picknicking on fish and chips, listening to old covers and fresher material of the Shovellors' own. Hundreds of fish and spuds beyond counting disappear. Is there alcohol? I can't remember anyone drinking.

In three days, among nine hundred people, there is no drunkenness. It's un-Australian.

LAST TIME I was here, I was honoured to make the acquaintance of an illustrious traditional owner. Aged and skeletal, gracious and enormously proud, the old man was a member of that group in Bidyadanga that has always resided here. There are four other groups whose ancestors were desert people.

I had not contemplated the resulting natural hierarchy: the coastal group has a moral authority over its ancestral lands, which is expressed in decidedly material ways. Tradition is tyrannous. Democracy is an alien concept. On this visit I hear murmurings of discontent. Those in power are 'holding the town back' in some unspecified way.

The desert mob are in perpetual exile. The result of this is great art. A painting movement has exploded over the past five years or so, as desert elders, the last of the generation of first contact, who 'came in' in the 1950s and '60s, paint their pain and longing onto canvases that sell out as soon as they reach the market.

Back in Broome, I go with my wife to the gallery in Short Street that is the painters' exclusive conduit to the public. This sort of monopoly might be anything from efficient to exploitative. The young woman in the office, Concetta, invites us to The Bungalow, where the old folks paint when visiting Broome. Here we encounter the works of Weaver Jack, the oldest of the oldies. Raw power, a passion for the land where she will never live again, cries out from the canvases. They grip us. Power of this sort threatens serious assault on the wallet.

We sit and listen as Concetta describes the painters and their work. Concetta confides that she was brought up in a home where much was taught, but religion was entirely absent. She and her sister are just starting to read the Bible. They want to encounter foundation stories of their own culture. Concetta's bearing is animated and almost yearning as she recounts the famous return to country of the old people, after fifty years or more of exile. She was a member of the convoy that travelled for days over trackless dunes, guided by the old people, who relied on their memory of that great trek to the coast when they were young. All the way, the old people sang, sang the land, its stories and contours, its shapes and its echoes.

Concetta breaks off her narrative now, leaning forward, smiling, as she listens to dim sound from the next room. 'They are singing now,' she says softly. 'They often sing as they paint. Weaver and her friends, they paint their country and they sing.'

Eventually, the old people arrived at the place of desert water. Concetta and the other whitefellas saw only the same unending dunes. The old people got out of the vehicles, and dug. Their uncovering of the *Jila*, the place of water, was a consummation. The people and their land were again one. That moment, that journey, sustains an art movement. It seems that this was Concetta's exposure to a defining spiritual life. She became a witness. As she gives her ecstatic account we sense not exploitation but its opposite. Concetta is in spiritual thrall of the custodians of that country.

WEAVER AND OTHER old ones paint like there is no tomorrow, knowing that to be true. Meanwhile, the young blade who led them back to the homelands on that epic return paints too. Although greatly in demand he refuses to paint fast. He is not tempted by commercial opportunity. 'He is young,' says Concetta, and smiles as if to say: the young have plenty of time.

Back in Bidyadanga, there are others who are working like there's no tomorrow. These are the builders. They start work at six in the morning and work through until nightfall. They work like this six days a week. 'I'd like to work Sundays too,' confides one. He comes from Victoria. He and his mates are erecting new houses in the community. They reckon they'll be here for the best part of a year. 'The money's good. Government money, you know...'

I do not see any blackfellas working on site in Bidgy. But in Beagle Bay, where streets of new houses are going up, I see blackfellas working sites in hard hats.

WHAT IS HAPPENING on this raft? Whitefellas are drawn to it, as if to encompass the mythic or the heroic. Whitefellas built it, to save non-whites. Somehow, we seek out the raft, in all our variety, and we clamber aboard and we seek to steer it. But the land, the spaces, the silences, the emptiness, all crowd in on us and we surrender, like drowning men, to our own salvation.

At the nurses' farewell party that first night I hear Kiwi accents, and a variety of British inflexions. They tell me the pay rates for outback nurses are 'pretty good, better than New Zealand'. The builders come from Victoria. The art assistant in Bidgy is from Malaysia. Concetta at the gallery is from Sydney; her offsider, Hermione, comes from South Africa, via Melbourne.

And what of the visiting doctor? They allocate me a new two-bedroom house, spacious and equipped with modern gadgets too advanced for me to operate. And the money's not too bad either. Elsewhere in the Kimberley, they give me a tiny slum shack without insulation.

While I am in Broome the local bookshop holds a book event featuring *Raft*. Afterwards people come forward bearing copies of my book for me to inscribe. As at all such events I meet young, eager people who have decided to teach or nurse or doctor in outback communities. These are not venal people.

All of these people from Somewhere Else, all of us congregating and deriving livelihood in Aboriginal Australia, all of us with our lofty motivations and our generous emoluments. It is confusing.

The raft is heavily laden, leaning on an uneven keel, its course uncertain. When we make our landfall who will have been helped?

Some names in this piece have been changed.

Howard Goldenberg is a writer who has practised medicine in a number of remote communities over the past twenty years. *Raft,* his account of these experiences, is published by Hybrid Publishers (2009).

Cory Taylor

Monkey business

    - Don't look them in the eye, she said. They find it confronting. With your build you scream dominant male.

    She was flattering me, as women often do. I tried to look at everything else, at the unpickable locks on the cages, at the newly disinfected floor, at the Fisher-Price toys that were changed once a week.

    - They take six months to adapt to cage life, she said, pushing her hair off her pretty forehead. It was warm in the lab and her skin was glistening.

    - Are all the researchers women? I said. I haven't seen any blokes.

    - There's probably a reason for that, she said, flashing me a smile. Her teeth were so straight I found myself staring.

    - How much do you charge per experiment? I said.

    - Around three times what the Chinese charge, she said.

    She paused in front of Sophie's cage. They all had names.

    - We like to think our methods are superior to theirs, she said.

    I'd seen monkey farms in China. I told her she wasn't wrong.

    - I wonder how much they know? I said. I tried not to look at the monkey while my guide placed a raisin on the floor of her cage. Sophie didn't move except to turn her head towards the wall.

    It was only when I glanced back that I saw her staring at me in her Fisher-Price toy mirror, for so long and with such shame that it was me who had to look away first.

This poem was shortlisted for the Bridport Prize.

Cory Taylor is a freelance screenwriter and author who divides her time between Brisbane and Japan. Her debut novel, *Me and Mr Booker*, will be published by Text in March and her essay 'Trouble at dolphin cove' appeared in *Griffith REVIEW 27: Food Chain*.

ESSAY

The play of days

Contemplating play through parenthood

Julienne van Loon

I AM sitting in the autumn shade at the edge of our long driveway. We always stop here on the way back from one of our walks because my son, ten months old, likes to play with the pebbles. We live in the midst of the jarrah forest that skirts the eastern suburbs of Perth, and one of the characteristics of the area is the gravelly laterite soils that produce a carpet of marble-sized burnt-orange pebbles rich in iron and aluminium. We sit here, and the boy crawls about, picking up one warm orange marble, then another, turning them over in his hands, weighing them up. Sometimes I offer my open palm and he places a small pebble there and I comment on it, how heavy or how small, or how orange or how round. Sometimes he piles them into his mouth, a knowing glint in his eye, mindful but defiant of my continued warnings about the threat of choking. But this is not a time for tension or dispute. I lean back. The sun has that subtle April warmth that makes you want to soak it up and there are red-capped robins flittering above us in the trees. The traffic on the main road is sparse and distant. After a while, the boy moves on, crawling up the steps, or else he is taken by a nearby bowl of water, dipping his hands in, shaking them about, calling out a small song of wonder. He and I have nowhere else to be, nothing else to do and I am grateful for that, but also, somehow, a little unsettled. We glimpse a fragile sort of joy here: bright and fleeting. It is one of the many aspects of this early relationship of ours that draws us together, imbricates one with the other. We drift together in play. Time falls away.

Before the child arrived, I used to wake fully rested each morning and know fairly quickly my tasks or goals for the day. I was always working at something. In the field of writing, where much of my attention has been focused during the past two decades, the endpoint was always a publication-ready work. Or alternatively, as a student or teacher, it was 'turning it in' or grading student work, and moving on. Either way, no matter how sidetracked I became by matters of process, my days were organised by a model based on plans, objectives, outcomes. At the university where I have worked for more than a decade the whole year is mapped out by schedules of one kind

---

PREVIOUS PAGE: Madeleine Winch. *Mother and child II*, 2005. Oil on canvas, 86cm x 86cm. Courtesy of the artist. www.madeleinewinch.com.au

or another, and your performance as a worker is constantly, almost neurotically, subject to measurement. Models and objectives provide structure and a sense of purpose. Applied collectively and on a much bigger scale, this kind of system is largely responsible for civil obedience in countries like Australia. But what happens when the capacity to maintain order or achieve outcomes is eroded?

I HAVE TAKEN twelve months' leave from my usual work to be at home with a new baby, and one of the biggest adjustments I have had to make is to arrive at a new understanding of time, one measured only by the fragile, mutable pattern of basic human needs: sleep, food, warmth, contact. In the contemporary suburban house, with all the conveniences of an automatic washing machine, heating at the flick of a switch, refrigeration and easy access to the supermarket, new motherhood can no longer be said to involve endless days of laborious household chores. Sometimes the only decision for the child and me to make is where to play for the next few hours and in what manner. Frequently there is no real decision made at all; we play indiscriminately. We play until the child is hungry, then we eat. We play until the child is tired, then we sleep. We play with the pink and green pushcart we've borrowed from the toy library until we end up sitting on a log and singing, or slotting small pebbles into the cracks between bricks. We play with the big green ball until it falls off the edge of the retaining wall, then we play with the soil from an upturned pot. And it doesn't matter. Unless you can't shake the itch for something more meaningful to do.

According to the pianist and essayist Stephen Nachmanovitch, play is sometimes conceived as a threat to normativity precisely because it wastes time. A game of amateur soccer or netball is measurably productive: it is good for our physical health, it develops teamwork skills. Similarly positive outcomes can be matched to more intellectual games like chess or cryptic crosswords. But if we devote too much time to this kind of play at the expense of family or work duties, we open ourselves up to criticism. I wonder about this, and about the double-edged nature of my radically altered state since play became such a large part of my everyday life. 'Play is not the way to maintain a tightly controlled society,' writes Nachmanovitch, 'or a clear definition of what is good, true or beautiful.' No, it isn't. And that's what makes it so delightful. That's what makes me want to defend it.

'THE FIRST AND perhaps most important thing to understand about newborn babies,' according to a state government pamphlet pressed upon me by the local community health nurse, 'is that they do not have any understanding of being a separate person inside their own skin…They have feelings of pleasure when they feed successfully or hear a soothing voice, feelings of pain when they are hungry or frightened – but they don't actually know that fear is what they feel and neither do they understand that there is a "them" to feel it.'

The infant, in other words, has not yet developed a sense of self. When I read this excerpt to a Buddhist friend, she laughs. 'And then we spend the rest of our lives trying to return to that state,' she says.

For a small child, play is a kind of biological imperative, just like sleep. It enables the emerging subject to form a separate sense of self. It also makes visible a bunch of developmental milestones that health and education specialists are always asking new mothers to look out for as markers of normality. But play is generally recognised, in animals as in humans, as a juvenile preoccupation. What of the adult, then, cast out – albeit temporarily – of the capitalist economy, and into the paradoxical state of play? How, and by what means, should she dwell there?

The American neuroscientist Stuart Brown calls play 'an altered state', which interests me because of the way we associate altered states with drugs and alcohol, or meditation, or trance, but also because my own frame of mind, post-birth, feels very much altered. Brown arrived at the subject of play through a background in criminology, and the desire to test out the theory that a particular mass-murderer evolved into the person he became because he was denied opportunities to play during childhood. 'The opposite of play is not work,' says Brown, 'it's depression.'

In a lecture available online Brown makes regular reference to 'hard science', saying things like: 'nothing lights up the brain like play.' He cites experiments with rats or cats, and I picture these animals wired up, and I shift in my seat and wonder, not for the first time, about the ruthless stupidity of so-called hard science. For whom is it hard? It's not difficult to guess the answer when Brown describes an experiment with a group of rats. Apparently rats are 'hardwired' (Brown's metaphor) to know that the scent of a cat equals danger. When a cat's collar is dropped into their cage, they run and hide. Such is the response of two separate groups of rats described in Brown's experiment. One of these groups has previously been 'allowed' to play, and the other group has been 'denied' play. He fails to go into detail about the means by which these allowances and denials have been achieved. In any case, the difference between the two groups, Brown states matter-of-factly, is that the rats that have been allowed to play poke their heads out of their hiding places periodically, after the appearance of the cat's collar. Eventually this group is able to assess that the danger has passed and they go back to their usual duties. The other rats, those 'denied play', never come out again. 'They die in their bunkers,' says Brown.

SOMETIMES I THINK identity is a very simple idea. It's who you start to become when you follow certain patterns. It's a habit you form.

A few months after my son turns one, we stay at my mother's small Aged Care Housing unit in Adelaide for two weeks. She seems at times impressed and sometimes disgusted by how much I play with the child. 'You're lucky to have a mother who plays with you,' she says to him. Or, 'You can't climb all over your mother all day. Go and amuse yourself.' We have become something other than ourselves, this baby and I. We have become a pair that plays too much.

Increasingly drawn to the theory of play, I seek out the writing of women thinkers on this topic, for surely it is mothers who have spent the most time playing with children under two. But try as I might, I find little serious philosophy written about this by women, except for work caught up in play as it relates to education and early childhood development. Reading the work of Maria Montessori, I find that her radical recasting of education for early childhood was based on her cynicism about notions of the imaginary. For Montessori, whose methods are said to have developed from observation, children do not play out of a desire for fantasy; rather, their so-called play is evidence of a strong desire to make sense of everyday reality. Montessori banned myth and fairytale in her classrooms, and worked instead to develop highly ordered environments in which children could 'play' at life skills such as cooking, cleaning, dressing. Her emphasis, in the classroom, was on presenting the children with interesting, age-appropriate, 'hands-on' materials, minimising interruptions and allowing freedom of movement. 'Freedom in intellectual work,' she wrote in her early research on spontaneous activity, is 'the basis of internal discipline.'

At the local Montessori playgroup where I take my eighteen-month-old son the playthings lined up neatly along the side of the room are called 'jobs'. He finds them each intriguing in an inquisitive mood, but something about the place disagrees with him; he spends so much time resisting the routines and rituals the facilitator is trying to set up that his attendance is a constant struggle for both of us. The boy throws himself to the floor and howls, or else wanders off, noisily off-task while the others are all lined up obediently on the mat to sing songs. I give up after about three weeks and stop taking him there.

AT THIS AGE my son is fascinated by cars and trucks, but sometimes despairs when he finds that there is no driver behind the wheel of a toy vehicle. He brings the toy to me and points inside the little cabin, saying, 'Gone, gone, gone.' He is the same age as Freud's famous grandson, Ernst, when he was observed playing the game of 'fort/da' (here/gone) with a cotton reel on a piece of string. I have never offered my son a cotton reel on a piece of string, but I now watch the same game, in principle, carried out across a number of contexts. He hides himself behind curtains or under blankets, amused when I pretend to look for him, then crying out with glee when he reappears to me; he lugs bags and containers around with him, stopping in the doorway to wave and call 'Bye! Bye! Bye!' – only to reappear again moments later and repeat the whole manoeuvre in a different part of the house. He hides little cars and tractors underneath the lounge or a blanket ('Gone! Gone! Gone!'), then gives a cheerful 'Oh!' when the disguise is retracted and the object reappears.

As Freud saw it, this game of fort/da, the wilful manipulation of an object to make it disappear and reappear over and again, is a game of mastery, converting the infant's hitherto passive role in relation to his mother into an active one. Freud understands the game as acting out an impulse 'suppressed in actual life, to revenge himself on his mother for going away from him'. He imagines the child's internal dialogue with the mother as one bound up in anger and frustration: 'All right, then, go away! I don't need you. I'm sending you away myself.' But feminist commentators have questioned this interpretation for its emphasis on a struggle for power and mastery. Jay Watson, for example, reads the fort/da game as an engagement with the mother's subject position via exploration and experiment, rather than as an attempt to overcome her. 'Fort/da confirms that growing up is more than just a matter of learning to live at a distance from the mother,' writes Watson. 'It is also a matter of learning to do the kinds of things she can do.' Considering the play between presence and absence in a broader sense as the play between life and death, Elisabeth Bronfen argues that the key objective behind fort/da is more likely the development of infant subjectivity. Linking the absence of the mother's body to the threat of death, the game becomes an experiment in both submitting to and resisting death, enabling the emerging infant to develop a sense of subjectivity without being overwhelmed by the fear of death.

In thinking this through, I am reminded of Stuart Brown's play-denied rats, dying in their bunkers out of fear of an imaginary cat. But also of the way in which my own identity has been radically altered since being immersed in – and hence subject to – infant play. For even while I find myself engaged with and by the child's play, I am also, always, distanced by it.

'The most irritating feature of play,' says Robert Fagan, a theorist in the field of animal play, is that it 'taunts us with its inaccessibility. We feel that something is behind it all, but we do not know, or have forgotten, how to see it.'

THE IDEA THAT infant play might be about exploration and experimentation, rather than about the kind of antagonistic mastery that Freud saw, fits in my mind with the kind of grown-up play I have always enjoyed through writing fiction. It also enables the idea that play is not just an aid to development and attainment, as the early childhood development school would have it, but a crucial and ongoing experiment that helps us to 'be' in the world. Most of us would agree, albeit with a slight tint of romanticism, that the condition of childhood requires what the ludologist David Golumbia calls 'a kind of unbounded, free play,' one that has the capacity to exist both within and beyond a specific set of rules, or both within and outside of organised institutions. Child's play, according to this understanding, can break its own rules and make up new rules frequently. It has been argued that it is this untameable aspect of play in childhood that enables not just adult creativity but perhaps adult language and representation more broadly.

In the six months before my son's second birthday, his ability to use language bursts forth in a barrage of single words and gobbledygook. Objects are named and words overheard, repeated, joined together, parodied. We take to calling out sounds like *oh* and *ee* and *ah* to one another as we zoom along the highway in the hatchback. The boy discovers many ways to make a single syllable imply meaning: excitement, despair, agreement, absurdity, stupidity, concern. We screech with laughter at one another's performance or at the sheer volume we can raise with voice alone. As Thomas Mann once said of art (quoting Goethe): 'This is very serious jest!'

At the end of summer, the boy says his first sentence. 'There it is!' he exclaims, pointing at an object he may or may not have been searching for. It is followed several days later, by a second, in the form of question: 'What is this?' he asks. 'Oh! What is this?' Repeated, again, again.

In his 1908 paper 'Creative Writers and Daydreaming' Freud equates the creative writer with the child at play, making clear the kind of emotional investment and energy that serious play demands from both writers and children. But Freud's understanding of play is strongly imbued with the idea of fantasy, the notion that play constitutes a *rejection* of reality. Somewhere between Freud and Montessori, there must a kind of middle ground that permits both understandings, that permits a multiplicity of relations between play, imagination and the real.

As the parent of an infant I have had my own reality, and with it my sense of self, profoundly interrupted. My once busy and fulfilling – you could also say insular – writing and academic life seems distant to me. I do not have the privilege of extended periods of isolation that both these roles require; and when, on occasion, the gift of time is given to me, a sense of disorientation pervades, so that my ability to concentrate flounders and falters. I cannot remember who I was prior to the arrival of the infant, and what it was I wanted to do. Sometimes this sense of disorientation is so pervasive that I find myself reluctant to separate from the boy. His play has become, over time, my play. It is curious that as he practises being me – here/gone, here/gone – I am practising losing myself, in a willing and not altogether unfulfilling way.

For Hélène Cixous, who has written extensively on the writing process, the kind of empathetic identification that a writer needs to make when representing another constitutes an extraordinary pilgrimage into another self. The purpose here is not about mastery, but rather about investigation and reflection. 'I become, I inhabit, I enter,' she writes. 'Inhabiting someone, at that moment, I can feel myself traversed by that person's initiatives and actions.' As Cixous understands it, identification with the other is not about erasure, but rather about 'permeability' or a 'peopling' of the self. You inhabit and are inhabited by turn. Or as Cixous puts it, 'one is always far more than one.' Writing, for Cixous, is the primary means by which we can engage in this to-and-fro. We can easily imagine how play between mother and infant might engage the same kind of alterity.

LATELY THE BOY and I have discovered the joy of repetition. We play a game in which he drops a tennis ball down the garden steps, traces its journey, then pursues and recaptures it before returning to the top of the steps and beginning the cycle anew. I am closely involved because of his inability to negotiate the steps on his own. So, side by side, we watch the ball's trajectory. It is never the same pathway twice. We descend the steps hand-in-hand and I stand by as he scrambles into the bush after the ball, then wait to hold his hand again for the ascent. We count the steps together, one through eight, or repeat the monosyllabic word *up, up, up*. At the top, he releases the ball again. It is curious how involved I become in this game, even taking comfort in the pattern of variation versus surety: the haphazard pattern of the ball's descent, the predictability of our progress through the cycle; the always tenuous grip of the boy's feet on the stairs, the ease with which we both begin again. There is barely any need for words.

'Mind is nowhere; play is nowhere,' writes Stephen Nachmanovitch.

Somewhere towards the end of the child's second year, the restlessness and boredom, the lack of ease I had earlier felt when engaged in play with the child, lifts away. This same period is matched by a gradual return of my desire and ability to write.

I'm not sure that writer's block adequately describes my writerly inactivity during the past two years. Over this period, I have been frustrated by not being able to write, but at the same time I have lacked the desire to produce new work. There was the practical issue of being able to make appropriate use of the small blocks of time in which I was able to write; but there was also what I have taken to thinking of as my altered state: a mixture of exhaustion, dislocation and a kind of giddy state of otherness, described by Cixous as simultaneously 'traversing' and being 'traversed by' another. Two novels into my writing career, it seemed at times to be all over. I was not interested in playing the game of authorpreneur required of writers in today's environment. But more than that, I felt I could not write because I was, indeed, nowhere. My altered state, while at times profoundly debilitating, remains a way of being I feel compelled to protect. I have unravelled, and though at times I have felt desperate to be more absolute, I have also been, mostly, unwilling to reconstruct my earlier (mis)understanding of selfhood. While my narrative self has unravelled, the baby's narrative self has been striving to land somewhere, to begin.

TWO YEARS AGO, cast outside meaningful production and into the role of mother/carer/playmate for a pre-lingual child, I entered quite abruptly a zone in which my previous understanding of self needed to be radically renegotiated. My altered state, though enlightening, pleasurable, challenging in the way of the best sorts of games, also enforced upon me a muteness of sorts. I have missed the sort of narrative play I had once believed myself good at, and have not easily found my way back to it. Immersed in the world of infant play, I have erased old habits. I have inhabited, instead, the world of the daydreamer who takes joy in the small pebble, the sound of a vowel, the chaos of the dropped ball's trajectory through space.

My initial unease was perhaps the result of a misunderstanding: play does not necessarily require mastery, subjection, waste, just as falling away from organised productivity does not necessarily involve falling away from meaning. Actually, the kind of play at which I have now become adept depends on narrative interruption. It is about being prepared to be taken away by another beyond the self-same and certain. It is, as the French philosopher Jean-Luc Nancy might say, an experience of being-in-common.

The commute to and from home to work and day care is lengthy, sometimes delayed further by an accident on the highway, or a heavy load being transported at a snail's pace up the gradual incline of the Darling Range. In the car, the boy and I share a packet of party blowouts between us. They are dazzling in metallic blues, silvers and reds. My occasional glances in the rear-view mirror are punctuated by the sight of a clownish paper tongue, unfurling, retracting, unfurling. Mostly our blowing into the mouthpieces produces only the sound of paper crackling and the whoosh of air forcefully exhaled. We are dilly-dallying. But sometimes at a change of gear we each produce a trumpeting sound with simultaneous force. The joint proclamation is ridiculously brassy and self-important. Then it tails off with a limp, almost melancholy change of tone. This amuses us.

References at www.griffithreview.com

Julienne van Loon is the author of *Road Story* (2005) and *Beneath the Bloodwood Tree* (2008), both published by Allen & Unwin. Her essays have appeared in *Griffith REVIEW: The Next Big Thing* and *Divided Nation*. She teaches writing at Curtin University. www.juliennevanloon.com.au

FICTION

THE RAFT

AMANDA LOHREY

IF asked then why I had not returned to London I could have – would have – given several clear reasons that, looking back, I recognised as mere rationalisations; transient structures of thought that clear a space for some deeper instinct or intuition to do its work. I didn't go back because it felt right not to; because some inchoate resistance – some feeling that didn't need a name and would never acquire one – welled up in my chest and said *stay*.

Sometimes you just did things. You surprised even yourself.

Within weeks of returning to Sydney I was working for a corporation with headquarters in North Sydney. Just a few kilometres away in Kirribilli, walking distance from the office, I rented a shoebox apartment overlooking a small park and began to settle in to my new life. Compared to what I had been doing with UTOPIA the work was dull – devising programs for the setting up of new accounting systems – but I intended within the year to break out into my own consultancy. When I had settled in. When I had found my line and length.

I didn't think about the sudden death of my brother, Barry, because when I did I felt as if I had had a psychic limb amputated. For the first time I began to suffer from insomnia. Each night I woke around four in the morning. Sometimes, if I couldn't get back to sleep, I would switch on the BBC World Service. News from remote borders, of the warring factions of the Mujahideen, rendered in civilised English tones, seemed calibrated to run exactly the right kind of interference on my zealous mind. Sometimes I would be dozing within minutes, but other data was less reliable. The English football results made me think of pleasurable hours on the West Ham terraces with Dave. Then I would wonder what my ex-girlfriend Mira was doing. Perhaps I should call her. What time was it in Montreal?

THE WEEKS PASSED. Occasionally I would have a drink with a friend. There were company social nights when I would turn up and play my role (and these were not unpleasant) and there was a regular game of squash with a group of old school friends at a local club. They invited me to dinners and barbecues, but these were the lowest level of distraction and, if I were not in the mood, would only aggravate my condition of restless grief. And then, out of the blue, I got a call from my cousin Julie, to say that she and her husband had been transferred back to Sydney from Auckland, where they had spent the past five years. Would I like to come over for dinner?

It was a Saturday evening in late November and, driving across to their house in Tamarama, I thought of the last time I had seen Julie, not long before I left to work in London. But my most vivid memory of her was of a holiday when our two families spent Christmas together at Terrigal. I remembered her then as a tomboy; a short, muscular girl with sun-streaked hair and a deep tan; a powerful swimmer who moved in the water with the slow, lazy focus of a fish.

That first night she came out to meet me in the driveway and I was relieved to see that she had scarcely changed, apart from a slight thickening around the middle. The house was a nondescript brick bungalow, and she led me through a cool hallway and out onto a concrete terrace overlooking the beach. The water was still, and shimmered in the hazy light. In one corner of the terrace a thickset man with a beard was wiping down the metal plate of a wood-fired barbecue. Below him, on the grass, two small boys in wet bathers chased a featureless brown mutt around the yard.

Julie introduced me to Kieran as 'my clever cousin' and I thought this was not perhaps the best start. Kieran shook my hand a touch too firmly and went on with his preparations for the barbecue while Julie and I looked out over the rooftops and spoke the lingua franca of Sydney life: real estate. All the while I was alert to Kieran, his slow and intense focus on the barbecue, the way he sighed as he adjusted the battens of wood and poked at loose twigs, and I wondered if Kieran was not so much gruff as tired; he moved with the stolid weariness of a man who has worked all day in the sun.

'Kiernan's been working on his boat all day,' Julie said, as if reading my thoughts. 'He bought this old whaling dinghy off a friend and now he's restoring it.'

'Huon pine, beautiful timber.' Kieran looked up from the waft of smoke.

'Why don't you show Rick the boat?'

Kieran poked at the fire again. 'Do you want to have a look?' he asked, and his asking was a courtesy, as if to say: I don't want to bore you with this.

'Sure.'

The boat, covered by a tarpaulin, sat in the side lane. Kieran became more animated as he removed the tarpaulin and ran his palm along the polished surface of the wood. Now he was at ease and happy to deliver a laconic discourse on glues and varnishes. Every now and then he would pat the side of the boat, as if it were an old friend, and nod his head in confirmation of its worth while I did my best to ask the right questions. I thought the shape of the boat was ugly, too wide in relation to its length, and this gave it a squat appearance, but the wood was ravishing, a golden honey hue with a soft plasticity that breathed. I saw that you could have a relationship with this wood, and was about to ask where it came from when Julie leaned over the terrace and said, 'Let's eat. The kids are getting ratty.'

'Such beautiful wood,' I said, looking up.

'Well, enjoy it,' she said tartly, 'because by the time they finish logging old-growth forests there'll be none of it left. They'll have to put boats like that in a museum.'

'Now then, Jules, you're winding up into a rave,' said Kieran, quietly, looking ahead. His eyes were hooded and his weathered lips set firmly against causes.

At this I felt a prick of annoyance; I did not like to hear my cousin rebuked. But Julie seemed oblivious. She had moved away to the other side of the terrace, where she was calling to the boys. Her husband had thrown out the net of his words but she was not caught.

Up on the terrace, bread and salads were laid out. Kieran set about the serious business of searing the meat while the boys, Ryan and Matthew, whooped around the garden. Conversation over dinner was broken but accommodating. The boys, though shyly deferential to me, were ragged with fatigue from a blustery afternoon on the beach with their mother. After they tired of tormenting the dog they whined and fought over who would ride the bike around the lawn and show off for the visitor. At last, Julie rose with deliberate calm and bundled them into a bath.

Despite the way they had interrupted my every sentence I was sorry to see them go. Watching them reminded me of the hours Barry and I had spent playing cricket in the backyard in that same enchanted hour of dusk, our subliminal sense of the light of the day falling away behind us, our innocent faith in its renewal.

With the boys in bed we settled into recliners on the deck and sniffed at the smell of meat and barbecue smoke, still wafting tantalisingly in the air. Kieran wasn't much of a talker and the wine soon sent him into a soporific slump. The small talk trailed off into companionable silence, and for a while we just sat and gazed out at the horizon. After a while I turned to Julie and said, 'Do you get much swimming in these days?'

'Not much. If it's hot, I go for a swim at night, when the kids are in bed, and if Kieran's home. That's the best time. The wind's dropped, there's no one on the beach.'

This struck me as somehow foolhardy. 'Can you see what you're doing?'

When she looked at me there was a gleam of the old mischief in her dark brown eyes. 'No,' she murmured. 'That's the point of going.'

I remembered how she used to wade into the surf at Terrigal, swimming beyond the breakers like a sleek porpoise, so evenly, so smoothly, as if she were in her element, as if she might never come back. It seemed to me then that there was a mystery in her, something unfathomable.

A warm breeze wafted up from the water and the sky glowed pink at the edge of the roofline. I saw that a trance came over these beach suburbs at night, a subtropical stupor in which all fear, all resistance was dissolved in the warm penumbra of dusk. Nature giveth, and Nature taketh away.

Beside us, Kieran snored gently on his recliner.

I drove home around nine, the last glow of daylight rimming the horizon. I wondered if I, too, could live like this, in the suburbs, a father of small children, with a sundeck and a barbecue, a double garage and a frangipani tree. These were the surfaces, and then there was the reality. Reality was the man polishing his boat on land and the woman swimming in the dark, but they were a riddle, one that I was not yet ready to unravel. Supposing I were to enter into this riddle? What would it make of me? Who would I be?

My mind drifted again to surfaces, the form of the thing. I saw my weary commute home in the evening, backyard cricket with my kids at twilight, supper on the beach on hot summer nights, an enigmatic wife who would form the impenetrable substratum of my dreams. This was the core of it. Everything depended on this last figure in the landscape: the woman on the beach. Without her I was just a cog in the machine. And with her? With her, we were mysterious creatures at the edge of the tide: liminal, amphibious, entwined.

I drove on, into the dark, and felt that I was some great displaced sea creature, splayed on a vinyl seat behind the wheel of a car; a beached merman waiting dumbly for the enveloping wave.

FOR THE NEXT eight months I did nothing but work and for all of that time I was celibate, the longest period in my life since I was seventeen. I began to frequent a Korean bathhouse near Taylor Square, in a rundown building that looked out onto the Doric columns of the Supreme Court. That bathhouse became a haven. You went up a seedy narrow staircase and into a foyer hung with paper scrolls. You rang a small brass bell and a chunky Korean who spoke no English would appear, nod and indicate the change room. Once undressed, you entered naked into the bathing area. This was a dimly lit room with two circular pools in the centre surrounded by wide tiles. The smaller of these pools was a warm spa bath filled with a pale brown infusion of ginseng with leaves floating on the surface, and as you stepped out and down onto the tiles (the baths were raised above the level of the deck) some of the dark leaves would cling to your skin, creating the brief illusion that you had just stepped out of a brackish lake.

After this you slipped into the larger pool, which was cooler, and bathed until you were ready for the Turkish steam room at the far end. At any given time there might be seven or eight men in the pools, some in the water, others sitting at the edge, dangling their feet and waiting to be rubbed down on one of the futons spread along the deck. Once you were prostrate on a futon another of the chunky Korean masseurs would come and kneel, and begin to scrub your body with a loofah, scouring the skin hard, almost to the threshold of pain but stopping every few minutes to sluice you down with warm water out of a long-handled bucket that an attendant kept refilled.

This was the best moment of all, the sluice of clean water across your shoulders, your lower back, thighs and feet. The warm, willing cascade of it; the luxurious blur of expectation just before the next deluge, the grateful exhalation of relief as you lay there like a slippery fish foetus in the womb of the pool room, with its dim steamy air and its becalmed bodies; warm, silent, anonymous.

And I would walk out of there, loose and light, and drive home, and often I would eat nothing that evening because I felt clean, purified.

One night after a session at the bathhouse I had a dream. I was in the big circular pool, or a space that resembled the pool, only it was not. And there was no one there but me, floating outstretched and naked on a raft at the centre of the water. And I dreamed that the raft was also my bed, so that it was not as if I were somewhere else; rather it was a sense of being on my bed in a state that was half-awake, and the surface of the bed was the surface of the raft. And all the while the raft was hovering, idly, on the surface of the pool… And every now and then I would wake… It was such a long, drifting dream, but even in the waking state a mirage of water persisted in my brain, like a hallucination, so that when I looked up in the dark I could see the water eddying across the ceiling and around the fan in a soundless swirl, rippling on and on across the blackness. And after a while it came to me. *I can't get off the raft.* Any moment now I will fall and sink to the bottom of the pool, and there's no one here and they'll never find me, and my body will be flushed away through one of the corner drains.

That's when I saw the woman with the baby. Standing at the end of the pool was a young woman in a white dress, and in her arms she was holding a baby, an amorphous white bundle swathed in swaddling clothes, swathed so tight that all I could see was its eyes. And the woman? She was familiar to me, I had seen her before. But where? And as I stared at them – thinking, who are they? and what are they doing here? – slowly, the baby began to glow. At first it had a faint glimmer but then it began to glow brighter, the white shimmer of the image growing more intense, until suddenly it flared into a blinding cone of light. At that moment I felt a tight nostalgic sweetness in my chest, a terrifying vertigo of joy, and I knew then that the light was coming to annihilate me –

And I woke with a gasp. And lay in the dark, open-mouthed and holding my breath. That feeling…that feeling was indescribable. For a moment I had felt as if I were falling…falling into bliss.

The feeling stayed with me for the whole of the day, until late afternoon when it began to fade. As it receded I tried to hold on to it, to wilfully recapture glimpses of the dream – the tilt of the raft, the hem of the woman's dress, the glow from the baby – but inevitably it grew more and more faint, like a silk fabric dissolving in the mind's eye. It could not be hung on to, and by late evening I had ceased even to try. The yearning around my heart had evaporated. The painful joy in my chest was gone.

MY VISITS TO Julie and Kieran's became a regular thing, and I grew fond of the boys, remembering on each occasion to bring them some small treat. One night, when Kieran was away on business, Julie packed some cooked sausages in buttered rolls smeared with tomato sauce and we walked to the beach. After our no-frills picnic on the sand the four of us played beach cricket until it began to grow dark. At one point Matt lobbed a ball into the water.

'I'll go,' I offered.

'No, I'll go,' she said, and in one supple movement she slipped out of her shorts, unselfconsciously, and waded into the surf.

Later, when the boys were in bed and we were sitting out on the deck, she asked me about Barry. I don't know why, but we'd never discussed it before. Suddenly a rush of pain ambushed me behind the eyes, like the prickly, needling onset of a migraine. I faltered mid-sentence and it was clear to her that I had tripped over an internal landmine.

Julie was unfazed. She turned her gaze away from the sea and stared at me. 'The only thing to do,' she said, 'is have a good cry. Just cry your eyes out for as long as it takes.'

'I can't.'

'Can't what?'

'Can't cry. I've never been able to cry.'

'You must have cried as a child!' She was looking at me in amazement.

'Not that I recall.'

She continued to stare at me. 'You know, Rick, you should talk to someone.'

'I'm talking to you.'

'I mean a professional.'

'Like who?'

'A friend of mine has been going to a therapist, a woman. Sue thinks she's really good. Do you want me to ring her and get the number?'

I shrugged resignedly.

I thought Julie must have misinterpreted the shrug because she made no effort to move, but a week later a business card arrived in the post with a note on the back in her handwriting. 'Thought you might want to hang on to this for future reference.'

I looked at the card.

SARAH MASSON
psychotherapist

It gave an address near the Manly Corso.

The next day I rang and made an appointment.

THE FIRST SESSION.

The house was set well back from the road behind a high cream brick wall. There was a Norfolk pine in the front garden, like the ones on the Manly Corso but with much more life in it, more density and spring. For a moment I was distracted by that tree; was willing to be distracted by almost anything since I had misgivings about being there. It was the realisation that I was becoming almost catatonically unable to speak to anyone about anything much that had finally driven me to this door.

Julie had said, 'You just need to talk to someone about the way you feel.'

That sounded reasonable. Unthreatening. Or so I thought when I rang and made the appointment. But on that first day, when I stood there, staring up into the radiating fronds of the Norfolk pine, it felt a good deal more confronting.

Yet I knew why I had come. I wanted to cry, and I couldn't. Perhaps she could teach me.

It was 1993. I was a week off my thirty-first birthday.

I stepped onto the veranda. Next to the stained-glass door was a brass plate that was inscribed 'Wholistic Therapy Centre'. Suddenly I felt nervous, like a child about to sit some kind of unorthodox examination. And I didn't like that word 'wholistic'. It had a phony ring to it. What'll I say? I thought. I'll just say that I have depression, that in the past year it's gotten worse. I'll just set out the facts, flatly. Describe the situation. Tell her about Barry and, before that, my ex-wife, Jo. And maybe about the dream, the one about the woman and the baby. Yes, definitely the dream. What could be difficult about that?

I pressed the brass button.

A short, muscular woman of about forty-five with prematurely white hair opened the door. 'Rick,' she said, as if she knew me. I looked at her, sizing her up sexually, as I did with any woman I'd just set eyes on. It was a reflex, even in this state; one I imagined would never leave me. To my relief there was nothing there for me. Good. It would make the encounter easier.

Sarah wore loose-fitting white pants, a white top and leather sandals. I noticed she had good skin, a good healthy tan, and deep green eyes. She put out her hand and I shook it. As I stepped in she indicated a room to her left. It was light and cool and carpeted, with a sofa and two nondescript armchairs. She gestured at one of the chairs and waited for me to sit down. We sat, facing one another, a metre apart. When I was settled, she looked at me and said, 'What is it that you want from this, Rick?'

That's when I leaned over and put my head in my hands. For a few moments the room blurred around me until I became aware of the silence. I couldn't speak. Something lurched and began to rise in my chest and I thought, then, with a pinprick of amazement, that I might be about to cry. Could it be this easy? But no, my eyes were dry. Finally I managed to open my mouth. 'I'm sorry,' I said. 'I'm tired. I've been working long hours. I'm not usually like this…' The truth was that I was increasingly like this: unwilling, or unable, to communicate.

'Everyone who comes here apologises for something.' She smiled. 'They always say they're tired and they're not usually like this.'

Opening my hands, just a little, I stared at the floor. I heard myself sigh, and that sigh seemed to come from a point just beyond my hands that were, unaccountably, still pressed up against my forehead, as if glued.

'What is it that you want, Rick?'

'I want to lose my fear.' I heard myself say this with surprising matter-of-factness. Out it came. Clear, sharp.

'What are you afraid of?'

'Everything.' I heard myself sigh again. This wasn't true. I hadn't been afraid of abseiling when my team had been ordered to go on one of those bogus corporate bonding programs some months before, nor was I afraid of many other things. *What was I talking about?* Where did these words come from? In my chest the black wind bellows were squeezed hard up against my ribcage. I sighed again.

'What does this fear feel like?'

At last I lifted my head. 'How do you mean?'

'What's your body telling you? Where can you feel this fear?'

'In my head, I suppose.' I paused. 'All over.' Silence. 'Nowhere in particular.' It was excruciating; my lips were made of sticky latex and I had to force the words out.

Sarah looked at me. 'All right. Let's get down on the floor.' She stood, and slipped out of her sandals.

I continued to sit, woodenly.

'You okay with that?'

At last I got my mouth open. 'Should I take my shoes off?'

'Whatever you're comfortable with.'

I left my shoes on.

Sarah pushed her chair back against the wall and walked over to a wooden chest standing by the door. It looked like a child's toy chest. She lifted the lid and took out a roll of pale blue foam. Glancing into the open chest, I could see a basketball there, and other things I couldn't identify before she closed the lid.

'My box of tricks,' she said, smiling, and unrolled the foam onto the floor. 'Just lie on your back, and get comfortable.'

I followed her instructions.

She knelt beside me. 'All right, now, take a deep breath.'

Breathing deeply was an effort. Plus it had always been my experience that as soon as someone told you to breathe deeply, you couldn't. I tried to make my mind go blank, to relax my stomach muscles. Then, with effort, I inhaled deeply – but the air seemed to get stuck above my navel. I turned my face from side to side, away from her, and began to sigh again, almost as if hyperventilating, though not quite. Then I covered my face with my hands.

'Why do you cover your face?'

'So I can't be seen, I suppose.'

'Why?'

'I thought for a minute I might cry.'

'What's wrong with that?'

'It's ugly. People look ugly when they cry. Ugly and weak.'

'Say, "I look ugly when I cry".'

'I never cry.'

'Alright then. Say, "I would look ugly if I cried".'

'I would look ugly if I cried.'

'Who mustn't see you cry?'

'Anyone.'

'Who's anyone?'

'What do you mean, "Who's anyone?" '

'Can you be specific? Name names? Who mustn't see you cry?'

'Friends…colleagues…my parents…teachers…friends…anyone.'

'What will happen if they see you?'

'I'll feel stupid…ashamed.'

'And?'

'They'll ask questions. I'll have to explain myself.'

'How does that feel?'

'How does what feel?'

'Explaining yourself.'

'I don't know. It feels tight.'

'You're holding your breath.'

'I know. I always hold my breath.'

'Holding the fort?'

Smiling, I exhaled, and the smile stayed with me. It occurred to me that I liked her. Had from the minute I set eyes on her. I started to relax.

She put her hand on my stomach, a large, square, practical hand. I liked the feel of it. 'If I do, or say, anything you're not comfortable with, tell me,' she said. 'Okay?'

'Okay.'

'Okay. Now, tell me…'

As I talked, occasionally she removed her hand and shook it away from her, as if she were flicking off some dross or contamination, some negative charge. It was weird.

BY THE TIME I walked out of there I felt lighter. I felt as if I had handed over my problems to someone else, had stored them in some kind of psychic safe. I felt also as if someone was on my side. Paying them to be on your side didn't matter. In fact, it helped: there was a freedom in the clarity of the transaction. For one thing, I didn't have to pretend to be interested in her. It wasn't a date. I could fall into myself and wallow about in the childish pain of all my stored-up sense of grievance, all my hatreds, my buried sense of outrage and grief (not just grief for Jo, and Barry, but every blow ever dealt to me). Though I still had the problem that I wanted to impress her; wanted her to think well of me, that I was a decent, sensitive, mature human being, so much more appealing than all her other clients — whoever they were.

And then she spoiled it. On the fifth visit she began to talk astrology. If there was one thing I couldn't bear it was prattle about the stars.

'You're an Arian,' she said, one hot afternoon, 'but you're holding your power in. Give yourself permission to be powerful. You're locking your energy away in your head and this creates a sadness in the heart area, this feeling you describe as boredom, as ennui. *Breathe.* Unlock the channels and the breath will flow through your body and enliven the surfaces of your skin. Enlarge your aura. If we lock our energy away, our skin is vulnerable. If we let the energy flow our surfaces are stronger; we're stronger all over; we're not contracted inwards, we radiate outwards. Our aura is enhanced. People *feel* our energy, our strength. They think twice about attacking us — if that's what you're worried about…'

There I was, beginning to trust her, and she started in on that astrology shit.

'…it's partly about learning to trust your environment. But only up to a point. There are times when something in the environment *is* hostile, *is* threatening. What you have to learn to trust is yourself. And your ability to deal with it.'

'It?'

'Whatever it is you're afraid of.' She got up off the floor. 'Let me look up your moons.'

My what?

She walked over to her bookcase and took a thick hardbound book off the middle shelf, began to flick through the pages, and stopped.

'You've got a moon in Capricorn,' she smiled, 'the goat. This means you're ambitious and single-minded. Ambitious, dogged, can be over-focussed...mmm, let's see...' Somewhere in the vault of my chest I gave a low, silent groan of dismay, but found myself listening intently, despite myself. I felt like Macbeth listening to the witches, but without the credulity.

It was after this session that I experienced a sense of massive letdown. I had been a fool to succumb, to get my hopes up. None of this stuff was going to work for me; for other people, maybe, but not for *me*. I had too sceptical an intelligence to enter wholeheartedly into the game, the spirit of it. Ninety per cent of it was faith in the cure. Faith. And no one with a first-class intellect (why be modest?) was going to come at that. Not that I hadn't at times been open to it, in a jokey kind of way. You got through the river of your day, sometimes wading, sometimes floating: sometimes it was a slow anguished crawl, sometimes an effortless sprint. And all the time you wondered if there was some other model that made sense of things, some other dimension that you were separated from by only a thin membrane. You felt this most when you were drunk, or stoned, like a mirage of the senses: a dreamy, floating state succeeded by a ravenous physical hunger that brought you down to earth with a pleasurable thud, and the plainest food tasted sublime, like manna. I remembered once eating a packet of ginger cookies that felt like the first meal, although the delayed effect, the wash-up, was more like the Last Supper and the taste of ashes. But that's all it was, a perpetual question mark in the mind, a disinclination to be a dogmatic naysayer rather than a yearning to be a true believer. *As if* the configuration of the planets meant something; *as if* there were a benign destiny moving through the heavens... Maybe all these counsellors were secret fruit loops, and behind those smooth, 'caring' facades were cultists who waved incense and burned cow dung at midnight.

The next week I cancelled my appointment. And then, when that felt hollow, I rang the following day to make another one. That night I dreamed about the baby again, almost the same dream in all its surreal detail...the floating on the water, the woman in white, the swaddled infant that began to glow. And then, tormentingly, the sweet, sharp pain behind the breastbone, so that I woke this time and sat bolt upright in bed with my chest heaving and my hand pressed hard against my heart. Was I having a heart attack? Was there some blockage or genetic weakness there that I didn't know about? Or was I just having a panic attack?

I came back to Sarah because I liked her, and because I couldn't think of anything else to do. Her house, that room, were soothing.

One evening when I knocked on her door I could hear the light soprano of a woman singing in German, and it was her. She was still humming and trilling the odd phrase as she unlocked the iron grille.

'Very nice,' I said.

'German lieder.' She grinned. 'It's an acquired taste.'

At the weekend I went into a specialist shop in Oxford Street and bought a CD of this lieder, only to find that while it had a certain charm, and the singer was no doubt more technically proficient than Sarah (I didn't have a musical ear and wouldn't know), it was not what I had heard from *her* lips. It was too studied; it lacked the same…the same *blitheness*. Did this mean I was becoming attached? I didn't think so, not really. While I might think of her between appointments in an 'I must raise this with Sarah' way, there was no more to it than that.

But there were layers to her that I would not have guessed at. I discovered that she had once been an industrial chemist and worked for the Bayer firm in Frankfurt, and that she spoke fluent German. In many ways she was salty and down-to-earth. After my initial surprise I realised it wasn't so out of character; there was that hard-headedness about her that I'd sensed in the first session, and that had made me trust her, something about that basketball in her box of tricks – and then she'd come up with that astrology drivel, though only that one time, as if she sensed I didn't like it. She never mentioned it again.

But she did eventually get the basketball out of the box and, with me stretched out on the futon, we began what Sarah called 'bodywork'. Lots of deep breathing, some massage, some acute pain in surprising places. I never knew what to expect, or where it was supposed to go. Sometimes I thought it wouldn't have mattered much what she did; it was her weekly dose of dispassionate warmth that kept me going, like taking the car into a garage to get the battery recharged.

TO BEGIN WITH I went to Sarah once a week, every Monday evening after work, and then once a fortnight, and then more irregularly. And it seemed to help. Not in any dramatic way, but with each visit some kind of minor catharsis took place, some discharge of toxic energy or emotions. I joked with her that she was a sixteenth-century physician of the psyche, that she bled me with leeches, that she saw to it that I was opened up just enough to leak out enough of my angst, my black blood, to keep the circulation moving, to stop all the circuits congealing with the thick bile of despair, the grey clag of sadness. It was, I imagined, a bit like being on a dialysis machine, like having your psychic blood rinsed.

One evening I found myself rambling to Sarah about Leni Croupe. Leni was the third wife of my boss in London, Jim Croupe, and she had invited me to spend a summer with them at their villa in Tuscany. The villa – more like a palace, really – was Leni's obsession. Her life's work, she told me, was to restore the building to its former glory, and she talked of nothing else, in long-winded detail, until I began to see that it was a form of mania.

Sarah listened, and then: 'Were you attracted to Leni?'

'Not sexually. She wasn't my type. Too skinny. And obsessive.'

'But she made an impression on you, obviously.'

'She sought perfection. In everything. I'd never met anyone before who was so uncompromising about it.'

'You admired her?'

'Yes and no. I felt a kind of weird kinship with her but I felt she was barking up the wrong tree.'

'And what would be the right tree?'

This was one of those times when I was lying on the mat, staring up at the ceiling. Now I looked sideways and up at Sarah, kneeling above me and sitting back on her haunches like a relaxed muse. 'If I knew that,' I said, smiling, 'I wouldn't be here.'

'From what you say it sounds like Leni was simply trying to create beauty, and unlike most of us she had the means to do it.'

I knew that. I wasn't a clod. I had no objection to beauty; it was a worthwhile project. I had no objection to comfort either, as in Jim's London office, a converted warehouse, with its jacuzzi and in-house barista and sculptor-in-residence. I had loved working there. Every morning that I walked into the atrium of that building I felt my spirit quicken. There was a lot to be said for a personal barista.

Talking about Leni was a dead end. I wanted to ask Sarah about my recurring dreams, about the woman and the baby. 'Why the baby?'

'I don't know,' she said, reflectively. 'In some schools of thought the baby is said to represent the self.'

'So the baby is me?'

She smiled, mischievously. 'Maybe. Some dream therapists believe that everyone in the dream is you: the baby, the woman, even the water. You can see the logic of this – if it's coming out of your brain, *your* mind, it must be you, all of it. *You* create the dream.'

'What do you think?'

'I think it's possible to pay too much attention to dreams. If you wake up and the meaning is clear, then listen to it. If not, forget about it.'

LOOKING BACK NOW I think of Sarah as a kind of transient angel in my life, someone I'd had the luck to find when I needed her. In some way I've never quite comprehended she had kept me from drifting heedlessly over the edge. She hadn't 'cured' me, but she had stopped me becoming more careless and self-destructive. It had been a conservation phase, a shoring-up of the best of what was already there.

Of course we had dealt with 'issues': my emotionally remote father, for one. Didn't everyone have one of these? I had asked.

'I'm not treating everyone,' she had said, 'I'm treating you.' Whenever I attempted to generalise she would always pull me up and bring me back to myself: what *I* experienced, what *I* felt. I could see the logic of it.

But what I was to recall later, in the light of subsequent events, was the time I told her about my inability to cry.

'You can't recall a time when you cried, as a small boy?'

'No.'

'Never?'

'Not that I remember.' What I remembered was being beaten at school and standing alongside other boys, and how they cried and I didn't, and how elated I had been at the hardness of my heart. Whatever else they did to me, they could not reach me there.

Sarah shook her head.

'I've wanted to cry, many times. But I just can't do it. I remember once, when I was nineteen, this girl dumped me. I felt I was on the edge of tears, and when they wouldn't come I put my fist through a wall.'

'A wall?'

'It was plasterboard.'

Sarah was silent for a while. Then she tapped me lightly on the arm. 'Don't worry,' she said, 'tears will come in their own good time.'

This is an extract from 'The Beloved', a novel-in-progress.

Amanda Lohrey writes fiction and essays. Her most recent work is the short-story collection *Reading Madame Bovary* (Black Inc., 2010).

A novel about the extraordinary true story of one man's attempt to stop the Holocaust, THE MESSENGER dramatises questions about our collective humanity and shows us man's moral bravery.

'Strong and intelligent, a huge act of empathy. A brilliant book.'
JOAN LONDON

AVAILABLE FROM ALL GOOD BOOKSHOPS

Text Publishing, Melbourne Australia
TEXTPUBLISHING.COM.AU

A powerful collection of stories based on true cases, from one of Germany's most prominent defence lawyers. This book may change the way you judge the world.

*Translated from the German by
Carol Brown Janeaway*

'A wonderful storytelling voice, dry, clear, restrained; but beneath the unshockable surface, a current of indignation and compassion.'
HELEN GARNER

AVAILABLE FROM ALL GOOD BOOKSHOPS

Text Publishing, Melbourne Australia
TEXTPUBLISHING.COM.AU

ASIA LITERARY REVIEW

The best writing from and about Asia

Your personal Asian literary festival – every quarter

Featured recently:

**Gao Xingjian | Hanif Kureishi | Su Tong
Miguel Syjuco | Margaret Atwood
Henning Mankell | Qiu Xiaolong | Nam Le
Dipika Mukherjee | Anne Enright | Ma Jian
Xiaolu Guo | Mahmoud Darwish | Yu Hua**

Subscribe for four issues, pay for three ... can you afford not to?

www.asialiteraryreview.com

Subscribe now and you won't miss out on Edition 32: Wicked Problems, Exquisite Dilemmas.

As complexity increases, so does the number of variables. Sequential steps are not enough, but unlike a crossword puzzle a wicked problem has no absolutely right or wrong solution – there are many possibilities. And sometimes the problem can only be understood once the solution has been found...

Take advantage of this special offer and choose a **FREE COPY** of a previous edition[†] as well.

Visit our website to subscribe online with the promo code **ED31FEB**[*] or simply fax/post the Subscription Form on page 264.

www.griffithreview.com

[*] Online code only available up until publication of Edition 31.
[†] Past editons available while stock lasts.

Save 20% with a 1 or 2 Year Subscription plus receive a FREE copy of a past edition of your choice*

☐ I would like to subscribe   ☐ I wish to give a subscription to: (please tick ✓ one)

Name: _____

Address: _____

_____ Postcode: _____

Email: _____ Telephone: _____

Please choose your subscription package (please tick ✓ one below)

☐ 1 year within Australia: $80.00 (inc gst)   ☐ 2 years within Australia: $150.00 (inc gst)
☐ 1 year outside Australia: $130.00 AUD   ☐ 2 years outside Australia: $250.00 AUD

I wish the subscription to begin with (please tick ✓ one below)

☐ CURRENT EDITION[†]   ☐ NEXT EDITION

For my FREE copy, please send it to ☐ me   ☐ my gift recipient (please tick ✓ one)

EDITION TITLE* _____

Select from past editions at www.griffithreview.com *While past edition copies remain in stock.*

PAYMENT DETAILS

Purchaser's Address (*if not the subscription recipient*):

_____ Postcode: _____

Email: _____ Telephone: _____

☐ I have enclosed a cheque/money order for $_____ made payable to **Griffith REVIEW** (Payable in Australian Dollars only)

☐ **Card Type (*please circle one*):** Bankcard / Mastercard / Visa / Amex

Card Number: ☐☐☐☐ ☐☐☐☐ ☐☐☐☐ ☐☐☐☐

Expiry Date: __ __ / __ __

Cardholder name: _____

Cardholder Signature: _____

MAIL TO:
Business Manager - Griffith REVIEW
REPLY PAID 61015
NATHAN QLD 4111 Australia

FAX TO:
Business Manager - Griffith REVIEW
07 3735 3272 (*within Australia*)
+61 7 3735 3272 (*International*)

● The details given above will only be used for the subscription collection and distribution of Griffith REVIEW and will not be passed to a third party for other uses. For further information consult Griffith University's Privacy Plan at www.griffith.edu.au/ua/aa/vc/pp ● [†] Current Edition only available for subscriptions received up until 2 weeks before Next Edition release date. See www.griffithreview.com for release dates.

ED31-1600011210